Penny Warner

Kids' Party Games and Activities

Hundreds of Exciting Things to Do
at Parties for Kids 2–12

Illustrated by Kathy Rogers

Meadowbrook Press
Distributed by Simon & Schuster
New York

Library of Congress Cataloging-in-Publication Data

Warner, Penny
    Kids' party games and activities/by Penny Warner; illustrated by Kathy Rogers.
        p.   cm.
    1. Games.   2. Amusements.   3. Children's parties.   I. Rogers, Kathy.   II. Title.
    GV1203.W33   1993
    793'.01922—dc20   92-41900
                                                                                    CIP

ISBN: 0-88166-199-6

Simon & Schuster # 0-671-86779-2

Editor: Elizabeth H. Weiss
Production Coordinator: Matthew Thurber
Desktop Publishing Coordinator: Jon C. Wright
Designer: Tabor Harlow
Illustrator: Kathy Rogers

Published by Meadowbrook Press, 18318 Minnetonka Boulevard, Deephaven, MN 55391.

BOOK TRADE DISTRIBUTION by Simon & Schuster, a division of Simon and Schuster, Inc.,
1230 Avenue of the Americas, New York, NY 10020.

98 97 96   6 5

Printed in the United States of America

DEDICATION

To Tom, Matt, and Rebecca, who still love to play games.

ACKNOWLEDGMENTS

There were many parents and teachers who generously contributed their favorite games to this book. Many thanks to Kelly Ball, Linda Barde, Edith Bassett, Kirstin Branton, Cathy Bray, Heather Buchanan, Trude Evans, Christine Hunter, Jill Johnson, Michele Kane, Terry Kelly, Bruce Lansky, Jim Bohen, Marianne Mendonsa, Tawna Redick, Julie Roberts, Heather Thorton, and Doreen Warner. A special thanks to Elizabeth Weiss and Jay Johnson.

CONTENTS

PRETEEN 10–12

INTRODUCTION

IT'S PARTY TIME!

Whether it's a birthday party, a club meeting, or a classroom event, you want to have the best party ever. You've planned the theme, sent the invitations, and bought the goodies. The party room will be decorated, the cake will be a masterpiece, and the crowd will gather for a fun-filled event.

It sounds great. But how do you guarantee a terrific time for all? And what do you do between the time the kids arrive and the time they go home?

The answer is simple: plan plenty of games and activities to keep the kids entertained and delighted. And it's easy, with the help of *Kids' Party Games and Activities.* This book contains hundreds of exciting things to do during any children's gathering. The games and activities are appropriate for ages 2–12, the instructions are clear and simple, and the preparation is inexpensive and easy.

The book is divided into three major age groups, with each section containing a wide range of age-appropriate activities. The Preschool section (ages 2–5) offers easy-to-learn and easy-to-master games and activities for children who are gaining better control of their bodies and acquiring stronger language skills. The School Age section (ages 6–9) contains lots of physical and mental challenges for children who are skilled at both fine and gross motor activities and who enjoy races, puzzles, and creative fun. The Preteen section (ages 10–12) has games and activities

that are more sophisticated for kids leaving childhood and entering adolescence. You'll find that many of these games can be enjoyed by kids older and/or younger than the age range specified. You know the guests best—read over some of the selections and decide what your group can handle.

Within each of the book's three major sections you'll find five types of party activities, including traditional games, contemporary games, group activities, outings and events, and entertainers. Whether you choose timeless favorites, new classics, or creative events, plan ahead! If you choose games that are too simple, the crowd will get bored. If the activities are too difficult, the kids might get frustrated, fight, or cry. If it rains during your outdoor games, the kids will be disappointed, and if they are cooped up inside too long, they'll wear you down. And if you don't have enough for the kids to do at the party, *everyone* will watch the clock in despair. Remember, be prepared, creative, and ready for anything, then approach the event with humor and patience. That way the party will be fun for you, your child, and the excited throng of guests.

How do you decide what types of activities to plan? It's easy! Just decide how much time you have for preparation and how many materials you want to buy, then let your child help you choose the games, activities, or events. And always have a contingency plan! For example, if you choose to have a stay-at-home party, pick a variety of indoor and outdoor games, active and quiet games, and competitive and noncompetitive games. If a game doesn't seem to be working, abandon it and go on to another—memorize the instructions so you don't have to consult the directions during each game. Group activities are fun for a creative crowd and work best

with lots of supervision and parental help. Entertainers provide a fun show-and-tell celebration and can make it easier on you, if entertaining a group of children isn't up your alley. Or take the kids on a party outing for an exciting, fun-filled day.

PARTY HINTS

These helpful tips will ensure a successful time:

- Choose a theme for the party. Ask your child what he or she would like as a focal point for the event and decorate around that theme. Perhaps a favorite toy, a special movie, or an often-watched TV show would make a good theme, complete with food, favors, and fun to match.

- Let your child help with the party planning. Find out what your child wants to do, and plan the event around that theme. If it's something outrageous, such as "go to Disneyland," suggest alternatives that incorporate his or her ideas and match your budget (such as a "Mickey Mouse Party," with a cake, decorations, and activities to match).

- Think the party through. Plan your time—two hours in the afternoon is best—and try to imagine how long each part of the party will take: the welcome, games and activities, opening of presents, cake and ice cream, and good-byes. Let the guests' parents know when the party ends so you won't have to entertain beyond a set time.

- Invite your child's good friends and try to keep the group manageable. You don't have to invite everyone your child has ever met to the party. But then again, you may have to include an entire class at a classroom event. In either case, have a few parents on hand to help keep the event under control.

- Hire a babysitter to help during the party if you can't round up adult volunteers. Helpers will be invaluable during game time. They can work with kids who have difficulties with the activities, supervise play while you lead the game or decide the winners, and watch the kids while you prepare the food.

- Plan to have both quiet and active games to balance the kids' energy levels. Start out with a quiet introduction game, if the kids don't know each other, then let them release all that party energy with an active game or two. Then settle down again with a quiet game. When you're finished playing, have cake and open presents.

- Over-plan the games. A party can turn to chaos if there aren't enough games and activities planned, so be sure to have a few alternatives if the games run short.

- Tie in the games and activities to the party theme by renaming the games or using props to complement the theme.

- Have prizes for both the winners and losers, and don't place too much emphasis on winning. Preschoolers don't need competitive games and might get upset if they have to leave the game because of a mistake. Preteens, however, usually enjoy competition. School-age kids fall somewhere in between, so use your own best judgment when choosing games.

- Keep the sweets to a minimum and provide some healthy snacks, so the kids don't get too strung out on sugar. This will help keep the games under control, too.

- Let the weather be your guide. Make sure your activities can be adapted to indoor or outdoor play, if necessary.

- Keep the cameras handy (both video and still cameras) so you have a record of all the fun. If possible, take Polaroid snapshots to hand out to the guests as they leave.

- Expect problems—and roll with them. Be prepared to make adjustments if the kids don't enjoy a game or have trouble following the game's rules. Adapt to fit the needs of your guests, and change the rules to please the group. The goal is to have fun!

I hope the ideas in this book will help you plan a wonderful party for your child. May your event be a success!

Penny Warner

Preschool 2-5

DUCK DUCK GOOSE

Duck Duck Goose is a game that's popular with preschoolers because it's easy to learn and packed with lots of action and suspense.

For Ages: 2–5

Optional Ages: 6–9

Players Needed: 5 or more

Object: To get to the safety zone without getting tagged

HOW TO PLAY

All of the players sit cross-legged in a wide circle—they are the Ducks. Pick one child to be the Fox. The Fox walks slowly around the outside of the circle, tapping the top of each Duck's head lightly while saying "Duck" with each tap. After a few moments of this, the Fox chooses a Goose by tapping one player's head and calling out, "Goose!" The Goose must quickly rise and chase the Fox around the circle, trying to tag him before he reaches the spot where the Goose was sitting. If the Fox reaches the spot and sits down before being tagged, he is safe, and the Goose becomes the Fox. If the Fox is tagged while running, he must start the game again. Play continues until everyone has played the part of the Goose and the Fox or until the players are too tired to play anymore.

CREATIVE OPTIONS

- Change the Duck, Goose, and Fox to other animals or pets. The characters can be more contemporary—choose three characters from "Duck Tales," "Teenage Mutant Ninja Turtles," or *The Little Mermaid.*

- Make a simple tail from fake fur or construction paper and attach it to a belt for the Fox.

- Make the game more complicated for older children by having the Fox say the name of each player as he goes by and then call out the *wrong* name to signal the chase.

- Another variation is to play Duck Duck Gray Duck, with the kids saying "Gray Duck" to signal the chase. For added fun, they can put other adjectives in front of the word "Duck" as they go around the circle. For instance, a child could say, "Red Duck," "Sleepy Duck,"

"Silly Duck," and then say, "Gray Duck," to signal the chase.

PRIZES AND FAVORS

• Give each Fox who returns to the circle without getting tagged a small rubber duck or duck sticker.

• When the game is over, give everyone an animal sticker or small stuffed animal.

• Give all of the players a treat bag. Fill them with wrapped hard candies, jelly beans, M&Ms, or cookies and label the bags "Duck Chow." Or fill the bags with tasty crackers and label the bags "Quackers."

TROUBLE-SHOOTING TIPS

• Play this game outside, if possible. That way no one will bump into any furniture and get hurt.

• If the game must be played indoors, make sure it's played on a carpeted area. Linoleum can be slippery, and carpeting provides a softer surface if anyone falls.

• Draw pictures of ducks (or have the kids do it) and use the drawings to mark the circle. Sometimes during the chase, the Fox and Goose get confused about where the safety zone is. A picture, or even a piece of paper marked with an "X," can help eliminate confusion.

• Encourage the Fox to tap (rather than slap) the Goose's head or to just tap the person's back or shoulder—players can get carried away by the excitement of the upcoming chase and become careless!

PIN THE TAIL ON THE DONKEY

Pin the Tail on the Donkey is a classic for preschool party-goers—you can make it even more fun with a few creative updates. It's a good indoor game that's appropriate for a small or large group.

For Ages: 2–5

Optional Ages: 6–9

Players Needed: 3 or more

Object: To "pin" the missing tail back on the donkey

HOW TO PLAY

Before the game, tape a poster of a donkey to the wall of the party room (make sure the area in front of the poster is clear of furniture). Prepare a tail for each player by writing her name on the tail she'll use. This will prevent confusion over who wins.

At game time, have the players form a line in front of the donkey poster. One by one, hand them a donkey tail, blindfold them, and spin them in a circle three times until they are facing the donkey again. (When you blindfold children, make sure the blindfold isn't too tight and that it covers their eyes completely.) They must stick the tail where it belongs on the donkey—the player who gets closest to the correct spot on the poster is the winner.

CREATIVE OPTIONS

• Use a different animal poster—try a rabbit and have the kids stick a cotton ball onto the poster for the tail. You can find animal posters at any poster shop and at some card and stationery stores, or draw your own.

• Draw a funny monster shape on a large sheet of paper and have each child pin a different body part to it (such as an eyeball, mouth, foot, or hoof) to create a creepy-looking creature. You can cut out these body parts from construction paper for a colorful effect.

• Cut tails out of fabric or felt and let the kids decorate them before the game with glitter, paint, and other art materials. The kids can also draw the tails and/or help draw the picture of the animal.

Materials Needed:
- A wall
- A large picture of a tailless donkey and a donkey tail for each player (available at party supply stores, or draw your own donkey and tails)
- A blindfold, bandanna, large scarf, or eye mask with the peepholes covered with black construction paper
- Tape

PRIZES AND FAVORS

- Blindfold the guest of honor, spin her around three times, and have her place a small goody bag on each guest (pin the goody bag on the indicated spot yourself to prevent anyone from getting pricked). The goody bags will probably end up on the guest's sleeve, collar, belt loop, or another funny place!

- The homemade decorated tails make nice mementos of the party.

- Offer prizes and favors related to the game— for example, a donkey stuffed animal, like Eeyore, or horse stickers.

- Give each child a small poster to take home.

TROUBLE-SHOOTING TIP

- If a child is reluctant to wear a blindfold, let her be the last one to take a turn so she can see it's not too threatening. If she still refuses, allow her to play with her eyes closed.

TREASURE HUNT

Pirates aren't the only ones who love to look for treasure—kids do, too. A treasure hunt is a wonderful activity for any type of party, and best of all, everyone gets to take a bit of treasure home.

For Ages: 2–5

Optional Ages: 6–9

Players Needed: 4 or more

Object: To find the most hidden treasure in a set period of time

HOW TO PLAY

Before the guests arrive, hide the treats and toys all around the party room. (It's best to play this game before any others because the kids might inadvertently discover some of the treasure while playing other games.) Hide the items in plain sight by matching the colors or shapes of the objects with the objects in the party room. For instance, if you're hiding a red jelly bean, put it next to a red book on the shelf so it's camouflaged but still easy to find. Hide the items *behind* or *beside* furniture or other objects instead of inside drawers or between seat cushions.

At game time, gather the kids together, hand them lunch bags to hold the treasure, and tell them to find the hidden goodies. Give them three minutes (or more or less time, depending on the group) to find the items. Every time they find a toy or treat, they should put it in their sack and quickly move on. When the time is up, count the items in each child's bag and see who found the most—that child is the winner.

CREATIVE OPTIONS

- Rather than having the kids keep what treasure they find, you can keep hiding the items and play again and again. Use recyclable items such as plastic Easter eggs, shells, or colorful beads instead of candy so the kids won't be tempted to snack between rounds. After each round give the player who finds the most items a prize.

- Let the kids take turns hiding all the treasure— it's fun for them to watch the rest of the gang try to discover their creative hiding places.

- Instead of letting the treasure hunt be a free-for-all, write up some cryptic clues to lead the kids from one site to the next (it's best for younger kids to work as a team). If you've

Materials Needed:

- A collection of small toys and treats (try jelly beans, M&Ms, wrapped hard candies, stickers, felt-tip pens, baseball cards, small plastic animals, pennies or nickels, small rubber balls, or inexpensive party toys)
- 1 small brown paper lunch bag per child
- A timer

hidden treasure in the bathtub, write a clue that says: "Rub-a-Dub-Dub," and let the kids try to figure out where to go next to find the reward. You'll need to read the clues to pre-schoolers or use pictures of objects cut out of magazines for clues, and you may have to coach them if they get stuck. Have a big prize waiting for them in one spot, such as a collection of goody bags, one for each child, or a bag of mini candy bars for everyone.

PRIZES AND FAVORS

- Let the kids keep the treasure they find.

- Give the kids bags of "pirate treasure" (gold-foil-wrapped chocolate coins tied with ribbon).

- If you use plastic Easter egg shells, fill them with goodies and give everyone a "goody shell" to take home.

TROUBLE-SHOOTING TIPS

- Make sure the treasure is hidden in plain sight and is no higher than preschoolers' eye level, so the kids can see and reach the items easily. If the kids are older, you can make the hiding places more obscure, but if they have trouble finding the items, give them hints such as, "Read any good books lately?" if you have an item hidden on the bookshelf.

- Let the kids know which areas are off limits so they won't wander to different places and waste their time.

- If one of the players doesn't find *anything*, hide a couple of trinkets in plain view when the rest of the kids are occupied with their own treasure hunting and give him a little help.

HOT POTATO

Hot Potato is a game that will really keep things "moving" at your preschooler's party. You can play indoors or outdoors—it's the perfect game for a large, energetic group.

For Ages: 2–5

Optional Ages: 6–9

Players Needed: 5 or more

Object: To catch and toss the Hot Potato quickly without getting caught holding it

HOW TO PLAY

The players sit cross-legged in a circle, facing the leader who is seated in the middle. The leader (you or one of the kids) starts the game by throwing the Hot Potato to a player of her choice, and then closes her eyes once the game gets underway (she must close her eyes so she can't tell who has the potato at any given time). The first player must catch the Hot Potato and toss it to another player quickly. Play continues with the Hot Potato getting tossed at random throughout the circle. If the Hot Potato is tossed out of play, the last person who touched it should be the one to fetch it.

After a short period of time, the leader shouts out, "Hot!" Whomever is caught holding the Hot Potato at that moment leaves the circle and is out of the game. The game continues in this

manner with the players gradually being eliminated. The last player left is the winner.

CREATIVE OPTIONS

• If the game is played outdoors, use a water balloon for the Hot Potato so that the kids must handle it more gently—if it's dropped during play, it will break and splash water on everyone, adding an element of suspense to the game! Just be sure to tell the guests to bring bathing suits or old clothes to the party if you choose this game option. (To make a water balloon, stretch the opening of a deflated balloon and attach it to a faucet. Holding the bottom of the balloon, turn on the faucet and slowly fill the balloon with water. Turn off the water, take the balloon off the faucet, and tie it closed.)

• Have the players toss hollowed, confetti-filled eggshells. Carefully poke two holes on either

Materials Needed:
- Enough space for the players to form a wide circle
- A potato, tennis ball, stuffed sock, beanbag, or water balloon

end of an egg and clean out the yolk by holding the egg upright and blowing through one hole. The yolk will drip out of the other hole—you might need to use a pin or needle to break up the yolk if it won't come out. Then rinse the eggshell with water and let it dry thoroughly. Once it's dry, use a funnel to fill it with confetti, tape both holes closed, and give it to the kids to toss back and forth—until the unexpected happens!

- Make a beanbag out of glittery or neon fabric and tell the kids they're tossing "hot lava" from a volcano. You can use different fabrics and your imagination to create other untouchable items, such as "pond slime" or "gopher guts"—the more disgusting the better!

PRIZES AND FAVORS

- If you're making a "hot" beanbag for the kids to toss, sew some extras for everyone.

- Make confetti-filled eggshells for each guest.

- Offer the grand prize winner a Mr. Potato Head kit.

TROUBLE-SHOOTING TIPS

- If you're worried about the kids randomly tossing the Hot Potato, have them pass it quickly around the circle one by one instead.

- Some players might get upset about having to sit out of the game because they got caught with the Hot Potato, so you can plan to play the game without having a winner. Kids who get caught with the Hot Potato can also take a turn as the leader. They will enjoy the pace of the game more than the competition.

- If you're using water balloons and some of the kids don't want to get wet, provide raincoats or plastic garbage bags for them to wear.

RED LIGHT, GREEN LIGHT

The suspense of Red Light, Green Light has made it a favorite for years. It's best to play this game outdoors in an open area, but it's possible to play indoors—if you have lots of space!

For Ages: 2–5

Optional Ages: 6–9

Players Needed: 3 or more

Object: To be the first one to tag the Police Officer without getting caught

HOW TO PLAY

Before the game, draw two parallel chalk lines or lay two ropes a good distance apart on the play area. Make sure there is plenty of space for the kids to run around between the chalk lines or ropes (twenty feet is a good minimum distance). Choose one player to be the Police Officer and have him stand in front of one line. All of the other players stand behind the opposite line.

The game starts with the Police Officer facing the other players. He turns his back to the other players and yells, "Green light!" Then he counts to five out loud as quickly as he can. The other players must run or walk quickly toward the Police Officer while he counts. When the Police Officer has counted to five, he shouts, "Red light!" and the players must freeze instantly.

The Police Officer whirls around to catch any players who are moving. Anyone who moves must return to the starting line. Play continues until one of the players crosses the line while the Police Officer's back is turned. That player then becomes the Police Officer.

CREATIVE OPTIONS

- Provide the kids with a special prop, such as a hat, shirt, or jacket when it's their turn to be the Police Officer. This makes it seem a little more official. A plastic "police" whistle is a fun prop, and the kids can use it instead of shouting the stop and go commands (give one to each child to prevent spreading germs).

- Have the Police Officer wave a scarf (or other light material item) in the air to make the other players move and drop it down when he wants everyone to freeze. This version is good

Materials Needed:
- A large playing area
- Chalk or 2 long lengths of rope

when the game is being played indoors because it's a little quieter.

- Make the kids do something silly when they get caught by the Police Officer such as hop, zoom like a car, or make animal sounds as they're going back to the line.

PRIZES AND FAVORS

- Let the kids keep their whistles or other props after they've been the Police Officer.

- Offer each player a book or coloring book about traffic signs, or make some homemade stop signs from red construction paper for the kids to play with at home.

- Pass out small red and green flashlights.

TROUBLE-SHOOTING TIPS

- Make sure that everyone gets a turn to be the Police Officer. If a player wins twice, have him pick another player so everyone has a chance to lead the group.

- Supervise the game to see that everyone plays fair. Some kids will cross the line at all costs and may need a little extra guidance so they don't gang up on the Police Officer.

- Choose a play area that's clear so the kids won't trip over the rope or run into anything.

MUSICAL CHAIRS

Kids love the classic game of Musical Chairs because it's full of excitement. You'll love it because it's a great way for a group of kids to let off some steam without getting out of control. Try some creative options if the kids don't want to stop playing!

For Ages: 2–5

Optional Ages: 6–9

Players Needed: 4 or more

Object: To be the last player in a chair when the music stops

HOW TO PLAY

Arrange the chairs in a line with every other chair facing in the opposite direction. If there isn't much space available, put the chairs back to back or in a circle. The players stand by the chairs, all facing the same direction.

Choose one player to be the leader, or play the leader yourself. The leader stands away from the players and is in charge of the music. When the leader starts the music, the kids march around the chairs in single file. As soon as the leader stops the music, the players scramble for the nearest empty chair and sit down quickly. Whomever is left without a chair leaves the game. One chair is then removed from the line so that there is one less chair than players. The game continues until two players are left to battle over one chair. The player who sits down first (when the music stops) is the winner.

CREATIVE OPTIONS

• Instead of chairs, use pillows or sofa cushions.

• Play music the kids will like, such as tunes from "Sesame Street" or the music of popular children's folk singers. Or prerecord a variety of songs, spaced at ten-second intervals, so no one has to monitor the music. You can also spin the radio dial and have the kids scramble for chairs when you get to a song.

• Tape an inflated balloon to the seat of each chair before the game and tell the players that they not only have to sit in the chair but also pop the balloon! This should prevent any disputes over who is actually sitting in the chair (the one sitting on top of the popped balloon gets to stay in the game). After each round, tape another inflated balloon to each chair. The kids will love the sound effects!

Materials Needed:
• Chairs for all but one player
• A cassette player and musical tape, or a radio

• For a really different version, toss items of clothing on the floor and spread them out so each piece is visible. Have one less item than players. Then use the basic rules of Musical Chairs to play, with the kids putting on a piece of clothing quickly when they hear the music stop. The player who doesn't get an article of clothing to put on is out of the game. Remove one item every time a player leaves the group.

PRIZES AND FAVORS

• Give each player a noisemaker or kazoo.

• If you play the clothing version of the game, purchase some special hats or inexpensive T-shirts that everyone can wear home.

• Give the kids cassette tapes featuring popular children's artists.

TROUBLE-SHOOTING TIPS

• When setting up, place the chairs about six inches apart to avoid a pile-up each time the music stops.

• If arguments over who's really sitting in the chair occur, repeat the round—this will prevent hurt feelings.

• Provide the kids who are out of the game with a small toy or treat so they won't feel bad about losing. Or let each one take a turn monitoring the music.

• Make sure the music is loud enough so everyone can hear it clearly.

SNATCH!

Kids love to be sneaky, and this game gives them a chance to be crafty—without getting into trouble. What's special about this game is that it's designed not to have a winner, so there's no direct competition between the kids!

For Ages: 2–5

Optional Ages: 6–9

Players Needed: 6 or more

Object: To secretly snatch an item from the party table

HOW TO PLAY

While the guests are in another room, place the objects on the party table (arrange them any way you want). Make sure the kids don't get to see what's on the table until you're ready to start the game.

The kids are to sit at the table, take a good look at the small items, and remember what they are. A chosen player then turns his back and closes his eyes. While his eyes are closed, point to another player and have this player quietly sneak one of the toys or treats off the table and put it in his lap, hidden from view. The first player can then face the group again—he must determine which item is missing from the table, and who snatched it. Allow him a few guesses and then have the culprit confess and show the stolen item. Return the item to the table before beginning the next round. The player who snatched

the item leads the next round, closing his eyes and facing away from the group. Select another player to snatch an item. Play continues until everyone has had a chance to snatch and guess.

CREATIVE OPTIONS

• If it's too difficult for the kids to guess the snatcher *and* the missing item, just have the kids try to identify the snatcher. After every wrong guess, have the guesser close his eyes again while the snatcher sneaks another item. Continue to allow guesses until the culprit, with a lap full of goodies, is identified.

• While the guesser has his eyes closed, have the snatcher give him something personal instead of taking something away from the table. The player could take off a shoe or sock and set it in front of the guesser's place. The guesser must identify who the shoe or sock belongs to—without looking under the table!

Materials Needed:
- A table
- A variety of small, fun items, such as candy or tiny toys—1 item per player

- If the players are older, place lots of items on the table to make identifying the missing item more difficult. In addition to the small toys and treats, you could fill up the space with a cake, paper plates, cups, or napkins.

PRIZES AND FAVORS

- Let each player take home a toy or treat from the party table. If you don't want the kids to grab for items at the same time, tell them you'll pick a number from one to twenty and whomever chooses the correct number can pick an item first. (The player who is closest to the number is the second to pick an item, etc.)

- Play a final round where the prizes are hidden away in different-colored goody bags. As each player snatches a bag, let him keep the goodies inside once he has been identified. Place the empty bag back on the table for the next player's guess.

TROUBLE-SHOOTING TIPS

- Sometimes kids get so excited, they almost give away the "thief" by their body language. They can't help turning their heads toward the culprit, glancing at him several times, or even pointing. (Sometimes the "thief" even gives himself away by giggling!) Warn the players about being too obvious *before* the game, and it might help control their impulses a little.

- If younger players have trouble identifying the item taken from the table, just omit that part of the game. The real fun is trying to find the culprit!

COPY CAT

Kids love to copy each other, until they drive themselves (and everyone else) crazy! If you're looking for an indoor game that's quiet (except for the giggling), try Copy Cat.

For Ages: 2–5

Optional Ages: 6–9

Players Needed: 6 or more

Object: To imitate an increasing number of body movements

HOW TO PLAY

All of the kids sit in a circle so they can see each other clearly. The starting player makes a body movement such as wiggling her nose, clapping her hands, pinching her ears, shaking her head, shrugging her shoulders, or waving her hand—it's her choice. The next player in the circle copies the starting player's movement and adds a new movement. The third player must copy the first two movements in the order they were made and then add a third movement. Play continues in this manner around the circle.

If a player can't remember a movement or copies a movement incorrectly, she is out of the game and must leave the circle. The last remaining player wins.

CREATIVE OPTIONS

• The kids can say words instead of making body movements. Or they can make animal sounds, silly sounds, or even sing a line of a song.

• With kids who are older, play Copy Cat using the alphabet as a guide. For instance, the first player might say, "Apple," the second player, "Bus," and so on through the alphabet with the kids repeating the previous words and adding one of their own. You can coach the kids along by saying "A," "B," or whatever letter they're working on, if they seem to hesitate a little.

• If you'd prefer to play a game that doesn't eliminate players, have the kids sit in a circle and take turns adding a line to a story started by the leader. Ghost stories can be told at a Halloween party and, for a birthday party, a

Materials Needed:
• Enough space for the players to sit in a circle

silly autobiography can be made up about the guest of honor.

PRIZES AND FAVORS

• Provide favors that have a cat theme—cat stickers, stuffed toy cats, or cat posters.

• Give the winner a prize that relates to body awareness, such as the Invisible Man kit, an anatomy poster (available at educational supply stores), or a kids' exercise video.

• If animal or silly sounds are used in the game, choose prizes and favors with an animal theme or make them completely silly—an assortment of joy buzzers, funny spectacles, fake lips and noses, rubber thumbs, and other gag gifts.

TROUBLE-SHOOTING TIPS

• Instead of having players leave the circle if they make a mistake, just say, "Oops, you goofed," and either move on or have the player who missed start a new sequence. There won't be a winner, but the game will still be lots of fun!

• If some players have trouble with memory skills, give them hints or let the other kids give assistance during the game.

• Don't pressure the players to imitate the movements exactly. Some kids are less coordinated than others—accept the best they can do.

SIMON SAYS

Simon Says is traditionally popular with pre-schoolers, but even preteen players can get fooled by tricky Simon! This game is great indoors and outdoors and keeps kids entertained for long periods of time.

For Ages: 2–5

Optional Ages: 6–12

Players Needed: 3 or more

Object: To follow the correct commands and stay in the game as long as possible

HOW TO PLAY

One player is chosen to be Simon. Simon's job is to call out, "Simon says (describe an action)," while demonstrating the action that the group should mimic.

Everyone in the group must do what Simon says *only* if he begins his command with the phrase "Simon says." If Simon describes and demonstrates an action but doesn't say "Simon says," the group should ignore the command. For instance, if Simon says, "Put your hands on your head," any player who puts his hands on his head is out and must leave the group. (It sounds easy, but many will be fooled!) Another way Simon can trick the other players is by simply doing a movement without saying anything at all. Any kids who copy the movement are out. The faster Simon's commands, the more confused the other players get! The last player remaining wins the game and becomes Simon in the next round.

CREATIVE OPTIONS

- You can play Simon if the group is made up of really young kids. Sometimes playing the role of Simon is difficult, and the kids might find it more fun to be in the main group. Be sure to include some silly commands like "Simon says burp" or "Simon says do a silly dance." This is especially fun and silly when the kids come to the party in costume!

- Have the kids use their own names when calling commands to personalize the game a little. Or use a funny name like "Terminator says . . ." to give them the freedom to giggle and act silly.

Materials Needed:
• Enough space for the players to spread out

• Instead of doing body movements, the kids can use a piece of paper and a pencil to draw the commands. Simon can say, "Simon says draw a circle," "Simon says cross the circle out," "Simon says draw a square," and so on.

• For a larger group, divide the kids into pairs for a team play. The leader gives directions that each team member should do to the other team member—"Simon says mess up your teammate's hair" or "Simon says give your teammate a hug."

PRIZES AND FAVORS

• If you're only playing one round, give the kids who are out a consolation prize while the game goes on—candy, stickers, or small toys work well.

• Give the last remaining player something special—perhaps a T-shirt, videotape, or a gift that goes along with the party theme.

TROUBLE-SHOOTING TIPS

• If you're playing Simon, don't go too fast for the younger kids because it takes them a little longer to process the commands.

• Have some coloring books and crayons set aside to entertain players who are out—this will help them feel better about leaving the game and will keep them busy.

• If a child insists he followed a command, but you saw him make a mistake, give him the benefit of the doubt—after all, it's just a game.

OCTOPUS

Octopus is a variation of Tag that's really fast-paced and full of action. You need a lot of outdoor space to play this game. It's a great way for the kids to burn off some extra energy!

For Ages: 2–5

Optional Ages: 6–9

Players Needed: At least 8

Object: To get across the Ocean without being tagged by the Octopus

HOW TO PLAY

Before the game, draw two parallel chalk lines or lay two ropes a good distance apart on the play area. Make sure there is plenty of space for the kids to run around between the chalk lines or ropes (twenty feet is a good minimum distance).

Pick one player to be the Octopus and have her stand in the area between the lines (the Ocean). The other players are the Little Fishes, and they stand behind one of the lines. Their objective is to cross the Ocean and reach the other line without getting tagged by the Octopus.

To start the game, the Octopus yells, "Cross!" and all of the Little Fishes run across the Ocean to safety. Any Little Fish who is caught stays with the Octopus until the next round and becomes a Tentacle. The next round begins when the Octopus yells, "Cross!" and all the Little Fishes run across the Ocean, trying to avoid the Octopus and her Tentacles. Any Little Fish who is caught joins the Octopus and Tentacles. Play continues until the Little Fishes are rounded up.

CREATIVE OPTIONS

- Instead of yelling, "Cross!" the Octopus can call out an item of clothing, and any Little Fish wearing that clothing must cross the Ocean. Or the Octopus can shout out types of pets, and anyone with such a pet must run across—any category will do for this game, so get creative!

- Once they're caught, have the Tentacles stand still in various spots around the Ocean, and allow them to use only their arms and hands to tag the Little Fishes.

Materials Needed:
- A large outdoor area
- Chalk or 2 long lengths of rope

- For a longer game, let the Tentacles become Little Fishes once they've tagged someone. Play until everyone is too tired to run anymore!

PRIZES AND FAVORS

- Send everyone home with stickers or magnets that have fish on them.

- Give the Little Fishes (and the Octopus) Gummi worms to enjoy after the game.

- Offer the kids "Shark Bites" candies.

TROUBLE-SHOOTING TIPS

- Don't make the play area *too* large or those little legs will get tuckered out too soon. You can easily redraw the chalk lines or move the ropes to suit the activity level of the group.

- Stand behind the goal line so that the kids will be sure to know where to go—you don't want them running in the wrong direction or into a neighbor's yard!

- If a child gets confused about the clothing item or category called out by the Octopus, help her by whispering or gesturing that she is to run.

- If you're worried about the kids' safety, play on a soft lawn that doesn't have any debris on it, rather than on cement.

GIGGLE AND HOWL

Here's a silly game that puts everyone in a good mood! It doesn't require any preparation and can be played indoors or outdoors.

For Ages: 2–5

Optional Ages: 6–9

Players Needed: 3 or more

Object: To giggle and laugh when the handkerchief is in the air and to keep a straight face when it hits the ground

HOW TO PLAY

The kids stand "frozen" in a circle and can't move until freed by the "magic handkerchief." When you toss the handkerchief up in the air, they must giggle and laugh out loud until the handkerchief hits the ground—then they have to stop *instantly* and become frozen again. If any player breaks into a smile, giggle, or howl after the handkerchief hits the ground, he must leave the circle. Continue until there is only one player left. That player wins the game.

CREATIVE OPTIONS

- Instead of using a plain handkerchief, you can use a small scrap of colorful fabric, a piece of tissue paper, a feather, or a small army figure attached to a toy parachute. You can also blow a soap bubble into the air—when it pops, everyone freezes.

- Use music in place of a handkerchief. Just switch on the music to make the kids come alive and stop the music to make them freeze.

- If you don't want to have a winner for this game, allow the kids who goof to remain in the game, and just keep playing until the kids stop giggling altogether.

PRIZES AND FAVORS

- Offer the kids a home version of Giggle and Howl by giving each of them a colorful bandanna to play with at home.

- Keep the silly mood of the party going by giving everyone a cassette tape of silly songs or a joke book.

- If you use the soap bubble option, give all of the kids a bottle of bubble solution and bubble wands to take home.

Materials Needed:
- Enough space for the players to move around freely
- A handkerchief or other lightweight cloth that will float down slowly when thrown into the air

TROUBLE-SHOOTING TIPS

- The kids might be unhappy if they have to leave the circle during the game, with so much giggling going on. If this happens, let those kids make faces and act silly outside the circle to make the other kids laugh (without tickling or other physical contact).

- Playing the game outdoors is preferable because the kids will have more room to spread out and run around. If you are playing indoors, clear away the furniture and make sure there's plenty of space for the kids to be able to express themselves.

- If the handkerchief falls too quickly to the ground, hold it from the top of a tall ladder (or piece of furniture if you're indoors) or toss it up in the air wrapped around a small object (toss it away from the kids so the object

doesn't hit anyone). The object will carry the cloth higher up but will detach itself on the way down so the handkerchief floats freely.

BALLOON BURST

Here's a science experiment disguised as a game that always ends with a "bang." You'll need sunny weather the day of the party or the game won't work.

For Ages: 2–5

Optional Ages: 6–9

Players Needed: 4 or more

Object: To be the first to pop a balloon, using only a magnifying glass

HOW TO PLAY

Before the game, inflate a balloon for each player and tack all of the balloons to a fence that will get direct sunlight during the party hours. Tack the balloons low to the ground, about a foot apart, so the kids can reach them easily. Or use a clothesline, and rig the line low to the ground in a sunny spot and tie the balloons to the line with string.

All of the players sit or kneel in front of a balloon, and on the count of three must hold their magnifying glasses about three inches from the balloon. The sun should shine through the magnifying glasses onto the balloons. After a while, a small bright dot will appear on the surface of each balloon. When this happens, each player must hold her arm and magnifying glass steady until the sun causes her balloon to pop. The first player to pop a balloon wins. (Don't stop the game once there's a winner— all of the other kids will want to pop their balloons, too.)

CREATIVE OPTIONS

• Let the kids pretend they're scientists during the game—provide accessories such as glasses (without lenses), pens, notebooks, and lab coats (men's white shirts) for everyone.

• For an indoor balloon burst, set the inflated balloons all over the party room floor and let the kids pop as many as they can by stepping or sitting on them.

• If the sun refuses to shine the day of the party, you can still have a balloon burst. Instead of having the kids heat the balloons until they pop, fill them with water and let the kids toss the water balloons back and

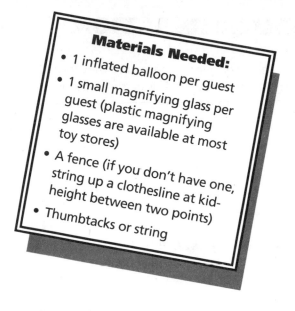

Materials Needed:
• 1 inflated balloon per guest
• 1 small magnifying glass per guest (plastic magnifying glasses are available at most toy stores)
• A fence (if you don't have one, string up a clothesline at kid-height between two points)
• Thumbtacks or string

forth until one eventually bursts, splashing everyone. (To make a water balloon, stretch the opening of a deflated balloon and attach it to a faucet. Holding the bottom of the balloon, turn on the faucet and slowly fill the balloon with water. Turn off the water, take the balloon off the faucet, and tie it closed.) For a really wet time, you can host a water balloon fight. (Just make sure that the guests don't mind a little water and that they bring an extra set of dry clothes.)

PRIZES AND FAVORS

• Give each guest a special Mylar balloon to take home.

• Let the kids keep the magnifying glasses to try the trick again at home.

• Give the game winner a science-related prize, such as a book about the weather or planets.

TROUBLE-SHOOTING TIPS

• Have lots of extra inflated balloons on hand in case any pop accidentally.

• If any kids are afraid of the loud popping noises, let them use tissues as earplugs.

• Sometimes it takes quite a few minutes for the sun to pop the balloons. If this happens, distract the kids with music or a story while they wait.

• Make sure to pick up all of the balloon pieces after any of these games—they can be dangerous around small children and animals.

• Thumbtacks can be dangerous so kids should use them under supervision.

CHAIN REACTION

Preschoolers love to dance, and they love to imitate one another. This game gives them the chance to do both!

For Ages: 2–5

Optional Ages: 6–9

Players Needed: 6 or more

Object: To guess which player is leading the dance

HOW TO PLAY

All of the players should be scattered around the party room in view of each other. Choose one player to be It and have him leave the room while you explain the game to the other players. Then choose one player to be the Dance Teacher.

Start the music so the Dance Teacher can begin a dance move that the other players must imitate. The rest of the players should immediately begin imitating his movements. The player who is It returns to the party room and tries to guess who is leading the dance. The Dance Teacher must keep changing his dance steps throughout the song, little by little, so it isn't obvious who's leading. And the other players should subtly imitate the Dance Teacher without giving away who it is. When the player who is It guesses who the Dance Teacher is, choose another player to be It and continue playing until everyone has had a chance to lead and to guess.

CREATIVE OPTIONS

• If you're looking for a less-active option, have the kids pretend to be statues, with the leader making a slight movement from time to time and the other players imitating the new pose.

• Seat the kids in a circle and choose one to be the leader and one to be It. The leader should move around a lot (from the waist up). He can clap his hands, pat his head, snap his fingers, or do any movement he wants. The other players must carefully watch the leader and copy everything he does until the player who is It guesses who the leader is.

Materials Needed:
- Enough space for the players to move around freely
- A cassette player and musical tape

PRIZES AND FAVORS

- Give each player a cassette single of a popular song.

- Provide favors that are dance- or music-related—posters featuring famous singers and dancers, music videos, or stickers that have a music theme.

- If you do the statue option, give the players a poseable figure or toy. It's also fun to make a batch of play clay or plaster of paris—the kids can make their own statues!

TROUBLE-SHOOTING TIPS

- Show the kids how to be subtle when imitating the leader. Tell them to *glance* at him once in a while and not to stare, or they will give the secret away too easily.

- Ask for volunteers instead of making each child be the Dance Teacher—some kids might feel shy about leading the group.

- The leaders should change their movements often and not keep one movement going for too long or everyone will get bored. But leaders should not confuse the group by changing their movements too often or too fast.

- If the game seems too easy for your particular group, have the players stand in a circle so it will be more difficult for the player who is It to guess who the Dance Teacher is.

SENSE-SATIONAL

Here's a fun noncompetitive game that preschoolers *love.* It's full of suspense and gives the kids a chance to get "grossed-out."

For Ages: 2–5

Optional Ages: 6–9

Players Needed: 4 or more

Object: To identify each item accurately by touch or smell

HOW TO PLAY

Prepare all of the "touch" and "sniff" items before the party by collecting them in bags and jars. Place the tactile items in zip-lock baggies first (don't seal the baggies) and then in lunch bags, and put the aromatic items in empty containers—cover the sides of the containers with aluminum foil if the labels don't fully hide the contents.

At game time, the players sit in a circle so the items can be passed around easily. Choose one player to start the game and pass the first "touch" item to her. She must reach into both bags and touch the item without looking at it or saying what it is. (The other kids will love watching her expression of surprise or disgust!) She passes the bag to the next player who must touch the mystery item without telling what it is. Once the bag has gone around the circle, the

kids take turns saying what they think is inside. After everyone has taken a guess, pull out the item so the players can see if they guessed correctly, and begin the next round with the new item.

Play the "sniff" version next. This game is played with similar rules—the players must smell each item with their eyes closed and try to identify it.

CREATIVE OPTIONS

- A fun variation is a tasting game where the kids taste a variety of mystery foods and try to identify them. To play, give each child a paper plate and place spoonfuls of mystery food on each one (choose food items that preschoolers will generally like but aren't always easy to identify, such as pizza sauce, frosting, cream cheese, or jelly). The kids have

Materials Needed:
- Fun-to-touch items, such as cooked spaghetti noodles, a package of Slime (available at toy stores), olives, cotton balls, soft bubble-gum, popcorn kernels, or a granola bar
- 1 small brown paper lunch bag for each "touch" item
- 1 zip-lock plastic sandwich bag for each "touch" item
- Fun-to-sniff items, such as catsup, mustard, pickles, a chocolate chip cookie, perfume, toothpaste, a flower, or baby lotion
- 1 clean baby food jar, juice can, or other container for each "sniff" item (no lids needed)
- *Optional:* aluminum foil

to taste each item (without smelling it or saying what it is) and then guess what it is once everyone has had a turn to taste.

- Gross the kids out with a game called Body Parts (this is a great game for older kids). Put a bunch of food items in zip-lock plastic sandwich bags and lunch bags, as in the game Sense-Sational, but this time tell the kids you're passing around body parts. (Use skinned grapes for "eyeballs," popcorn kernels for "teeth," cooked noodles for "guts," a small raw carrot for a "finger," and a skinned peach half for a "tongue.") Pass the items around and have the kids reach in and feel the body part. Once everyone has had a chance to touch the items, let them guess what the item *really* is.

PRIZES AND FAVORS

- Send everyone home with some scratch 'n' sniff stickers to wake up their senses.

- If you use Slime as one of your "touch" items, give all of the players a package to take home.

- Offer the kids fun-to-touch items like Koosh balls or Silly Putty.

TROUBLE-SHOOTING TIP

- If a player seems hesitant about touching or smelling anything, let her watch the other players first. She may want to join in later when she sees it's fun to play.

SURPRISE PACKAGE

This game takes some preparation, but it's fun and well worth the effort. It has humor, suspense, and a grand finale!

For Ages: 2–5

Optional Ages: 6–9

Players Needed: 6 or more

Object: To open the surprise package when the music stops and win a special prize

HOW TO PLAY

Before the game, place a grand prize in your smallest box and wrap it in gold gift wrap. Label it "Big Prize Winner!" so the kids will know it's the last box and the best gift. Set the gold box inside a larger box; include a booby prize, candy treat, or small toy, and wrap the package. Repeat until all of the boxes contain one gift, are wrapped, and are stored inside each other. When you're finished you should have one large wrapped box with all of the other boxes and prizes inside it.

The players sit in a circle, and when you start the music, the kids pass the box around the circle as quickly as possible. When you stop the music, the lucky player holding the box is allowed to open it. (Don't tell the kids there are other boxes inside the gift—they'll get the idea

soon enough, which is part of the fun.) Once a player opens a gift he must leave the circle. Play continues with the kids passing the box when the music is started and opening it when the music stops—you may want to warn the kids ahead of time that some of the gifts are a little strange! Soon there will be only two players left. The player who opens the second-to-last box gets to keep its contents and hands the gold grand prize box to the winner.

CREATIVE OPTIONS

• Instead of having a mixture of prizes hidden in the boxes, collect similar, theme-related items such as various candy bars, stickers, or comic books.

• Instead of playing with music, have the kids pick a number from one to twenty. The player who calls out the selected number opens the box. Continue playing this way until all of the boxes are opened.

- For an added surprise, have the kids close their eyes while passing the package around and then open them when the music stops, to see who got the gift.

PRIZES AND FAVORS

- For the nicer prizes, select candy or other treats, small toys, or board games.

- For the booby prizes, try giant underpants, a pacifier, dog biscuits, or any other silly gift you can think of.

- Choose a popular musical tape, book, or videotape for the big prize winner.

TROUBLE-SHOOTING TIPS

- If the big box is too heavy for the kids to pass around at the beginning of the game, they can push the box around the circle. To avoid this problem, buy lightweight prizes.

- When choosing the prizes, make sure to select generic items that all of the guests will enjoy, especially if there are both girls and boys invited to the party.

HANDY CANDY

No preschooler can resist this game—especially because the game pieces are pieces of candy!

For Ages: 2–5

Optional Ages: 6–9

Players Needed: 4 or more

Object: To guess the number of candies in a handful

HOW TO PLAY

The players gather in a circle around the bowl of jelly beans, and the first player reaches in and grabs a handful. Just when she thinks she gets to keep a whole handful of jelly beans, tell her the rules: she must first guess how many jelly beans she has and can only keep the number she guesses. If she has grabbed ten jelly beans, but guesses that she has five, she must return the extra five to the bowl. If she guesses *over* the amount in her hand, she must return them all and wait for the rest of the players to have a turn before she gets another try. Play continues until everyone has a handful.

CREATIVE OPTIONS

• Give everyone a special candy bag at the beginning of the party and attach it to their clothes with safety pins or to their belt loops with string. The kids can save their candy to take home.

• Place four different-sized bowls, one inside the other, on the floor with the kids gathered around them. Label the smallest center bowl "4," the next largest bowl "3," the next largest bowl "2," and the largest "1." Distribute ten jelly beans to each player. While kneeling, each player tosses the jelly beans into the bowls, trying to reach the bowl labeled "4" in order to get four points. At the end of each turn, see where the jelly beans landed and assign points based on the bowl numbers. For instance, two jelly beans in bowl "3" would be six points. When the points are all added up at the end of the toss, give the player that amount of jelly beans as a prize.

Materials Needed:
- A large bowl or wide-mouthed jar
- Enough jelly beans to fill the bowl or jar (or other small candies such as Skittles, M&Ms, or gum balls)

- Hang Lifesavers from the ceiling with string and tape, and let the kids try to eat them.

PRIZES AND FAVORS

- Send everyone home with a variety of candy.

- Give each child a bag of gourmet jelly beans.

- Other fun favors are stickers, memo pads, or toys with a candy theme.

TROUBLE-SHOOTING TIPS

- Be sure the kids wash their hands before playing since they'll be handling all the candy. Or, to avoid sticky hands, play the game using small wrapped candies instead of jelly beans.

- One way to avoid having the kids eat too much candy during the party is to tell them they can eat their candy *only* when they hear

the "candy bell" ring (you can use a bell or whistle for this purpose). If they are caught eating their candy at any other time, they must put one piece of their candy in the "candy pot" (a bowl or dish). Split the candy in the candy pot between all of the guests at the end of the party.

LOOSE AT THE ZOO

This version of tag is fun for kids because they really have to stay alert! It's a good outdoor game for an active bunch.

For Ages: 2–5

Optional Ages: 6–9

Players Needed: 6 or more

Object: To reach the other side of the line before getting caught by the Zookeeper

HOW TO PLAY

Before the party, cut out pictures of different zoo animals from magazines or coloring books (or draw them yourself) and glue them onto index cards. Make one animal card for each player. Then draw two parallel chalk lines or lay two ropes a good distance apart on the play area (twenty feet is a good minimum distance).

Select one player to be the Zookeeper—the rest of the kids are the Zoo Animals. The Zookeeper stands between the lines while the other players stand behind one of the lines. The Zoo Animals are each given an index card that tells them which animal they should pretend to be for the game. They should keep their animal identities from the Zookeeper.

The Zookeeper patrols the Zoo (the play area), walking back and forth between the rope or

chalk lines and making sure there are no loose Zoo Animals. At the same time, the Zookeeper must shout out the names of different zoo animals—any he can think of. Players whose cards match the animals called out must run to the opposite side of the play area before the Zookeeper tags them. Any child who is caught must freeze instantly, and all the other kids must run loose *around* him for a more challenging race. Any kids who make it to the other side go back to the starting line for another round. The game is over when all the animals have been frozen—the very last Zoo Animal to get caught is the winner.

CREATIVE OPTIONS

• For added fun, make a bunch of extra index cards with different animals on them so that the kids who make it across the line without

Materials Needed:
- A large outdoor area
- Magazines or coloring books featuring zoo animals
- 1 index card (3½ by 5½ inches) per player
- Glue
- Chalk or 2 long lengths of rope

getting caught can become a new animal right away and continue playing.

- Instead of having the kids who are tagged freeze, let the Zookeeper "lock up" the tagged kids behind the finish line with a special key—these kids can even act like caged animals so they won't get bored!

- Give the Zookeeper a prop to use (a special shirt, hat, or name tag) while he's in the middle of the field.

PRIZES AND FAVORS

- Give the kids small plastic or stuffed animals, animal coloring books, or animal masks to take home.

- Let the kids have any props used in the game.

- Give the grand prize winner a special theme-related prize, such as a big stuffed animal.

TROUBLE-SHOOTING TIPS

- Before the Zookeeper begins calling out animal names, give the kids a few moments to memorize which animal they are so they don't have to keep looking at the pictures.

- If the Zookeeper is too quick and always catches the other players, have him turn his back to the group, call out an animal, and then quickly turn around to catch runners.

- If you're worried about the kids' safety, play on a soft lawn that doesn't have any debris on it, rather than on cement.

DINOSAUR DIG

All kids love dinosaurs, so they'll be thrilled with this activity, which lets them dig for "dinosaur bones." For extra fun, plan a whole dinosaur party with dinosaur decorations and "prehistoric" food!

For Ages: 2–5

Optional Ages: 6–9

Players Needed: 2 or more

Object: To dig for "dinosaurs" and find the special prize

HOW TO PLAY

Before the party, bury some "bones" (pipe cleaners or popsicle sticks) in a sandbox or a sand-filled roasting pan. Also bury a special treat—toward the bottom of the sand so it takes longer for the kids to find it—and if you're using more than one roasting pan, hide a treat in each one so all of the kids have a chance at finding the prize.

Give the kids spoons, strainers, or shovels and tell them to pretend they're archaeologists digging for dinosaurs. Let them know there's one special item hidden in the sand, and that whomever finds it is the grand prize winner.

Once the kids have uncovered all of the bones, they can put together their dinosaurs. If they're using pipe cleaners, they can twist and shape the pipe cleaners into spines and ribs and bend

the pipe cleaners around one another for legs and feet. With popsicle sticks, all they need is some glue and imagination. Award ribbons (made from posterboard and colored with felt-tip pens) to each dinosaur when the activity is finished—under categories like "most creative," "scariest," or "best built." Display the dinosaurs and ribbons on a table in the party room for everyone to enjoy.

CREATIVE OPTIONS

- Hide plastic dinosaurs in the sand rather than "bones." Let the kids keep any they find.

- Hide a plastic Easter egg filled with jelly beans (call it a big dinosaur egg filled with lots of mini dinosaur eggs)—the player who finds it is the grand prize winner.

- Decorate the party room to look like a prehistoric land by hanging up pictures of

Materials Needed:

- Pipe cleaners or popsicle sticks (about 10 per child)
- A backyard sandbox or a large foil roasting pan filled with sand (1 pan for every 3 kids)
- Spoons, small strainers, or small plastic shovels
- A special treat that is well-wrapped (like a miniature candy bar, a small sticker pack, or a pack of bubblegum)
- Glue (if you're using popsicle sticks)
- Posterboard
- Felt-tip pens

dinosaurs cut out from construction paper and lining the table with plastic dinosaurs, along with the kids' dinosaur-bone creations. Place a dark paper tablecloth over a large table (or two small ones pushed together) so that it falls completely to the floor. Let the kids (or cave people) enjoy their party refreshments as they hide in this makeshift cave!

PRIZES AND FAVORS

- Let the kids keep their homemade dinosaurs or any other dinosaurs found in the sand.

- Pin the ribbon awards on the guests for them to wear home.

- Give everyone plastic or rubber dinosaurs.

- Send the grand prize winner home with a book about dinosaurs, a pack of dinosaur stickers, or another item featuring dinosaurs.

TROUBLE-SHOOTING TIPS

- Tell the players that archaeologists dig very carefully and that they should, too. That way the kids won't toss sand everywhere and make a mess in their excitement to find "bones" and prizes.

- If the kids will be constructing dinosaurs from pipe cleaners or popsicle sticks, have a few dinosaur books handy so the kids can copy them, rather than trying to create them from memory.

- If some of the kids don't find enough "bones" to create a dinosaur, have a few extras on hand to give them.

FUNNY PAPER RACE

The comics section of the Sunday newspaper is great for party activities—and it's inexpensive to use. This funny paper race gives the kids a chance to act silly!

For Ages: 2–5

Optional Ages: 6–9

Players Needed: 6 or more

Object: To cross the finish line before the rest of the players

HOW TO PLAY

Cut out a bunch of popular characters from the Sunday comics—two of the same character for each player. Cover the cut-outs with clear Contact paper or glue them to 3½-by-5½-inch index cards so they'll be sturdy enough to last the whole game. Then place one of each character into two separate boxes.

At game time, the kids line up side by side, facing the finish line (twenty feet is a good minimum distance—or choose a distance you feel is appropriate for the group). Make a finish line out of the Sunday comics for added fun!

Without looking, each player picks a character from the first box. Then the first player in the line chooses a character from the second box and shows it to the group. The player whose character matches the one picked gets to move toward the finish line by taking a step appropriate to the character. If the player's character is Garfield, he could take a step forward on all fours, meowing. If his character is Fred Flintstone, he could take a step forward and yell, "Yabba-Dabba-Do!" The player who chose the character then returns it to the box, and the next player in the line chooses one. (Bring the characters to the kids as they move closer to the finish line, so they won't lose their place.) The game continues until one player has crossed the finish line—that player is the winner.

CREATIVE OPTIONS

• Make necklaces out of the cartoon cards by punching two holes at the top of each one. Reinforce the area around the holes with tape, and string yarn through the holes (or let the kids do this at the party). The kids can

Materials Needed:
* A large playing area
* A few comics sections from the Sunday newspaper
* Clear Contact paper or index cards (3½ by 5½ inches)
* Glue
* 2 boxes

keep one cartoon identity throughout the race or trade necklaces.

* Instead of using the Sunday comics, buy coloring books that feature many different cartoon characters and let the kids color the pictures before the race.

PRIZES AND FAVORS

* Give each player a comic strip character covered in clear Contact paper to take home and make up several more so the kids will have lots to play with. They're fun to use in the bathtub!

* Give the kids items featuring favorite comic strip characters like Garfield, Snoopy, or Opus—Mylar balloons, T-shirts, stuffed toys, and play figures are popular.

* Pass out comic books to everyone and give the grand prize winner a gift certificate to a store that specializes in selling them.

TROUBLE-SHOOTING TIP

* Some kids may be less coordinated than others, so don't emphasize competition in this race—the kids will enjoy the challenge of the race just as much without the competition.

MAGIC "MOOSH"

This fascinating substance is fun to make and will intrigue the kids for a good part of the party. And if you're careful, it won't even make a mess!

For Ages: 2–5

Optional Ages: 6–9

Players Needed: Any group size

Object: To make a magic concoction

WHAT TO DO

Set up a big table (outdoors, if possible, to prevent a mess), and cover it with newspaper. The kids can stand up while making the "moosh" if there aren't enough chairs. Hand out sandwich bags and let the kids pick out a favorite shade of food coloring. When everyone has their materials, begin demonstrating the following steps, pausing often and checking that the kids are following directions properly: (1) Pour 1 cup cornstarch into the sandwich bag, and slowly add approximately ¼ cup water mixed with a few drops of food coloring, (2) Carefully press the excess air out of the sandwich bag and seal it shut, and (3) Knead the sandwich bag until the mixture is well-blended and smooth, but don't puncture the bag!

Watch their delight as the kids mix up the "magic" concoction, which slowly changes from dry to wet, from hard to soft, and from white to a color. Tell the kids to first squeeze the mixture firmly and quickly in the bag and then feel the mixture "melt" in their hands.

CREATIVE OPTIONS

• The kids can add two different shades of food coloring to the "moosh" to make a new color.

• Let everyone put glitter in the "moosh," at the same time the food coloring is added, for a little sparkle.

• Another fun and magical recipe is a catsup and mustard creation that the kids can work with to make designs. Just put a blob of catsup and a blob of mustard in a zip-lock plastic sandwich bag for each child, seal it,

Materials Needed:
- A large table
- 1 cup cornstarch per child
- About ¼ cup water per child
- Food coloring (many colors)
- 1 zip-lock plastic sandwich bag per child

and let the kids create colorful designs by pressing or "drawing" on the baggies with their fingers. The two colors will stay separated for a while. Once they've completely mixed, pour the contents into a bowl and use this special sauce to top hot dogs, burgers, or french fries.

PRIZES AND FAVORS

- Make fun "moosh" recipe cards for everyone so they can try the activity again at home.

- Give everyone some store-bought or homemade play dough to take with them.

TROUBLE-SHOOTING TIPS

- To be on the safe side, seal the sandwich bags with electrical tape to make sure they won't open during handling.

- If you have a large group, premeasure the materials so that all the kids have to do is pour and mix.

- Although the "moosh" mixture is nontoxic, it's not a good idea for the kids to put it in their mouth. Warn them ahead of time to touch but not taste.

- Provide the kids with old T-shirts to put over their clothing so the food coloring won't stain their good clothes.

CATERPILLAR CRAWL

In this activity the kids not only get to make their own caterpillar, but also make it crawl. It gives them a chance to create and control their own tiny world for a while—they'll love the experience.

For Ages: 2–5

Optional Ages: 6–9

Players Needed: Any group size

Object: To create a caterpillar and "magically" make it crawl

WHAT TO DO

Set up the materials at a table—this will make it easier for the kids to work on their projects. The kids can start by making either the caterpillar or the caterpillar's tail. To make the caterpillar, they need to tightly coil a pipe cleaner around a pencil. The coil should be about two inches long. While the pipe cleaners are still on the pencils, have the kids glue two wiggly eyes onto one end of the pipe cleaners. Set the caterpillars aside so the glue can dry.

Using felt-tip pens and crayons, the kids can create a winding caterpillar trail or maze on cardboard or paper plates. Encourage the kids to get creative and make a whole caterpillar environment with grass, flowers, rocks, and anything else they can think of.

When the trails are done, have the kids remove their caterpillars from the pencils and stick a piece of magnetic tape (cut to about one inch) on the underside of the caterpillars. Then show the kids how to bring the caterpillars to life! By holding a magnet underneath the cardboard surface and putting the caterpillar over the magnet, it will magically scurry along the cardboard trail as the magnet is moved.

CREATIVE OPTIONS

- For more "advanced" caterpillars, have the kids glue together three pom-poms, apply wiggly eyes, and use pipe cleaners for the antennae.

- Rather than using pieces of cardboard or paper plates, the kids can use shoeboxes or even larger-sized boxes. Just prepare the boxes ahead of time by cutting out the sides, leaving a two-inch border by each box corner.

Materials Needed:
- A table
- Pencils
- Felt-tip pens and/or crayons (assorted colors)
- Glue
- Children's scissors
- Magnetic tape (available at hardware stores)
- Colored pipe cleaners (the 12-inch chenille ones work best) 1 per child)
- Small plastic wiggly eyes (available at craft stores; 2 per child)
- 1 small magnet per child
- 1 piece of cardboard or 1 paper plate per child

Turn the boxes over and use the flat surface. The kids can reach up under the box, which resembles a table, to control the magnet and caterpillar. The benefit of using a large box is that four kids can use the box at once.

- Host an insect party—with the guests dressed as favorite bugs! Serve "insect" refreshments, such as sundaes with "chocolate-covered ants" (chocolate sprinkles) and "bugs on a log" (celery sticks spread with peanut butter, with rows of raisins on top).

PRIZES AND FAVORS

- Let the kids keep their caterpillars, trails, and magnets to take home and play with—the caterpillars make good refrigerator magnets.

- Give everyone a small metal toy to use with their trails.

- Offer coloring books with an insect theme,

books about insects, or a homemade "bug catcher" for studying bugs (a fancy jar with holes poked in the lid and a ribbon tied around the mouth).

TROUBLE-SHOOTING TIPS

- Test the magnets before the day of the party to be sure they're strong enough to work through a piece of cardboard.

- If you're using a cardboard box or a piece of cardboard box, make sure it's not too thick and has no seams. A thin, smooth surface works best.

- For safety, help the kids when they're using scissors.

- The magnets and small plastic wiggly eyes are dangerous if swallowed—supervise the kids carefully.

DAFFY DRESS-UP

It doesn't have to be Halloween for kids to dress up and pretend they're someone (or *something*) else. All they need are funny clothes and accessories, and a little imagination.

For Ages: 2–5

Optional Ages: 6–9

Players Needed: Any group size

Object: To encourage creativity and make-believe play

WHAT TO DO

To set up, just toss a bunch of clothes in a big, lidded box and cover it with wrapping paper so it looks like a giant gift. Then let the kids open it at once and pull out the clothing. Bring out some accessories and tell the kids they can dress up in the fancy clothing and pose in front of the mirror to their heart's content. You'll probably have to help them with the accessories, especially putting on make-up. Encourage creativity, and let the kids be as silly as they want.

Once the guests have on outfits they're happy with, let them have a parade. They'll love marching through the neighborhood modeling their new clothes—just go a short distance, like around the block. Let them keep their dress-up outfits on throughout the rest of the party, if they wish. It will be fun for them to act like grown-ups during refreshments and other party activities.

CREATIVE OPTIONS

• Have the kids dress each other, with half of the kids posing as "department store mannequins" and the rest of them playing "window dressers." Then let them switch roles so all of the kids are dressed up.

• Help the kids do a little skit after they're dressed up. They'll love pretending!

• Videotape the parade or take Polaroid snapshots of the kids in costume so they can see how funny they look.

Materials Needed:
- All sorts of fun adult clothing: flannel shirts, harem pants, sports or occupation uniforms, high-heeled shoes, oversized boots, floppy hats, and sailor caps (available at thrift shops, costume shops, and from your own closet)
- All sorts of accessories: wigs, scarves, fake jewelry, ribbons, ties and bow ties, and make-up (available at thrift shops)
- A full-length mirror
- A large cardboard box
- Wrapping paper (the Sunday comics can also serve as wrap)
- Tape

PRIZES AND FAVORS

- Before the dress-up activity, make some little award certificates or ribbons—one for each guest. These can be as simple or creative as you want. Label these awards with categories such as "silliest outfit," "most creative costume," or "most imaginative." Be sure they're all positive so that all the kids feel special.

- Give everyone their Polaroid snapshot.

- Give out favors that go along with the dress-up theme, such as T-shirts that feature a special party message or paper dolls.

TROUBLE-SHOOTING TIPS

- Be sure to have a wide variety of interesting and unique clothes for the dress-up activity. Don't collect clothing appropriate to only one gender—it limits creativity.

- On the invitations, tell everyone to wear snug-fitting clothes to the party, such as tights, bathing suits, or exercise wear, so they can easily put the dress-up clothes over their own.

MAKING WAVES

You've heard of a ship in a bottle—here's an "ocean in a bottle." This simple, unique activity is fun to do, and the end result is a long-lasting toy that kids will really enjoy.

For Ages: 2–5

Optional Ages: 6–9

Players Needed: Any group size

Object: To create a homemade toy that really lasts

WHAT TO DO

Before the party, wash and dry one bottle and cap for each child. If there are labels on the bottles, soak the labels in warm water for a half hour and try to peel as much of them off as you can.

Gather the kids at a table with the materials spread out before them. Using a funnel, pour six ounces of cooking oil into each child's bottle, followed by six ounces of vinegar. Let the kids observe the fluids interacting—the oil goes to the top and the vinegar to the bottom. Then pour several drops of blue food coloring into the bottles, and again let them watch the changes and separations.

Close the caps tightly and tell the kids to shake their bottles to make "waves." For added fun, give everyone tiny plastic toys to put inside the mixture so they can float in a homemade ocean. Plastic confetti and glitter will add sparkle, too. Once all of the materials are added, seal the caps shut with rubber cement or glue to prevent leakage.

CREATIVE OPTIONS

• The kids can make a tornado in a bottle instead of waves. The easiest way is by first purchasing a "Tornado Tube" (under three dollars at most educational supply stores) for each guest. Then clean out two large clear plastic soda bottles for each child and have the kids fill one of their bottles up with water and a pinch of glitter. Attach the "Tornado Tubes" to the bottles according to the package directions, and tell the kids to swirl the water-filled bottle and watch the tornado appear.

Materials Needed:
- A table
- 12-ounce plastic bottles with screw-on caps (1 per child)
- 6 ounces of cooking oil per child
- 6 ounces of vinegar per child
- Blue food coloring
- Glitter, plastic confetti (available at party supply stores), or tiny plastic toys
- A funnel
- Rubber cement or strong glue

- Send invitations with a beach theme. Seal ziplock plastic sandwich bags (filled with either water or sand) with some glue, and attach a piece of paper with the party details on it. You'll need to hand-deliver these!

- Decorate the party room with homemade starfish and seaweed cut out from construction paper and serve the food with plastic shovels. You can also serve a cake decorated like the beach.

PRIZES AND FAVORS

- Let the kids keep their new "wave makers."

- Give everyone water toys, such as pails and shovels, squirt guns, bathtub body paints, or small plastic boats.

- Offer books about tornadoes or send everyone home with their "Tornado Tubes."

TROUBLE-SHOOTING TIPS

- Tell the kids that, like the ocean, the liquids in the bottle aren't liquids they should drink. (The ingredients are nontoxic, but warn the kids anyway.)

- Glitter and plastic toys are dangerous if swallowed—supervise the kids carefully.

MYSTERY PUZZLE PIECES

Here's a quiet activity with a surprise twist. The identity of the person in the "mystery puzzle" always comes as a delightful surprise to the party guests—it's them!

For Ages: 2–5

Optional Ages: 6–9

Players Needed: Any group size

Object: To solve the identity in the mystery puzzle

WHAT TO DO

Before the party, collect photographs of all the guests scheduled to attend. You'll need to do this secretly, so call the guests' parents to arrange it. Suggest that they supply more than one photo so you can pick the one that will reproduce the best.

Take the photos to a copy store to have them reproduced in black and white and enlarged to a small poster size (about twelve-by-eighteen inches). Cut posterboard to the size of the photocopies and then spray the pieces of posterboard with spray adhesive. Next, lay the enlarged pictures of each guest on the posterboard, pressing down firmly. Allow the posters to dry for a few minutes, cover them with clear Contact paper if desired, and draw large-sized puzzle shapes on each one using a black felt-tip

pen. Then cut out the puzzle pieces, keeping them together, and slip each puzzle into a large envelope. You can write each child's name on the inside flap of the envelope so you'll know which puzzle belongs to whom.

When you're ready for a quiet-time activity during the party, pass out the envelopes and have the kids put the puzzles together. Tell them the finished result will be a special surprise. Wait until you see their expressions when they realize the face on the puzzle is their own!

CREATIVE OPTIONS

• If the puzzles aren't covered with clear Contact paper, the kids can color them with crayons.

• Serve a cake decorated with the race of the honored guest (call a bakery for details).

Materials Needed:
- A photograph of each child (school photos work well, or try to get one that features a full-body shot)
- 1 large sheet of posterboard per guest
- Spray adhesive
- A black felt-tip pen
- 1 large envelope per child (bright and colorful, if possible)
- Scissors
- *Optional:* clear Contact paper

• Another fun activity to do with the kids' school photos is to create a "Miniature Me" for each guest. Using a set of paper dolls, trace the paper doll on a large piece of posterboard several times. Make photocopies of each guest's headshot and glue the photocopy of each photo onto each paper doll's head. For a fun, quiet activity, present the kids with their very own miniature likenesses and let them color them in. They can also add glitter or other decorative items—let their creativity run wild!

PRIZES AND FAVORS

• Give the kids special gift certificates at a shop that creates magazine covers, T-shirts, or mugs featuring the customer's likeness.

• Send the kids home with their personalized puzzles and paper dolls.

• Many bookstores have storybooks, activity books, and coloring books with an "all about me" theme—these would make fun favors.

• Take Polaroid snapshots of the kids during the party and present them in small, inexpensive frames.

TROUBLE-SHOOTING TIP

• Be sure to make the puzzle pieces large enough for preschoolers to use. If they have too many pieces to work with, the activity won't be as much fun.

DOWN ON THE FARM

A nearby farm makes a great outing for a preschool party. Let those citified party-goers have a look at things they may not see too often—cows giving milk, pigs getting fed, or a farmer driving a tractor.

For Ages: 2–5

Optional Ages: 6–9

Preparation: Look in the Yellow Pages for farms that are open to the public and arrange a visit. Or ask your child's preschool teacher to recommend one.

WHAT TO DO

To get the kids in the mood for a trip to the farm, read them a story about farm animals or farming before you go, and sing a few verses of "Old MacDonald" during the drive.

Once you arrive, the owners of the farm or a farmhand will probably guide the group around (request this specifically when you call, if you wish), so just follow along and enjoy the experience. Ask ahead of time if it's possible to arrange some special activities, such as allowing the kids to milk a cow, brush the horses, pick some berries or corn, feed the hens, gather eggs, ride on a tractor, or take a hayride. Some farm owners provide tours of the house and barn, or they let the kids get involved in some of the easier farm tasks— others might just want the kids to watch. No matter what the day brings, the kids will have

a wonderful time being outdoors and seeing the animals in their picture books "come alive." Don't forget to bring a camera!

CREATIVE OPTIONS

- Find out if the farm you're visiting offers pony rides or maintains a fish hatchery, for added fun.

- While at the farm, give the kids some tasks to do as they tour the facilities. For example, give each child a different quest, such as finding out what kind of food the horses eat, what sound a goat makes, or how many cows there are. Have them share their discoveries on the car ride home.

- Send invitations cut out in the shape of farm animals, with a little plastic farm animal attached. Ask the guests to wear "farm" clothing (flannel shirts, jeans, and wide-

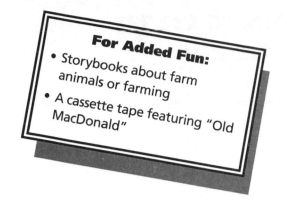

For Added Fun:
• Storybooks about farm animals or farming
• A cassette tape featuring "Old MacDonald"

brimmed hats) so they blend right in with the scenery.

• Back at the ranch, serve food like pork and beans, hot dogs, and apple cider, with a cake featuring plastic farm animals grazing on a meadow of green-tinted frosting.

PRIZES AND FAVORS

• Give the kids Polaroid snapshots of themselves with the animals to take home.

• Offer everyone plastic farm animals or a cassette featuring "Old MacDonald."

• If you can find some coloring books featuring farm animals or Golden Books that tell farm stories, give them to the kids as a memorable follow-up to their rural adventure.

TROUBLE-SHOOTING TIPS

• Get adult volunteers to accompany you on the outing to make sure the kids don't get hurt or wander off with a herd of cows. Never leave a child unattended on a farm!

• Before you leave for the farm, go over a few simple rules: no yelling because it might startle the animals, no running because it will stir up the dust, and no touching the animals unless permission has been given.

• Tell the kids to wear old clothes so they won't have to worry about mud or dirt.

• Use the buddy system on this outing—have the kids hold hands with a partner so they'll stay together.

ZOOMING TO THE ZOO

Kids and animals go together like cake and ice cream, so a day at the zoo will be a big hit with preschoolers!

For Ages: 2–5

Optional Ages: 6–9

Preparation: Call the zoo ahead of time to find out the hours of operation and to see if there are any special exhibits or shows that preschoolers might enjoy.

WHAT TO DO

If you have a plan of action ready before the kids arrive, the event should go smoothly. Preschoolers have a short attention span (and short legs!), so make sure they won't be walking around the zoo for more than about two hours. Choose the most exciting exhibits, and save time for the petting zoo, if there is one. If you plan to have cake and ice cream at home after the outing, give everyone little goody bags to take along to the zoo, so the kids won't want to stop each time they see a snack bar. Fill the bags with "animal" foods like peanuts, bananas, berries, and nuts. (Just make sure they don't try to give the goodies to the animals!)

Collect the kids together for a ride in the "zoo-mobile" to make the drive more fun, especially if the zoo is far from your home. Put a few bars made from black construction paper on the car windows and a sign in the rear window that reads: "Zoo-mobile—Do Not Feed the Animals." The kids will love singing animal-related songs like "I'm Being Swallowed by a Boa Constrictor" or "Five Little Monkeys Jumping on the Bed" and making animal noises.

At the zoo, keep the group together with simple planned activities. The kids can make the sound of each animal they see or walk and behave like animals as they go by the exhibits. Point out the various kinds of foods the animals eat, their habitats, and their different movements. After the zoo tour, have a picnic on the grass or open the goody bags and then head home for cake. Some zoos sponsor parties for kids, so you can have cake, ice cream, and the works right there—just call for a reservation.

For Added Fun:
- 1 small brown paper lunch bag per child
- A mixture of peanuts, bananas, berries, or nuts

CREATIVE OPTIONS

- Let the kids make animal masks to wear on the excursion or dress up in homemade animal costumes.

- Arrange for a special guided tour around the zoo, if possible.

- Books about zoo animals are fun to share with preschoolers, before and after the outing.

- Set up the party room to look like a zoo by drawing cages and animals on large sheets of paper and hanging them on the walls.

PRIZES AND FAVORS

- Send the kids home with animal stickers, animal coloring books, animal crackers, and small plastic animals.

- Let everyone pick out one special (but inexpensive) item from the zoo's gift shop.

- Bring along a Polaroid camera and take pictures of each guest in front of a favorite animal or exhibit. Give out the pictures at the end of the party as a special memento.

TROUBLE-SHOOTING TIPS

- Mention on the invitation that the kids should dress in casual clothes (appropriate for the weather conditions on the day of the party) and comfortable shoes.

- Make name tags for everyone (decorate them with animal stickers, if you wish) or assign partners so that nobody will get lost.

- For a large group of kids, ask other parents to attend the event and help keep everyone together and under control. If you can't round up any volunteers, arrange for a trusted babysitter to come along.

PUMPKIN PATCH PARTY

If you're planning a fall party, include a trip to a pumpkin patch and let the kids pick out their very own pumpkins to creatively carve and decorate.

For Ages: 2–5

Optional Ages: 6–9

Preparation: If you don't know the location of a pumpkin patch in your area, look in the Yellow Pages under "Orchards" to find one. Find out the hours of operation, the costs, and get directions to the field.

WHAT TO DO

On the invitation, request that the kids wear orange and green clothing (this will make it easier to keep track of everyone) or that they come in some sort of a pumpkin costume. Then, on the way to the pumpkin patch, keep the kids entertained with songs or stories.

When you arrive at the patch, let the kids explore the area, examine all the pumpkins, and pick out their favorite. A fun additional activity is a Pumpkin Hunt. Secretly put stickers on some pumpkins while the kids are wandering in the pumpkin patch. Once all the kids have chosen a pumpkin, send them back in the field to look for the special pumpkins with stickers on them. Tell them that whomever finds a sticker wins a prize (let the winner keep the extra pumpkin and give them each a sticker pack, too).

Plan extra time for pumpkin-carving/decorating activities after the trip, if you wish. Just put newspaper on a table for pumpkin-carving and show the kids what to do. Don't give them knives or other sharp objects—there are safe pumpkin-carving utensils at drugstores and grocery stores. It's also a good idea to draw faces on the pumpkins before doing any carving. Half the fun of this activity is opening the pumpkin shell and pulling out all the yucky stuff, so be sure to allow the kids to do this. Or for a less messy activity, give the kids colorful permanent felt-tip pens and let them draw faces on their pumpkins.

CREATIVE OPTIONS

• Here's a different pumpkin-decorating activity: cut up a bunch of vegetables and store them until you're ready to get started. Then let the kids use the vegetables to make

For Added Fun:
- Stickers
- A table
- Newspaper
- Safe pumpkin-carving tools or permanent felt-tip pens

faces on their pumpkins—use radish slices for eyes, a carrot stick for a nose, some bell pepper slices for a mouth, and celery tops for hair. Attach the vegetables with straight pins or thumbtacks (*supervise this activity!*).

- Rinse the pumpkin seeds once you scoop them out of the pumpkins. Bake the seeds on a cookie sheet in the oven at 350° for about five minutes (until they're crisp and lightly browned). Then let the kids gobble them up for a tasty snack. The seeds can be toasted plain, or shake on a little salt or other seasoning before baking to give them extra flavor.

- Invite the kids to the party by hand-delivering miniature pumpkins with the party details written on them with felt-tip pen, or mail the guests pumpkin-shaped invitations cut out from orange construction paper.

PRIZES AND FAVORS

- The personalized pumpkins make great mementos of the party.

- Send the kids home with small bags of candy corn and packaged pumpkin seeds or let them take the freshly-baked seeds.

TROUBLE-SHOOTING TIPS

- Adult supervision is necessary not only for the pumpkin-carving but also for decorating pumpkins with vegetables.

- If you plan to let the kids carve their pumpkins, it might be easier to have an adult volunteer help you with this project. That way, the kids won't get bored or frustrated waiting for help.

SCIENTIFIC EXPEDITION

Here's an exciting expedition into the fun side of science—an adventure that will fascinate the kids through hands-on experience.

For Ages: 2–5

Optional Ages: 6–9

Preparation: Most cities have a kids-style science museum that offers lots of science activities for kids to explore. Look in the Yellow Pages under "Museums" to find one near you. Call ahead of time to find out the hours of operation, costs, directions, and whether they have guided tours, group rates, or special classes.

WHAT TO DO

Give each guest a fun science toy to play with on the ride to the museum—a magnet, magnifying glass, telescope, kaleidoscope, prism, or other science gizmo—this will keep them busy and get them in the mood for their educational adventure.

Once you arrive at the museum, let the kids walk around and enjoy the science exhibits and displays. Let them look at everything, independently or in pairs, depending on their preference. After allowing enough time to see the exhibits, break for an activity called "What If." For this game you'll need to have prepared ahead of time a list of "What if . . ." questions. Write down questions that will get preschoolers thinking about fantastic possibilities— "What if your cat could talk?" "What if trees grew money?" "What if it rained popcorn?"

or "What if you could fly like a bird?" Give everyone a chance to answer and share their ideas. When it's time to leave, stop by the museum gift shop to get the kids a special (but inexpensive) science toy to play with on the ride home.

CREATIVE OPTIONS

- Allow extra time for doing some fun "science" experiments at home. Here's a good one: Give each child a glass of water— the amount of water in the glasses should vary. Show the kids how to make music by holding the glass steady with one hand, dipping a fingertip of the other hand in the water, and lightly rubbing the fingertip in a circular motion around the rim of the glass. The trick is to use slight pressure—it will produce a ringing sound. The sounds will be higher- or lower-pitched depending on the amount of water in each glass.

For Added Fun:
- Small science toys
- Paper
- A pencil or pen

- Let the junior scientists make some tasty peanut butter play dough! Mix together two cups smooth peanut butter, two cups powdered dry milk, and one cup honey. (You can double the recipe for a larger group.) The result will be a pliable and edible substance that the kids will love.

- If you plan to do a few science-related activities after the trip to the museum, have the guests come dressed in white lab coats (men's white shirts).

PRIZES AND FAVORS

- Give the kids a gift certificate to a store specializing in science and nature gifts.

- Offer do-it-yourself science activity and experiment books (available at bookstores). Two fun ones are James Lewis's *Measure Pour & Mix, Kitchen Science Tricks* and *Learn While You Scrub, Science in the Tub,* published by Meadowbrook Press.

- If you try the peanut butter play dough option, let everyone take a sample home in a baggie—if they haven't already eaten it, that is! Or write up the recipe for each child to try again at home.

TROUBLE-SHOOTING TIPS

- Keep a close eye on each child while visiting the museum. Ask the guests to wear red or yellow T-shirts to the party (the bright colors will be easy to spot) and provide giant name tags for all the guests with the address and phone number of the party host, in case anyone gets lost.

- Find adult volunteers to help on the trip because the kids will want to run off in different directions. If you can't round up any volunteers, arrange for a trusted baby-sitter to come along.

UNDER THE SEA

Some kids may hate eating fish, but all kids love looking at fish—so why not plan an "under the sea adventure?"

For Ages: 2–5

Optional Ages: 6–9

Preparation: If you live in a big city, you probably have an aquarium nearby. Call ahead of time to learn the hours of operation, costs, directions, and whether they have guided tours, group rates, or special classes. If there isn't an aquarium in your area, you can still have an "under the sea" party. Look in the Yellow Pages under "Fish Hatcheries" and plan a different outing that's just as fun.

WHAT TO DO

When the guests arrive, have them make "fish" to take along to the aquarium. Give everyone a mitten to decorate, with the fish's face at the fingertip end of the mitten and the fins at the knitted end. Using felt-tip pens, puffy paints, felt scraps (preferably pre-cut into small shapes), accessories, and any other art materials, the kids can create colorful, imaginative sea creatures. Once the decorations have dried, the kids can slip the fish mittens onto one hand and wiggle them to make the fish "swim." Some kids might prefer to make sharks—the thumb area of the mitten can serve as the fin.

When you arrive at the aquarium, let the kids explore the various exhibits, under supervision. If the aquarium also features a tide-pool area, feed-the-fish tank, or deep-sea diver show, be sure to visit these attractions. After viewing all the aquarium has to offer, head home, keeping the kids entertained with songs from the movie *The Little Mermaid*.

CREATIVE OPTIONS

• If there's time for more fun after the outing, play a new type of "Go-Fish" with the kids, tossing a fishing pole line (a stick with string attached, and a magnet on the string) behind a couch or chair and "catching" metal toys—Matchbox cars, metallic figurines, or refrigerator magnets.

• Decorate the party room walls with lots of fish cut out from colored construction paper, blue waves made from crepe paper, and creepy rubber sharks and octopuses (avail-

For Added Fun:

- 1 white (or any light colored) cotton mitten per child (available at hardware stores)
- Permanent felt-tip pens
- Puffy paints (available at art supply stores)
- Accessories such as ribbons, sequins, glitter, buttons, or felt scraps
- Glue

able at toy stores) hung with thumbtacks. For a hazy "underwater" effect, replace your regular light bulbs with blue or green ones and cover the lamp shades with inexpensive shades poked with tiny holes so the light peeks out.

PRIZES AND FAVORS

- Give the kids their homemade fish mittens and toys from the "Go-Fish" game.

- Give everyone items related to *The Little Mermaid* movie such as small figurines, books, and soundtrack cassette tapes.

- Let the kids pick out an inexpensive item from the aquarium gift shop.

TROUBLE-SHOOTING TIPS

- Use the buddy system on the outing—have the kids hold hands with a partner so they'll stay together.

- Depending on the size of the group, you might want to ask other adults to accompany you. If you can't round up any volunteers, arrange for a trusted babysitter to come along.

- Be sure the kids know they shouldn't tap on the glass at any of the aquarium exhibits (or disturb the fish at the hatchery). Reward those who behave well with stickers.

CLOWNING AROUND

All kids love to clown around! Turn your party into a really special event by inviting a professional clown to entertain!

For Ages: 2–5

Optional Ages: 6–9

Preparation: Find a clown by looking in the Yellow Pages under "Entertainers—Entertainment" or in kids' magazines. For a less-expensive alternative, arrange for a friend or family member to do the job. (Clown suits and make-up are available at costume shops.)

WHAT TO DO

You can find a clown through a special company or agency, or you can hire one that works independently. Interview several by phone ahead of time to determine which performance or act is right for your party and guests. Some clowns use props, and some pass out balloons or party favors.

Your clown party can be fun and simple—just let the clown do the entertaining and then have cake and ice cream afterwards. Videotape the performance if possible, and let the kids watch it once the clown leaves, for an added treat.

If you have extra time for preparation, provide the kids with clown accessories and let them dress up for the special guest. They'll have loads of fun putting on colorful oversized

clothes, funny shoes, wild wigs, and floppy hats. Put make-up on each child (you may want to invite another adult to help you with this), or if the guests are a bit older, let them make up themselves or each other. Once the clown leaves, have a parade, take lots of photos, and enjoy the kids' show.

CREATIVE OPTIONS

- Turn the party room into a big top circus! Create booths out of cardboard boxes, decorate the party area with streamers, hang pictures of clowns and circus animals on the walls, and play circus music in the background (the music of John Philip Sousa will work well). Have a special face-painting booth for turning the guests into clowns.

- Invite guests to the clown party with balloon invitations that they have to inflate to read

For Added Fun:

- Wigs
- Colorful shirts
- Baggy pants
- Oversized shoes
- Floppy hats
- Rouge
- Eyeliner
- Eye shadow
- Lipstick
- "Clown white" make-up (These materials are available at costume shops, thrift shops, or drugstores.)
- A camera or videocamera

(write the party details on inflated balloons, deflate, and mail).

- Serve hot dogs or corn dogs for the main refreshment, and popcorn and peanuts for a snack. Serve a "circus" cake shaped like a carousel and covered with brown sugar "sawdust" and plastic horses.

PRIZES AND FAVORS

- Give everyone a Polaroid snapshot of themselves dressed as a clown before they leave.

- Pass out helium-filled or Mylar balloons.

- Give each guest a book or coloring book about the circus.

- Provide bags of peanuts or popcorn.

TROUBLE-SHOOTING TIPS

- Some kids are afraid of clowns—all that make-up and wild clothing can be scary—so explain to them what the clown will look like and that a clown is really a person in disguise. Some clown entertainers might also be willing to clean off their make-up and change clothes in front of the kids when they're done performing—kids find the transition amazing.

- If the kids will be dressing up like clowns, have them draw their clown faces on paper first so they'll have a good idea how they'll look. Encourage a lot of creativity—traditionally, no two clown faces are supposed to look alike!

FIRE FIGHTER!
FIRE FIGHTER!

Kids love the hero image of a fire fighter, and many local fire stations are happy to send someone over to talk with the kids, show them the equipment, and teach fire safety.

For Ages: 2–5

Optional Ages: 6–9

Preparation: Call a local fire station to see if a fire fighter can come to the party in uniform with some equipment.

WHAT TO DO

When you call the fire station, find out what items the fire fighter can bring for the presentation (such as fire-fighting equipment, handouts, or posters). Be sure to determine the amount of time the fire fighter will be able to spend at the party—if it's a short time, plan other activities.

As the guests arrive, give them fire-fighter hats to wear. Encourage them to ask the fire fighter questions if they want. When the special presentation is over, gather the kids for a "fire check" activity. Have the group walk around the house and yard searching for possible (but imitation) fire hazards that you have set up ahead of time—piles of newspaper, a gas can, matches—and award a sticker for each potential hazard found. After the fire

check, have the kids create a fire safety poster using posterboard and felt-tip pens, with a thank-you message for their favorite fire fighter. Then load the kids into the car, and drive to the fire station to drop it off.

CREATIVE OPTIONS

- Ask the fire fighter if it would be possible to arrive in a fire truck (one of the small ones) that the kids can explore, under supervision, during the party.

- Have the kids act out a skit involving a fire scene with some of them pretending to be fire fighters and some of them needing to be rescued.

- Send out invitations in the shape of a fire hat or fire truck.

For Added Fun:
- Fire-fighter hats for each guest (available at toy stores)
- Posterboard
- Felt-tip pens
- Stickers

- Decorate the party room with ladders, hoses, fire-fighter hats, and axes—all made from construction paper.

PRIZES AND FAVORS

- Let the guests wear their fire-fighter hats home and keep any items the fire fighter passed out during the presentation.

- Give everyone a book or coloring book about fire fighting or fire safety.

- Pass out bags of red hot candies.

- Give the kids dalmatian dog stuffed animals.

TROUBLE-SHOOTING TIP

- Remind the kids to be good listeners when the guest arrives, and reward those who listened quietly with a special sticker.

'TOON TOWN

Mickey and Minnie Mouse, Fred Flintstone, the Tasmanian Devil—all are favorites with kids. Your guests will love watching a cartoon character come to life!

For Ages: 2–5

Optional Ages: 6–9

Preparation: You can hire a costumed cartoon character for your event through special companies and agencies listed in the Yellow Pages under "Entertainers—Entertainment." For a less-expensive alternative, arrange for a friend or family member to rent a cartoon character outfit from a costume shop.

WHAT TO DO

If you plan to hire a cartoon entertainer through a special company or agency, find out what kinds of services they will provide. Some entertainers will have a special act, and some offer photo and videotaping services. If you plan to have a friend dress up, you'll need to have games and activities—the "special guest" can join in the party rather than put on a show.

Encourage the kids to ask the visitor questions (yes or no questions are best), shake hands, or give hugs. The character can pass out favors, too. For the main event, take Polaroid snapshots of each guest sitting on the lap of the special entertainer.

Later, have the kids make their own creative cartoon panels using white posterboard cut into six-inch squares. They can color a back-ground scene with the felt-tip pens or crayons and fill in the scene with the cartoon characters from comic and coloring books (cut these out before the party so the kids won't be using scissors). They can either glue the characters onto the scene for a display or do creative play by moving the characters around. When the cartoon panels are complete, the kids can arrange them in an interesting sequence and make up a connecting story.

CREATIVE OPTIONS

• Rent a favorite cartoon video if you have a VCR. Disney movies are popular, but short cartoon videos are also available.

• Purchase a coloring book featuring some favorite cartoon characters, cut a few different characters out, and place them in a large envelope. At game time, pull out a

For Added Fun:

- White posterboard cut into 6-by-6-inch squares
- Comic books or coloring books featuring favorite cartoon characters
- Felt-tip pens and/or crayons
- Glue
- Scissors
- A Polaroid camera

little bit of the character at a time, and have the kids try to be the first to guess who it is.

- Purchase a cartoon coloring book and cut one scene up into large puzzle-shaped pieces (one piece for each child). Give each guest a piece of the puzzle to color with felt-tip pens. To play, place the pieces in a large envelope, have one child reach in and pull out a puzzle piece and guess what character it might be, and then place the puzzle piece on the table. Repeat this with all of the guests, having them try to connect the pieces as the game progresses. Continue until the cartoon character is revealed and the puzzle is put together.

- Invite the guests with homemade cartoon character invitations. The party details can be placed in a speech bubble.

PRIZES AND FAVORS

- Let everyone take home the Polaroid snapshot of themselves with the special guest.

- Give the kids comic books, cartoon coloring books, small plastic cartoon figurines, or stickers featuring cartoon characters.

- Video rental stores often have cartoon posters or inexpensive cartoon movies that would make fun favors.

TROUBLE-SHOOTING TIPS

- If any guests are frightened by the larger-than-life cartoon character, take them aside and privately explain that it's just a person dressed up in a costume.

- To keep the kids from wrestling over the cut-out cartoon characters for their cartoon panels, make sure you have extra cut-outs of the most popular characters on hand.

TELL ME A STORY

Stories hold a magical quality for everyone—especially children. A storyteller can bring magic to a party—and it's usually an inexpensive form of entertainment.

For Ages: 2–5

Optional Ages: 6–9

Preparation: Contact a children's bookstore, library, or preschool for storyteller referrals.

WHAT TO DO

True storytellers are a real treasure. They make up stories or tell them from memory, with a lot of movement and expression. Depending on the situation, you may be able to request a specific story, arrange for a telling of several preschool-level stories, or have the storyteller dress up as a character. If you are unable to find a storyteller for the party but would still like to have one, arrange for a friend or family member to play the role. Have a few practice runs before the party for a smoother, more animated reading. To get the kids in the mood for a story, request on the invitation that they dress as their favorite story character and bring a favorite book to the party.

Plan some special activities to do after the storyteller is finished. The kids can take turns telling the other guests which character they are dressed up as or acting out the story their character is from (videotape this, if possible). Then let the kids create their own storybook (using blank books you've prepared ahead of time by covering pages made from plain white paper with covers made from tagboard). Poke some holes about two inches apart where the bookbinding would normally be and tie all of the pages together with yarn. The kids can draw scenes on the pages with pencils, crayons, and felt-tip pens. If there's time, read to them from storybooks they brought, or show them the videotape you made.

CREATIVE OPTIONS

• Serve a storybook cake shaped like an open book, with frosting words and illustrations.

For Added Fun:
- Tagboard
- Plain white paper
- A hole-punch
- Felt-tip pens
- Pencils
- Crayons
- Yarn

- Show a selection from Shelley Duvall's *Faery Tale Theatre* after the storyteller has gone.

- Invite the kids to the party with invitations made to look like miniature storybooks.

- Decorate the party room with books and posters from a library or children's bookstore.

PRIZES AND FAVORS

- Send everyone home with a special book as well as their own homemade book.

- Offer posters that promote reading or feature storybook characters.

- Give each child a bookmark.

TROUBLE-SHOOTING TIPS

- To promote good listening, remind the kids not to talk or disturb the storyteller during the presentation.

- If any of the kids are inattentive during the story, let them quietly draw pictures that go along with the story.

- Some younger children will need individual attention while making their storybooks. Older guests can pair up with younger ones to offer help and encouragement, or parents can help their youngsters.

MAKING MUSIC

"Come to a party!" can be music to a child's ears—especially if the party promises a musical entertainer. Invite a professional musician or singer to entertain the kids for a really memorable event.

For Ages: 2–5

Optional Ages: 6–9

Preparation: You can hire a musical entertainer through special companies and agencies listed in the Yellow Pages under "Entertainers—Entertainment." For a less-expensive alternative, invite a friend or family member with special talent to entertain. Or call a preschool or a music store for musician or singer referrals.

WHAT TO DO

If you plan to find a musician or singer in the Yellow Pages, be sure to ask if the entertainer performs music that preschoolers will enjoy. If someone you know will be doing the entertaining, have a few practice runs to make sure the performance will go smoothly. See if your musical guest can bring along some preschool songs and fingerplays to teach the kids. The entertainer could also bring a few musical instruments to share and cassette tapes or videos that feature performers for the very young (or provide these materials).

Plan lots of activities before and after the performance. The guests can perform songs or fingerplays or play musical instruments and form a little band (videotape this, if possible). If you don't have any real musical instruments,

let the kids create some. They can make drums from oatmeal canisters, maracas from spice bottles and dried rice or beans, and kazoos from empty toilet paper rolls with one end covered with waxed paper and secured with a rubber band. After the musical guest leaves, show the kids the videotape you made. Or let the kids can listen to music and dance.

CREATIVE OPTIONS

• Show a video featuring lots of music, such as *Annie* or *Beauty and the Beast.*

• Have the kids take turns being a "one-man band," playing as many instruments as possible—all at once!

• Invite the guests with a musical invitation—a card in the shape of a musical note, a harmonica, or a kazoo with the party details tied on.

For Added Fun:

• A cassette player and musical tapes appropriate for pre-schoolers

• Musical instruments—real or homemade

• A collection of songs and fingerplays

• Supplies for homemade instruments: oatmeal canisters, spice bottles, dried rice or beans, empty toilet paper roles, waxed paper, and rubber bands

• Request that the guests bring along their favorite cassette tape or a musical instrument to play at the party if they have one, so they can share the music they love.

• Play a round of Musical Chairs if there's any extra time (see p. 12 for directions).

PRIZES AND FAVORS

• Let the kids take their homemade instruments with them when they leave.

• Give everyone an inexpensive musical instrument to take home such as a kazoo, harmonica, or set of musical spoons.

• Offer cassette tapes of popular children's songs or videos featuring a famous singer.

TROUBLE-SHOOTING TIPS

• Be sure you have an instrument for every guest so no one is left out. If that's not possible, supervise to make sure the kids take turns.

• Don't worry about musical ability—this party is bound to sound a little off-key sometimes. Instead, focus on enhancing cooperation between the members of the "band," watching the kids learn new skills, and letting them have fun with music.

School Age 6-9

GUMBY LOTTO

Gumby Lotto is a homemade version of the popular party game Twister. Kids love this game because it gives them a chance to get all tangled up like a Gumby doll!

For Ages: 6–9

Optional Ages: 2–5, 10–12

Players Needed: 3 or more

Object: To be the last remaining player on the board

HOW TO PLAY

Prepare the Gumby Lotto board by painting a grid on a plastic sheet with twenty-four squares, each twelve-by-twelve-inches wide (six-by-six-inches for younger kids). Then paint a different sticker design, using the sticker packs as a guide, inside each square. Cut tagboard or paper into twenty-four small squares and put a different sticker on each one—these will be the playing cards.

When the guests arrive, place several different stickers from the matching sticker set on their hands, feet, elbows, and knees, making sure each player gets the same number of stickers. At game time, have the first player choose a card. The card must match one of the stickers on her body in order for her to move onto the board—if it doesn't match, the card is passed to the next player or on down the line until

someone has a match. When a match is made, the player must put the body part on the corresponding Gumby Lotto square. For instance, if a player has a matching sticker on her elbow, she must bend over and put her elbow on the grid. Play continues with the players taking turns putting their hands, feet, elbows, and knees on the board as cards are chosen (keep shuffling and reusing the cards). If a player is unable to get a body part in the appropriate square or loses her balance, she is out. The last remaining player on the board wins.

CREATIVE OPTIONS

- If you don't have time to make the game materials, purchase the board game Twister at a toy store instead.

- Videotape the kids getting all tangled up with each other and show the video later. Or take Polaroid snapshots—one for each guest.

Materials Needed:
- A large sheet of clear or white plastic, about 6 feet long (an old shower curtain or plastic bedding will work)
- Acrylic paints
- 2 sets of 24 matching stickers with simple designs
- Tagboard or paper
- Scissors

• After a few rounds of Gumby Lotto, use the plastic grid as an English Hopscotch board. Just use six of the squares, and have the kids hold a marker (a rock, rubber ball, or any small object) between their feet while taking turns jumping through the path of squares.

PRIZES AND FAVORS

• Give everyone a sticker pack to take home.

• If you play Hopscotch, give each of the kids a small toy to use as a marker such as a fancy eraser, key chain, or rubber ball.

• Give the winner of Gumby Lotto the board game "Twister."

TROUBLE-SHOOTING TIPS

• Be flexible with the rules so the kids will have a good time. If a player chooses a card that doesn't match any of her stickers or simply can't reach a square, allow her to choose another card for a second chance.

• Lay the grid on a soft surface so the kids won't get hurt when they topple over during the game.

SUITCASE RELAY

This relay race will have everyone laughing! It's especially fun for going-away parties, but it will be a big hit at *any* party.

For Ages: 6–9

Optional Ages: 2–5, 10–12

Players Needed: 6 or more

Object: To be the first team to reach the finish line after completing the required challenges

HOW TO PLAY

Before the game, pack two suitcases with a collection of crazy, mismatched clothing, making sure that each carryall has an equal amount of clothes. Divide the kids into two teams, with the same amount of players on each side, and set up a starting line and goal line (twenty-five yards between the two lines is a good distance)—masking tape or pieces of rope work well for this.

To start, the kids line up in their teams and the first player in each line runs toward the goal carrying a suitcase. When those two players reach the goal line, they open their suitcases, put on *every* item of clothing, pick up the empty suitcases, run back to the starting line, undress, put all the clothes back in the suitcases, close them, and hand them off to the next teammates in line. The next players repeat these steps, passing the suitcases on to the next kids in line. All the players have to do is put the clothing items on their bodies—it's okay if they wear flippers on their hands or put a shirt on backwards (it's a race for fun, not to see who can correctly dress themselves). The game continues until one team has finished the race—that team is the winner.

CREATIVE OPTIONS

• A variation is to divide each team in half and have one half stand at the first line and the other half stand at the second line. The race starts with the first players on each team opening the suitcases, putting on the mismatched clothing, closing the suitcases, and running to their teammates at the other line. The same players then take off the clothes, and the first teammates waiting at

Materials Needed:

- 2 small suitcases, tote bags, or brown paper grocery bags
- Crazy, mismatched clothing, including footwear (high heels, galoshes, or even flippers), an oversized item (a big shirt, smock, or coat), and a funny accessory (goggles, mismatched knee-high socks, or a bathing cap)
- Something to mark the starting line and goal line (masking tape or pieces of rope work well)

the other line pack the clothing into the suitcases and sprint back to the first line. The race continues until every player has had a chance to pack and dress, and the quicker team wins.

- For a simpler race, have the first runners pack the suitcases with items you've provided (clothing, accessories, toiletries—anything goes), carry the suitcases to the goal line, run back to the starting line, unpack the suitcases, and hand them off to the next players. The game continues until the faster team finishes.

PRIZES AND FAVORS

- Give everyone a funny accessory to remind them of the race—goggles, flippers, a bathing cap, or a pair of silly socks.

- Offer each child an inexpensive lunch box (a mini suitcase). Put goodies like candy and bubblegum inside, for an added surprise.

- Make travel goody bags for the kids by filling small brown paper lunch bags with gum, mini bags of peanuts, little activity books, or toy vehicles like cars or trains.

TROUBLE-SHOOTING TIPS

- For younger kids, have extra adult helpers on hand in case any of the kids have trouble putting the clothes on.

- Avoid clothing items that might be difficult to put on such as belts, turtleneck shirts, or long underwear.

TWENTY QUESTIONS

Twenty Questions is a classic game that's fun to play in a large or small group. Try some variations to give the game a new twist.

For Ages: 6–9

Optional Ages: 10–12

Players Needed: 3 or more

Object: To guess the person, place, or thing within twenty yes or no questions

HOW TO PLAY

Before the game, write the names of real or fictional people, places, or things on cards cut from tagboard. You can add an element of humor to the game by labeling the cards with people, places, or things that will make kids laugh—the Terminator, the Principal's office, or underwear.

The first player chooses a card (without looking at the other cards) and tells everyone whether her secret word is a person, place, or thing. One by one, the other players ask yes or no questions to figure out the answer. The group can only ask a total of twenty questions. Each player can try to solve the mystery when it's her turn, but an incorrect guess means she's out of the game. (An incorrect guess doesn't count toward the twenty questions.)

Continue to play until twenty questions have been asked. If no one has guessed correctly by then, the card-holding player reads the answer and wins a prize for stumping the group. Anyone who guesses the correct answer within the twenty questions wins.

CREATIVE OPTIONS

- Let each player come up with a person, place, or thing rather than putting the answers on cards.

- Instead of using person, place, and thing categories, play the game using animal, vegetable, or mineral categories. (This version works better with older kids.)

- Play a version of Twenty Questions called Virginia Woolf. The players must select famous people, living or dead, for everyone to guess.

Materials Needed:
- Tagboard
- A pencil or pen
- Scissors

• If the kids really like the game, you can break them up into pairs and let them play Twenty Questions quietly together—perhaps while everyone is waiting for parents to arrive at the end of the party.

PRIZES AND FAVORS

• Send each guest home with a small wrapped box with a secret "thing" inside. Fill the boxes with candy or small toys.

• Give the kids postcards, posters, or buttons featuring famous celebrities. Make a game of it and have them guess what their prizes are, one at a time, before they go home!

• Give each guest twenty stickers, twenty gum balls, or twenty wrapped hard candies.

TROUBLE-SHOOTING TIPS

• To make the game easier, have the player holding the card give a hint after every question. For instance, if someone guesses "Is he famous?" and the answer is yes, a hint such as "But he's only famous if you watch TV" can be given. The game will move faster, and the kids will win sooner. You can even write up some hints ahead of time on the back of the cards.

• If the kids have trouble guessing the correct answers within twenty questions, allow them to just keep guessing until everyone gives up.

BLIND MAN'S BLUFF

How well do the party-goers really know their friends? This fun game will help them find out! Blind Man's Bluff is best-suited for a large group of kids that know each other.

For Ages: 6–9

Optional Ages: 10–12

Players Needed: 8 or more

Object: To guess the identity of another player while blindfolded

HOW TO PLAY

Choose one player to be the Blind Man and blindfold him. (When you blindfold children, make sure the blindfold isn't too tight and that it covers their eyes completely.)

All of the players form a circle around the Blind Man with their hands joined. The players start moving in one direction until the Blind Man claps three times. At that time, the players in the circle must stop, and the Blind Man points to one of them and is given one guess to name that person. If the Blind Man guesses correctly, the two players switch places, and if he guesses incorrectly, the player steps into the middle of the circle with the Blind Man.

The Blind Man stays blindfolded and tries to catch his chosen player, who in turn tries to avoid being caught. Once the Blind Man

catches the player in the circle, he must try to identify the player by touching the player's clothing, hair, and other features (the player must stand still while the Blind Man does this). When the player is correctly identified, the Blind Man removes the blindfold and joins the circle, and the identified player becomes the Blind Man. Play continues until everyone has taken a turn being the Blind Man.

CREATIVE OPTIONS

- During the chase part of the game, the child in the circle with the Blind Man can make funny sounds to attract—or distract—the Blind Man.

- A fun variation eliminates the chase part of the game—instead, the players move in a circular motion around the Blind Man, while singing a song of their choice. When the

Materials Needed:
- Enough space for the players to form a wide circle
- A blindfold, bandanna, large scarf, or eye mask with the peepholes covered with black construction paper

song ends, the Blind Man points to one of the players and gives a funny command such as "Howl like a wolf," "Sing like Michael Jackson," or "Talk baby talk." The Blind Man then tries to identify the player, and if he does, the two switch places. Otherwise, the game continues with the players circling and singing again.

- Let the Blind Man touch only the hands, clothing, face, or hair of the player in the circle to make guessing more difficult.

PRIZES AND FAVORS

- Give everyone a bandanna "blindfold" to take home.

- Take Polaroid snapshots of each player as the Blind Man and give the photos as souvenirs at the end of the party.

- Offer all of the kids cassette singles of popular songs.

TROUBLE-SHOOTING TIPS

- Make sure the play area is free of any obstacles (like furniture or lawn debris) so the kids won't trip or hurt themselves.

- If a child is reluctant to wear a blindfold, let him be the last to take a turn so he can see it's not too threatening. If he still refuses, allow him to play with his eyes closed.

- If the game is too difficult with the Blind Man getting only one guess, allow three guesses instead.

UP, JENKINS!

This classic game hasn't gone out of style with today's kids because it has all the suspense, excitement, action, and surprise that kids love.

For Ages: 6–9

Optional Ages: 10–12

Players Needed: 8 or more

Object: To discover which player has the hidden coin

HOW TO PLAY

Divide the players into two teams and have them sit on opposite sides of the table. Pick one child on each team to be the leader and give one team a coin. Have a piece of paper and a pencil handy for keeping score.

To start the game, one team begins passing the coin back and forth among each other, underneath the table. After a short period of time, the leader of the other team shouts, "Up, Jenkins!" The team with the coin must quickly raise their closed fists above their heads. The leader of the other team then shouts, "Down, Jenkins!" and the team with the coin slaps their opened hands on the table, palms down. The team without the coin should listen carefully for the coin hitting the table so they can identify the player who is

concealing the coin. (They can discuss their guesses in secret before announcing who they think the culprit is.)

One by one, the leader of the team without the coin says the names of the players on the opposing team, trying to eliminate those players who *don't* have the coin. When a player's name is called, she must lift her palms from the table to show the coin isn't there. If the coin is revealed before the last player's name is called, that team gets to hide it again. However, if the team correctly identifies the culprit, the players on that team take the coin to hide.

Play as many rounds as possible in an allotted amount of time (twenty minutes or so) and give each team a point when they identify the culprit correctly. The team with the most points wins.

Materials Needed:
- A table
- A coin
- A piece of paper and a pencil or pen

CREATIVE OPTIONS

- To make the game more difficult, have the guessing team identify the person who has the coin *and* which hand the coin is in.

- Instead of calling "Up, Jenkins!" the kids can shout "Up, Chuck!" to add a little humor to the game.

- Use a jellybean instead of a coin so that the kids will get a giggle when it gets flattened on the table. (You'll need a plastic tablecloth or a card table that can be wiped off for this option.) Replace the squished jellybean with a fresh one after each round.

PRIZES AND FAVORS

- Give all of the kids gold foil-wrapped chocolate coins to eat at the party or take home.

- If you try the jellybean option, offer small bags of jellybeans or other candy.

- Send everyone home with a couple of real coins and a small piggy bank.

TROUBLE-SHOOTING TIPS

- Tell the kids not to slap the table *too* hard or their hands will be sore!

- If you're using a table with a wood finish, place a padded tablecloth on it to prevent scratches and to cut down on noise.

- Demonstrate how to slap your hand on the table without dropping the coin or letting it slip out.

PENNY PITCH

The sport of pitching pennies goes way back, but it's still lots of fun. And the game pieces (a handful of pennies) are always easy to find.

For Ages: 6–9

Optional Ages: 2–5

Players Needed: 3 or more

Object: To pitch and win the most pennies

HOW TO PLAY

Put ten pennies in a paper cup for each player (write the players' names on the cups to avoid confusion during the game). Then spread ten extra pennies on the ground (or floor, if you're playing indoors) in front of a wall.

At game time, give each player a cup of pennies and tell the first player to gently toss a penny against the wall, aiming it so the penny will ricochet and hit one of the pennies on the ground. If the tossed penny touches one of the pennies on the ground, the player who made the toss retrieves his penny and the one he hit. (If the tossed penny touches more than one penny on the ground, the player may keep all the pennies hit.) However, if the shot is missed, the player loses the tossed penny (it stays on the ground where it lands), and the

next player takes a turn. Play continues until all of the pennies are emptied from the cups or all of the pennies are gone from the ground. The player who has the most pennies at the end of the game wins.

CREATIVE OPTIONS

• Draw a grid on a large piece of paper and put it on the ground in front of the wall. Mark some of the squares with stars, some with circles, and some with triangles (or any design will do). Then fill small brown paper lunch bags with candy or small toys and mark each bag with one of the designs in the grid. Any time a player's penny lands in one of the boxes containing a design, let him reach into the bag with the corresponding design for a prize.

Materials Needed:

- A wall
- 10 pennies per child, plus an extra 10 pennies
- 1 paper cup or other container per child
- Enough space for the kids to spread out
- A pencil or pen

- Instead of spreading only pennies on the ground, include a variety of different coins—nickels, dimes, quarters, half-dollars, and even some fake coins or wooden nickels.

- Allow the players to continue tossing pennies if the tossed penny hits another penny, stopping only when their coins miss the mark.

PRIZES AND FAVORS

- Let the kids keep all of the coins won during the game.

- Give everyone a collection of gold foil-wrapped chocolate coins to eat during the party or to take home.

- Give the winner a piggy bank for storing his winnings.

TROUBLE-SHOOTING TIP

- Show the kids how to toss the pennies gently and take aim—the pennies will tend to bounce off the wall and roll away if thrown too hard.

AIRPLANE

Here's a fun game for older kids that's a variation of Pin the Tail on the Donkey. They'll love the suspense!

For Ages: 6–9

Optional Ages: 10–12

Players Needed: 6 or more

Object: To pin your airplane to the map, farthest from the "takeoff" spot

HOW TO PLAY

Before the game, make an airplane for each player by cutting airplane shapes out of tagboard (write the players' names on the airplanes to prevent confusion over who wins). Hang a map on the wall of the party room and mark a "takeoff" spot in the middle of it.

At game time, line up the players at the opposite end of the room from the map and, while they're watching, put several obstacles in the middle of the room (furniture, throw pillows, or wastebaskets will work well—nothing breakable!). Give the players some time to study the placement of the obstacles and the "takeoff" spot.

One by one, hand the players an airplane, blindfold them, and point them toward the

map. (When you blindfold children, make sure the blindfold isn't too tight and that it covers their eyes completely.) Each player must cross the floor without touching any obstacles and pin the airplane to the map as far away from the "takeoff" spot as she can. If a player runs into an obstacle before reaching the map, it's considered a plane crash and the player is out. If she reaches the map but pins her airplane to the water, it's considered a crash-landing and she is out. The player who reaches the map safely and pins her airplane farthest from the "takeoff" spot is the winner.

CREATIVE OPTIONS

• Provide crayons, paint, glitter, and other art supplies and let the kids decorate their airplanes before the game. Or let the kids create their own fantasy maps.

Materials Needed:
- A large playing area
- A large map of the world
- A blindfold, bandanna, large scarf, or eye mask with the peepholes covered with black construction paper
- Tagboard
- A pencil or pen
- A tape measure or ruler
- Scissors
- Tape
- Obstacles

- Spin the kids around before their turn so they get even more mixed up about where to go. (Don't spin them too hard or too long!)

- For an easier game, just have the kids try to reach the map and pin their plane on it rather than trying to avoid the water, too.

PRIZES AND FAVORS

- Let the kids take their airplanes home.

- Give each child a colorful map of the United States.

- Offer everyone toy airplanes or airplane stickers (available at toy and discount stores).

- Give the kids bandanna "blindfolds."

TROUBLE-SHOOTING TIPS

- When setting up the obstacles, make sure you don't use any small items the kids could trip over or low tables they could bang their knees on. Encourage them to walk across the room slowly so they won't get hurt.

- If a child is reluctant to wear a blindfold, let her be the last one to take a turn so she can see it's not too threatening. If she still refuses, allow her to play with her eyes closed.

MARCO POLO

Marco Polo is a classic game for a pool party. If you don't have a swimming pool, play the game in the shallow end of a public pool—with lots of adult supervision.

For Ages: 6–9

Optional Ages: 10–12

Players Needed: 3 or more

Object: To avoid being caught by Marco

HOW TO PLAY

Choose one player to be Marco. He must close his eyes and count to ten, giving the other players a chance to scatter throughout the pool. Then, with his eyes closed, he must find and tag one of the other players.

To find the other players, Marco swims blindly around the pool, calling out "Marco!" to which the other players respond all at once, "Polo!" Marco can call out as often as he likes—even if he is inches from one of the other players—and the other players *must* respond. Once Marco tags another player, that player becomes Marco, and the game begins again. The kids will probably want to play many rounds!

CREATIVE OPTIONS

• Play a "silent" version of the game with Marco calling out "Marco!" and the players responding with movement only. The players can swim, splash, or gently ripple the water—Marco must listen very carefully to find the others.

• Have one player be Jaws! All of the players, including Jaws, must close their eyes. Jaws swims around the pool trying to "attack" the other players. With everyone "blind," the tension and suspense increases.

• If you're playing at a public pool, have the kids stay in the shallow end only. (A larger shallow end can be a fun advantage, too—more space to hide in!)

Materials Needed:
• A swimming pool

PRIZES AND FAVORS

• Give all of the kids a pair of swimming goggles to wear during the party and take home later.

• Send everyone home with favors that remind them of a fun day at the pool—a pair of sunglasses, beach ball, water toy, snorkel, or flotation device.

• If you try the "Jaws" option, offer the kids Shark Bites candy and shark toys.

• Give everyone a beach towel to use at the pool and to take home.

TROUBLE-SHOOTING TIPS

• Adult supervision is vital for all pool activities. If you have a large group, make sure you have more than one lifeguard.

• Call all of the guests' parents ahead of time to find out if their kids can swim. Ask any parents of weak swimmers to provide flotation armbands and make sure the kids wear them.

• Provide sunscreen for all of the kids, and encourage them to apply it frequently.

TUG OF WAR

A good old-fashioned Tug of War is a great way to help kids work off their excess party energy. Half the fun is losing as one team tumbles to the ground in a laughing heap!

For Ages: 6–9

Optional Ages: 10–12

Players Needed: 6 or more

Object: To pull the opposing players over the center line

HOW TO PLAY

Before the game, draw a chalk line or lay a rope on the grass to mark the center line. (Make sure the playing area is level and free of debris.) Divide the kids into two teams with an equal number of players who share approximately equal physical strength and weight. Have the players line up in single file on each side of the center line, with a few feet of space between each player. Tie a bandanna or scarf around the middle of the tugging rope and set this marker over the center line.

Each player grabs onto the tugging rope and, on the count of three, tries to pull the first member of the other team over the center line. The game may end right away if the first player on either team steps over the center line—however, it's more likely that all of the players on one team will be pulled across the line and collapse in a giggling pile!

CREATIVE OPTIONS

• Instead of using a line to mark the center, use a big piece of red or brown cloth and call it "hot lava" or "quicksand." The kids will have fun trying to avoid the "dangerous territory."

• Play a second game with only the winners of the previous game. Divide them up into another two teams and start the Tug of War again. When one side wins, divide those winners in half and play again. Continue until there are only two players left to pull on the rope.

• Tie a few sheets together and use them for a rope—it will be easier and softer to hold.

Materials Needed:
- 1 long, sturdy rope (about 8 to 10 feet in length)
- A bandanna or scarf
- A large grassy outdoor area
- Chalk or a long length of rope

PRIZES AND FAVORS

- Give the winning team a big bag of candy to share, and be sure to provide the losers with a fun consolation prize.

- Give the guests fun bandannas to wear at the party or to take home.

- If you use the "dangerous territory" option, give all of the kids books about volcanoes to take home.

TROUBLE-SHOOTING TIPS

- Sometimes the kids get rope burns from the tugging, so choose a smooth rope and ask the players to bring gloves to the party.

- After each round, mix up the team members so the sides aren't lopsided in strength.

- Position bigger kids on the ends of each rope to act as team "anchors."

HA HA HA

In this game, the rules are easy, but the challenge (keeping a straight face) is almost impossible!

For Ages: 6–9

Optional Ages: 10–12

Players Needed: 4 or more

Object: To keep a straight face while the other players try to make you laugh

HOW TO PLAY

The players sit or stand in a circle, and one player begins by saying "Ha," as solemnly as possible. The next player in the circle says, "Ha Ha," and the player after that, "Ha Ha Ha." Play continues with each player adding a "Ha" during his turn. The players must all keep a straight face throughout the game.

Any player who smiles or giggles must leave the circle; however, he can now move around the circle trying to make the other kids laugh. He can make funny faces or noises, but cannot touch the other players. The game ends when only one player remains in the circle by having kept a straight face through all the laughter.

CREATIVE OPTIONS

- Have the players lay on the floor at right angles, with each child's head resting on another's tummy. Once one player's tummy starts shaking from laughter, the other kids will have trouble controlling their giggling!

- Instead of saying "Ha," the kids can say a silly word like "belly button" or "burp." Let the kids choose or make up their own silly words, too.

- Give the kids fake noses or funny hats to wear during the game. It will be harder for everyone to control their impulse to laugh.

Materials Needed:
• Enough space for the players to form a circle

PRIZES AND FAVORS

• Give the kids silly gag gifts to take home—fake noses, joy buzzers, or rubber bugs.

• Offer everyone joke and riddle books to get them laughing again.

• Give the grand prize winner a funny cartoon videotape.

TROUBLE-SHOOTING TIPS

• Make sure the kids who are out don't try to tickle or touch the other players to make them laugh.

• This is a quick game, so play a few rounds or have other activities planned, too.

3-D TIC-TAC-TOE

All kids love the challenge of Tic-Tac-Toe. Here's a 3-D version that they'll want to play again and again.

For Ages: 6–9

Optional Ages: 2–5

Players Needed: 2 or more (2 play at a time)

Object: To be the first player to get three squares in a row—up, down, or diagonally

HOW TO PLAY

In traditional Tic-Tac-Toe, a grid is divided into nine squares, and two players take turns marking an X or an O in the squares. To win, a player must get three of her marks in a row—up, down, or diagonally. If no one gets three in a row, the game is a draw.

The 3-D version takes a little more skill. Before the game, draw a Tic-Tac-Toe grid on the pavement, closing the grid up by connecting all of the unconnected lines (if you can't play outdoors, use masking tape to create a closed-up Tic-Tac-Toe grid on a tile floor). Then collect beanbags (you can buy them at toy and craft stores, or make them yourself by filling old socks with dried beans or rice and tying a knot in the sock tops). Mark three of the bags with X's and three with O's.

At game time, the kids stand several feet away from the grid, and two players begin—one with the X beanbags and one with the O beanbags. They alternate turns tossing the beanbags into the grid, trying to get three of their bags in a row. If a player tosses one of her beanbags away from the grid, she can take another turn—the beanbag *must* land in a square. If her beanbag lands in a square occupied by another player's beanbag, the other beanbag is removed and must be tossed again. The player who gets three in a row first is the winner.

CREATIVE OPTIONS

• Let the kids make the beanbags before the game—just provide the socks and "beans" and show them what to do. (Let each player create three beanbags for her own use during the game.)

Materials Needed:
- Pavement or a tile floor
- Chalk or masking tape
- 6 beanbags (available at toy and craft stores, or make your own)

• Play a Tic-Tac-Toe variation in which the player who gets three bags in a row first is the *loser.*

• Number the grid squares one to nine and have silly instructions to go with each number: "Jump backwards on one foot," "Bark like a dog," "Make a weird sound without moving your lips," and so on. When the kids toss their beanbags onto the grid, they must do the corresponding action.

PRIZES AND FAVORS

• Let the kids take their beanbags home.

• Fill some homemade beanbags with jelly beans, and let the kids open the beanbags and eat the candy.

• Give all of the winners activity books filled with Tic-Tac-Toe games.

TROUBLE-SHOOTING TIPS

• If any of the kids have trouble with their aim, allow them to stand closer to the grid.

• To avoid boredom and having guests wait for turns, draw several Tic-Tac-Toe grids in your playing area. Have at least one adult supervising the games at each grid.

BINGO

Everyone loves to play Bingo! The game preparation takes a few minutes, but the fun is long-lasting, and the cards can be used again and again.

For Ages: 6–9

Optional Ages: 2–5

Players Needed: 3 or more

Object: To be the first player to cover five spaces in a row—up, down, or diagonally

HOW TO PLAY

Before the party, make some Bingo grids on white paper by drawing five squares across each horizontal row and five squares down each vertical row. At the top of each grid write B-I-N-G-O, and fill in the squares by writing any numbers from one to fifty. Each grid should have a random sampling of numbers when you're done. Then make some Bingo caller cards out of different-colored pieces of paper cut into small squares and labeled with the letter/number combinations on the grid—B-21, I-36, N-11, G-50, etc. (all the letter/number combinations must be added to the caller cards).

At game time, you'll play the role of the Caller. Give each player a handful of small tokens to hold on to (try pennies, buttons, or

Hershey's Kisses); then mix up the Bingo caller cards, draw one, and announce it to the players. Any player who has a corresponding letter/number combination on his grid, covers the spot with a token. Continue to draw caller cards and announce letters/numbers until one of the players has filled a row with tokens—up, down, or diagonally. That player shouts, "Bingo!" and wins the game.

CREATIVE OPTIONS

• Let the kids take turns being the Caller.

• For a longer game, see which player can fill up an entire grid first.

• Make Bingo grids that have squares filled with different letters of the alphabet and call out letters in a random order. The player who gets five in a row first wins.

Materials Needed:
- Paper (plain white and colored)
- Scissors
- A pencil or pen
- Small tokens (try pennies, buttons, or Hershey's Kisses)
- *Optional:* clear Contact paper

PRIZES AND FAVORS

- Give each player a homemade Bingo grid and playing cards.

- Let the kids take home their tokens.

- Give the big winner a special prize, such as a store-bought Bingo game, a bag of Hershey's Kisses, or a piggy bank.

TROUBLE-SHOOTING TIPS

- If you play more than one round, have the players switch playing cards—you'll be more likely to get a variety of winners.

- Put the Bingo caller cards aside after you draw them so you can check to make sure the player who calls, "Bingo!" has really won.

- Cover the Bingo playing cards with clear Contact paper so they won't get ripped in the excitement.

SLAP, CLAP, AND SNAP

Slap, Clap, and Snap is a classic twist on the traditional game Categories. It takes some coordination and quick thinking, and will keep the kids entertained for a long time.

For Ages: 6–9

Optional Ages: 10–12

Players Needed: 4 or more

Object: To be the last remaining player in the circle

HOW TO PLAY

Have the players sit cross-legged in a circle and choose one player to start. The first player chooses a category like "colors," "names," "foods," "TV shows," or any other one she can think of. Then she begins to slap, clap, and snap in rhythm by slapping her legs twice, clapping twice, and snapping her left fingers and then her right in an even rhythm. All of the other players do the same actions in the same rhythm so that everyone in the circle is slapping, clapping, and snapping at once.

The starting player then calls out an item from the chosen category, saying it just after she snaps, without changing or losing the rhythm. The next player in the circle follows in turn, naming another item in the category just after snapping. Play continues in this manner around the circle and doesn't stop until a player can't think of an item, repeats an item, or misses the beat—that player is out of the game and must leave the circle. The next round begins with a new category. The game is over when only one player remains in the circle—that player is the winner.

CREATIVE OPTIONS

• Play the game without a winner to avoid competition. Just continue the game after a player misses, but start a new category.

• To add some suspense, have each player point to another player to signal that it's her turn, rather than taking turns in a circle. For example, the first player calls out an item while clapping and points to any other player while everyone else is snapping. That player must keep the rhythm, call out an item after snapping, and point to another

Materials Needed:
• Enough space for the players to form a circle

player. It's easier to make a mistake in this version, producing lots of giggles!

• Play an active, outdoor version by having the kids bounce a ball back and forth between players. Each time a player catches the ball, she must name an item in the category and quickly bounce the ball to another player.

PRIZES AND FAVORS

• Give all of the kids cassette singles of popular songs to snap and clap to at home.

• If you play the outdoor version, give the kids sports balls or small, bouncy rubber balls to take with them.

• Give the grand prize winner a board game.

TROUBLE-SHOOTING TIPS

• Have the kids slap, clap, and snap at a slow pace so each player will have a few seconds to come up with a category item. Once everybody gets the hang of it, the pace can speed up.

• Keep a list of simple category suggestions handy in case the players have trouble coming up with any.

MUMMY WRAP

Kids love to act like scary monsters, and this game gives them a chance to do just that. It's also a great icebreaker for kids who don't know each other very well.

For Ages: 6–9

Optional Ages: 10–12

Players Needed: 6 or more

Object: To be the first player to wrap your partner from head to toe like a mummy

HOW TO PLAY

Divide the kids into pairs, with one player as the Mummy and the other as the Mummy Wrapper. On the count of three (after a warning that the toilet paper is "very old and delicate"), all of the Mummy Wrappers must race to wrap their Mummies with the rolls of toilet paper as fast as they can.

To win, a Mummy Wrapper has to be the first to wrap his Mummy from head to toe (except for the face). In the hurry and excitement of wrapping, the players will soon find that the toilet paper will tear, causing all kinds of delays, do-overs, and giggles. To make the mummy wrapping easier, provide tape.

CREATIVE OPTIONS

• Use rolls of crepe paper (available at party supply stores) for a more heavy-duty wrapping. Choose different colors for each "mummy" pair.

• Buy extra rolls of "mummy wrap" and play another round so everyone gets a chance to be "mummified."

• Have a mummy-wrapping contest and award a prize to everyone for fun categories like "freakiest," "silliest," or "most ghoulish." Decorate the party room with fake cobwebs, monster posters, and glow-in-the-dark accessories, and play scary music in the background (all of these materials are available at party supply stores).

Materials Needed:
• 1 roll of white or colorful toilet paper for every two kids (avoid scented brands)
• *Optional:* tape

PRIZES AND FAVORS

• Take Polaroid snapshots of the completed mummies and send everyone home with a fun photo.

• Give the winning pair a roll of gag-gift toilet paper (available at party supply stores).

• Give everyone a scary action figure (preferably a mummy) from a toy store.

• Offer all of the guests tiny pieces of candy in small plastic pill bottles and tell them it's ancient Egyptian candy that's been sealed in an old tomb for centuries. (Be sure to wash out the pill bottles before adding the candy.)

TROUBLE-SHOOTING TIPS

• If the kids don't seem to be making much progress with the wrapping, you might want to provide tape so they can put any ripped toilet paper back together.

• Be sure to tell the kids to wrap only their partner's body, leaving his face uncovered.

PRICE IT RIGHT

This home version of the classic TV game show is a winner! Kids will love the suspense, and best of all, they'll all win a prize.

For Ages: 6–9

Optional Ages: 10–12

Players Needed: 6 or more

Object: To win a prize by guessing closest to its actual price

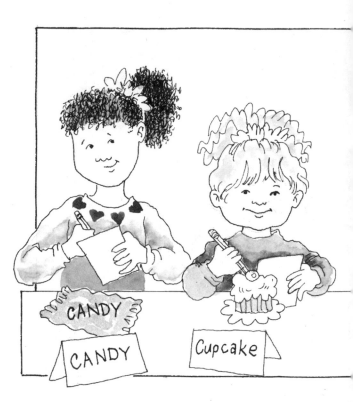

HOW TO PLAY

Before the party, set out prizes in the party room (make sure the actual prices are covered up). Then make price tags from construction paper, write the prices on them, and fold them over so the prices are hidden. For added fun, write lavish descriptions of each item on the front of the tags.

At game time, the kids must guess the price of each item, secretly writing their answers on pieces of paper. Once everyone has written down the price of the first item, have the kids read their estimates aloud. Then open the price tag and announce the price of the item. The player whose guess is closest to the actual price wins the item and is out of the game. Play continues until all of the gifts are won and everyone has a prize.

CREATIVE OPTIONS

• Allow the kids to hold a gift exchange after the game—they can trade prizes with one another if they want.

• Ask the guests to bring a white elephant gift from home along with the price of the item (they may have to do some research to find out the price). Have the rest of the kids guess the values—whomever guesses closest to the actual price has to keep the item!

• Have the kids pretend they're game show contestants. Provide adult dress-up clothes or ask the kids to come in costume. You can make name tags with funny names, using construction paper, for each guest, too.

Super Ball YO-YO Gummy Worms

Materials Needed:
- 1 inexpensive prize per guest (try paperback books, small toys, candy, or sticker packs)
- Construction paper
- A pencil or pen for making price tags
- A piece of paper and a pencil or pen for each guest

PRIZES AND FAVORS

- Along with the prizes they've already won, provide a few extra bonus prizes like bubblegum or fun pencils and erasers.

- If you have the kids dress up, let everyone keep an accessory or item of clothing, such as sunglasses or a fun hat.

- Give all of the kids inexpensive calculators to take home. They'll love playing with them during the party, too!

TROUBLE-SHOOTING TIPS

- If there is a tie for a price estimate, have the kids guess a number from one to ten to decide the winner.

- When choosing the prizes, make sure you select generic items that all of the guests will enjoy, especially if there are both girls and boys invited.

TOY MOUSE

PUZZLE HUNT

This fast-paced, silly race is fun for a large or small group. You can make the challenge as easy or difficult as you want, depending on the ages of the guests.

For Ages: 6–9

Optional Ages: 10–12

Players Needed: 4 or more

Object: To be the first to get rid of your puzzle pieces

HOW TO PLAY

Before the game, decide how many pictures and pieces of tagboard you'll need based on the number of guests. Draw puzzle shapes (about the size of a child's palm) with a felt-tip pen over each picture, leaving the middle portions of the pictures intact and a puzzle border around the edges. Then coat the back of each picture with spray adhesive and stick the pictures onto tagboard. When the adhesive has dried, cut out the puzzle pieces along the border. Make sure your homemade puzzle *looks* like a puzzle and that all the pieces will fit together again!

At game time, place the pictures, minus their "puzzle" borders, on flat surfaces around the party room and divide the mixed-up puzzle pieces equally among the guests. On the count

of three, the kids must scramble around to the different puzzle borders to find where their pieces fit. The kids will soon find that they have to cooperate with other players to figure out where their pieces go, even though they're racing against each other—that's part of the fun. The first player to fit her last puzzle piece into a puzzle border before anyone else (whether the puzzle itself is complete or not) is the winner. When you have a winner, let the rest of the guests complete the puzzles.

CREATIVE OPTIONS

• If you have a really large group, allow the kids to work in pairs.

• Photocopy school photos of the guests, have them enlarged at a copy store, and use them as the puzzle pieces.

Materials Needed:

- Large, colorful pictures that you can turn into "puzzles" (posters, coloring book pages, or magazine photos)—1 or 2 pictures per guest
- Large sheets of tagboard—enough to back each picture
- Spray adhesive
- Scissors
- A felt-tip pen

- Make the game more difficult for older kids by cutting out smaller puzzle pieces or using similar pictures (for example, posters of the four Teenage Mutant Ninja Turtles).

PRIZES AND FAVORS

- Give the winner all of the completed puzzles to try the game again at home.

- Give everyone a fun box puzzle.

- Send everyone home with a coloring book or poster.

TROUBLE-SHOOTING TIPS

- Make sure the puzzle pieces are large enough for the kids to handle so they won't get frustrated.

- For a race with less confusion, allow the kids to look at the puzzles and pieces for a few minutes before the game begins.

SWITCH

This is one of those "What's wrong with this picture?" activities that kids are familiar with from school—but this one is much more fun!

For Ages: 6–9

Optional Ages: 2–5

Players Needed: 6 or more

Object: To figure out which guests are wearing the wrong clothes

HOW TO PLAY

Divide the kids into two teams and take the first team into another room. This team must switch various items of clothing (or accessories) with one another so that each team member has traded something she was wearing with another team member. (Tell the kids to switch items like shoes, belts, barrettes, socks, or sweaters—not shirts or pants—and let boys trade items with girls.) If you think the kids will have trouble remembering any accessories that were traded, write them down on a piece of paper. This will prevent confusion when it's time to switch back.

Once the first team has switched clothing, the players return to the party room and the other team must guess what's different. When a player thinks she might know what switch has

been made, she can shout out the answer. If she's right, give her a candy treat. See if the kids can correctly identify all of the "switches" on your list. Then let the second team try to stump the first team.

CREATIVE OPTIONS

- For a bigger challenge, have the team that's guessing identify the items that have been switched *and* the players who did the switching.

- Instead of having the kids switch their own clothes, gather some items of clothing and accessories for the kids to put on over their own outfits (try a pair of socks, a watch, a necklace, a vest, and so on). Let the kids dress up, return to the party room, and try to fool the other team.

Materials Needed:
- A piece of paper and a pencil or pen
- Candy or other treats

- Have the team members switch only their shoes with each other. The other team must guess which shoes belong to whom.

PRIZES AND FAVORS

- Give all of the kids an accessory to wear home such as a pair of funny socks, some costume jewelry, or a silly hat.

- Give everyone a funny dress-up outfit such as a grass hula skirt, an occupational uniform, or a long dress. You can find all sorts of fun and inexpensive clothing at thrift shops. The kids will have a ball wearing these outfits during the party.

- Offer the kids fun jewelry items such as barrettes or surfer bracelets.

TROUBLE-SHOOTING TIPS

- Remind the kids to exchange only outer clothing—nothing embarrassing.

- If the game seems too easy for the guests you're inviting, ask them ahead of time to dress in mismatched clothes with lots of extra accessories.

PUMPING IRON

Here's another great party icebreaker. The kids have to work together to win this fun and silly challenge.

For Ages: 6–9

Optional Ages: 10–12

Players Needed: 4 or more

Object: To stuff the most balloons into your team's "Weakling" to create "muscles"

HOW TO PLAY

This game takes some preparation beforehand, but it's well worth the effort! If you don't want to blow up a bunch of balloons yourself, rent a helium machine or recruit some helpers.

At game time, divide the kids into two teams. Select one guest from each team to be the Weakling—the remaining guests are the Personal Trainers. Have the teams gather on opposite sides of the room and divide the balloons up equally among them. Then have each Weakling put on a union suit (a pair of one-piece long underwear) over his clothes.

On the count of three, the two teams of Personal Trainers must make their Weaklings grow some instant muscles by stuffing as many balloons as possible into the union suits.

Give the teams two minutes on a timer to do this. When the time is up, let everyone admire the Weaklings' new muscles (be sure to have a camera ready!). Then remove the balloons from the union suits one at a time, counting as you go. The team that stuffed the most balloons wins, but popped balloons don't count toward the total.

CREATIVE OPTIONS

- Buy or borrow union suits for half of the guests and divide the kids into partners instead of teams. After one pair has won, let the kids switch roles so they each get a turn posing and stuffing (you'll need extra balloons for this option).

- Instead of having a race, let the kids stuff one Weakling to see how many balloons they can use up. If you have enough balloons, let everyone take a turn getting stuffed.

Materials Needed:
- About 50–100 small inflated balloons
- 2 adult-size union suits (one-piece long underwear)
- A timer

PRIZES AND FAVORS

- Send everyone home with a poster of Arnold Schwarzenegger as the "Terminator."

- Give the guests books or activity booklets about exercise.

- Hand out helium or Mylar balloons to all of the kids.

TROUBLE-SHOOTING TIPS

- Use small balloons (or don't inflate the balloons very much) because you want the kids to be able to stuff them into the union suits easily.

- Make sure to pick up all of the balloon pieces after the game—they can be dangerous around small children and animals.

TONGUE TEASERS

Have a camera ready for this game—you're sure to get some great photos of funny faces!

For Ages: 6–9

Optional Ages: 10–12

Players Needed: 4 or more

Object: To identify the most "mystery" foods by tasting them

HOW TO PLAY

Place some mystery foods in separate bowls and add serving spoons. Then write the numbers one through eight clockwise on paper plates (one number for each food item). Pass out the paper plates and spoons to the guests. Have the kids sit in a circle so they will be able to see each other's expressions.

At game time, put a dab of the first food by the first number on each player's plate. Once everyone is served, the kids must taste the mystery food and secretly write down what they think it is on pieces of paper. (Wait until you see their expressions!) Repeat these steps for every food item. At the end of the taste tests, see which guest got the most correct answers—that player wins.

CREATIVE OPTIONS

• For younger kids, allow everyone to shout out what they think the mystery food is (after everyone has tasted it) rather than writing the answers down.

• Tint the mystery foods with food coloring to disguise them a little.

• Play the tasting game with breakfast cereals. Buy a variety pack of cereals, pour them into small brown paper lunch bags so the kids can't see them, and have the kids sample them one by one and try to guess the brand.

• With a more adventurous group of kids, use food items that are difficult to identify, such as mashed garbanzo beans or pureed vegetables.

Materials Needed:
- About 8 fun-to-taste items, such as yogurt, pudding, flavored oatmeal, salad dressing, pizza sauce, a mashed banana, or mashed rice
- 1 paper plate per guest
- 1 plastic spoon per guest
- Bowls for each taste item
- Serving spoons for each taste item
- A piece of paper and a pencil or pen for each guest

PRIZES AND FAVORS

- Give all of the kids mini boxes of cereal from variety packs.

- Send everyone home with a mystery food, such as a few homemade cookies or an unwrapped candy bar sealed in aluminum foil and tied with a ribbon.

- Give the grand prize winner a kids' cookbook, a fast food gift certificate collection, or a book of kids' mysteries.

TROUBLE-SHOOTING TIPS

- When selecting food items, avoid foods that are tart or that kids don't like.

- If a player seems hesitant about tasting anything, let her watch the other players first. She may want to join in later when she sees it's fun to play.

THE INVISIBLE GIFT

This game is a fun combination of Telephone, Gossip, and Charades. It's a good noncompetitive activity for an indoor party.

For Ages: 6–9

Optional Ages: 10–12

Players Needed: 6 or more

Object: To identify the "invisible" item

HOW TO PLAY

The players form a circle—they can sit or stand. The first player secretly thinks of an object such as a toy, an animal, or a food item and must pretend to handle it and pass it to the next player in the circle. For instance, if he has chosen a cat for his object, he could pretend to scoop it up, hold it, kiss it, pet it, and feed it a can of cat food. He must do all of this without talking and then hand the mysterious item to the next person.

The next player must pretend to take the item, indicate what it is without talking, and pass it to the next player. Play continues around the circle until the last player receives the item. The last player announces to the group what he thinks the item is. If he's wrong, the second-to-last player can take a guess. If that

player is also wrong, the third-to-last player gets a guess, and so on, until someone gets the correct answer. If no one gets the answer right, the first player reveals what the intended object was. Play a new round, so a new player can choose the object.

CREATIVE OPTIONS

- Instead of having the kids try to think of an object, fill a bag with all sorts of items and have each player secretly choose one when it's his turn to act. (Remove the items after each round so they won't be chosen twice.)

- After the kids have played the game using objects, have them demonstrate a whole invisible activity, such as eating breakfast or taking a shower.

Materials Needed:
- Enough space for the players to form a wide circle

- For a fun twist, have all of the players close their eyes while the demonstration is going on *except* for the player who's acting and the one who's going to relay the information. The guesses should be pretty funny by the end of the game!

PRIZES AND FAVORS

- Send everyone home with a mystery present wrapped in gift wrap or hidden in a small brown paper lunch bag.

- If you choose to do the option with the bag full of goodies, fill it with fun items for kids. After each player has chosen one, let him keep it.

- Give everyone mystery books or pads of paper and "invisible ink" pens.

TROUBLE-SHOOTING TIP

- If the kids have trouble thinking up items that are easy to describe with actions only, make a list of appropriate items and whisper one to each player when it's his turn. Include simple, concrete items, such as a scarf, book, plant, ball, or can of soda.

TICKET, PLEASE

This fun game takes quick thinking. You'll find that it's a good indoor game for an active group of kids.

For Ages: 6–9

Optional Ages: 2–5

Players Needed: 7 or more

Object: To travel from one spot to another safely

HOW TO PLAY

Arrange some chairs in a circle facing inward, with enough room in the center of the circle for the kids to run around in. Choose one player to be the Conductor. The Conductor stands in the middle of the circle.

Mix up postcards and pass them out to every player but the Conductor. Tell the players to keep their destinations (the places featured on the postcards) a secret. Then give the Conductor a list of the destinations indicated on the postcards, as well as a few that aren't (prepare this list before the game). The Conductor calls out one of the destinations on the list, and the two players holding the postcards that match the destination must jump up and switch places *before* the Conductor can take one of their empty seats. If the Conduc-tor reaches an empty chair first, the player who's left standing becomes the Conductor.

CREATIVE OPTIONS

- For younger kids, use pictures of zoo animals instead of places, and call the Conductor the Zookeeper. Provide the Zookeeper with a list of animal stickers so she can glance at those instead of trying to read words.

- For older kids, choose postcards with similar-sounding destinations so they have to listen carefully, or just add similar-sounding places to the Conductor's list (Iowa, Idaho, Ohio, Hawaii, etc.).

- Have the Conductor sit in the circle rather than stand so she has to quickly scramble for an empty seat.

Materials Needed:

- Chairs for all but one player
- Enough space for all of the kids to form a wide circle
- Pairs of identical postcards featuring different destinations—enough for all but one player (for instance, 6 postcards for 7 players, with 2 of Disneyland, 2 of London, and 2 of Rome)
- A piece of paper and a pencil or pen

PRIZES AND FAVORS

- Send the world travelers home with posters of foreign countries or maps of the world.

- Give the kids souvenirs like British candy or Chinese puzzles.

- Offer everyone fun postcards, stamped and ready to send to a friend or relative.

- If you try the option for younger kids, send everyone home with stickers featuring zoo animals.

TROUBLE-SHOOTING TIPS

- Spread the chairs out in a wide circle so there's plenty of room. That way there's less risk of the kids crashing into each other.

- If the Conductors always find a seat first and seem unchallenged, have them close their eyes while calling out destinations and open them when they hear the other players scrambling for chairs.

ALPHABET GAME SHOW

This quick-paced quiz game will keep the kids on their toes. They'll want to play it over and over.

For Ages: 6–9

Optional Ages: 10–12

Players Needed: 4 or more

Object: To be the first player to name items in categories and win the most alphabet cards

HOW TO PLAY

Before the game, write each letter of the alphabet on a separate index card. Then think up fun categories that kids can relate to (animals, names, TV shows, sports and hobbies, cartoon characters, etc.) and write each one separately on index cards. Next, put the alphabet cards in a separate pile from the category cards and shuffle both piles.

At game time, choose one player to be the Game Show Host. He must pick a card from the category pile and hold it up for all of the other players to see. He then chooses an alphabet card, holds it up for everyone to see, and announces the letter. The first player to name an item in the category that begins with the alphabet letter wins the card. For instance, if the host chooses candy bars as a category

and pulls the letter M from the pile, the first player to call out, "Milky Way," or, "Mounds," wins the alphabet card. At that time, you can choose another Game Show Host or let the same one choose another two cards. The player with the most alphabet cards at the end of the game is the winner.

CREATIVE OPTIONS

• If you want to have a noncompetitive game, just omit the part where the kids keep the alphabet cards. Instead, shuffle the alphabet cards back into the pile and continue.

• Let the kids think up their own categories instead of making the cards ahead of time.

• For a more challenging version of the game, make up Bingo grids with five squares across and five squares down. Write the same five

Materials Needed:
- 26 index cards (3½ by 5½ inches), plus at least 2 extra per player (to write categories on)
- A felt-tip pen

categories by each square on the left side of the grids and five different alphabet letters by the squares at the top of the grids. To play, the players must fill in the squares of the grids, matching categories with alphabet letters as quickly as possible (set a two-minute time limit). After time has been called, have the players read off their answers for each letter.

PRIZES AND FAVORS

- Send the kids home with items that relate to the categories, such as comic books if the category is cartoon characters or giant Hershey bars if the category is candy bars.

- Give the winner the board game "Scattergories."

TROUBLE-SHOOTING TIPS

- To make the game go more smoothly, you can omit letters that are especially difficult such as Q, X, and Z.

- You can also allow the kids to use the difficult letters *within* a word, rather than at the beginning of the word.

MYSTERY MASTERPIECE

The kids will love the surprise result of this activity. And it's so easy, they'll be able to try it at home again after the party!

For Ages: 6–9

Optional Ages: 10–12

Players Needed: Groups of 4

Object: To create a crazy creature one part at a time

WHAT TO DO

Before the activity, divide pieces of paper into four panels by folding each one over from the short edge three times. Or demonstrate to the kids how it's done and let them do the folding themselves. Seat the kids around a table.

Have each child draw the head of a favorite animal, person, or creature in the top panel with felt-tip pens, making the neck extend into a small portion of the second panel. (For added fun, suggest that the kids try to draw the body parts of cartoon characters, space creatures, robots, or monsters.) They should then fold the paper over so that the head isn't visible but the bottom of the neck is. After that, they must pass the folded piece of paper to the child on their right who adds a body and arms in the second panel, beginning with the neck and ending with the waistline. (The kids must not peek at the previous drawing!) Tell the kids to extend the creature's waistline below the panel, and pass the folded piece of paper to the right. The third panel of each piece of paper will feature legs, and the last panel will have the feet. When the drawings are complete, the kids can unfold their "masterpieces" and share them with the rest of the group. The results will be some crazy creatures and lots of laughter!

CREATIVE OPTIONS

- Divide the paper into six panels for extra fun. The first panel can feature the top of the head, eyes, and nose; the second panel, the face, mouth, chin, and neck; the third panel, the upper torso and arms; the fourth panel, the lower torso; the fifth panel, the legs; and the sixth, the feet.

Materials Needed:

- A table
- Several sheets of 8½-by-11-inch paper per child
- Lots of felt-tip pens in a variety of colors

- The kids can cut the body parts out and swap them to create even more silly combinations. Give them tape to hold the creatures together.

- Provide art supplies such as paint, crayons, glitter, and glue so the kids can really go wild with the drawings.

PRIZES AND FAVORS

- Let each of the kids keep a completed picture. Before sending the pictures home with the kids, glue them to posterboard and write the names of the artists near the different body parts.

- Give the kids felt-tip pens, pads of paper, paint sets, or other art supplies.

TROUBLE-SHOOTING TIP

- If the kids worry about not being good at art, tell them it's not a contest and that the pictures are supposed to look silly anyway.

PUPPET FUN

Kids love to make things that they can use over and over—a puppet-making party will give them this opportunity. And they're easy to make using the simplest household materials!

For Ages: 6–9

Optional Ages: 2–5

Players Needed: Any group size

Object: To create reusable puppets

WHAT TO DO

Set up the art materials at a table—this will make it easier for the kids to work on their projects. The kids can start by making puppet bodies using socks, bags, cups, or wooden spoons.

For a paper bag puppet, have the kids draw the eyes and nose over the bag's bottom flap—the underside of the flap becomes the mouth. Let the kids use glitter, ribbons, and yarn to give the puppets some sparkle and flair. For a wooden spoon puppet, the kids can simply create a face on the spoon part, using felt-tip pens, and hold the handle to control the puppet's movement. They can make fun soft puppets with socks, simply adding buttons or pom-poms for eyes. To make a small paper cup puppet, just have the kids cut two holes

below the cup rim, turn the cup upside down, and insert two fingers in the holes for crazy puppet legs—a face and decorations can be added with crayons and other art supplies.

When the puppet-making activity is finished, give the kids some time to come up with a script, and put on a puppet show for the parents (have them pick the kids up twenty minutes early and enjoy the production).

CREATIVE OPTIONS

• Make some awards for the kids, using fun categories such as "silliest-looking puppet," "most decorative," or "funniest puppet voice." Make sure to pick out something special about *each* project so every child will feel special.

Materials Needed:
- A table
- Socks
- Wooden spoons
- Small paper cups
- Brown paper grocery bags or small brown paper lunch bags
- Glue
- Children's scissors
- Buttons and/or pom-poms
- Ribbons and yarn
- Glitter
- Felt-tip pens and/or crayons (assorted colors)

- Have the kids make a simple puppet stage by spreading sheets over the table. They can hide behind it for their puppet show.

- Write a funny puppet show script before the party, with a part for each guest's puppet. Have the kids learn their parts, or provide photocopies of the scripts so everyone can follow along.

PRIZES AND FAVORS

- Let the kids keep their puppets.

- Give everyone a collection of puppet supplies for creative puppet-making at home.

- Offer books that teach kids how to make more advanced puppets.

TROUBLE-SHOOTING TIPS

- Ask adult volunteers to help with the puppet-making activity. This will prevent the kids from getting confused or frustrated waiting for help.

- If the kids worry about not being good at art, tell them it's not a contest and that the puppets should look silly or fun anyway.

FACE PAINTING

Face painting has become a popular activity with kids of all ages. It's an especially fun activity for a party because the kids will have a place to show off the decorations.

For Ages: 6–9

Optional Ages: 2–5, 10–12

Players Needed: Any group size

Object: To create fun artwork on your partner

WHAT TO DO

Before the activity, gather all of the face-painting materials—pens, paper, and mirrors—and put them on the table. Then make awards out of construction paper for categories such as "most creative," "funniest," or "best use of color"—one for each guest.

Divide the kids into pairs or let them choose partners for face painting. This activity works best if the kids sketch some designs first, so let them take their time experimenting on paper. When they're ready, have the artists begin painting their partners' cheeks, avoiding the eye and mouth area. If you prefer to use accessories like make-up and stickers, let the kids use the stickers for a basic design and paint colorful scenes around them. Or let them freely experiment with color, using the stickers for body designs. When they're done painting, allow their partners to admire their new faces in the mirror for a while, and let the artists show off their work to everyone. Then have the partners try their hand at face painting. The kids won't want to stop there! Let them paint designs on their hands or use partners again. Give everybody a special award at the end.

CREATIVE OPTIONS

• Buy packages of temporary tattoos (available at discount and toy stores) and let the kids go crazy putting tattoos all over each other's bodies—on their ankles, arms, wrists, and tummies.

• Give the artists specific themes to create, such as monsters, flowers, or animals, and

Materials Needed:

- A table
- Face paints (available at craft, party supply, toy, and art supply stores)
- *Or face-painting accessories, such as lipstick, eye shadow, "clown white" make-up, (available at costume shops or drugstores), and stickers*
- White paper
- Felt-tip pens
- Mirrors
- Construction paper

have the rest of the group guess what the artist has painted.

- Have a jar of cold cream and a box of tissues on hand so the kids can clean up and do the activity again with different partners. Take Polaroid snapshots of each design before cleanup, if possible.

PRIZES AND FAVORS

- Give the kids several tubes of face paint to take home.

- Offer everyone fun stickers and temporary tattoos to use at the party or take home.

- Send everyone home with their awards and Polaroid snapshots.

TROUBLE-SHOOTING TIPS

- If freehand painting is too difficult for the kids, provide picture books or magazines and let the kids copy designs of their choice.

- If the kids worry about not being good at art, tell them it's not a contest and that the goal is just to have fun.

- Provide the kids with old T-shirts to protect their clothing.

WATER FROLIC

You don't need a swimming pool to have a water frolic. Here are some fun ways for the kids to beat the heat, get wet, and stay entertained for hours.

For Ages: 6–9

Optional Ages: 2–5, 10–12

Players Needed: Any group size

Object: To stay cool and entertained for hours

WHAT TO DO

Specify on the invitations that the guests bring bathing suits and towels to the party. Then set up one area of the lawn for a water war, one for sprinklers and hoses, and one for a water slide. For the water war, you'll need squirt guns, basters, squirt bottles, plastic pails, and sponges. Set up the hose and sprinkler in another area (if possible, poke holes in an old garden hose so there's lots of spray to run through). Make a slippery water slide by cutting several large plastic garbage bags open to form long rectangles and taping them together with waterproof tape. Place the "slide" on the lawn (preferably on a gentle incline). If you prefer not to make a slide, you can buy one at a toy or discount store. Set a hose at one end to create a rush of water.

At party time, let the kids start off with a water war. Divide them into teams and when you say "Go!" they can squirt the water guns, throw the sponges, or even haul around the pails full of water to get their opponents soaking wet. They can also try squirting party hats off each other's heads with squirt guns (remove the elastic bands from the hats beforehand and tell them *not* to aim for the face). Next, let the kids give the water slide a try. To prevent long lines at the slide, divide the kids into teams again and have one team play in the sprinkler and the other on the slide. Switch after fifteen minutes. The kids should be tired out by the end of the day!

CREATIVE OPTIONS

• During the water war, have the kids try to capture an object sitting in the middle of the other team's territory (the object

Materials Needed:
- A lawn or grassy area
- A hose or sprinkler
- Plastic pails
- Squirt guns
- Basters
- Squirt bottles
- Sponges
- Several large plastic garbage bags
- Scissors
- Waterproof tape
- Party hats

shouldn't be held by anyone). The player who's brave enough to make a mad dash toward the object will get soaked by the other team.

- Make a "water snake" by holding the spout of the hose and moving it back and forth along the ground. Have the kids try to run across the area without getting touched by the water snake.

- The kids can play Follow the Leader down the water slide, with the leader doing a different approach each time. They might slide backwards, face first, or on their knees. Switch leaders after each turn.

PRIZES AND FAVORS

- Give all of the kids a pair of swimming goggles to wear during the party.

- Hand out squirt guns or other water toys.

- Give everyone plastic water bottles featuring fun designs (available at sports stores).

TROUBLE-SHOOTING TIPS

- Supervise the water play to make sure it doesn't get too rough—make sure the kids don't aim for anyone's face during the water war and tell them that only *one* child can be on the water slide at a time.

- Provide sunscreen for all of the kids and encourage them to apply it frequently.

- If the water slide rips, repair it with some waterproof tape. Keep a few extra garbage bags on hand so you can replace torn parts.

- Clear the entire area of any debris so the kids won't get hurt, and warn them to avoid running on wet, slippery grass.

SUPER SUNDAES

Delicious desserts are always a kid-pleaser—especially when *they* get to make them!

For Ages: 6–9

Optional Ages: 10–12

Players Needed: Any group size

Object: To create a yummy treat!

WHAT TO DO

At party time, set the ingredients, bowls, and spoons out on the table and let the kids go to work making their own ice cream sundaes. Tell them that they can make the sundaes as big or as small as they want, but that they need to eat every bite. (Don't actually force the kids to eat until they're too full—you just want to make sure that they don't build a mountain of ice cream.) If you want to make homemade ice cream, let everyone partic-ipate. Read the instructions aloud, perform the steps, and get the ice cream maker turning.

For added fun, let the kids do a taste test of each sundae and judge for themselves which one is the yummiest (provide everyone with a tasting bowl and serve a dab of each sundae in the bowls, to prevent spreading germs).

After that, pass out awards made from con-struction paper to all of the kids for categories such as "tallest sundae," "most creative," or "best use of whipped cream."

CREATIVE OPTIONS

• Instead of making sundaes, give the kids cones and let them make ice cream clowns. The cones can serve as clown hats on top of a round scoop of ice cream. Have the kids create clown faces using the sundae ingre-dients. Line the clowns up on a cookie sheet and take a picture.

• Let the kids make ice cream caterpillars. Give each child three scoops of ice cream in a row (the caterpillar body) and let them use pep-permint sticks for the antennae. Using the sundae ingredients, they can add the eyes, nose, and any other features.

Materials Needed:

- A table
- Bowls
- Spoons
- Ice cream scoopers
- Ice cream or frozen yogurt (various flavors)
- Sundae sauces (various flavors)
- A variety of toppings (colored sprinkles, frozen strawberries or raspberries, mini marshmallows, coconut shavings, chopped nuts, chocolate chips, granola, and whipped cream)
- Construction paper
- Felt-tip pens

- Buy a bunch of bananas and let the kids make banana splits. Just cut the bananas lengthwise, lay the halves in a dish, and place scoops of vanilla, chocolate, and strawberry ice cream on top. The kids can add any sauces or other ingredients.

PRIZES AND FAVORS

- Give everyone gift certificates for treats at an ice cream or yogurt shop.

- Send all of the kids home with ice cream cones filled with small candies and treats.

- Offer the kids small containers of ice cream or cool pops to eat at home.

TROUBLE-SHOOTING TIPS

- Warn the kids not to nibble while creating the sundaes or to eat too much too fast—you don't want anyone to go home with a tummyache.

- Tell the kids to wear old clothes to the party if you're worried about chocolate or other food stains. Or provide old shirts so they won't wear any ice cream home.

- Tell the kids to work quickly—ice cream melts fast!

DAY AT THE BALLPARK

Baseball is an American favorite, so why not treat the kids to a day at the ballpark? Here's an easy party that you can adapt to almost any sporting event.

For Ages: 6–9

Optional Ages: 10–12

Preparation: Purchase the tickets ahead of time and be sure to ask if group rates are available. Inquire about special kids' party activities, too, such as player signings, locker room tours, or getting the guests' names on the scoreboard.

WHAT TO DO

Before the party, have the guests create a team banner, using a large sheet of paper and felt-tip pens. They can hold it up every time their team scores or makes a good play.

Ask all of the guests to wear clothing in the favored team's colors and to bring along their baseballs, mitts, caps, or team pennants. Keep the kids entertained during the ride to the ballpark by giving them each a pack of baseball cards and leading them in a few rounds of "Take Me Out to the Ball Game." (If you've arranged special activities such as a tour of the locker room or autograph signings, you'll need to arrive at the park early.)

During the game, keep a betting pool going, with penny or treat bets on who will hit the first home run, who will steal a base, or even which food vendor will come by first (record the kids' answers on paper to keep track). Then hand out a penny or treat to each guest who wins a bet. Baseball games usually last a few hours, so be sure to bring some snacks or offer to buy hot dogs and sodas.

CREATIVE OPTIONS

• Buy "ballpark" food (hot dogs, hamburgers, peanuts, and soda) and take along a hibachi for a tailgate party in the parking lot. While the hot dogs are cooking, let the kids toss around a baseball in a safe area.

• Make up a list of baseball trivia questions to ask during the car ride to the park or during the game. Award stickers or bubblegum to the guests who get the right answers first.

For Added Fun:
- Baseball cards
- Pennies (or candies and gum)
- A piece of paper and a pencil or pen
- Banner-size paper
- Felt-tip pens

- If you don't have a ballpark near your home, host the party around another sport, such as football, basketball, or hockey. Or go to an unusual sporting event, such as a wrestling match or a high school activity.

PRIZES AND FAVORS

- Send the guests home with inexpensive baseball theme items such as stickers, key chains, or erasers.

- Send the kids off with a big bag of fresh peanuts in the shell.

- Give the trivia star a glove, cap, or bat, signed by all of the party guests.

TROUBLE-SHOOTING TIPS

- Find adult volunteers to join you on the trip because the kids will need to go to the bathroom and shouldn't go alone. If you can't round up any volunteers, arrange for a trusted babysitter to come along.

- Use the buddy system on the outing—have the kids choose partners so they'll stay together.

- If the game gets rained out at the last minute, rent a movie about baseball, and keep the kids happy with lots of ballpark food. (Indoor sporting events like basketball, hockey, swimming, and wrestling will not be affected by cold or wet weather.)

OUTDOOR OVERNIGHT

Camping in the great outdoors is an activity kids can't resist. With a little planning, an outdoor overnight can be a great adventure, even if it's just in the backyard.

For Ages: 6–9 (best for more mature six-year-olds)

Optional Ages: 10–12

Preparation: Get out the tent, camping cookware, flashlights, and sleeping bags (you can rent or borrow these items if you don't own them). You'll also need materials for making a camp fire (or use a grill), plus fun food for dinner and breakfast.

WHAT TO DO

Ask the guests to bring along any clothes and gear (don't forget toothbrushes!) needed for overnight camping. Before they arrive, set up the tents, camp fire, and sleeping bags, and have all of the food items ready to go. Or, wait till the kids get there, and make setting up camp a featured activity.

While it's still light out, have a Scavenger Hunt. Divide the kids into two teams and provide each team with a list of items to find outdoors, including both easy- and hard-to-find items (for instance, a white flower, three pine cones, a gray stone, etc.). The team that finds all of the items first wins.

When the sun goes down, serve food cooked on the camp fire or grill, and roast marshmallows for dessert. For before-bed fun, read a few ghost stories and pass around plastic bags full of "body parts"—cooked noodle "guts," eyeballs made from grapes or olives, a Jell–O liver, and a shriveled finger that's really just a raw carrot. Have the kids feel inside the bags to get really grossed-out. When everyone's good and scared, have the kids read comic books by flashlight and tell jokes and riddles so that they won't be too scared to sleep. Let everyone wake up to eggs frying over the fire, or pass out mini boxes of cereal.

CREATIVE OPTIONS

• Have an outdoor "Blind Walk" where some of the kids hold hands and walk around the yard with the guidance of their "sighted leaders." Tell the guides to be careful so no one trips. This activity will help the kids appreciate the sounds and smells of the outdoors a little more.

For Added Fun:
- Food items (grapes or olives, cooked noodles, carrots, and Jell–O)
- Zip-lock plastic sandwich bags
- Paper and a pencil or pen
- A book of ghost stories
- Comic books

- Show the kids how to make shadow figures on the tent walls, using flashlights.

- Give each guest a turn to read a ghost story or make one up.

PRIZES AND FAVORS

- Give the kids packages of freeze-dried food to snack on all night (available at camping and sporting goods stores).

- Give the kids toy compasses, mini flashlights, or plastic magnifying glasses for studying bugs and leaves.

- Give the kids on the team that wins the Scavenger Hunt a few joke books, and give the other kids consolation prizes.

TROUBLE-SHOOTING TIPS

- Some kids might feel afraid to spend a whole night away from home or sleep outdoors. Be sure to camp out with them so they'll feel more confident.

- The party doesn't have to end if it suddenly rains or gets too cold. Be prepared to move indoors if bad weather hits. If the kids are dressed warmly and tents are covered properly with waterproof slicks, however, there's no reason for the fun to go indoors!

- Depending on the size of the group, you might want to ask other adults to spend the night, too. If you can't round up any volunteers, arrange for a trusted babysitter to come over.

STARSHIP TO THE PLANETARIUM

All kids are interested in the mysteries of outer space. A trip to the planetarium can be a cosmic celebration!

For Ages: 6–9

Optional Ages: 10–12

Preparation: Contact a nearby planetarium—they're usually located in a science museum or at a college or university. Call ahead of time to learn the hours of operation, costs, directions, and whether group rates are available.

WHAT TO DO

Before the party, ask all of the guests to bring a plain white T-shirt that can be painted. Pull each shirt over a sheet of cardboard and use thumbtacks to hold the shirts down. Then give the kids paintbrushes and let them go wild painting designs on their shirts with glow-in-the-dark paint. While the paint is drying, let the kids stick glow-in-the-dark stickers all over the shirts for a special effect.

You can also keep the kids busy with a fun activity called "Draw in the Dark." Give the guests a piece of paper and a pencil and have them draw a simple design, such as a star or the sun. Then turn off the lights (you'll need a dark room) and tell the kids to draw the same design. They'll be surprised by the results!

When the shirts are dry, let the kids wear them to the planetarium. They'll shine in the dark as they watch the show. Keep the kids entertained on the ride back home with paperbacks or comic books about outer space. Or bring along the horoscope section from the newspaper and have the guest of honor read all of the fortunes aloud.

CREATIVE OPTIONS

- Before or after the planetarium show, create a spectacular at-home planetarium and surprise the party's guest of honor at the same time. Secretly place a bunch of glow-in-the-dark star stickers on the ceiling of the honoree's bedroom. Gather the guests in the bedroom, turn out the lights, and surprise everyone. Be sure to have the kids wear their glow-in-the-dark shirts!

For Added Fun:
- Glow-in-the-dark paint (available at art, hobby, and paint stores)
- Paintbrushes
- Glow-in-the-dark star stickers (available at science and nature shops or toy stores)
- Cardboard
- Thumbtacks
- Paper and a pencil for each child

- Give each guest a package of freeze-dried astronaut food (ice cream is best) to eat before or after the show (available at camping and sporting goods stores).

PRIZES AND FAVORS

- Send the kids home with their decorated T-shirts and glow-in-the-dark stars.

- Offer books about the stars and planets or wall charts of the galaxy.

TROUBLE-SHOOTING TIPS

- When the kids are painting their shirts, make sure they don't apply the paint too thickly, or the shirts won't dry in time for the show. If the paint hasn't dried in time, place the shirts outside in the sunlight for a few minutes, or use a hair dryer to dry them.

- Remind the kids to be quiet at the planetarium so they won't disturb others.

- Depending on the size of the group, you might want to ask other adults to accompany you. If you can't round up any volunteers, arrange for a trusted babysitter to come along.

TAKEOFF TO THE AIRPORT

The airport offers an afternoon of exciting sights and activities for all ages. If you've got a future pilot in the family, turn this fascination for flight into an airport adventure.

For Ages: 6–9

Optional Ages: 2–5, 10–12

Preparation: Contact your local airport (large or small) to arrange for a tour of the airplanes, control tower, and other facilities. Or, if the weather permits, plan to just have a picnic on the grass in an area by the airport where the planes fly overhead.

WHAT TO DO

The best way to plan an airport outing is to make a preliminary trip to the airport to see what kind of arrangements they have for kids' tours. Find out if it's possible to look inside an airplane, meet a few pilots, see the control tower, go up on the observation deck, or go behind-the-scenes at the baggage claim area. If you can do just one or all of the activities, it's worth it.

Before leaving for the airport, give the guests skycaps and wing pins, and tell them they've just been appointed as pilots and flight attendants. Take an airport transportation bus to the airport, if you can afford the extra cost. If the group is too large for this, drive the kids in your own "airport limo" with posterboard signs that read: "(Your last name) Airlines—

First Class." Have the kids decorate the signs with pictures of airplanes.

When you arrive at the airport, tour the facility as arranged, and then watch some planes take off. If you're planning to have a picnic on the grass instead, pack a basketful of "airline food"—small bags of peanuts, cans of soda, and sandwiches and coleslaw (or potato salad) wrapped in plastic, with plastic silverware on the side. Buy an airplane-shaped cookie cutter and press it on the sandwiches for airplane-shaped sandwiches. Give the kids balsa wood airplanes to assemble and play with outside.

CREATIVE OPTIONS

- Set up a mini-airport at home to greet the guests. Give them their skycaps and wing pins, and usher them into your baggage

For Added Fun:
- Wing pins and skycaps for each child (available at party supply stores and airport gift shops)
- Balsa wood airplanes for each child (available at toy stores)
- Posterboard
- Felt-tip pens

claim area to exchange their party gifts for a baggage claim check (made from construction paper). Have them wait in the "departure room" for the flight call, and draw names to see who gets to be the pilot and sit up in the "cockpit" (the front seat of the car). Everyone else will be flight attendants or passengers. Provide fun dress-up clothes, for added fun.

- If there's some extra time, play Airplane (see p. 84 for directions).

PRIZES AND FAVORS

- Send the kids home with their balsa wood airplanes, wing pins, and skycaps.

- Let each child pick out one inexpensive item from the airport gift shop.

- Offer everyone small toy airplanes.

TROUBLE-SHOOTING TIPS

- Keep a close eye on each child—airports are big, crowded places, and you don't want anyone to get lost. Provide name tags for all of the guests, with the address and phone number of the party host—just in case!

- Find adult volunteers to join you on the trip because the kids might be tempted to run around in all that open space. If you can't round up any volunteers, arrange for a trusted babysitter to come along.

KITES AT THE PARK

You don't need a gusty day to have a kite-flying party at the park—a little breeze will give your kites and kite-flyers a lift.

For Ages: 6–9

Optional Ages 2–5

Preparation: Look in the Yellow Pages under "Kites" for kite stores, and purchase ready-made kites. You can also find kites in hobby and craft stores. Find a park that's free of trees and telephone poles.

WHAT TO DO

If you plan to fly store-bought kites, you can still do a kite-making activity before you head to the park. Gather art materials together and give each child a small brown paper lunch bag. Begin demonstrating the following steps, pausing often to check that the kids are following directions properly: (1) Fold the open edge of each bag back approximately one and a half inches, (2) Tape a piece of string about five inches long to each corner of the open end of the bags, and join these strings with a knot, (3) Add a long piece of string (about five feet) to each knot. (The bags should fly when the kids hold the strings and run.) For some really fun kites, have the kids decorate the paper bags using felt-tip pens, glitter, and stickers.

When you get to the park, tell the kids to, "Go fly a kite!" After all that running around, the kids will be hungry, so pack a picnic basket and spread the lunch out on a picnic table or on the grass. Take along sandwiches cut into diamond shapes and decorated to look like kites—dip a toothpick in food coloring and paint lines on the bread.

CREATIVE OPTIONS

• Before the outing, play a game of Pin the Tail on the Kite. Draw a picture of a tailless kite and give construction paper tails to the kids. Play using the rules of Pin the Tail on the Donkey (see p. 4 for directions).

• Have a kite contest with lots of prizes for "craziest kite," "funniest kite-flying technique," "most likely to get off the ground," or other silly categories.

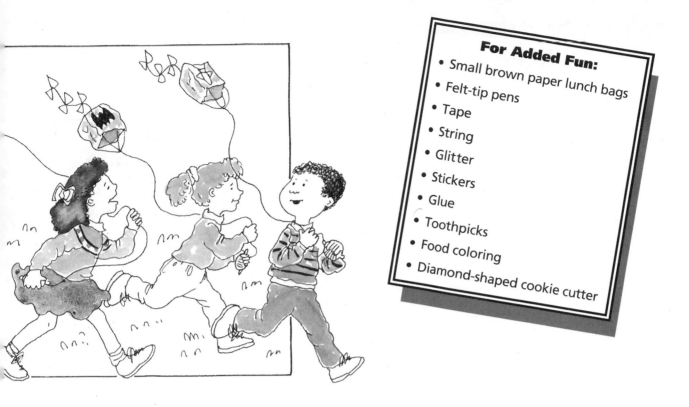

For Added Fun:
- Small brown paper lunch bags
- Felt-tip pens
- Tape
- String
- Glitter
- Stickers
- Glue
- Toothpicks
- Food coloring
- Diamond-shaped cookie cutter

- Bring along other gadgets that are guaranteed to stay airborne, such as Frisbees, parachute toys, and boomerangs, in case the kites don't fly as planned.

PRIZES AND FAVORS

- Let the kids keep their kites and give everyone an extra ball of string.

- Offer everyone their own pack of felt-tip pens for the kite-decorating activity.

- Give the winner of Pin the Tail on the Kite a book on kite-making.

TROUBLE-SHOOTING TIPS

- Bring at least one "reserve" kite along, in case a child's kite rips or blows away.

- It's probably necessary to have an adult volunteer to help the kids make their kites.

That way, the kids won't get bored or frustrated waiting for help.

- Find adult volunteers to join you on the trip because the kids will want to run off in different directions outside. If you can't round up any volunteers, arrange for a trusted babysitter to come along.

ABRACADABRA— A MAGICIAN!

All kids love magic and have dreamed of being a magician. Invite a real magician to turn your party into a magical event.

For Ages: 6–9

Optional Ages: 2–5

Preparation: Find a professional magician by looking in the Yellow Pages under "Entertainers—Entertainment." You might also find magicians in the classified ads of your local newspaper or by calling magic shops for recommendations.

WHAT TO DO

You can find a magician through a special company or agency, or hire one that works independently. Interview several by phone ahead of time to determine which performance or act is right for your party and guests.

Your magician party can be fun and simple—just let the magician do all of the entertaining, and then have cake and ice cream afterwards. Videotape the performance if possible, and let the kids watch it once the magician leaves, for an added treat.

Before the magician arrives, pass out capes, hats, and wands and let the kids pretend to be magicians. Magic shops have lots of fun tricks, jokes, toys, cards, and books about magic that will keep the kids busy until the special entertainer arrives. (Or check out a magic book from the library and have some fun tricks ready to show the kids.) Take lots of photos before and during the show.

CREATIVE OPTIONS

- Instead of having tricks to hand out to the kids when they arrive at the party, ask the kids to prepare two or three tricks ahead of time to present when they arrive.

- Serve a "magic" dessert such as Jell–O with surprise fruit or candy inside, or pieces of cake with a surprise toy inside (warn them ahead of time!).

- Include a little magic trick inside the invitations to get the kids in the mood for a magical event.

For Added Fun:

- Magician's clothing (top hats and black capes) for all of the guests (available at magic shops and toy stores)
- Magic wands (available at magic shops and toy stores)

• Invite the guests with invitations written in invisible ink (available at toy stores) or milk that has dried on the paper (use a cotton swab for writing the party details). Give the guests instructions for reading the invitations (for the dried milk option, the paper must be heated until the letters appear).

PRIZES AND FAVORS

• Send the little magicians home with their new magic tricks.

• Let them keep the top hats, capes, and wands.

• Give everyone a Polaroid snapshot of themselves posing with the magician.

TROUBLE-SHOOTING TIP

• Remind the guests to be good listeners during the magic act and not to shout out solutions to the tricks.

CALL THE POLICE!

Kids see crime shows on TV all the time—invite a police officer to the party so the kids can find out what it's *really* like to be a cop. For an extra-special activity, have the kids solve a mysterious crime complete with clues, evidence, and a clever solution.

For Ages: 6–9

Optional Ages: 2–5, 10–12 for guest speaker; 10–12 for mystery

Preparation: Call a local police department to see if a police officer can come to the party in uniform with some equipment.

WHAT TO DO

When you call the police station, find out what items the police officer can bring for the presentation (such as "Wanted" signs, handouts, or posters). Be sure to determine the amount of time the police officer will be able to spend at the party—if it's a short time, have other activities planned.

As the guests arrive, give them police badges and hats to wear. Encourage them to ask the police officer questions if they want. When the special presentation is over, gather the kids for a "mystery activity" (you'll need to secretly set up a crime scene beforehand).

To create a crime scene (such as the mysterious disappearance of the cake), hide the cake and leave a note that says: "I have stolen the cake, and you'll never find it! Ha! Ha! Ha!—The

Shadow." Then secretly take one of the kids aside to be the culprit and set up some clues—leave some flour spilled on the kitchen counter and floor, and have the culprit leave some fingerprints and a footprint in the mess; then borrow a couple of hairs from the culprit to leave at the scene, as well as an accessory or article of clothing. Once the scene is complete, send the culprit back to the other room with instructions not to let on about the mystery.

Once the special guest leaves, tell the kids it's time for cake. When everyone is ready to eat, exclaim that the cake has been stolen and that the kids must solve the crime! Pass out some magnifying glasses and let them search for clues. If they're stumped, have the culprit confess. Once they have solved the crime, let them feast on the stolen property.

For Added Fun:
- Police hats and badges (available at toy stores)
- Plastic magnifying glasses
- Flour
- A piece of paper and a pencil or pen

CREATIVE OPTIONS

- Ask the police officer if it is possible to arrive in a squad car that the kids can explore, under supervision, during the party.

- Give the kids posterboard and felt-tip pens for creating "Wanted" posters.

- For the mystery, you can have the culprit take one of the gifts instead of the cake. Plant a piece of wrapping paper on the bottom of the thief's shoe (use tape to make it stick), or have the culprit leave a mysterious, inky thumbprint on the note.

PRIZES AND FAVORS

- Let the kids take their police hats, magnifying glasses, and badges home.

- Give the kids other police accessories, such as whistles, handcuffs, or doughnuts.

- Send everyone home with comic books that feature "super cops."

TROUBLE-SHOOTING TIPS

- Remind the kids to be good listeners when the guest arrives and reward those who listened quietly with a special sticker.

- If you find out ahead of time which items the officer will be bringing to the presentation, you can alert the kids so they won't be disappointed if they don't get to see real weapons.

KARATE KIDS

Kids love action movies that feature karate masters, so invite a martial arts expert to show off some moves and teach your crowd self-defense.

For Ages: 6–9

Optional Ages: 2–5, 10–12

Preparation: Find a professional martial arts instructor by looking in the Yellow Pages under "Karate." Ask whether a professional teacher or student can give the kids a brief introduction to the sport and do a demonstration of karate, judo, kung fu, or another martial art.

WHAT TO DO

When looking for an instructor, try to find one who is accustomed to teaching and working with kids. Interview several martial arts experts by phone ahead of time to determine which one is right for your party and guests. Some of these instructors will entertain your party guests at no charge because it's a form of free advertising for their business, but others might charge a fee. They might also recommend one of their top students if they're too busy to make the visit.

Arrange for the martial arts expert to do a demonstration for the kids, and to teach them a few simple moves. The entertainer will probably want to share a little bit of the history and philosophy of the martial arts, too. As soon as the guests arrive, provide them with karate-style clothing (some oversized white T-shirts tied at the waist with white strips cut from sheets). Have the kids put on the outfits and remove their shoes and socks to make it a little more authentic. Then let the kids watch the demonstration and try a few moves. If they're really lucky, the instructor might show them the trick of chopping a brick or board bare-handed (just be sure to warn the kids not to try the trick at home!).

CREATIVE OPTIONS

- Clear away the furniture and let the kids try the karate moves they learned. If the instructor has time to work with the kids individually, arrange for this, and keep the other kids busy with comic books featuring martial arts heroes.

For Added Fun:
- 1 oversized white T-shirt per guest
- A white sheet
- Scissors

- Take Polaroid snapshots of each guest with the martial arts instructor. Tell the kids to pose in karate positions, for added fun.

- Rent the movie *The Karate Kid* and show it after the special guest leaves.

PRIZES AND FAVORS

- Give the kids books or comic books about the martial arts to take home.

- Let the kids wear their karate outfits home.

- Offer the kids Polaroid snapshots of themselves with the special entertainer.

TROUBLE-SHOOTING TIPS

- Remind the kids that the martial arts are a form of self-defense and should only be used as a defense against an attacker. (You don't want them to start roughhousing in the excitement!)

- Allow the kids lots of room to practice their kicks and karate chops so they won't hurt each other or themselves.

FUNNIEST HOME VIDEOS

Host a home version of the popular TV show, "America's Funniest Home Videos." Just invite a professional videotaper to create a great party video, and you'll have an event to remember!

For Ages: 6–9

Optional Ages: 10–12

Preparation: Find a professional video-taper by looking in the Yellow Pages under "Video." For a less-expensive alternative, rent or borrow a video camera and let a friend or family member do the job. If you don't have a VCR, you'll need to rent or borrow one.

WHAT TO DO

When trying to find a video expert, make sure the person you hire has a camera that's compatible with your VCR so you can play the tape during the party. Try to find a videotaper who can show the kids how the camera works and who is comfortable working with kids.

Before the special guest arrives, divide the kids into two groups and give them some time to come up with ideas for their own funny home video. (Or, for a smaller group, let all of the kids work together.) Put on some music and let the kids come up with a silly skit, commercial, or dance for the video. Provide costumes and old clothing to help them get inspired. Then let the videotaper record the first group of kids while you keep the other group entertained in a separate room, with comic books

or joke books. The videotaper can then film the second group. Later, bring everyone into the party room for a private screening complete with popcorn.

CREATIVE OPTIONS

- After the main event, ask the videotaper to go around the room and record each guest giving a special message or greeting to the guest of honor. This will provide priceless memories of the party!

- Have the kids bring their own home videos and show some clips to the crowd. Encourage the kids to choose something funny from their video collection and have them vote for the funniest home video of all.

- Move the guests one at a time into a separate room and have the videotaper get

For Added Fun:
- Costumes or old clothes (available at costume and thrift shops)
- Comic and joke books
- Popcorn
- Cassette tapes or records and a stereo

close-ups of body parts such as feet, fingers, or noses. Then have the guest talk in a funny voice. Repeat for all of the guests, then show the video to the crowd so they can try to guess who's who.

PRIZES AND FAVORS

- Send the kids home with inexpensive used videotapes from a video rental store.

- Give each guest a big bag of popcorn (store-bought or homemade) to eat while watching a favorite video at home.

- If you try the guessing game option, hand out prizes such as movie treats to anyone who shouts out a correct answer.

TROUBLE-SHOOTING TIPS

- Encourage the kids to be as silly as they want for the videos but not to get too rambunctious. Give special encouragement to any kids who seem shy in front of the camera.

- Take care of the videos brought from the kids' homes—they are very valuable to the owners.

ARTIST PARTY

Kids love making things with their hands. It's fun, enhances self-esteem, and creates a personalized, one-of-a-kind product. Invite an artist for a creative event!

For Ages: 6–9

Optional Ages: 2–5, 10–12

Preparation: Decide what type of artist you'd like to invite (try artists who specialize in ceramics, clay sculpture, painting, or collage). Contact an art store, college, or your child's teacher for artist referrals.

WHAT TO DO

When looking for an artist, try to find one who is accustomed to teaching and working with kids. Request that the artist bring samples of his or her work, and be sure you know ahead of time what type of art materials you'll need to have on hand for the kids to use (the artist might provide supplies, too). Specify on the invitations that the kids wear clothes that can get a little messy or that they bring smocks or old shirts.

Set up some tables in the party room (or the garage, if you're worried about a mess) and put newspapers over them. Then just let the artist take it from there. While the kids are busy doing their projects, make up some ribbons—one for each guest—that give a special award or honor for each project. (Make the

ribbons out of construction paper and felt-tip pens.) Don't turn the activity into a contest—instead find something good about each piece of artwork.

CREATIVE OPTIONS

• Ask the kids to wear oversized white shirts to the party. Buy fabric paints (available at art supply stores) and let the kids paint their shirts after the artist leaves.

• Have the kids make their own stationery. Just buy rubber stamps and ink pads (available at toy stores, art supply stores, and card shops) and paper by the pound (available at card shops and party supply stores). Let the kids go wild!

• Purchase yards of shelf paper and have the kids make a mural! They can do body

For Added Fun:
- Construction paper
- Felt-tip pens
- Tables
- Newspapers
- Any art supplies needed for working with the artist

tracings and color all of the self-portraits—it makes a great gift for the guest of honor.

PRIZES AND FAVORS

- Send all of the kids home with their artwork and ribbons.

- Give everyone a supply of art materials—felt-tip pens, colored paper, or a box of paints and paintbrushes.

- Give the guests craft how-to books or posters by famous children's illustrators.

TROUBLE-SHOOTING TIPS

- Ask adult volunteers to help if the type of work the artist does is complicated. This will prevent the kids from getting confused or frustrated waiting for help.

- If the kids worry about not being good at art, tell them it's not a contest and that the goal is just to have fun.

- Give the guests special cleanup tasks after the activity (*e.g.*, washing paintbrushes or putting supplies away). This will make cleaning up easier for everyone, especially the guest artist.

Preteen 10–12

CHARADES

Kids love charades as much as adults do—it's a classic party-pleaser. Older kids might find the creative options even more fun and challenging.

For Ages: 10–12

Optional Ages: 6–9

Players Needed: 6 or more

Object: To guess the phrase or sentence your team is acting out, in the shortest period of time

HOW TO PLAY

Before the party, write some simple phrases, sentences, or book, movie, or song titles (appropriate for your party crowd) on slips of paper. Fold the papers up and place them in a hat, bowl, or other container.

At game time, divide the guests into two teams and seat them across from one another. Show the various pantomime signs used in Charades: open hands signify a book title; a cranking motion (for a pretend camera) signifies a movie title; and waving a hand before an open mouth signifies a song title; cupping a hand behind an ear means "sounds like"; holding up one finger means "first word" of the saying (two fingers, second word, and so on); and one finger inside the elbow means "first syllable"; a beckoning motion tells the audience they're close to the right answer; a pushing away motion tells them they're off base; and touching the nose indicates a correct response.

Have someone from the first team pick out a slip of paper and silently read the title or phrase. Give her one to three minutes, depending on the group's ability, to stand up before the group and communicate the information to her teammates without speaking. (The other team may watch the action, too.) Then let a player from the second team choose a slip of paper and communicate the information to her team, while everyone watches. Continue to trade off turns in this manner. Record the time it takes each team to get the right answers—the team with the least total amount of time wins the game (after everyone has had a chance to play performer).

Materials Needed:
- A hat, bowl, or other container
- Paper and a pencil or pen
- A timer

CREATIVE OPTIONS

- Play a specific form of Charades, such as "Rock Music Charades" or "Scary Movie Charades," using any phrases, titles, or sentences from those categories.

- Play "One-Word Charades" with the players acting out a single word, such as "flat," "headache," "corner," and so on. (If you have trouble thinking up words, look at some of the one-word clues in the board game "Pictionary.")

- Play "People Charades" and have the players act out famous people instead of phrases and titles (include cartoon characters, politicians, movie stars, child actors, and historical figures).

- Allow the kids to write up the titles and phrases themselves, so they can have a shot at stumping the group.

PRIZES AND FAVORS

- Give the winning team small plastic "Oscar" awards (available at party supply stores).

- Hand out cassette singles of songs used in the game, or give away the board game version of Charades.

- Buy or make a large bag of popcorn for each guest to take home.

TROUBLE-SHOOTING TIPS

- Make a chart before the game showing the various Charades signals so there won't be any confusion.

- If a player is shy about performing for the others, just let her help with the guessing.

- If the teams write their own titles and phrases, screen them to weed out any that are too difficult.

149

GOSSIP

This party favorite always produces lots of laughs. You'll get the best results when you play it with a large group.

For Ages: 10–12

Optional Ages: 6–9

Players Needed: 8 or more

Object: To whisper a piece of gossip down the line of players and see how well the message was carried

HOW TO PLAY

Before the game, write out ridiculous bits of gossip about each of the guests on slips of paper—the more ludicrous the better. For example: "Yesterday, Nicole quit school, eloped with Luke Perry, and is planning to have eight children"; "Tom spent a year in jail when he was nine for stealing Snickers bars from the Snack Shack"; or "Rebecca got muscle implants, hair extenders, and a nose ring so she could look really cool."

At game time, arrange the players in a line or circle and show the first player one of the slips of paper. After he stops laughing, he must whisper the rumor to the next player, who whispers it to the next player, and so on down the line until the last player has heard the story. Have the last player recite the piece of gossip *exactly* as he heard it—see how close to the truth he gets! Send the first player to the end of the line after the round and play again.

CREATIVE OPTIONS

• Let the kids make up their own outrageous rumors to be passed down the line (make sure to write them down so the comparison can be made).

• Cut out phrases from the tabloids, glue them to pieces of paper (substituting the names of the guests for the famous names), and use them for the gossip starters. The kids will get a kick out of hearing that "Heather is pregnant with the fifty-pound baby of an alien" or "Joey's botched facelift makes him look like Willard Scott."

Materials Needed:
- Enough space for the players to form a long line or large circle
- Paper and a pencil or pen

- Make the gossip appropriate to your party theme. If it's a dance party, write down rumors about rock groups or add the guests' names to song titles or lyrics. Or just make the pieces of gossip into tongue twisters so the message is sure to get mixed up.

PRIZES AND FAVORS

- Send everyone home with the piece of gossip about them taped to a goody bag or made to look like an award certificate.

- Give the kids the funny tabloid headlines with their names on them.

- Offer the guests teen magazines full of gossip (and remind them that everything they hear and read may not be true).

TROUBLE-SHOOTING TIPS

- When writing the rumors, don't make the sentences too long (the kids might get confused) or too short (the kids might find the game unchallenging).

- Don't write any rumors that could be true or embarrassing for the players—keep them completely silly.

- Remind the kids to whisper softly so only the receiver will hear the message. Play music in the background to obscure the messages.

SCAVENGER HUNT

What do an old shoelace, a paper clip, and a rock have in common? They're great items for a scavenger hunt. Searching for unusual items is the challenge, so when making your list, be creative—and a little crazy!

For Ages: 10–12

Optional Ages: 6–9

Players Needed: 3 or more

Object: To locate all the items (or as many as possible) on the list

HOW TO PLAY

Prepare a list of items for the kids to locate and photocopy it for each guest, or for each team, depending on how big the group is. You can play this game indoors or outdoors— just make sure your list reflects your choice. Try these suggestions or use your own: an old shoelace, a paper clip, lipstick, a tea bag, a party item, a rock, a bobby pin, an old paperback, a used eraser, some litter, a flower, unopened junk mail, a business card, dog food, a colored pencil, a receipt, a candy bar, and/or some sand.

At game time, define the area where the players can search and set a time limit; then divide the players into pairs, teams, or let them play solo. Pass out lists and bags and let them get started. When the players return,

dump out each bag and review the items to see if they brought back exactly what was on the list. The player or team with the most "acceptable" items wins.

CREATIVE OPTIONS

• Let each player make her own list, then pass it to another player who must find the items (teams can make up and exchange lists, too). Advise the kids not to make the items too easy or too hard, and review the lists to weed out impossible-to-find items.

• Offer bonus opportunities by making lists of generic items (for example, a shoelace) and adding beside them optional bonus items (a *colorful* shoelace). The kids can double their findings!

• Have a "white elephant scavenger hunt" where the teams go door-to-door asking for

Materials Needed:

• A timer

• 1 large bag per player or per team

• A photocopied list of items for each player or team to find (see suggestions in How to Play)

• Paper and a pencil or pen

a donation of anything strange, bizarre, and unwanted. (This option works best when you know the neighbors well.) Have the kids return to the party and see who collected the strangest stuff.

PRIZES AND FAVORS

• Give the winners a fun item from the scavenger hunt list.

• Give the losers a funny item from the list as a consolation prize.

• Send everyone home with goody bags full of small things like mini candy bars, Hershey's Kisses, small rubber balls, fun buttons, or sugarless bubblegum.

TROUBLE-SHOOTING TIPS

• Find adult volunteers to go along with the kids if you're having an outdoor hunt.

• Make some rules—"Be careful crossing streets," or "No searching in drawers and other private areas," etc. Set any other limits you think might be necessary.

• Don't make the scavenger items too difficult—the kids have more fun when they can find most of them.

ROMANCING THE STORY

Here's a game that doesn't have competition, but does create lots of laughs! All it takes is some imagination and creativity.

For Ages: 10–12

Optional Ages: 6–9

Players Needed: 5 or more

Object: To have the group create a humorous story

HOW TO PLAY

Give paper and pencils to all of the guests and have them sit in a circle. Let them know they are going to write a "best-selling romance story," section by section, working as a team.

Each player writes part of the story, following your instructions. Start the story with the girl character's name—have each player write her name and a description of her, then fold the paper over, and pass it to the next player. Next, have the writers come up with a boy's name and description, then fold the paper over, and pass it again. The kids should continue writing and passing the paper, using the following plot turns: how the boy and girl met, the first words the boy said to the girl, how the girl replied to the boy, what happened next, what the neighbors said, the consequences, what the newspapers printed about them, and their future. When everyone has finished with the last paragraph, let them unfold the papers and read the funny stories aloud, one by one.

CREATIVE OPTIONS

• Distribute different-colored paper and pens to make the game even more fun.

• Get more creative with the plot lines, having animals or famous people as the characters. Or have the kids write a murder mystery or spy story.

• Host a "writer" party, with the guests starring as authors (you could provide fun props for them such as sunglasses or oversized pens or pencils to get them in the mood). Serve a cake shaped like an open book.

Materials Needed:
• Enough space for the players to form a circle
• Paper and a pencil or pen for each player

PRIZES AND FAVORS

• Give everyone popular preteen, joke, or cartoon books.

• Offer the kids journals and fancy pens so they can practice their writing at home.

• If you have a "writer" party, let the kids wear the props home.

TROUBLE-SHOOTING TIPS

• Divide each piece of paper into ten sections so the writers know exactly how much they can write and where the words should go.

• Set a time limit so the players will write quickly and spontaneously. If they get stuck, give them a few creative ideas.

SPOONS

The kids will soon find that half the fun of playing this exciting game is trying to quickly grab a spoon—and the other half is discovering they're the last to get one! This game is full of fast-paced fun.

For Ages: 10–12

Optional Ages: 6–9

Players Needed: 6 or more

Object: To secretly steal a spoon before anyone else

HOW TO PLAY

The players sit in a circle on the floor or at a table, with some spoons placed in the circle's center in a star-burst design (for easy access). There should be one less spoon in the middle of the circle than the number of players. Deal four cards to each player, put the remaining cards in a draw pile, and choose a leader (or play the leader yourself). The kids must collect four matching cards to pick up a spoon.

To play, the leader first chooses the top card from the draw pile and decides if she wants to keep it. Whether or not she keeps it, she must discard one card to the player on her right. That player, who is also trying to collect four matching cards, can keep or discard that card or another from her own hand. Play continues in this manner, with the players continually passing cards to their right. Here's where it gets tricky: the player to the *left* of the leader doesn't discard to the leader but to a discard pile. (What usually happens is that the leader runs out of cards from the draw pile before anyone gets a set of four—she then begins pulling from the discard pile, and the player to her left starts a new discard pile). This game should move fast, and players should never have more than four cards at once. To keep the game going at a steady pace, shout: "Pass!" every so often to make the kids pass the cards quickly. The first player to get four matching cards must quickly and quietly grab a spoon from the middle of the circle. All of the other players must then grab one, too.

Usually the players get so carried away with collecting cards that they forget to watch the spoons and/or the other players. When all of

Materials Needed:
- A spoon for all but one player
- A deck of cards

the spoons are gone, and the last player is left with nothing but a look of surprise, begin another round with the loser starting the deal.

CREATIVE OPTIONS

- You don't have to play with spoons—any item that's easy to see and grab will work.

- Have the kids do a funny action rather than grabbing spoons or other items. For example, they can stick out their tongues or touch their noses once they've collected four matching cards.

- Have the player who didn't get a spoon stand up and do something silly, such as bark like a dog, or spin around like a ballerina.

PRIZES AND FAVORS

- Give the kids fun food items that must be

eaten with a spoon—pudding, Jell-O, or ice cream, for example—along with decorative or plastic spoons.

- Give everyone a deck of cards.

TROUBLE-SHOOTING TIPS

- Remember to use items that can withstand getting grabbed and squeezed by energetic hands (candy bars, for example, may get mushy if the kids aren't careful). Avoid paper items—they're apt to get mangled and torn.

- Be sure to enforce the "Pass" rule as much as possible. Otherwise, it's not fair for the kids sitting to the right of slow passers.

QUICK DRAW

This fast-paced drawing game has been a favorite for years. It doesn't require any artistic talent—the worse the kids draw, the more fun they'll have during the game.

For Ages: 10–12

Optional Ages: 6–9

Players Needed: 4 or more

Object: To guess the phrase, object, title, or sentence your teammate is drawing before the time is up

HOW TO PLAY

Before the party, write some simple objects, phrases, or sentences (appropriate for your party crowd) on slips of paper. Fold the papers up and place them in a hat, bowl, or other container. Try single words such as "spring," "hamburger," "basement," or "bride"; common phrases such as "Raining cats and dogs," "Quiet as a mouse," or "Not guilty"; or movie, TV, or song titles.

At game time, gather the guests around a table and divide them into two teams. A player on the first team must choose a card without looking and draw a picture that represents the word or phrase. (He must *draw* only—talking or gesturing is not allowed.) Set the timer for one, two, or three minutes, depending on the skill level of the kids. The player's teammates must try to guess what the word or phrase is before the time runs out. Give each team a point for a correct answer, and award a prize to the team with the most points at the end of the game. Or play a noncompetitive version without points—just let the next team choose a new slip of paper and move on.

CREATIVE OPTIONS

- Let the teams make up their own words and phrases for the other teams to guess—screen them to weed out any that are too difficult.

- If a team is unable to guess what their player is drawing and the time runs out, pass the drawing to the other team to see if they can guess correctly.

Materials Needed:
- A table
- Large sheets of paper
- Felt-tip pens or pencils
- A hat, bowl, or other container
- A timer

- Play the game based on a specific category or theme, such as music, movies, or book titles.

- For a really silly game, have the kids draw with the hand they don't usually use, or with their eyes closed.

PRIZES AND FAVORS

- Give each player a pad of paper and a fun pencil so they can play the game at home.

- Send everyone home with drawing supplies—sketch pads, charcoal, or colored pencils (available at art supply stores).

- Offer the kids packs of felt-tip pens.

TROUBLE-SHOOTING TIPS

- Make sure the players have enough time to draw, but not too much time or the game won't be challenging.

- Switch team members around if one team continually wins.

RELAY RACES

Preteens love doing relays—the sillier, the better! They'll enjoy the exercise and the craziness of these zany games.

For Ages: 10–12

Optional Ages: 6–9

Players Needed: 6 or more

Object: To be the first team to reach the finish line after completing the required challenges

HOW TO PLAY

Get ready for your day of relays by preparing all of the materials ahead of time—first gather sacks, spoons, clothing, and oranges, and then hard-boil some eggs. Lay ropes on the grass (twenty-five feet apart is a good minimum distance) or, if you play indoors, clear away the furniture and mark starting and finishing lines with masking tape.

Start off with the Sack Relay. Divide the kids into two teams and have them line up behind the starting line. Have the first player on each team stand in a sack or pillowcase. The first players must hop to the finish line in the sacks, step out of them at the finish line, run back to the starting line with their sacks, and pass them to the next players in line. The race continues in this manner until every player on one team has completed the challenge.

Next, move on to some even sillier relays. For the Egg on the Spoon Relay, divide the kids into two teams and give each player a spoon. Give the first player on each team an egg (don't tell the kids the eggs are hard-boiled), and have them walk as quickly as possible to the finish line and back to the starting line, balancing the eggs on the spoons. Once the players reach the starting line again, they must carefully pass the eggs to the next players in line without touching the eggs! The race continues in this manner until every player on one team has completed the task. (If a player drops an egg, she must get a new egg and start again.)

The Orange Relay is sure to make the kids laugh, too. To play, divide the kids into two teams and have them form two lines; then have them pass an orange from the beginning of each line to the end, using only

Materials Needed:
- 2 burlap sacks or 2 large pillowcases
- A spoon for each player
- Hard-boiled eggs (the relay requires 2, but some might break)
- 2 oranges
- Ropes or masking tape to mark the starting and finishing lines

their chins and necks! If a player drops the orange at any time, she must pick it up without using her hands and continue.

CREATIVE OPTIONS

- Invite the guests' parents to join in the relays! The kids will love watching their parents compete in the races, and the games are great fun for adults, too.

- In the Orange relay, have the kids line up alternating male and female, if you wish. This game can serve as a good icebreaker.

PRIZES AND FAVORS

- Award small plastic trophies to everyone (available at party supply stores).

- Give the grand prize winner a book about a popular athlete.

TROUBLE-SHOOTING TIPS

- Play the games on a grassy surface and clear away any lawn debris. Or clear a large in-door area and remove any obstacles.

- If one team consistently wins, switch the players around after each race to make the competition more challenging.

- Don't put too much focus on competition.

TRUTH OR CONSEQUENCES

Here's a kids' game that's so fun even adults like it! It gives the guests a chance to take a dare and act really silly.

For Ages: 10–12

Optional Ages: 6–9

Players Needed: 6 or more

Object: To tell the truth or take the consequences

HOW TO PLAY

Before the game, write up some silly questions on slips of paper—some that are *slightly* embarrassing, and some that are easy. For example, you might ask: "Who is your girl-friend (boyfriend)?" or "What's the worst thing you ever did?"; or ask: "Is the sky blue?" or "How much is two plus one?" Fold up the slips of paper and place them in a small box, with the word "Truth" written on the outside.

Next, write up a set of stunts and tricks and place them in a separate box labeled "Consequences." Make up tricks that are silly and fun, such as "Sing the chorus of a popular rock song," "Call your mom and apologize for the last bad thing you did," or "Hop around the room like a kangaroo."

Gather the guests in a cozy circle and have the first player pick a slip of paper from the "Truth" box. He must read the question aloud to the group and make a choice—to answer the question truthfully or to lie. If he doesn't tell the truth, he must pick a consequence from the other box and perform the stunt. Once he has told the truth or taken a consequence, move on to the next player.

CREATIVE OPTIONS

• Write up consequences that take two players to perform, and then have a player choose another player to take the consequences with him. For example, have the two players race across the room on one foot, buzz like bees (seeing who can buzz the longest without taking a breath), or sing out loud.

Materials Needed:
• Room to form a cozy circle
• Paper and a pencil or pen
• 2 small cardboard boxes

• Instead of asking personal questions or ones that are really easy, ask trivia questions about sports, U.S. capitols, or music. When a player can't answer a question correctly, have him do a funny stunt.

• Allow the guests to make up their own questions and stunts for each other. Screen them before the game to weed out any that are too difficult or embarrassing.

PRIZES AND FAVORS

• Send the kids home with boxes filled with small goodies.

• Give everyone a diary for keeping their secrets or lockets for storing personal photos.

• Take Polaroid snapshots of the kids doing silly stunts and pass them out at the end of the game.

TROUBLE-SHOOTING TIPS

• If the kids take too long deciding whether to answer the questions truthfully, use a timer.

• Some kids might need a little encouragement to do the tricks or stunts. Try modifying the "consequences" a little if it makes the kids feel more comfortable.

• Make the questions fun and silly, rather than too personal; make the consequences entertaining, rather than embarrassing.

CHAOS CARDS

This fast-paced, action-packed card game is great for a group of quick thinkers—just when they think they've got it down, it's chaos!

For Ages: 10–12

Optional Ages: 6–9

Players Needed: 4 or more

Object: To have the most cards when the time is called

HOW TO PLAY

Have the players sit in a circle (on the floor or at a table) and deal all of the cards face down. If you have more than four players, use two decks of cards, and if there are more than eight players, use three decks. Tell the kids not to look at their cards. On the posterboard, draw symbols of the four suits: a heart, a diamond, a club, and a spade, as well as a symbol for numbers—"#." Ask the players to name a category, such as "girls' names," and write that category next to the first symbol. Next, ask for another category, such as "boys' names," and write it beside the next symbol. Repeat this three more times, until each symbol has a different category next to it. (Some fun categories are candy bars, cars, singers, or foods.) Have the players memorize the categories, but keep the chart visible.

Whenever you say, "Chaos!" all of the players must flip over one card *at the same time,* then scan the overturned cards to see if their card matches the suit or number of any other cards. The players who match suits must shout out an item in the category that corresponds with the suit. For example, if two players flip cards showing hearts, they must race to name an item in the "girls' names" category; if three players flip cards showing clubs, they must race to name an item in whatever category has been assigned to clubs. Here's the catch: any cards with matching *numbers* take precedence over cards with matching suits. So, if two players flip matching fives, and two others flip matching diamonds, the kids with matching fives are the ones to race to name an item from the "#" category. As you can see, this game is chaos! The player who correctly yells out a category item first wins all

Materials Needed:
- A deck of cards for every 4 players
- A sheet of posterboard
- A felt-tip pen
- A timer

♥ Girls' Names
♦ Boys' Names
♣ Junk Food
♠ Songs

of the cards that were turned face up during the round. Set a timer for twenty minutes and see who has the most cards at that time—keep playing if the kids love the game.

CREATIVE OPTIONS

• For a simpler game, assign categories for suits only. In other words, only cards that match suits count.

• Tell the players that words used to win a round cannot be repeated. For example, if a player calls out the name "Mary" before any other players to win the round, that name can't be called when the girls' names category comes up again.

• After the kids have played using the first set of categories, stop the game and write in new ones on the back of the posterboard.

The kids will have to learn a new set of categories and forget the old set—more chaos!

PRIZES AND FAVORS

• Give everyone their own deck of cards to take home.

• Send them home with some items from the categories, such as candy bars, small toys, or snacks.

• Offer the game winner a fancy deck of cards.

TROUBLE-SHOOTING TIPS

• Don't wait too long to shout "Chaos!" or the kids will have time to prepare their answers, rather than thinking them up spontaneously.

• Jot down any category items used, so that repeat items can be disqualified.

PUZZLE BAGS

If you have a big group of guests who don't know each other very well, this is the perfect game for you. It's a quiet icebreaker that will help your group get ready for more games and activities.

For Ages: 10–12

Optional Ages: 6–9

Players Needed: 6 or more

Object: To be the first team to figure out their puzzle bag's theme

HOW TO PLAY

Prepare some "puzzle bags" by deciding on a fun theme for each bag and gathering the appropriate items. Here are some suggestions: School (ruler, pencil, dunce cap, apple, lunch bag, late slip); Pizza (olives, flour, water, cookbook, cheese, Italian spices); Monopoly (an iron, a shoe, a hotel receipt, dice, money); "Beverly Hills 90210" (sunglasses, money, a postcard from Minnesota, a zip code, a picture of sideburns); or the Beach (sand, water, tanning oil, a bikini top, a lifeguard whistle, "Shark Bites" candy). Just make sure the themes relate to preteens and that the items aren't too abstract.

At game time, divide the guests into teams and give each team a bag of items. They must take the items out of the bags, look them over, and decide what they have in common. The first group to figure out the theme of their bag wins.

CREATIVE OPTIONS

- Have the teams write down their answers instead of calling them aloud. When the teams have written down their answers, they can hand them to you, exchange bags, and play again.

- Play the game using words written on slips of paper, rather than using actual items.

- Play as one large group, holding up one item at a time from the bags and allowing everyone to guess the theme.

- If the party has a special theme, design the "puzzle bags" with that theme in mind. For example, if it's a dance party, fill each of the bags with items related to different musical groups or song lyrics.

PRIZES AND FAVORS

• Buy colorful bags from a party supply store, fill them with goodies, and let the kids on the winning team take them home after the party (or give one to each child).

• Fill a bag with snacks for a "Junk Food" theme, and distribute the goodies after the game. Or let the kids reach in the bag without looking and pick their "prize."

• Give the kids some of the items from the bags—but only the fun stuff.

TROUBLE-SHOOTING TIP

• Try to put together "puzzle bags" with the same degree of difficulty. It isn't fair to the other teams if one team's bag is really simple.

"SCHOOL"

MYSTERY MELODIES

Much like the old TV game show "Name That Tune," this musical game is fast, frenzied, and lots of fun.

For Ages: 10–12

Optional Ages: 6–9

Players Needed: 3 or more

Object: To be the first to correctly name the most tunes

HOW TO PLAY

Prerecord lots of sample lyrics from your preteen's music collection or record bits of various songs from her favorite radio station. (Make sure to write down the song titles and musical artists, if you're not familiar with them.) Record about thirty seconds of silence between the songs, too.

To start the game, have the guests sit in a circle and play only the first set of notes for the first song. The first player to call out the name of the song wins a point (she can earn a bonus point for correctly naming the singer or group). If none of the players can get the answer, play a little bit more of the song. If that doesn't help, move on. Continue in this manner until the whole tape is played. Make sure to record each player's points to see who got the most at the end of the game.

CREATIVE OPTIONS

• When recording songs for the tape, throw in a few oldies, some country music selections, or some famous tunes from musicals. Award extra points to players who guess the titles correctly.

• In addition to naming the song title and artist, have the guests identify the year the song came out or another bit of trivia.

• Have a rock-and-roll party with a dance or lip-sync contest. For added fun, hang musical decorations in the party room and ask the guests to dress as favorite pop stars.

PRIZES AND FAVORS

• Give the game winner a gift certificate to a record store or an inexpensive music video.

Materials Needed:
- Cassette player
- A blank cassette tape
- A selection of various recorded songs and artists
- Paper and a pencil or pen

- Send the gang home with blank cassette tapes, or buttons and/or postcards with popular performers on them.

- Give each guest a rock star poster or popular cassette single.

TROUBLE-SHOOTING TIPS

- If it's too chaotic when everyone calls out the song title at once, let the players guess one at a time. Just make sure each player has a turn to be the first guesser.

- Be sure to record enough of each song so that the players will eventually be able to get the right answer.

CRAZY OLYMPICS

Here is a great idea for an outdoor preteen party—host a Crazy Olympics with lots of fun challenges. The kids will love the physical exercise!

For Ages: 10–12

Optional Ages: 6–9

Players Needed: 6 or more

Object: To be the first to complete the challenges in each event

HOW TO PLAY

Divide the kids into teams of two, and start the Olympic games with a crazy obstacle course. Have two players compete at the same time on two identical courses. You'll have to set up a series of starting and finishing lines all around the yard so the kids can go from one challenge to another without stopping. Also tie a string or rope around two trees or two clothesline poles for the limbo (the trees or poles should be about five feet apart, and the rope about four feet off the ground).

For the first obstacle, have the kids balance an apple on their head and walk to the finish line, without dropping it. If the apple falls, it's back to the starting line for that player. For the second challenge, have the kids run backwards on all fours (crab-walking)—it's crazy,

but it can be done. Next, make the kids do the limbo! Show them how to bend backward and walk under the rope without letting the rope touch their stomach. For the final event, have the kids get on tricycles and pedal to the finish line as quickly as possible. After the first two players have completed the course, the next two players can begin.

For the last event, have the kids play a game of Leapfrog. After the kids have completed the other challenges, divide them into two teams, and put ropes on the ground to mark the starting and finishing lines. To play, the first player on each team must squat down, with shoulders and head tucked. The other players on each team line up single file and, one by one, "leapfrog" over their teammate (to leapfrog, a player simply places his hands on the stooped-over player's back and vaults

Materials Needed:
- A large, grassy outdoor space
- 2 tricycles
- 2 apples
- Ropes to mark the starting and finishing lines, plus an extra rope for the limbo
- 2 trees or 2 poles for the limbo

over him, legs apart). After the first players have completed the leapfrog, they must bend into a stooped position a few feet in front of the players they leaped over, and the next players must leapfrog over *two* players. Play continues like this until one team leapfrogs all of its players over the finish line.

CREATIVE OPTIONS

- Before the events begin, play a cassette tape of the Olympics theme music (or any music that is similar).

- Take lots of Polaroid snapshots of the kids performing during the events (the photos are fun for the kids to keep and compare during the party, and they serve as nice mementos). Then take one photo of the whole group of "Olympic Stars" and send reprints to everyone later, if you wish.

- If you can't set up two identical courses, have each player perform the feats separately. Use a timer to see who finishes first.

PRIZES AND FAVORS

- Give each guest a ribbon that says "First Place," "Second Place," "Honorable Mention," etc. You can find these at sports stores or make them yourself.

- Offer the grand prize winner a piece of sporting equipment.

TROUBLE-SHOOTING TIPS

- Demonstrate all of the challenges before the events begin so that the players understand what they must do.

- Play the games on a grassy surface and clear away any lawn debris.

- Don't put too much focus on competition.

171

BOX OFFICE TRIVIA

Kids love following the lives of celebrities and teen idols. Here's a fun trivia game that features questions about the stars. For extra fun, add a personal twist to the game by playing Friend Trivia, as well.

For Ages: 10–12

Optional Ages: 6–9

Players Needed: 4 or more

Object: To correctly answer the most trivia questions about celebrities or friends

HOW TO PLAY

Before the game, collect pictures and postcards of various celebrities, and find some information about these stars, using magazines or books. You might use information like birthdates, hometowns, real names, girlfriends' or boyfriends' names, film/TV show titles, names of their film/TV characters, and some of their most famous lines. (Make sure you choose celebrities that preteens know well.) Write up the trivia questions on slips of paper, and place the postcards and pictures around the party room.

At game time, pass out the paper and pencils and tell the guests to answer each question secretly on paper. Ask the trivia questions, giving the guests some time to write down their answers. Plan on asking about twenty-five questions total. When all of the questions have been asked, let each guest reveal her answers. Award a prize to the guest who answered the most correctly. Then play a bonus round—this time with trivia questions about the various guests. (You'll have to come up with some questions ahead of time and secretly phone the guests' parents for the correct answers—try some about their favorite stuffed animals, which movie stars they have a crush on, what they did the last time they got in trouble, their favorite dessert, their favorite rock group, their best subject in school, etc.) Let the guests answer aloud in this version. See how well they know each other!

CREATIVE OPTIONS

• Write up some bonus questions that are a little more difficult, and award extra points for them. Try trivia about older movie stars or music groups to test the kids.

• Have the kids dress up as movie stars (you can provide sunglasses or other props). Serve star-shaped cookies and a star cake.

• Write up some trivia questions about the guest of honor and have the guests try to answer them. You can make them difficult or easy, but not too embarrassing!

PRIZES AND FAVORS

• Let each trivia game winner pick a celebrity picture or postcard to take home; or buy a special celebrity poster for the winner.

• Give all of the guests teen magazines, posters, or giant bags of popcorn.

• Award a small prize to any guest who answers a "friend trivia" question correctly (try cassette singles or celebrity buttons).

TROUBLE-SHOOTING TIPS

• If you plan to use dialogue from the movies for extra trivia questions, rent a few movies and jot down some of the best lines. Record several, so that if guests miss one, they can try again.

• When calling parents to find out trivia information about the guests, don't ask embarrassing or private questions.

• Ask an equal number of questions about each guest so no one feels left out. Tell each guest to remain silent when they're the subject of a question.

MURDERER

This game is scary, suspenseful, and full of surprises. Who will be the victim? And who will be the murderer? The answers are in a deck of cards.

For Ages: 10–12

Optional Ages: 6–9

Players Needed: 6 or more

Object: To solve the murder mystery before the other players

HOW TO PLAY

Write down a short and silly murder synopsis (small enough to fit on a playing card) on a slip of paper. Include the weapon, the motive, and the murder location. For example, you might write down the following: "The victim was killed with a squirt gun in an alley because she was blackmailing the murderer about the money stolen from the ice cream truck." Tape the slip of paper securely onto the face of the Ace of Spades. (Don't wrap the tape around the sides of the card.) Shuffle the cards and pass them out to all of the guests. Tell the players to look over their cards secretly to see if they have the Ace of Spades or the Joker. The player holding the Joker is the Victim, and the player with the Ace and information sheet is the Murderer. The Murderer must discreetly memorize the crime

information, and everyone must tuck their cards out of sight.

Flick the lights off and on for a moment. While the lights are out, the Victim must fall to the floor, pretending to be dead. When the lights are turned on again, have the rest of the players ask each other questions about the murder (including the Murderer, who remains anonymous). The Murderer must answer any questions truthfully, according to the information on the card. The other players should try to fool one another as they're asking and answering questions. The one question they can't ask, however, is: "Are you the Murderer?" The players can write down any information in their notebooks. The person who first discovers the culprit, weapon, motive, and murder location wins the game.

Materials Needed:
- A deck of cards with 1 Joker
- Tape
- A pencil or pen for each player
- A small notebook for each player

CREATIVE OPTIONS

- Write up funny scenarios on all of the cards. For example, you might write: "You're the maid. You were out of town during the murder. Your hand is too shaky to handle a weapon." The players can use these alibis as answers during questioning to make the game more intriguing.

- Write some instructions on the Joker card to add a little humor, such as "Roll over and play dead."

PRIZES AND FAVORS

- Give the "detectives" a sleuth kit, with a plastic magnifying glass and a "Holmes" hat.

- Offer the kids mystery novels (like Nancy Drew or the Hardy Boys mysteries), or solve-it-yourself mystery books.

- Give the kids mystery movie videos or the board game "Clue."

TROUBLE-SHOOTING TIPS

- If the kids have trouble knowing what type of questions to ask each other, offer suggestions and ask a few questions yourself. Or write up some sample questions on cards and pass them out.

- If the "sleuths" are completely stumped, ask each player to offer a clue to the group—all but one will be false.

"SNIFF SNIFF"

JINGLES AND SLOGANS

Preteen kids generally know the words to as many commercials as pop songs. Here's a fun way for them to use that knowledge.

For Ages: 10–12

Optional Ages: 6–9

Players Needed: 4 or more

Object: To correctly name the most products after hearing their jingles

Catch a wave...

HOW TO PLAY

Before the game, prerecord a collection of commercials (perhaps ten to fifteen total) from radio or TV. Leave a few seconds of silence between each jingle, and blank out the product's name in each song.

Gather the players together and distribute paper and pencils. Play the first jingle on a cassette tape, presenting a few notes of the music and lyrics (but not the product name). Have the players write down the name of the product the jingle is advertising. Once you've gone through all the jingles, read off the answers and see who got the most correct.

Next, play the "slogan" version of this game by writing down some old and new product slogans. For example, you might include "Catch the Wave!" (Coke), "I love what you do

for me!" (Toyota), and "It's Grrrreat!" (Frosted Flakes). Have the kids identify the product from the slogan.

CREATIVE OPTIONS

• Make a visual presentation by videotaping portions of TV commercials. Since seeing the commercials makes them easier to identify, record only a few seconds so the game will still be challenging.

• Instead of having the kids write their answers down on paper, have them call out their answers and race to see who can name the product first.

• Play the slogan version, letting the kids come up with their own slogan challenges.

• Instead of recording only a small amount of each jingle, record the entire jingle and play

Materials Needed:
- Blank cassette tape
- Cassette player
- Paper and pencils for each player

a little bit at a time. Have the players write down their answers as soon as they know the product, and record whether they got the correct answer on the first, second, or third play.

PRIZES AND FAVORS

- Give the kids one of the products mentioned in the jingles and slogans, such as a candy bar, a box of cereal, or a toy.

- Give everyone a gift certificate for a drugstore or toy store so they can pick out their favorite products.

- Let the grand prize winner take home the board game "Adverteasing."

TROUBLE-SHOOTING TIP

- Use commercials that kids are familiar with, and try to choose ones that feature products that preteens use. Avoid products for adults only, such as cigarettes and alcohol.

♪ I Love What You Do For Me...
...Things go better with

ROB YOUR NEIGHBOR

Here's a memory game that's fun for older kids since it has an element of suspense. It gives them a chance to win prizes that kids of all ages love—candy!

For Ages: 10–12

Optional Ages: 6–9

Players Needed: 6 or more

Object: To remember which player has stolen your favorite treat so you can get it back

HOW TO PLAY

Gather the kids in a circle on the floor and place a pile of candy bars in the center of the circle. Shuffling a deck of cards thoroughly, pass out three cards to each player and have the kids place the cards face up in front of them. Using a second deck (also shuffled), pick cards from the pile one at a time and hold them up for the kids to see. If a card matches one of the player's cards, he may take his favorite candy bar from the center pile. (Tell him to tuck the candy bar out of sight, so the other players can't see it, and tell the others to remember what he took). Continue in this manner until all of the candy bars are gone— each player should end up with three.

Next, reshuffle the first deck and give each player one card, telling the kids to peek at

them secretly. Return to the second deck of cards and display one card at a time—until one of the players has a match with his hidden card. After he proves it's a match, he can choose a candy bar to "steal" from another player, but he must first identify the candy bar and who originally took it. This isn't easy considering how many candy bars have been distributed! If he is able to name another player's hidden candy bar in one try, he may rob that player of it, leaving that player with only two candy bars. But if he incorrectly identifies the player who took a particular candy bar, he must give one of his own candy bars to that player. Play continues until everyone has had a chance to rob their neighbors.

CREATIVE OPTIONS

• Try small toys or other fun items, rather than candy bars, for the kids to "steal." Or play

Materials Needed:
• 3 mini candy bars for each player (different brands)
• 2 decks of cards

with wrapped hard candies, different brands of gum, trading cards, stickers, or buttons.

• Increase the number of candies or toys to make the game more difficult. (Reduce the number of candies for younger kids.)

• Instead of giving the kids only one guess when robbing their neighbors, give them two or three.

PRIZES AND FAVORS

• Let the kids keep their "loot"—make sure you have extras for any player who was left with no candy.

• Send the kids home with decks of cards.

• Make goody bags for the kids to store their candy, or buy goody bags at a party supply store.

TROUBLE-SHOOTING TIP

• If a player loses all of his candy and seems upset, tell him an insurance policy covered the loss. Then give him a giant candy bar for being a good sport.

EYEWITNESS

Preteens will love the drama and challenge of Eyewitness. The game can be played as many times as the kids like, always with a different outcome.

For Ages: 10–12

Optional Ages: 6–9

Players Needed: 4 or more

Object: To recall the most details of a crime

HOW TO PLAY

You'll have to do a little planning before the party to make sure this game is a success. First, find an adult volunteer who will act as the robber during the game, and put an appropriate costume together. Set the stage for the crime by creating a scene or display, using various props. For example, if the crime is a jewelry heist, set up display tables with costume jewelry, make price tags, and put up a jewelry store sign.

When the guests arrive, choose one to play the sales clerk, and give her a name tag made from construction paper that tells who she is. The rest of the kids can be customers at the jewelry store. Have them take their places in the scene and tell them to expect the unexpected! This is your volunteer's cue—he or she

enters the scene dressed as a robber, causes a commotion, steals a piece of jewelry, and leaves the scene, all within a few seconds. After the crime has been committed, ask the guests a series of questions about the robbery such as: "What was the robber wearing?" "What time did the robber enter the scene?" "What piece of jewelry was taken?" and "What did the robber look like?" Have the kids call out their answers, and record them to see who got the most correct—award a prize to that "super sleuth." You can play again, with the robber stealing a different item and changing his or her appearance. The second time you play, the kids will know that something is going to happen. They'll be more observant, which is fine, because they'll solve the crime sooner.

Materials Needed:

- A burglar costume: a mask, dark clothing, a "loot" bag, etc. (available at thrift shops and toy stores)

- An object to be stolen: a toy, a piece of jewelry, or a goody bag

- Props for the scene of the crime (see How to Play, for ideas)

- Construction paper

- Felt-tip pens

- Paper and a pencil or pen

CREATIVE OPTIONS

- Use other scenarios, such as a "fist fight" between two people, a murder, a different type of robbery, or a rude party-crasher.

- Create other crime scenes by turning your party room into a dance hall, a bank, a cruise ship, or another fun scene.

- Allow the kids to interview the suspect so they can solve the crime (the robber can lie or tell the truth, depending on how difficult you want the game to be).

PRIZES AND FAVORS

- Give everyone a magnifying glass.

- Present the big winner with a mystery game, such as "Clue" or "Lie Detector."

- Send the kids home with mystery books or give them items related to the crime scene, such as jewelry for a jewelry heist.

TROUBLE-SHOOTING TIPS

- If the kids don't pay close attention and miss some of the details the first time around, have the robber repeat the crime.

- If the kids have trouble figuring the mystery out, ask more specific questions such as, "Was the robber wearing a baseball cap or a sailor's hat?"

BABY BOTTLE RACE

Once the party-goers get warmed up with a few challenging games, they'll be ready for some hilarious activities. The kids will love getting a chance to act silly!

For Ages: 10–12

Optional Ages: 6–9

Players Needed: 2 or more

Object: To empty the baby bottle first

HOW TO PLAY

Before the race, fill each baby bottle with about two inches of water. Divide the kids into pairs (or play relay-style if you have a really big group, with the first set of players going first and other sets of players starting when they're done—just make sure everyone gets their own bottle). Have them put on baby bibs, if you choose to use them. At the starting signal, each of the two players must empty their bottles—by drinking out of them like a baby! The first one to drink all of his water wins. Then have the next pair race.

Since the bottle race is short, you might want to have the kids do another silly activity as long as they're in a silly mood. One at a time, have each guest close his eyes and have another guest speak to him in baby talk. The

first player must guess who is speaking. Play until everyone has had a turn to guess and talk baby talk.

CREATIVE OPTIONS

• Fill the baby bottles with more water for a longer race.

• Use juice or another liquid, rather than water.

• Try an activity called "Only a Face a Mother Could Love." Give the guests some tape and have them tape up their faces in funny ways. Tell them this is the way they looked when they were first born. Take Polaroid snapshots of each guest with a funny face.

• Serve teething biscuits and Cheerios, drinks in baby bottles, and a cake with all of the

Materials Needed:
- 1 baby bottle per player (use new nipples, if possible, for a more challenging game)
- *Optional:* baby bibs

kids' names on it, decorated with pink and blue frosting.

PRIZES AND FAVORS

- Send everyone home with their baby bottles.

- Give the big babies boxes of animal crackers to take home.

- Give each race winner a small stuffed animal, baby rattle, or pacifier.

TROUBLE-SHOOTING TIP

- If you want to use another beverage for the bottle race, try juice or punch, rather than a bubbly drink.

PRODUCT-ABILITY

Here's another fun icebreaker to get the kids in a party mood. Play more than once if the kids really like it.

For Ages: 10–12

Optional Ages: 6–9

Players Needed: 6 or more

Object: To guess which product you've been assigned

HOW TO PLAY

Cut out a product advertisement for each guest at the party. Try to choose items that will appeal to the kids to make the game more fun. You might include advertisements for products like Snickers bars, Coke, and *Seventeen* magazine, or various toothpastes and cereals. Keep the product ads in a bag by the front door, and as each guest enters the party, tape or pin the product ad to her back. Tell the kids there's something "going on behind their backs," but they can't look over their shoulders, use a mirror, or bribe other guests to tell them what it is.

To guess the products they have on their backs, the guests must ask questions such as, "Can this product be eaten" or "Is the product something to wear?" They are not allowed to

ask any direct questions such as, "What product am I?" Players can also give each other clues. For example, for a player who has a picture of a Coke can on her back, someone could say, "Are you thirsty?" "Can I get you a soft drink?" or "What a classic you are." When each guest finally guesses her product, she collects a prize.

CREATIVE OPTIONS

• Instead of using magazine ads, use the actual product packages and wrappers. For example, use a Snickers wrapper, a cover from *Seventeen* magazine, or an empty toothpaste tube.

• Use products in the same category. If your category is candy bars, find wrappers or ads for all different brands. This will make it a little easier for the kids to guess.

Materials Needed:
• 1 product advertisement per guest, clipped from a magazine
• A bag
• Tape or pins

• Play a version of this game with the kids guessing their "new identity" rather than a product name. Just pin the name of a sports star or celebrity on each player's back and have the players ask questions or give clues accordingly.

PRIZES AND FAVORS

• Give each guest the actual product once they guess what it is. But if a player is "toothpaste," for instance, you might want to give her a small treat, too.

• Give the kids favors related to their products, such as giant candy bars to match the small wrappers on their backs.

• If you play the celebrity identity version, give each player an item featuring their celebrity, such as a poster, postcard, or button, etc.

TROUBLE-SHOOTING TIPS

• In case the kids have trouble coming up with clues for the products, have a few clues ready ahead of time to help the players.

• Make sure the products are fun and well-known to kids (try products related to food, music, make-up, sports, clothes, or school subjects). Avoid ads for adult products only, such as cigarettes or alcohol.

REWRITE

Here is a homemade version of the popular game "Madlibs." Kids love the wacky results of Rewrite!

For Ages: 10–12

Optional Ages: 6–9

Players Needed: Any group size

Object: To create a crazy story

WHAT TO DO

Clip out articles or stories from teen magazines or other sources (one for each player). Choose articles that will take approximately sixty seconds to read aloud. Using White-Out, remove a number of adjectives, adverbs, nouns, and verbs from each story; or, if you have a typewriter or computer, type up the stories with those parts of speech missing. Underneath each blank, write whether the missing word was a noun, verb, adjective, or adverb. (If the articles have small type and seem hard to read after you erase some of the words, take them to a copy store and have them slightly enlarged.)

At game time, divide the kids into pairs and give a different story to each team. Have one team member read aloud the missing parts of speech (*not* the rest of the story though) for the other team member to fill in. In other words, Player One says, "Noun," and Player Two chooses a random noun for Player One to write in. This continues until each blank is filled in. When all of the kids have finished their rewrites, have them take turns reading their funny stories aloud. The result will be some crazy stories and lots of laughter!

CREATIVE OPTIONS

- Rather than erasing only nouns, verbs, adjectives, and adverbs, blank-out some complete quotations, names, or other appropriate items for the kids to fill in.

- Have all of the teams use the same story; then let them read their different versions. The kids will enjoy seeing how different the stories turn out.

"buggy?"

Materials Needed:
- Articles from teen magazines, newspapers, or tabloids
- Liquid correcting fluid (e.g., White-Out)
- A pencil for each player

- Gather the kids in a circle and read out the missing parts of speech yourself, letting the kids shout out their suggestions. Write in the first one that you hear. It's fun when the game is a group effort.

PRIZES AND FAVORS

- Let the kids keep the funny stories—make sure you have one for each child.

- Give each guest a "Madlibs" activity tablet to take home.

- Give everyone a popular teen magazine or funny tabloid newspaper.

TROUBLE-SHOOTING TIPS

- If the kids have trouble thinking up words, quickly write up a list of suggestions to get them going.

- Encourage the kids to think up silly words to fill in the blanks—for instance, words like "giant" or "pig" make funnier stories than words like "man" or "person."

- Before the game, review the different parts of speech to help avoid confusion.

FREAKY FRIDAY

This crazy activity is inspired by the classic Disney film, *Freaky Friday.* You'll have to do some careful planning before hosting this delightfully twisted party—but the results are memorable! Everyone will have fun when the preteen guests come dressed as their parents and vice versa.

For Ages: 10–12

Optional Ages: 6–9

Players Needed: A group of kids *and* parents

Object: To have the kids and their parents switch roles

WHAT TO DO

This party requires both the preteens and one of their parents to attend, so call ahead of time to make sure both can come. Ask them to arrive dressed as one another, and encourage them to exaggerate as they're dressing up, for added humor. Be sure to let the guests know that daughters can dress as their fathers and sons as their mothers—either parent can attend! Also, have all of the guests answer some trivia questions that you've prepared ahead of time such as, "What time does your daughter really go to sleep at night?" "What kind of after-shave does your dad wear?" or "What's your child's favorite rock group?" Make sure the parents and kids answer these questions secretly so the answers will be a surprise at the party.

When the guests arrive, tell them they must talk and act like one another for the duration of the party. The parents will enjoy using slang, and the kids will like telling their parents what to do for a change! Play a trivia game by asking the questions you prepared before the party. Go around the room, letting the guests answer the questions in turn. Award prizes for questions answered correctly.

CREATIVE OPTIONS

- Instead of giving the guests time to come up with a Freaky Friday outfit, invite them by phone, asking them to arrive as one another—as they appear at the moment of the call.

- Play a general trivia game about parents and kids. Prepare some questions ahead of time

Materials Needed:
• Paper and a pencil or pen
• Trivia questions about all of the guests

that the parents must answer, and some that the kids must answer. For example, you might ask the parents, "Is Skid Row the name of a song, a rock group, or a jeans label?" You might ask the kids, "How much does gas cost per gallon?" Each group can confer before answering—award a point for each correct answer. The group with the most points at the end of the game wins.

PRIZES AND FAVORS

• Give the guests items appropriate to their new "identities" and let them trade when they get home (teen idol posters for the adults and cookbooks for the kids, etc.).

• Offer everyone joke gifts that stereotype parents and kids, such as teen magazines or copies of *Good Housekeeping.*

TROUBLE-SHOOTING TIPS

• If a parent is unavailable for the party, tell the child to bring a grandparent, relative, or adult friend.

• Encourage the guests to *really* exaggerate their imitations of one another—it helps them get into the spirit of their new roles.

TALENT SHOW

Kids love to show off, and what they lack in talent, they make up with enthusiasm. Give them a chance to put on a show for one another with a come-one, come-all talent show.

For Ages: 10–12

Optional Ages: 6–9

Players Needed: Any group size

Object: To put on a fun talent show

WHAT TO DO

When you invite the talented guests, don't tell them that you're planning a talent show. Half the fun is coming up with ideas on the spur of the moment. Arrange a stage by spreading sheets on the floor and tacking them to the wall for a background, and set up chairs for the audience.

Welcome the guests to the talent show by telling them they have just been hired by a famous producer to put on a show. Show them your collection of props, fashions, makeup, and music and tell them to get creative. They can work in teams or solo—just be sure to give them at least twenty minutes to prepare. Make suggestions to get them thinking about their talent: lip-sync to a pop song, sing a camp song, act out a skit, do a popular dance, perform a parody of a TV show or musical, write and read a scary poem, show off some card tricks, or do a comedy routine. Then set up the video camera and start the show. When the show is over, play the video for more laughs.

CREATIVE OPTIONS

• Borrow some short plays from the library or rent video musicals that feature a number of roles for kids or teens (such as *Grease* or *Annie*). Then make up scripts, let the kids choose characters to act out, and let them put on a play or musical! Or rent a Karaoke machine so the kids can sing along.

• Videotape the performance and keep the camera rolling during the rehearsals, moving from room to room as the kids prepare for

Materials Needed:
- All sorts of fun clothing, costumes, props, and make-up
- A cassette player and musical tapes
- Chairs
- Sheets
- Thumbtacks
- *Optional:* a video camera and VCR

the show. You'll capture a behind-the-scenes look at the world of "show business."

- If you don't have a video camera, take Polaroid snapshots of the kids in costume, putting on their performances.

PRIZES AND FAVORS

- Give each performer a bouquet of flowers or a single rose when they come off the stage.

- Give everyone movie magazines, celebrity posters, inexpensive videos, or cassette singles of popular songs.

- Give everyone a copy of their embarrassing Polaroid snapshot.

TROUBLE-SHOOTING TIPS

- If the kids have trouble coming up with acts, prepare some possibilities on slips of paper, put them in a box, and have the kids draw them, one by one—whatever they pick, they must perform.

- Tell the kids not to worry if their act isn't perfect—the more mistakes and flubs, the funnier it will be.

191

DESIGNER T-SHIRTS

Decorating T-shirts is a wonderful activity for a preteen party—and all of the guests will get to take fun, long-lasting mementos of the party home with them.

For Ages: 10–12

Optional Ages: 6–9

Players Needed: Any group size

Object: To decorate T-shirts with paint

WHAT TO DO

Cover the table with newspapers to prevent a mess and set out all the art materials. Then insert a sheet of cardboard between each T-shirt to make painting easier. It helps to let the kids create designs on paper first, or have a finished T-shirt for them to look at.

The kids can paint the T-shirts using many different techniques. Just read the directions on the paint packages beforehand to know what to do. Another decorating technique, called batik, is also fun. To batik the easy way, buy several packs of crayons, pick out a few primary colors, peel off the wrappers, and break them into pieces. Place the pieces separately in an old muffin tin, along with a piece of paraffin the size of a sugar cube. Hold the muffin tin over a pot of boiling water to melt the ingredients; then set the tin on a hot plate to keep the crayons melted while the kids use them for painting. When the T-shirts are painted, have the kids crumple them into a ball and dip the entire shirt into a large container of fabric dye. The dye will color the unpainted areas and seep into the cracks created from crumpling the shirts. Remove the shirts from the dye, rinse them thoroughly in cold water, and allow them to air dry until they're just slightly damp. Lay the T-shirts on an ironing board covered with an old towel, and place several paper towels on top of and underneath the painted area of the T-shirts. Iron off the wax by heating the painted area, pulling off the paper towels when soaked, and repeating until the crayon area is soft. Set the finished T-shirts in indirect sunlight or fresh air to dry.

Materials Needed:
- Newspaper
- Cardboard
- Containers for paint
- 1 white T-shirt for each guest
- A variety of T-shirt decorating materials (available at hobby, fabric, and art supply stores)
- Paintbrushes and sponges
- Batik supplies (crayons, paraffin, a muffin tin, a boiling pot, a hot plate, an iron and ironing board, fabric dye, a large container, paintbrushes, an old towel, and paper towels)

CREATIVE OPTIONS

- Rather than painting T-shirts for themselves, the guests can paint special T-shirts for the guest of honor.

- Make simple awards out of construction paper to give to each guest under fun categories like "most colorful," "strangest," or "funniest." Pin the awards to the T-shirts so the kids can wear both home.

- Have the kids make T-shirt designs that go along with the party theme or that are signed by all of the guests—this will help them remember the special day!

PRIZES AND FAVORS

- Send the guests home with their new designer T-shirts.

- Give everyone some T-shirt paints to try the activity again at home.

- Offer the kids T-shirt accessories such as pins or buttons.

TROUBLE-SHOOTING TIPS

- Make one T-shirt ahead of time, using the decorating ideas you plan to try at the party, so that you know how to do the technique. This will help prevent mistakes during the real event.

- The batik process requires adult supervision at all times. Working with hot wax and an iron can be dangerous, so do these steps yourself. If you need help, ask for adult volunteers to come to the party.

SECRET INGREDIENTS

Kids in the kitchen make for a lot of creative fun. Here are the right ingredients for a great time, a good snack, and a grade-A party.

For Ages: 10–12

Optional Ages: 6–9

Players Needed: Any group size

Object: To create delicious treats!

WHAT TO DO

Set the ingredients on the table, and when the kids arrive, divide them into two teams. Tell them they must create an original snack using only the ingredients they find in front of them; then set the timer for fifteen minutes. Let them know their snacks will be judged and that appearance counts as well as taste. Pass out index cards and pens and let the kids give their concoctions a creative name (if there's time, they can decorate the cards, too).

When the time is up, tell the cooks to stop mixing, and have them present their snacks. Pass out paper to all of the guests and have them walk around the table to inspect and taste the snacks. Have them record, out of a possible ten, what each snack is worth in three areas: name, appearance, and taste. Count up the points and award a prize to the best snack-making team—then let the cooks gobble up the rest of the contest entries!

CREATIVE OPTIONS

- Give each group a different set of ingredients so the snacks will taste different. Be sure to give each group a soft food that will hold the other foods together, and make sure the flavors are compatible.

- Instead of having the cooks judge their own foods, invite a few surprise taste-testers at the end of the cook-off and have them make the final judgement.

- Award prize ribbons for the snacks under categories such as "most original," "most creative," "most unusual," "funniest," "largest," "most like pet food," and so on.

Materials Needed:
- A table
- Food items (peanut butter, yogurt, applesauce, jam, juice, bananas and other fruit, raw vegetables, cheese singles, cereal, crackers, coconut shavings, and chocolate chips)
- Kitchen utensils (spoons, forks, knives, measuring spoons, measuring cups, bowls, plates, cutting boards, mixers, etc.)
- Index cards (3½ by 5½ inches)
- A timer
- Felt-tip pens
- Paper

- Host a "Cook-Off Party"—invite the guests with invitations on recipe cards, and ask the kids to wear aprons or dress like chefs.

PRIZES AND FAVORS

- Send the cooks home with ingredients for chocolate chip cookies and a few samples of the finished product.

- Give the kids samples of the party treats to take home, along with their award ribbons.

- Offer the guests fast food coupons or other food-related gifts.

TROUBLE-SHOOTING TIPS

- Be around to supervise and help, especially if the kids want to use the microwave or other appliances.

- Give the guests special cleanup tasks after the activity—this will make cleaning up easier on everyone, especially you.

PETS ON PARADE

Kids and animals are a winning combination. Take your group of preteen party-goers to a pet show.

For Ages: 10–12

Optional Ages: 6–9

Preparation: Contact a humane society or civic center to find out if any pet shows are scheduled; be sure to ask about times, costs, and directions.

WHAT TO DO

Whether your group is going to a dog, cat, or exotic pets show, the guests will love the experience. Tell the kids ahead of time to bring photos of their pets to show everyone before the outing.

At the show, give the kids ballots (a piece of paper and pencil) so they can vote for the pets they like the best. Have them judge the dogs, cats, or other animals on a variety of serious and silly traits such as best fur color, most fluffy, strangest haircut, best disposition, weirdest-looking, or even most abundant drooler. Also have the kids predict the real winners and award prizes to the kids who guess correctly. Then, for a special treat, give the guests a chance to photograph their favorite animal, using a Polaroid camera. The

kids can share their voting results and snapshots on the ride home.

CREATIVE OPTIONS

- If going to a pet show is not possible, you can still have a pet-viewing event. Ask the kids to bring their own pets to the party (just be prepared to take care of them!). Or take the kids to a horse show or county/state fair.

- If there's time left after the outing, hold a "barking" or "meowing" contest. Give all the guests a chance to show their stuff—be sure to videotape this, if possible.

- Send the guests invitations written on the back of a photo of the family pet, or on cards shaped liked a dog or cat. Serve hot dogs with "cat-sup," a cake in the shape of a doghouse (call a bakery for details), and let

For Added Fun:
- Paper and pencils for each guest
- A Polaroid camera
- Photos of each guest's pet

the kids eat their meals out of "dog" or "cat" bowls.

PRIZES AND FAVORS

- Send the guests home with squeaky toys for their pets, special pet treats, or, for the kids who don't have pets, stuffed animals.

- Give the guests stickers or posters featuring all sorts of pets.

- Give the winner of the "animal sounds" contest a book about pets or a cartoon book featuring Garfield or Marmaduke.

TROUBLE-SHOOTING TIPS

- Check to see if any of the guests have allergies to fur or specific animals before you plan the event.

- Find adult volunteers to join you on the trip so the kids can walk around freely without getting lost or into trouble.

SLUMBER PARTY

Slumber parties are a tradition, and at some point, almost every child wants to have one. Here are some ideas to make your slumber party fun and trouble-free.

For Ages: 10–12

Optional Ages: 6–9

Preparation: Ask the guests to bring their own sleeping bags, but have a few extras on hand in case someone forgets. Plan lots of activities so the kids won't be tempted to play pranks on each other (or on your neighbors!).

WHAT TO DO

When planning a slumber party, it's best to have the guests come during the early evening, rather than the afternoon—the kids will be spending enough time together as it is! If you provide dinner for everyone, have something simple, such as "make-your-own tacos" (this works well for snacking too, which kids love to do at overnighters). Just set the ingredients out in bowls and let the kids prepare their own tacos assembly-line style.

After dinner, play Swami's Secret. Choose one guest to be the Swami and one to be the Swami's Assistant (put a towel "turban" around the Swami's head, for added fun), and secretly tell these guests the trick of the game. The Swami must leave the room so the Assistant can choose another child to be It; then the Swami returns to amaze everyone by naming that guest. Here's the trick: the Assistant says a sentence beginning with the first letter of It's name when welcoming the Swami back into the room. For example, the Assistant could say, "Just tell us who is It, great Swami," if the person's name is Jennifer. If there are a few guests whose first names begin with the same letter, instruct the Assistant to say a sentence with the first two words beginning with the initials of It's *first* and *last* names. Play until one of the guests figures out the trick.

Later in the evening, let the kids have a good old-fashioned pillow fight. Clear away the furniture and lamps (or send them outside, if the weather permits) and let them pound each other with pillows. Show a movie before bed, if you wish, to help them wind down.

For Added Fun:

- Taco fixings (shells, ground beef, cheddar cheese, tomatoes, lettuce, salsa, sour cream, olives, etc.)
- Bowls
- Lots of pillows
- Extra sleeping bags
- A towel
- *Optional:* a VCR and rented videotape

CREATIVE OPTIONS

- Keep the kids entertained throughout the evening with popular slumber party games, such as Truth or Consequences (see p. 162) or Gossip (see p. 150).

- Provide a cereal buffet in the morning. Just set various kinds of cereal and fruit out, and give each guest a spoon and bowl. All they have to do is add milk—instant breakfast!

- Telling ghost stories is always a popular activity at slumber parties. Turn down the lights and give the storytellers flashlights to shine on their faces as they tell tales.

PRIZES AND FAVORS

- Give the guests Magic Eight Balls (available at toy stores) so they can tell their fortunes all night.

- Offer everyone personalized toothbrushes or pillowcases.

- Send the kids home with boxes of cereal from variety packs, or goody bags filled with cassette singles of popular songs and bubblegum.

TROUBLE-SHOOTING TIPS

- If you rent a scary movie, consider whether the kids will be too scared to sleep.

- Discourage the kids from playing traditional slumber party pranks (such as toilet-papering yards).

BICYCLE RALLY

Combining fun with adventure makes for a great party outing. This bicycle trip has lots of surprises to keep the riders moving along, while providing good exercise.

For Ages: 10–12

Optional Ages: 6–9

Preparation: Make sure the guests have bicycles that are in good working order and that they wear helmets. Scout and map out a safe route for a group of bicycling kids.

WHAT TO DO

Once you choose the route for the party, travel it once on your own bike and make notes about the length of the course, turns, landmarks, and other points of interest along the way. Look for places to securely hang paper plates.

On the day of the party, write up some directions on each paper plate that will help the cyclists find their way to the end of the course. For example, on one paper plate you might instruct the riders to turn at a fork in the road—if they miss the turn, they'll end up going out of their way (hang plates that say, "Oops, go back," in case this happens). You can make the clues simple or complex, depending on how long you want the bike rally to last. Then mount the plates (using a staple gun, tacks, or tape) to the landmarks you've chosen, having them all point to a fun destination, such as a restaurant or picnic area. Always make sure the plates are at eye level so the kids won't miss them, and be sure that the plates won't be defacing property.

For added fun, write up some riddles or trivia questions on each paper plate for the kids to solve and answer. Tell them to secretly write their answers on paper—but be sure they understand that they can confer with other cyclists on the course directions. Gather the "bikers" together and tell them the rules of the bike rally. Then watch them go! If their destination is a picnic area, plan for another adult to welcome them with a picnic lunch you've packed ahead of time. Or, enjoy lunch at a restaurant.

For Added Fun:
- Paper plates
- Felt-tip pens
- Paper and a pencil or pen for each rider
- A staple gun, tacks, or heavy tape

CREATIVE OPTIONS

- Instead of using paper plates to mark the route, give each cyclist a map of the course. Make it more challenging to follow by omitting street names and using directions such as "Turn left at first chance." Mark the map with landmarks so they won't get lost.

- If it's not possible to have the cyclists end up at a restaurant, take them on a circuitous route that leads them right back to your home. While they're biking, arrange for another adult to set up the party room with "Welcome Home" balloons, a fun meal, and plenty of cold drinks.

PRIZES AND FAVORS

- Give the guests small, personalized bicycle license plates with their first names on them (available at bike shops or toy stores).

- Give them all T-shirts to wear on the rally, with the inscription: "I Survived the Bike Party!"

TROUBLE-SHOOTING TIPS

- Check the kids' bikes to make sure they're in good working order before the trip. (Bring along a patch kit and tire pump, in case there's trouble.)

- Find some adult volunteers to help keep everyone on track and safe. For a longer distance, follow along in a car or other vehicle to rescue any bikers who get a flat.

- Be sure to go over the rules of the road before the trip begins. Bike safety is very important, even on secluded roads.

PAJAMA BREAKFAST

Wake up—it's time to party! This surprise pajama breakfast is a hoot—for the hosts, the guests, and anyone else who's lucky enough to share in the fun.

For Ages: 10–12

Optional Ages: 6–9

Preparation: Make reservations at a restaurant that specializes in breakfast food, and tell them about your party plans (make sure they don't have a "No-Pajamas" dress code!). Let the parents know about the surprise, but don't tell the guests.

WHAT TO DO

After you've warned the restaurant staff of your plans, call the guests' parents and explain the details of the event. Tell them not to inform the kids of the plan, but to make sure they wear decent pajamas the night before.

Early on the morning of the party (six or seven a.m.), awaken the guest of honor, hop in the car, and collect the party guests, one by one. At each house, have the guest of honor go up to the door to alert the parent that it's time for the party, then awaken the sleeping guest. Make sure the guests wear only their pajamas, robes, and slippers or tennis shoes and socks (no changing clothes unless they're absolutely *not* decent).

As the party crowd gets larger, let them all awaken and greet the other snoozing guests.

Once you have everyone, head for the next surprise—breakfast at a restaurant! The event is silly and only slightly embarrassing, and it's lots of fun for the guests to enter the restaurant in their pajamas. Let the guests order whatever they want, enjoy the scene they're making, and return home to begin the rest of their day.

CREATIVE OPTIONS

- If you'd prefer not to go out in public, you can kidnap the "sleeping beauties" for a breakfast buffet at your home.

- Coordinate with the other parents to hold a "progressive" breakfast party. After gathering all of the guests, drive the route again, this time stopping at each home for a part of the breakfast meal—go to one house for juice; one for fruit; one for cereal; one for

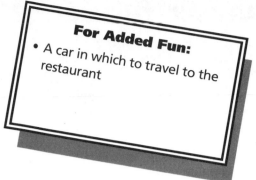

For Added Fun:
• A car in which to travel to the restaurant

pancakes, eggs, and bacon; and one for cake or dessert. Then drop off the satisfied guests at their own homes again.

• Host an overnight party and wake the kids early for the surprise pajama breakfast.

PRIZES AND FAVORS

• Give the pajama-wearing gang some hair accessories to manage their "morning hair."

• Give everyone inexpensive slippers, fun toothbrushes, and bubblegum-flavored toothpaste.

• Hand out mini boxes of cereal from variety packs.

TROUBLE-SHOOTING TIPS

• Be sure the guests are wearing pajamas, a robe, and slippers so they won't be too embarrassed—restaurants require footwear of some kind, so slippers or tennis shoes are a must.

• Be sure to prepare the restaurant staff for your visit, to avoid any problems. Ask if they have a banquet room available to ensure privacy and to keep the noise level down.

• Tell the guest of honor to wake the guests gently, allowing them to brush their teeth and hair—you don't want any crabby, messy guests!

DAY AT THE BEACH

Any ocean, lake, river, or pool will make a perfect setting for a beach party. Just gather the kids, add water and sunshine, and serve up a great time!

For Ages: 10–12

Optional Ages: 6–9

Preparation: Find an ocean, lake, river, or pool for the party. Recruit some adults or older teen volunteers to act as lifeguards.

WHAT TO DO

Plan the beach party during a sunny season (but have an alternative plan, in case Mother Nature is having a bad day). Specify on the invitations that the guests bring their bathing suits and towels to the party. Then hop in the car and head to the beach.

When you arrive, organize some group beach games such as volleyball, Frisbee, and jai alai (for jai alai, rinse and clean bleach bottles thoroughly and cut them into scoops, leaving the handles intact—have the kids stand in a circle and toss a small ball to one another using the scoops to catch and throw). When the kids are ready to get wet, break for a swim or a squirt gun fight.

While the kids are swimming, get the hibachi going and cook hot dogs, burgers, or s'mores.

When everyone runs out of energy, hold a sand-sculpting competition. Divide the kids into teams and have them make super sand castles and sculptures—they can use the jai alai scoops as tools. Spend about two hours in the sun; then shake off the sand, collect the gear, and wave good-bye to the beach.

CREATIVE OPTIONS

- Instead of having organized games, just provide the guests with rafts or other flotation devices and let them ride the waves and soak up the sun.

- If the weather turns bad, have a beach party anyway—even at home! Ask the guests to wear their bathing suits, and spend the day watching a beach movie, eating party food, and listening or dancing to music.

For Added Fun:
- A Frisbee
- A volleyball and net
- Beach balls
- 1 large, empty bleach bottle per guest
- Squirt guns
- Small balls for everyone
- A hibachi or grill, with plenty of food to cook

- Invite the guests to the party by sending inexpensive sunglasses or beach balls with the party information attached. Or send the guests postcards featuring the ocean; tuck them into envelopes with the party details, add a little sand, and mail.

PRIZES AND FAVORS

- Send the kids home with beach toys—jai alai scoops, squirt guns, or Frisbees.

- Give everyone a pair of sunglasses and some sunscreen.

- Offer beach towels or T-shirt cover-ups.

- Give everyone a beach ball to use during the event or to take home.

TROUBLE-SHOOTING TIPS

- Make sure the kids wear shoes to the beach, in case the sand is hot or there is broken glass or litter around.

- Provide sunscreen for all of the guests and encourage them to apply it frequently.

- Adult supervision is vital for all swimming activities. If you have a large group, make sure you have more than one lifeguard.

FABULOUS FORTUNE-TELLER

There's something fabulous and fascinating about fortune-tellers (even if they can't predict so much as the weather!). You can "predict" a fun event when you invite a fortune-teller to your party.

For Ages: 10–12

Optional Ages: 6–9

Preparation: Find a professional fortune-teller by looking in the Yellow Pages under "Entertainers." For a less-expensive alternative, arrange for a friend or family member to do the job (clothing and make-up are available at costume shops).

WHAT TO DO

You can find a fortune-teller through a special company or agency, or you can hire one that works independently. Interview several by phone ahead of time to determine which performance or act is right for your party and guests. Some fortune-tellers tell fortunes with crystal balls or cards, some read palms, and some even read tea leaves! Prepare some fun predictions on paper for the guests ahead of time, such as who the guests will marry (name some teenage heartthrobs), where they'll live (a shack or a mansion), what careers they'll have (grave digger or movie star), what kind of car they'll drive (an old school bus or a limousine), and other fun fortunes.

For extra fun, work with the fortune-teller to set up some predictions that actually come true during the party—thanks to some sneaky planning ahead of time. You might predict that a guest's mother will call at a certain time (and she does!—with an arrangement beforehand), that a certain song will come on the radio at a certain time (tape record a station ahead of time and play it during the party), and that someone at the party will spill or drop something (it's bound to happen!).

CREATIVE OPTIONS

- Create some fun horoscopes to give to the guests to read aloud (find out their birth-dates before the party), and let them play with a Ouija board.

- Make the atmosphere of the party mysterious—place dry ice around the "crystal ball," lay out some tarot cards, and hang

For Added Fun:
- Paper and a pencil or pen
- A cassette player
- Blank cassette tapes for pre-recording songs

astrological charts on the wall; then play spooky music, dim the lights, and light some candles.

- Serve fortune cookies to the guests. You can fill them with fun fortunes that you create yourself. Just type up some witty or silly predictions, cut them into small strips, pull out the original fortunes with tweezers, and insert your own (personalize them as much as possible).

PRIZES AND FAVORS

- Give the guests their own Magic Eight Balls, an astrology chart, a book of horoscopes, or other fortune-telling items.

- Send the kids home with their fortune cookies and fortunes.

- Take Polaroid snapshots of the guests with the fortune-teller to give away.

TROUBLE-SHOOTING TIP

- When choosing a fortune-teller, make sure you choose one who will be compatible with the fun spirit of a kids' party. Explain that the fortunes can't be too serious or scary in any way—especially if the medium is doing a tarot card reading.

BAKE ME A CAKE

A decorated cake is a special part of every party, and it's extra special if the kids can do the decorating themselves. Here's a party that really takes the cake!

For Ages: 10–12

Optional Ages: 6–9

Preparation: Contact a bakery to find a cake-decorating expert. For a less-expensive alternative, make arrangements with a friend or family member who is an expert in the decorating craft.

WHAT TO DO

When looking for a cake decorator, try to find one who is accustomed to teaching and working with kids. Request that the cake decorator bring samples of his or her work, and be sure you know ahead of time what type of decorating materials you'll need on hand (the decorator might provide supplies, too). Specify on the invitations that the kids wear clothes that can get a little messy or that they bring smocks or old shirts.

Depending on the decorator you hire, he or she might bring a cake that all of the kids can work on, and show them how to make frosted flowers, leaves, and other fun decorations. If you wish, you can also prepare cupcakes or a couple of large sheet cakes (cut into squares) for the kids to decorate—freeze the cakes ahead of time to make it easier to spread the frosting. Tint the cake frosting a variety of colors, using food coloring, and set out the decorating items on a table for easy access. Take pictures of the frosted cakes before the kids gobble them up!

CREATIVE OPTIONS

- If you decide to use sheet cake squares, let the kids decorate the squares individually; then put them back together to form one large "patchwork" cake.

- For simpler cake decorating, buy an easy-to-operate decorating kit from a grocery store. Then just twist on a decorating tip and squeeze out the pre-made frosting.

- Invite the guests by hand-delivering a large cookie with the party details written in

For Added Fun:
- Cakes or cupcakes to decorate
- Cake-decorating tubes, papers, and accessories
- Ready-made frosting or frosting ingredients
- Food coloring
- A variety of cake decorations
- A camera or videocamera to take pictures

frosting. Or send them a "recipe for party fun" with the party details written like a recipe card.

PRIZES AND FAVORS

- Send the guests home with any extra cakes or cupcakes.

- Give everyone a box of cake mix, a tube of frosting with a decorator tip attached, and some sugar decorations.

- Give each child an apron and chef's hat to take home (available at department stores).

TROUBLE-SHOOTING TIPS

- Be sure the kids wash their hands before handling the food.

- Tell the kids to wear old clothes to the party, if you're worried about chocolate or other food stains.

- Remind the kids to be courteous when waiting their turn to decorate.

DANCING WITH A DJ

Kids love to dance, so why not host a dancing party complete with a disc jockey playing popular tunes? Have your guest of honor help choose the type of music, then clear the dance floor and let the kids dance all night.

For Ages: 10–12

Optional Ages: 6–9

Preparation: Find a professional disc jockey by looking in the Yellow Pages under "Disc Jockeys." For a less-expensive alternative, arrange for a family member or teen to do the job. The guests can bring their own musical selections, too.

WHAT TO DO

When hiring a disc jockey, shop around, because fees vary. You can have the disc jockey bring music or you can provide your own. Hire a disc jockey who is accustomed to working with kids and who can help "break the ice" at the beginning of the party.

Ask the guests to wear their dancing clothes—they can go fancy or trendy, as long as they can move around in what they're wearing! Then decorate the party room with posters of rock groups and singers, hang a strobe light or Christmas lights for atmosphere (dim the overhead lights), and, for extra fun, rent a bubble machine. Once the stage is set, let the kids dance to their hearts' content.

For added fun, have a lip-sync contest before the dancing begins (have the kids volunteer

for this). Just play a popular song and let the kids show off their "musical skill" for a few minutes. This will help everyone get in the mood for dancing and fun.

CREATIVE OPTIONS

- Hold a dance contest with you or the disc jockey as the judge.

- Find a volunteer (a friend, family member, or neighborhood teen) to teach the kids some fun new or old dances.

- Videotape the kids dancing, then play the tape later for fun. Pretend you're taping a televised dance show (such as "American Bandstand") and "interview" the kids about the music, their favorite singers, and their special requests.

- Take Polaroid snapshots of the kids dancing to hand out as favors later.

For Added Fun:
- A big room with a floor fit for dancing
- Posters of rock groups or singers
- A strobe light or Christmas lights
- *Optional:* a bubble machine

- Provide party food and drinks while the disc jockey takes a break.

PRIZES AND FAVORS

- Give everyone a cassette single of a popular song.

- Send dance contest winners home with a rock group poster, record, or CD.

- Give everyone inexpensive items with a musical theme—key chains shaped like musical notes, buttons featuring singers, or pins shaped like guitars.

TROUBLE-SHOOTING TIPS

- Move furniture and breakables out of the way to prevent any accidents.

- Make sure the disc jockey's sound system is compatible with the amount of space you have in the party room.

- Don't force the guests to pair off into couples at mixer parties—depending on the age and maturity level of the group, they might be shy about boy/girl dancing.

- Have the disc jockey play slow songs regularly, so the kids don't get too worn out.

Order Form

Qty.	Title	Author	Order No.	Unit Cost	Total
	Bad Case of the Giggles	Lansky, B.	2411	$15.00	
	Best Baby Name Book	Lansky, B.	1029	$5.00	
	Best Baby Shower Book	Cooke, C.	1239	$7.00	
	Best Party Book	Warner, P.	6089	$8.00	
	Best Wedding Shower Book	Cooke, C.	6059	$7.00	
	Dads Say the Dumbest Things!	Lansky/Jones	4220	$6.00	
	Free Stuff for Kids	Free Stuff Editors	2190	$5.00	
	Familiarity Breeds Children	Lansky, B.	4015	$7.00	
	Grandma Knows Best	McBride, M.	4009	$6.00	
	If We'd Wanted Quiet/Poems for Parents	Lansky, B.	3505	$12.00	
	Kids' Holiday Fun	Warner, P.	6000	$12.00	
	Kids' Party Games and Activities	Warner, P.	6095	$12.00	
	Kids Pick the Funniest Poems	Lansky, B.	2410	$15.00	
	Moms Say the Funniest Things!	Lansky, B.	4280	$6.00	
	Mother Murphy's Law	Lansky, B.	1149	$5.00	
				Subtotal	
			Shipping and Handling (see below)		
			MN residents add 6.5% sales tax		
				Total	

YES! Please send me the books indicated above. Add $2.00 shipping and handling for the first book and 50¢ for each additional book. Add $2.50 to total for books shipped to Canada. Overseas postage will be billed. Allow up to four weeks for delivery. Send check or money order payable to Meadowbrook Press. No cash or COD's, please. Prices subject to change without notice. **Quantity discounts available upon request.**

Send book(s) to:

Name _____ Address _____

City _____ State _____ Zip _____

Telephone (_____)_____ P.O. number (if necessary) _____

Payment via:

❏ Check or money order payable to Meadowbrook Press (No cash or COD's, please)

Amount enclosed $ _____

❏ Visa (for orders over $10.00 only)   ❏ MasterCard (for orders over $10.00 only)

Account # _____ Signature _____ Exp. Date _____

A *FREE* Meadowbrook Press catalog is available upon request.

You can also phone us for orders of $10.00 or more at **1-800-338-2232.**

Mail to:

Meadowbrook, Inc.
18318 Minnetonka Boulevard, Deephaven, MN 55391

(612) 473-5400   Toll-Free 1-800-338-2232   Fax (612) 475-0736

KIDS' HOLIDAY FUN

Great Family Activities
Every Month of the Year

By Penny Warner
Illustrated by Kathy Rogers

Meadowbrook Press
Distributed by Simon & Schuster
New York

Library of Congress Cataloging-in-Publication Data
Warner, Penny.
    Kids' holiday fun : great family activities every month of the year / Penny Warner ; illustrated by
Kathy Rogers.
                p.   cm.
    Includes index.
    1. Holidays—Juvenile literature.   2. Special days—Juvenile literature.   [1. Holidays.
2. Handicraft.]   I. Rogers, Kathy, ill.   II. Title.
    GT3933.W36   1994
    393.2' 6—dc20   94-28477
                                                                CIP
                                                                AC

ISBN 0-88166-214-3
Simon & Schuster Ordering # 0-671-89981-3

Creative Advisor: Bruce Lansky
Editor: Cathy Broberg
Managing Editor: Dale E. Howard
Production Manager: Amy Unger
Art Director: Erik Broberg
Desktop Publishing Coordinator: Patrick Gross
Illustrator: Kathy Rogers

Published by Meadowbrook Press, 18318 Minnetonka Boulevard, Deephaven, MN 55391.

BOOK TRADE DISTRIBUTION by Simon & Schuster, a division of Simon and Schuster, Inc.,
1230 Avenue of the Americas, New York, NY 10020.

99 98 97 96 95   6 5 4 3 2

Printed in the United States of America.

DEDICATION

To my family, Tom, Matthew, and Rebecca, the ones who
make every day a holiday and every moment a celebration.

ACKNOWLEDGMENTS

I'd like to thank the following kids for sharing the holidays with us: Chad Anderson, Brenton Burpo, Craig Clemetson, Jason Cosetti, Tara Cubel, Jonathan Ellington, Steven Ellington, Brian Hurley, Geoffrey Pike, Brie Saunders, Brooke Saunders, Kelli Saunders, Kristin Saunders, Sean Saunders, Jana Swec, Joseph Swec, Tim Swec, Mia Thiele, Heather Thornton, Holly Valdez, Samuel Valdez, Zachary Valdez, Jennifer Ware, Alexander Warner, Nicholas Warner, and Simonie Webster.

Thanks to my Early Childhood Education and Special Education students at Diablo Valley College, Chabot College, and Ohlone College for sharing their wonderful ideas. Thanks especially to students Marianne Mendonsa, Stacey Norris, James Rudder, and professors Dr. Linda Barde, Deya Brashears, Barbara Burri, Norma Meyerholtz, and Peyton Nattinger.

Thanks to Jonnie Jacobs, Margaret Lucke, Lynn MacDonald, and Sally Richards, my inspirational writing group.

Thanks to Sonja Brown, Laurie Erickson, Ann Fate, Irma Kelley, Deb Sieber, Gail Sorenson, Lisa Steinman, and Beth Thompson for reviewing the manuscript.

And a special thanks to Bruce Lansky and my wonderful editor at Meadowbrook Press, Cathy Broberg.

CONTENTS

INTRODUCTION

The holidays around my house have always been a time for family gatherings, festivities, food, and fun. Anytime we can celebrate a special day, we do—all year-round from New Year's Eve to Christmas Day. Every month offers more opportunities for merriment!

After years of hosting family holiday celebrations and collecting great ideas for things to do, play, eat, and enjoy, I've put together all the best ideas in this easy-to-follow, how-to book called *Kids' Holiday Fun*. Its thirty-four popular holidays feature lots of favorite traditional ideas you may recognize, with many new ideas added for today's new interests. I've provided a wide range of activities that families can do together, or that older kids can do by themselves. The book contains suggestions for decorations, activities, arts & crafts, recipes, and party ideas, along with practical tips, variations, and more—all with an emphasis on fun!

So check the date on your calendar, flip open the book to the appropriate month, and find a special day to celebrate with your family.

Happy Holidays!

Penny Warner

January

NEW YEAR'S EVE & NEW YEAR'S DAY
December 31 & January 1

New Year's Day is one of our oldest holidays, but it hasn't always been celebrated on January 1. In fact, January wasn't even a month until the first century B.C., when Roman Dictator Julius Caesar created a new calendar. Most of the world now uses the Gregorian calendar, a revision of Caesar's calendar that Pope Gregory XIII introduced in 1582.

The New Year prompts people to look back over the year past and forward to what the future may hold. Some people take time to make resolutions to improve their lives. Many others set aside New Year's Eve for parties, celebrating with confetti and noise-makers and singing "Auld Lang Syne" at midnight, when the New Year officially begins. New Year's Day, a national holiday, is a day to watch football games and parades and to gather with family and friends. It is also a holy day for many religions.

Confetti Bags

5, 4, 3, 2, 1. . . Celebrate! Preparing for the big countdown is half the fun of New Year's Eve. And smashing these confetti-filled bags will be a favorite part of the celebration. It's messy, but lots of fun.

Time: 30 minutes

Complexity: Easy

What to Do:

1. Use the markers to draw festive designs on the paper bags.
2. Cut the crepe paper up into tiny pieces to use as the confetti.
3. Put the confetti into the bags.

Materials:
- Markers (all colors)
- Paper bags (lunch-size)
- Crepe paper (all colors)
- Scissors
- String

4. Blow the bags up and tie them shut with the string.
5. Pop the bags when the clock strikes twelve.

Variation: Use balloons instead of bags. Be careful not to inhale when blowing up the balloons, and be sure to pick up all the balloon pieces after the party so toddlers won't swallow them.

Practical Tip: Have a clean-up race after the confetti explosion.

Party Hats

Have a blast creating these wacky party hats! They're a must for New Year's Eve.

Time: 30 minutes

Complexity: Easy

What to Do:

1. Cut the construction paper into 4-inch-wide strips, long enough to wrap around your head with a little extra to overlap.
2. Cut a zigzag design along one side of each strip.
3. Decorate with the glitter, sequins, ribbons, and crayons or markers.

Materials:
- Construction paper
- Scissors
- Glitter, sequins, and ribbons
- Glue
- Crayons or markers
- Tape

4. Measure the strip to fit your head and then tape it together.

Variation: Make a cone-shaped hat or any other shape you want.

Noisemakers

Strike up the band, the New Year is here! These kazoo noisemakers are a great way to celebrate the New Year.

Time: 30 minutes

Complexity: Easy

What to Do:

1. Decorate the toilet-paper tubes with the glitter, sequins, ribbons, and crayons or markers.
2. Cut one saucer-size circle out of the cellophane for each tube.
3. Wrap a cellophane circle over one end of each tube and secure with rubber bands.

Materials:
- Toilet-paper tubes
- Glitter, sequins, and ribbons
- Glue
- Crayons or markers
- Cellophane
- Scissors
- Rubber bands
- Tape

4. Hold the open end of a tube up to your mouth, and then hum or make other noises.

Variation: Make other noisemakers by placing candies, popcorn kernels, or beans in small metal boxes or paper plates folded in half and stapled shut.

Resolution Book

Say good-bye to the past and hello to the future. This activity is a good way for your family to share feelings and find solutions to problems.

Time: 30–60 minutes

Complexity: Easy

What to Do:

1. Using the ruler and pencil, draw vertical lines down a piece of light-colored construction paper, creating a column for each family member.

2. Have the family members write their names on the top of the columns.

3. Discuss resolutions, and then have the family members write their resolutions under their names with pens. The parents' resolutions could parallel the children's.

4. Fill the other pages of the book with drawings or pictures, cut from old magazines or catalogs, that illustrate the resolutions. For example, a picture of a couple waltzing will encourage parents to learn how to dance and a picture of a child playing a piano will stimulate children to practice.

Materials:
- Construction paper (light-colored)
- Ruler
- Pencil
- Pens (all colors)
- Paper punch
- String or notebook binder
- Scissors
- **Optional:** old magazines or catalogs

5. Use the paper punch to punch three holes along the left side of the pages, and then bind the pages together with string or put in a notebook binder.

Variation: Do this activity using a video camera or tape recorder. Just record your family members talking about their resolutions. Pull the tapes out whenever you need a reminder.

Practical Tip: Keep the resolutions simple so there will be little pressure. For example: "Keep room clean" or "Start a new hobby."

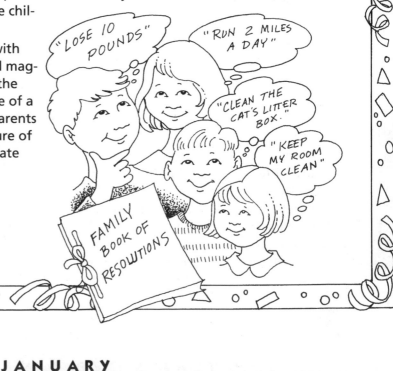

Family Calendar

So many fun things to do, so little time. Fit it all into your busy schedule by making plans now on a family calendar. And then do them!

Time: 1 hour

Complexity: Moderate

What to Do:

1. Select thirteen family photos from the past year, one for each month and one for the cover. Try to choose photos that represent a particular time or season: a snowball fight for December, a day at the beach for July, and a family vacation scene for August. If they don't match a season, just choose your favorites.

2. Glue or tape one photo to the top of each of twelve pieces of tagboard, leaving room to draw in the days of the month below. Glue your cover photo in the middle of the last piece of tagboard and decorate as you wish.

3. Label each month, and then use the ruler and felt-tip pen to draw in a grid for the dates. Fill in the appropriate dates for the upcoming calendar year.

4. Mark special family dates like birthdays, anniversaries, family vacations, and anything else family members want to remember.

5. Punch holes in the top of the tagboard and bind together.

6. Hang the calendar up in a central location for your family to use and enjoy throughout the year.

Materials:
- 13 pieces of tagboard (all colors)
- 13 family photos (one for each month plus one for a cover)
- Glue or tape
- Ruler
- Black felt-tip pen
- Paper punch
- Fastener or binder

Variations: Make personal calendars for each family member.

Make a calendar as a gift for grandparents. (They'll love it!)

Practical Tip: Preserve your keepsake photos by having color reproductions made at a copy store. Then return original photos to your albums and use the copies for your calendar.

BUNCH OF BEVERAGES

This special night calls for extra-special refreshments. Everyone will love toasting in the New Year with these yummy drinks.

Cherry Sparkler

Here's a traditional favorite also known as a "Shirley Temple."

Ingredients:
- 1 32-ounce bottle ginger ale
- 1 6-ounce bottle cherry juice
- 4 maraschino cherries
- **Optional:** ice

Materials:
- Large spoon
- Pitcher
- 4 tall glasses
- Straws

Serves: 4

Time: 5 minutes

Complexity: Easy

What to Do:

1. Pour the ginger ale and cherry juice into the pitcher and stir well.
2. Pour the mixture into four tall glasses.
3. Drop a cherry into each glass.
4. Serve with a straw and ice, if desired.

New Year's Frost

Mmmm! This delicious drink tastes like apple pie à la mode.

Serves: 4–6

Time: 5 minutes

Complexity: Easy

Ingredients:
- 1 16-ounce can applesauce
- 1/4 teaspoon cinnamon
- 1 pint frozen vanilla yogurt
- 1-1/2 cups milk

Materials:
- Blender
- Glasses
- Straws
- Spoons

What to Do:

1. Put half of the ingredients into the blender, cover, and blend until smooth.
2. Pour the blended mixture into glasses, and then blend the second half.
3. Serve in glasses with straws and spoons.

Hot Chocolate Mint

Here's a warm, creamy drink with a hint of mint.

Serves: 4

Time: 5 minutes

Complexity: Easy

Ingredients:
- 4 cups milk
- 8 tablespoons cocoa mix
- 4 drops peppermint flavoring

Materials:
- Spoon
- Saucepan
- Stove
- Mugs

What to Do:
1. Combine the ingredients in the saucepan and warm over low heat, stirring occasionally.
2. Pour into mugs and serve.

Winter Warmer

Brrrr . . . this warm berry drink is sure to warm you up on this frozen and frigid night.

Serves: 6

Time: 10 minutes

Complexity: Easy

Ingredients:
- 1 32-ounce bottle cranberry-juice cocktail
- 1 16-ounce bottle apple juice
- 3 cinnamon sticks

Materials:
- Large spoon
- Saucepan
- Stove
- Mugs

What to Do:
1. Combine the ingredients in the saucepan and warm over low heat, stirring occasionally.
2. Pour into mugs and serve.

Time Capsule

Here's a great way to capture time in a bottle—or rather a box. This activity helps the whole family remember fun times over the last year, and the capsule becomes a cherished collection of childhood treasure in years to come. Make it a yearly tradition.

Time: 30–45 minutes

Complexity: Easy

What to Do:

1. Collect memorabilia from the past year's events such as a vacation, birthday party, moving day, last day of school, Halloween, visit to the hospital, trip to the zoo, and Valentine's Day.

2. Make an inventory list of all the items you want to include in the time capsule for future reference. For example: postcard from June family vacation to Yellowstone, program from Susan's first clarinet recital, balloons from David's fifth birthday party, and so on.

3. Talk about each item and the event it's from before placing it in the box.

4. Store the box in the attic or another safe place. Look through the box at the beginning of the next year before creating a new time capsule.

Materials:
- Memorabilia from the year's events, such as photos, ticket stubs, vacation postcards, programs from plays or school recitals, letters, invitations, party favors, Halloween masks, and so on
- Dress or shoe box
- Paper
- Pen or pencil

Variations: Make a family scrapbook or yearbook out of the year's memorabilia.

Make a collage out of memorabilia to hang up and enjoy.

Practical Tip: Decorate the box with construction paper, markers or crayons, glitter, and so on.

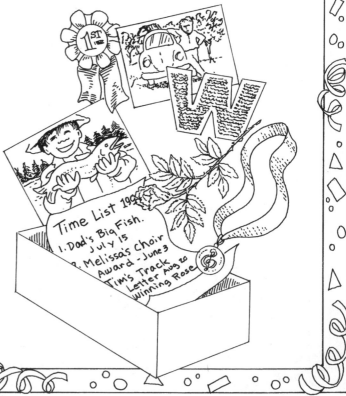

Memory Clock

Tick-tock, tick-tock. Watching the clock on New Year's Eve can make kids restless and wild. Here's a good party activity to settle things down a little. It's also a good way to reminisce about the fading year.

Time: 30 minutes

Complexity: Easy

What to Do:

1. Cover the table with the paper tablecloth or piece of tagboard.

2. Using a dark-colored felt-tip pen, draw a large clock on the tablecloth or tagboard. Fill in the hour markers with both numbers and months. For example, write "1" and "January" at the first spot, "2" and "February" at the second, and so on.

3. Using a felt-tip pen, draw Mickey Mouse–style hands (one short and one long) on the construction paper. Cut the hands out and either glue them onto the clock pointing to the "12" or attach them to the center of the clock with a brass fastener.

4. Outside of the clock face and next to the corresponding month, have the guests take turns writing in memorable events that happened over the year. Include both personal events, such as "Jackie made the soccer team," and news events, such as "Earthquake."

5. Continue taking turns adding memories until the tablecloth is filled with the past.

Materials:
- Table
- Paper tablecloth or large piece of tagboard
- Felt-tip pens (all colors)
- Construction paper
- Scissors
- Glue or brass fastener

Variation: Fill the clock with events your guests are looking forward to in the upcoming year, such as a summer vacation, an upcoming birthday, or the day when the braces will come off.

Practical Tips: Make sure your table is protected if pens are permanent and could soak through.

Use heavy-duty paper so it won't tear.

Save the memory clock to show the next year.

MARTIN LUTHER KING DAY
January 15

Martin Luther King Jr. was born in Atlanta, Georgia, on January 15, 1929. A Baptist minister, he led the American civil rights movement in the late '50s and '60s, believing that equality could be achieved through nonviolent action. His dream of equality and brotherhood became a vision for the nation. King received the Nobel Peace Prize in 1964. On April 4, 1968, he was assassinated in Memphis, Tennessee. His birthday was designated as a national public holiday in 1986.

This is a day to remember a great civil rights leader. It's also a day to recognize the rights and freedom we have in this country and to continue the fight for true equality. On this day many communities hold programs to honor King, and individuals participate in various marches and prayers in an effort to bring King's dream closer to reality.

Singing "We Shall Overcome"

Honor Martin Luther King by learning this song that was a major anthem of the civil rights movement. It's a good way to focus on civil rights and equality

We Shall Overcome

We shall overcome, we shall overcome,
We shall overcome someday.
Oh, deep in my heart, I do believe
We shall overcome someday.

We are not afraid, we are not afraid,
We are not afraid today.
Oh, deep in my heart, I do believe
We shall overcome someday.

We are not alone, . . . (today)

The truth will make us free, . . .

We'll walk hand in hand, . . .

Black and white together, . . . (now)

We shall all be free, . . .

WE SHALL OVERCOME

Musical and Lyrical Adaptation by Zilphia Horton, Frank Hamilton, Guy Carawan and Pete Seeger. Inspired by African American Gospel Singing, members of the Food and Tobacco Workers Union, Charleston, SC, and the southern Civil Rights Movement.

TRO –©– Copyright 1960 (Renewed) 1963 (Renewed) Ludlow Music, Inc., New York, New York

Royalties derived from this composition are being contributed to the We Shall Overcome Fund and The Freedom Movement under the Trusteeship of the writers. Used by Permission.

Flag of Freedom

Flag-tastic! Make a colorful flag to carry in a Martin Luther King Day march or to display year-round. It's easy, and it will remind all who see it what this holiday means.

Time: 30 minutes

Complexity: Easy

What to Do:

1. Using the markers, draw a design on the fabric. Try to reflect the themes of equality and fellowship in the design. For example, draw two members of different races holding hands, a profile of Martin Luther King, or the slogan "We Shall Overcome." (You can make your design as elaborate or as simple as you desire.)
2. Glue the fabric to the wooden dowel or pole. Allow to dry.
3. Hang the flag outside your house or bring it to a parade.

Materials:
- Fabric (muslin works well)
- Wooden dowel or pole
- Markers (all colors)
- Glue

Variation: Make a poster instead of a flag. Hang it up at home or bring it to school to share.

Practical Tip: Read information on Martin Luther King to inspire ideas for the flag.

Portrait Studio

Martin Luther King stressed that all people should be accepted and loved no matter what their differences. This fun activity helps kids understand how unique each one is and yet how much alike we all are.

Time: 45–60 minutes

Complexity: Easy

What to Do:

1. Have one person lie down on a large sheet of paper and have someone else draw the outline of the person. Take turns until all have been outlined.

2. Draw in features, such as clothes, facial features, and hair styles. Have the artists look in the mirror if they forget to add ears, freckles, fingernails, and so on.

3. Cut the portraits out and tape them to the wall, with each one holding the hand of another one.

4. Talk about how all of the portraits are similar and how they are all different.

Materials:
- Sheets of white paper as large as a child's body (available at arts-and-crafts stores and stationers)
- Crayons or felt-tip pens
- Scissors
- Mirror
- Tape

Variations: Have everyone draw in someone else's portrait so they can notice the similarities and differences firsthand.

Draw portraits of famous figures in history or fantasy, such as Martin Luther King, Abe Lincoln, or Superman.

Draw costumes from other countries.

Practical Tip: If you can't find large enough paper, tape together several small sheets.

February

CHINESE NEW YEAR
(Date Varies)

Gung Hei Fat Choy! That means "Good Luck" in Chinese and is the usual Chinese New Year's greeting. The New Year is the biggest celebration for the Chinese—the festivities go on for fifteen days. This lunar holiday begins at sunset on the day of the second new moon following the winter solstice (usually between January 21 and February 20).

As the Chinese New Year approaches, families clean their homes to escape bad luck in the upcoming year. Feasts are held on New Year's Eve, and all stay up late, believing that doing so brings a longer life to parents. People dress in their best clothes and new shoes on New Year's Day and give small gifts to each other. The celebration continues until the first full moon is celebrated with the great Feast of the Lanterns. Carrying homemade lanterns, people fill the streets, joining a great parade led by an enormous dragon, which closes this grand holiday.

Chinese Wand

Bright colors are a favorite part of the Chinese New Year celebration. Join in the festivities by waving these colorful Chinese wands, made out of ribbon or crepe paper, at a Chinese New Year parade or just at home.

Time: 10 minutes

Complexity: Easy

What to Do:

1. Cut a piece of ribbon or crepe paper as long as each person is tall.
2. Securely tape the ribbon to a pencil or chopstick.
3. Wave the wand in the air, making different patterns, shapes, and movements. Write names or make circles, figure eights, and other designs.

Materials:
- Ribbon or crepe paper
- Scissors
- Pencil or chopstick
- Tape

Variation: Have several friends over to make the wands and to develop a group "drill" to perform for family or neighbors.

Practical Tip: Trim the ribbons if their length is troublesome.

Paper Lantern

Red, a lucky color in China, is the predominant color in all New Year's decorations. The Chinese believe that red not only conveys wishes of a great start to the New Year but also brings good will, harmony, and beauty. Trim your party room in red and make these Chinese paper lanterns to hang from the ceiling.

Time: 45 minutes

Complexity: Moderate

What to Do:

1. Fold a piece of red construction paper in half, lengthwise.
2. Use the pencil and ruler to draw lines every 1/2 inch along the folded edge. Cut on these lines from the fold to within 1/2 to 1 inch from the edge of the paper.
3. Open the paper. Curl it into a cylinder with the short ends at the top and the bottom.
4. Glue or staple the edges of the paper lantern together.
5. Draw four rectangles 1-1/4 inches by 3-1/2 inches on the blue construction paper. Cut these out for your candles.
6. Draw and cut out from the construction paper eight large yellow flames and eight small red flames.
7. Glue a yellow flame on both sides of the blue candles; then glue a red flame in the center of each yellow flame.
8. Glue the paper candles to the inside of the lantern.

Materials:
- Construction paper (red, yellow, and blue)
- Pencil
- Ruler
- Scissors
- Glue or stapler

9. Cut a piece of construction paper into a strip about 1 to 2 inches wide by 8 to 10 inches long. Glue or staple the strip to the top of the lantern for a handle.

Variations: Use tissue paper instead of construction paper.

Instead of candles cut out traditional Chinese animal shapes like the rat, ox, or dog.

Practical Tip: For smaller children, pre-cut the paper for easier handling.

Chinese New Year Masks

Put on a happy face, or a sad one, or a scary one—the possibilities are endless with homemade masks. Masks are a playful part of Chinese New Year parades, and making these festive disguises lets you stretch your imagination.

Time: 45–60 minutes

Complexity: Easy—Adult assistance recommended.

What to Do:

1. Prepare the stiff paper plates ahead of time by cutting them into interesting shapes and cutting out eyeholes with the scissors or Exacto knife.

2. Cut the soft paper plates into large shapes; then staple, glue, or tape these pieces to the outside of the foundation (stiff paper plate) to make the mask larger and more interesting.

3. Decorate the masks with the materials listed above to create bright, scary, or crazy faces.

4. Glue or tape pieces of ribbon or yarn (about 6 inches long) to the base and sides of the masks.

5. Staple or glue a wooden dowel, ruler, tongue depressor, or Popsicle stick to the side of each mask.

6. Hold a mask in front of your face and have a parade.

Materials:
- Stiff white paper plates
- Soft white paper plates
- Construction paper (all colors)
- Decorations, such as sequins, glitter, stars, ribbons, stickers, confetti, and puffy paints
- Poster paints, felt-tip pens, or crayons
- Paint brushes
- Stapler, glue, or tape
- Scissors or Exacto knife
- Ribbon or yarn
- Wooden dowels, rulers, tongue depressors, or Popsicle sticks

Variation: Use pieces of cardboard or tagboard instead of paper plates.

Practical Tips: Provide lots of arts-and-crafts materials.

Cut out different shapes from the colored construction paper that the artists can use on their masks.

Chinese New Year Firecrackers

These Chinese New Year Firecrackers don't explode, but they're great for party-room decorations or for just playing with.

Time: 15–30 minutes

Complexity: Easy–Moderate

What to Do:

1. Tie a piece of string around a small gift, such as a Chinese finger trap, a Chinese fan, or some rice-paper candy.

2. Insert the gift into a toilet-paper tube. Be sure the free end of the string is long enough to dangle out from one end of the tube.

3. Cover the tube with red crepe paper, leaving 2 inches extra at each end and still allowing the string to dangle out.

4. Twist the ends of the "firecracker," still leaving the string dangling out.

5. Use the felt-tip pen to write a name on each "firecracker" or hang them up in a party room and let the guests choose one; then have them pull the string to pull out the gift.

Materials:
- String
- Small gifts
- Toilet-paper tubes
- Red crepe paper
- Felt-tip pen

Variations: Put New Year's fortunes inside the firecrackers instead of gifts.

Use cellophane instead of crepe paper for a crackly effect.

Decorate the firecrackers with stickers.

Practical Tip: Make sure all of the gifts are of equal value.

Almond Cookies

A Chinese dessert tradition that kids of all ages like indulging in, these almond cookies will melt in your mouth. They're also perfect for dipping in tea or milk.

Yields: 4 dozen cookies

Time: 30 minutes

Complexity: Challenging—Adult assistance recommended

Ingredients:
- 3-1/2 cups flour
- 2 cups sugar
- 1 teaspoon baking powder
- 2 cups margarine
- 1 egg, beaten
- 2 teaspoons almond extract
- 1 teaspoon vanilla
- 2–3 tablespoons whole blanched almonds

What to Do:

1. Sift the flour, sugar, and baking powder together in the medium bowl.
2. Add the margarine, egg, almond extract, and vanilla.
3. Mix the dough with your hands until smooth and blended.

Materials:
- Medium bowl
- Rolling pin
- Floured board
- 2" round cookie cutter
- Cookie sheet
- Oven, preheated to 375°

4. Roll the dough until it's 1/4-inch thick on the floured board.
5. Cut with the cookie cutter.
6. Place one almond in the center of each cookie.
7. Place the cookies 1-1/2 inches apart on the ungreased cookie sheet.
8. Bake until lightly browned (about 12 minutes).

Practical Tip: Use caution around heat.

Homemade Fortune Cookies

Will the new year bring riches to your family and friends? Only time will tell. In the meantime, write your own predictions to put in these homemade fortune cookies. They're sure to supply smiles.

Serves: 8

Time: 30 minutes

Complexity: Challenging—Adult assistance recommended

Ingredients:
- 1/4 cup cake flour
- 2 tablespoons sugar
- 1 tablespoon cornstarch
- Dash of salt
- 2 tablespoons oil
- 1 egg white
- 1 tablespoon water

What to Do:

1. Write fortunes on the slips of paper. Set aside.
2. In the medium bowl sift together the cake flour, sugar, cornstarch, and salt.
3. Add the oil and egg white, and stir until smooth.
4. Add the water and mix well with an electric mixer or by hand.
5. Make one cookie at a time by pouring 1 tablespoon of the batter on a lightly greased frying pan. Spread to a 3-1/2-inch circle.
6. Cook over low heat until lightly browned (about 4 minutes).

Materials:
- 8-1/4" x 1" slips of paper
- Pen or pencil
- Medium bowl
- Frying pan, lightly greased
- Spatula
- Large spoon
- Pot holder
- Muffin pan
- Stove
- **Optional:** electric mixer

7. Turn with the spatula and cook for 1 more minute.

8. Quickly place the cookie on the pot holder.

9. Put a paper fortune in the center of the cookie and fold the cookie in half.

10. Fold the cookie again over the edge of the bowl to make a crescent shape.

11. Place the cookie in the muffin pan to cool.

VALENTINE'S DAY
February 14

Though it's believed to be the day birds choose their mates, nobody knows for sure how Valentine's Day came into being. Some say it's been celebrated since the Middle Ages, and most agree it's celebrated in honor of St. Valentine, but *which* Valentine? As many as eight St. Valentines have been identified! According to one popular story, a jailed Valentine fell in love with the jailer's daughter and sent her letters signed, "From Your Valentine." Commercial valentines appeared about 1800.

Cards, kisses, and, yes, chocolates are popular gifts to give to your loved ones on this day, but you can express your love in many ways—hugs, kisses, and just sharing your time. Gift or no gift, Valentine's Day is the perfect time to tell your family and friends how much you love them.

Heart Mobile

Hearts galore! Here's the perfect decoration to get everyone in the mood for this loving holiday.

Time: 30–60 minutes

Complexity: Easy–Moderate

What to Do:

1. Cut billions and billions (well, a lot!) of hearts out of the construction paper in all different sizes.
2. Lay out a piece of the ribbon, and glue the paper hearts to both sides of it to make a long valentine mobile.

Materials:
- Construction paper (red, pink, and white)
- Scissors
- Ribbon (red, pink, or white)
- Glue

3. Make as many of these ribbon-heart mobiles as you like, then hang them from the ceiling to create a magical, romantic room of hearts.

Variation: Use fabric scraps instead of construction paper.

Practical Tip: For smaller children, pre-cut the hearts and let them glue them together.

Heart Pin

If you can't afford anything from a jewelry store, here's an inexpensive way for you to make jewelry you'll be proud to give to your valentines.

Time: 60 minutes (plus baking time)

Complexity: Moderate—Adult assistance recommended

Ingredients:
- 4 cups flour
- 1 cup salt
- 1-3/4 cups water
- Red food coloring

What to Do:

1. Make up a batch of baker's clay by combining the flour, salt, and water and kneading it until well mixed.

2. Add a few drops of the red food coloring and mix well.

3. Roll the dough out and cut it into heart shapes, using a cookie cutter or cardboard pattern.

4. Insert a safety pin in the back of each heart and bake 2 to 3 hours (until firm). Allow to cool completely.

Materials:
- Heart-shaped cookie cutter or cardboard pattern
- Oven, preheated to 250°
- Acrylic paint and paint brush or permanent felt-tip pens
- Safety pins
- Varnish (such as Verathane)

5. Use acrylic paint or permanent felt-tip pens to personalize or add designs to the pins.

6. Varnish the pins and allow to dry.

Variations: Instead of coloring the dough with food coloring, just paint the hearts after they're baked.

Use your imagination and make anything you want, such as letters of a loved one's name, a reproduction of a loved one, a special message spelled out, or game pieces for chess or checkers.

Practical Tip: Work the dough on foil so you won't have to transfer it to the cookie sheet. Foil peels off nicely.

Giant Heart Cookie

This family-size cookie will get loved ones' hearts beating faster and show them how much they're loved!

Time: 30–40 minutes (excluding baking time)

Complexity: Moderate—Adult assistance recommended

Ingredients:
• Chocolate-chip cookie dough
• Tube of icing

What to Do:

1. Mix up your favorite chocolate-chip cookie recipe and spread the entire bowl of batter onto a large cookie sheet, forming it into a heart shape.
2. Bake a little longer than usual—about 15 to 20 minutes, until golden brown.
3. Remove from the oven and let cool.
4. Cover the heart-shaped piece of cardboard with tin foil and a paper doily.
5. Carefully transfer the cookie onto the cardboard.
6. Write "I love you" or another special message on the cookie with the icing.

Materials:
• Large cookie sheet
• Oven
• Cardboard shaped like a heart
• Tin foil
• Paper doily

Variation: Use another cookie dough that's firm, such as sugar cookies, gingerbread cookies, or oatmeal-raisin cookies.

Practical Tip: If your cookie heart comes out less than perfect, use a knife to trim and shape the heart while it is still warm. Eat the trimmings!

Chocolate Dipped Goodies

Whoa! Valentine goodies can be expensive. Here's a way for kids to give scrumptious goodies to their valentines without breaking into their piggy banks.

Time: 30–45 minutes

Complexity: Easy—Adult assistance recommended

Ingredients:
- 12-ounce bag of chocolate chips
- 1 tablespoon margarine
- Goodies to dip (cherries, caramels, marshmallows, nuts, dried fruit, raisins, pineapple, Chex cereal, banana chips, strawberries, or peanut butter mixed with coconut and granola)

What to Do:

1. Melt the chocolate chips with a little margarine in a double boiler or microwave, stirring often.

2. Dip your favorite goodies into the melted chocolate.

3. Place the chocolate-covered items on the waxed paper and set in a refrigerator to firm up.

Materials:
- Double boiler or microwave-safe bowl
- Stove or microwave
- Waxed paper

Variation: Use white chocolate or butterscotch chips instead of chocolate chips.

Practical Tip: Work quickly but away from heat, so chocolate doesn't set or burn. Use toothpicks or tongs for dipping the items.

Lovebugs

Real lovebugs are small black flies that live in states near the Gulf of Mexico. These lovebugs are much cuter and easier to love. And kids will love bugging their loved ones with them on Valentine's Day.

Time: 30 minutes

Complexity: Easy

What to Do:

1. Cut two 2-inch hearts and one 1-inch heart out of the felt.

2. Draw a funny face on the smaller heart with the black felt-tip pen.

3. Draw a design on the larger hearts. (These will be the bug's wings.)

4. Glue two short pieces of pipe cleaner to the top of the small heart and twist the ends. (These will be the bug's antennae.)

Materials:
- Felt (red, pink, purple, white, and blue)
- Scissors
- Felt-tip pens (black and other colors)
- Pipe cleaners
- Glue
- Tongue depressors

5. Glue the larger hearts (wings) across from each other on a tongue depressor.

6. Glue the small heart (head) onto the top of the tongue depressor.

Variations: Create other bugs using pompoms, felt, and tongue depressors.

Attach magnet tape to the back of the tongue depressors to create refrigerator magnets.

Practical Tip: Cut the felt into hearts ahead of time for younger kids.

"I Love You" Coupons

Here's a great way to give yourself as Valentine gifts. A coupon book full of proposals and promises, written on heart-shaped pieces of paper, is endearing and lasts a lot longer than a box of candy.

Time: 30–45 minutes

Complexity: Easy

What to Do:

1. Cut 3-by-3-inch hearts out of the construction paper.
2. On the hearts write things to do for loved ones. A parent might include such things as "Good for one batch of favorite cookies," "Good for ten readings of your favorite story," and "Good

Materials:
- Scissors
- Construction paper (all colors)
- Felt-tip pens (all colors)
- Stapler or decorated envelope

for one full lunch box of favorites." A child's coupons might include: "Good for one car-washing," "Good for one week's menu-planning of healthy stuff I'll eat," and "Good for one poem or song written by me just for you."

3. Staple the coupons together into a coupon book or simply put them into a decorated envelope marked "Valentine Coupons."

Practical Tip: When presented with a coupon, perform the requested activity with good humor.

Treasure Hunt

Make your family work for their Valentine gifts—send them on a treasure hunt. They'll feel like secret agents as they decode the clues and discover the hidden treasure.

Time: 30 minutes

Complexity: Easy

What to Do:

1. Use inexpensive valentines or cut hearts out of construction paper.
2. Write instructions on the valentines like those on candy conversation hearts, such as "Be Mine . . . On Time" to get the hunters headed toward the clock,

Materials:
- Kid valentines or construction paper (red, pink, and purple)
- Pen
- Special Valentine gift

where you've hidden the next clue, "I'm True . . . In a Shoe," to get them to look in shoes, or "Hug Me . . . By the Tree," to have them look outside.

3. Hide the gift in the designated spot.

Practical Tip: Write puzzling notes for older family members and draw pictures for younger children who can't read.

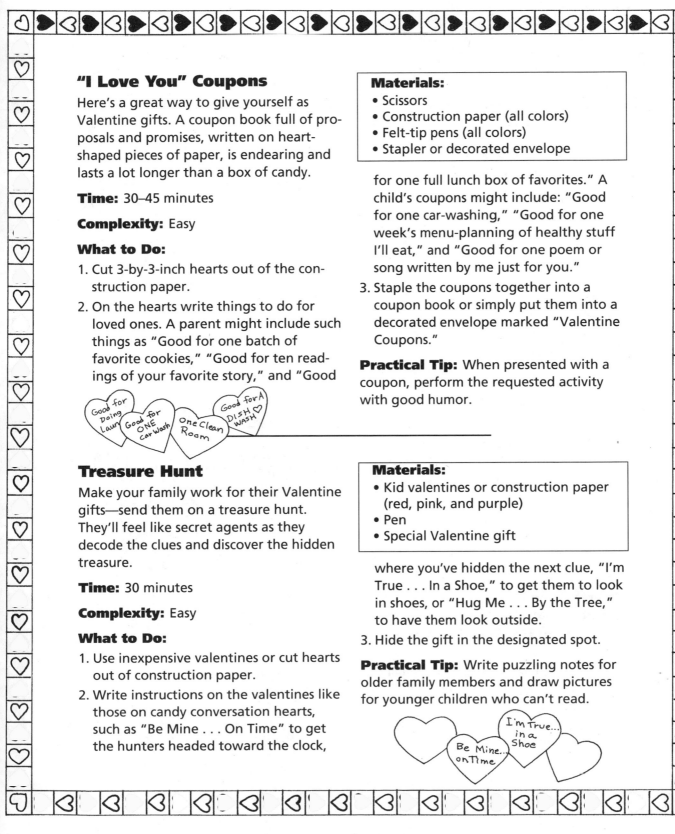

ASSORTMENT OF HEARTS AND CRAFTS

Have a make-your-own valentine marathon session with these fun-to-do arts and crafts. Just pile the materials up and let young artists create their own masterpieces.

Patchwork Heart

What to Do:

1. Cut a large heart out of the fabric.
2. Cut the heart into large pieces.

Materials:
- Fabric
- Scissors
- Glue
- White paper

3. Mix the pieces up.
4. Glue the heart back together on a large sheet of white paper.

Valentine Collage

What to Do:

1. Cut large hearts out of the red construction paper.
2. Glue a variety of the craft items onto the paper hearts.
3. Glue each heart onto a paper doily.

Materials:
- Red construction paper
- Scissors
- Craft items, such as rickrack, sequins, glitter, lace, ribbon, yarn, fabric, stickers, and paper
- Glue
- Paper doilies

Heart Prints

What to Do:

1. Cut a heart shape out of a sponge or potato.
2. Stamp the heart into the ink pad and then onto the white paper.
3. Cut the paper into a Valentine's Day card and write a poem or special message inside.

Materials:
- Sponge or potato
- Pink or red stamp pad
- White paper
- Scissors
- **Optional:** paring knife

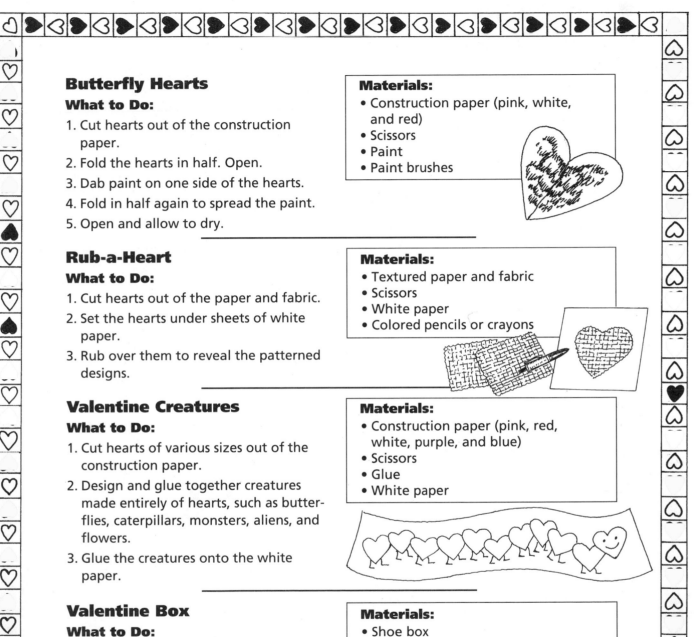

Butterfly Hearts

What to Do:

1. Cut hearts out of the construction paper.
2. Fold the hearts in half. Open.
3. Dab paint on one side of the hearts.
4. Fold in half again to spread the paint.
5. Open and allow to dry.

Materials:
- Construction paper (pink, white, and red)
- Scissors
- Paint
- Paint brushes

Rub-a-Heart

What to Do:

1. Cut hearts out of the paper and fabric.
2. Set the hearts under sheets of white paper.
3. Rub over them to reveal the patterned designs.

Materials:
- Textured paper and fabric
- Scissors
- White paper
- Colored pencils or crayons

Valentine Creatures

What to Do:

1. Cut hearts of various sizes out of the construction paper.
2. Design and glue together creatures made entirely of hearts, such as butterflies, caterpillars, monsters, aliens, and flowers.
3. Glue the creatures onto the white paper.

Materials:
- Construction paper (pink, red, white, purple, and blue)
- Scissors
- Glue
- White paper

Valentine Box

What to Do:

1. Wrap the shoe box with the wrapping paper.
2. Decorate the box with paper hearts, lace, and other items.
3. Cut a slit in the top of the box and use to collect valentines.

Materials:
- Shoe box
- Tape
- Valentine wrapping paper
- Construction paper, lace, and other craft items
- Scissors
- Glue

Puzzle Card

Love can be very puzzling. Here's a Valentine puzzle with a secret message that's easy to put together—kids will love making and solving it.

Time: 30 minutes

Complexity: Easy

What to Do:

1. Cut a large heart out of the white tagboard or construction paper.

2. Cut a heart out of the red tagboard or construction paper about an inch larger than the white one.

3. Glue the white heart onto the center of the red heart.

4. Write a Valentine message on the heart with the white candle or crayon. You won't be able to see what you're writing, so plan ahead carefully.

5. Cut the heart into puzzle pieces and slip them into the envelope with instructions to put the heart together and color over the white paper lightly with a dark crayon or paint to read the surprise message.

6. Deliver the valentine to someone special.

Materials:
- Large sheet of white tagboard or construction paper
- Large sheet of red tagboard or construction paper
- Scissors
- Glue or spray adhesive
- White candle or crayon
- Large envelope

Variation: Use just a red sheet of paper and write the messages with a red crayon or candle.

Practical Tip: Using spray adhesive ensures that the white paper will be completely secured to the red paper. If you use glue or paste, be sure to cover the back of the white heart completely so the pieces will not come off when you cut it up.

Heart Bingo

Here's a game of matching hearts for this heartfelt day. Reward the winner with a jar of heart-shaped candies.

Time: 30–45 minutes

Complexity: Easy

What to Do:

1. To prepare a game board for each player, cut one heart out of each piece of fabric for each board plus one extra set for the caller.

2. Glue the ten different hearts in two rows of five on each board.

3. Place the last ten hearts in a small bowl or box.

4. Give each player a game board.

5. Have someone pull a heart from the bowl or box and show it to the players.

6. Players must look at their cards and point to the hearts on their boards that match the heart that was drawn. Whoever points to the right spot first gets to place the drawn heart over the matching board heart.

7. Continue playing until all of the hearts have been drawn. Whoever collects the most hearts, wins.

Materials:
- 10 fabric scraps
- Tagboard, about 8-1/2" x 11" (one sheet for each player)
- Glue
- Scissors
- Heart-shaped cookie cutter
- Small bowl or box

Variations: If you have enough fabric scraps, cut out different hearts for each player's board. Then when hearts are drawn from the bowl, they will only match one card.

Instead of using fabric, color hearts on the game boards in all different ways and have matching ones to draw from the bowl.

Practical Tip: Make the game boards well in advance of the time you plan to play the game.

PRESIDENTS' DAY
Third Monday in February

Presidents' Day began as a day to honor George Washington and Abraham Lincoln. George Washington (1732–99) became the father of our country by leading the American army in revolution against the British. Sometimes it seemed that only his courage, faith, and strong will kept the ragtag army together. After winning the war, Washington presided over the Constitutional Convention in 1787. He then became our first president. After two terms he retired to his estate, Mt. Vernon, Virginia, where he died on December 14, 1799.

People called Abraham Lincoln (1809–65) "Honest Abe." He once walked through a snowstorm to return change to a customer of his store. He later became a lawyer in Illinois and was respected for his integrity. As our sixteenth president, Lincoln guided our country through its bitter Civil War. He is especially remembered for issuing the Emancipation Proclamation that freed slaves in the rebellious states. His Gettysburg Address clearly and simply stated the major goal of the war—to preserve the union and democratic government "of the people, by the people, for the people."

These two great presidents are still the main focus of this holiday, but it has also become a time to honor all presidents of the United States.

Singing "Yankee Doodle"

"Yankee Doodle Dandy!" This song, written during the American Revolution, was intended to ridicule the soldiers' uniforms. "Macaroni" does not refer to pasta but instead to an overdressed "dandy" (someone who pays a lot of attention to how he dresses). For whatever reason this folk song came into being, it is still fun to sing today. Give it a try!

Yankee Doodle

Yankee Doodle went to town
A-riding on a pony,
Stuck a feather in his cap
And called it macaroni.

Fath'r and I went down to camp
Along with Captain Goodwin.
There we saw the men and boys
As thick as hasty puddin'.

There was Captain Washington
Upon a slapping stallion,
Giving orders to his men;
I guess there were a million.

Refrain:

Yankee Doodle keep it up,
Yankee Doodle dandy.
Mind the music and the step
And with the girls be handy.

Papier Mâché Piggy Bank

Here's a safe place for kids to put their Washington dollars and nickels so they won't disappear so fast. It's a messy but fun project.

Time: 30–45 minutes

Complexity: Moderate—Adult assistance recommended

Materials:
- Balloon
- Tape
- 6 small paper cups
- Scissors
- Liquid starch
- Paint brush
- Tissue paper
- Permanent felt-tip pens
- Sharp knife

What to Do:

1. Blow up a balloon and tape on four small paper cups for the pig's feet and one paper cup for the pig's snout. Cut a paper cup in half and tape the two halves on for the pig's ears.

2. Brush a small amount of liquid starch over part of the balloon and place torn pieces of tissue paper on top of the starch. Continue until the balloon, including the paper cups, is covered with tissue paper. Cover the balloon with a second coat of starch and tissue paper.

3. When dry, stand the pig up, draw on eyes, and deco-rate its face with permanent felt-tip pens.

4. Cut a slot in the top of the pig's back.

Variation: Make a bust of Washington instead of the pig, or use a round hatbox covered with tissue and decorated like a large nickel.

Practical Tips: The more layers of tissue paper you use, the sturdier the bank will be.

Allow to dry thoroughly before adding details.

Edible Log Cabin

Abraham Lincoln was born in a log cabin in Kentucky. This cabin is a little smaller than Lincoln's cabin but tastes a lot better.

Time: 30 minutes

Complexity: Easy

Ingredients:
- Bag of large pretzels
- Peanut butter

What to Do:

1. Empty the small milk carton. (Drink the milk and nibble on the pretzels.)
2. Wash and dry the milk carton.
3. Staple the milk carton shut and spread peanut butter along one of its sides.
4. Stick pretzels along the peanut-butter side to form a wall. Repeat for all four walls and the roof, and you'll soon have a "log" cabin. (You may have to bite off the ends of some pretzels to make them the right size.)

Materials:
- Small (8-ounce) milk carton
- Stapler
- Table knife or spatula

Variations: Use graham crackers instead of the milk carton, and stick the cabin together with peanut butter. Use pretzels as a foundation at the corners.

Stick on sesame seeds instead of pretzels.

Practical Tips: Keep a few pretzels and peanut-butter dip to munch on while you're building your cabin.

Destruct and eat the cabin before it gets too hard.

If I Were President—
Hat and Speech

Roll out the red carpets! This activity offers kids a chance to wear a different hat—that of President of the United States.

Time: 30 minutes

Complexity: Easy

What to Do:

1. First, make a presidential stovepipe hat. Roll a large sheet of construction paper into a cylinder that will fit head securely and tape it closed.

2. Set the cylinder on another sheet of paper and draw an outline of the circle.

3. Draw another circle about 2 inches wider than the first to make a ring that will form the base of the hat.

4. Cut 1/2-inch slits all the way around the bottom and top of the cylinder.

5. Fold the bottom slits outward.

6. Glue the ring on top of the slits to make the base.

7. Cut another circle to fit the top of the cylinder, fold the slits inward, and glue the circle to the slits to close off the top of the hat.

8. Cut a 2-inch band to wrap around the bottom of the cylinder and glue it on.

9. Cut out a 3-inch square, cut the center out of it, and glue it to the front of the hat to form a decorative buckle.

10. Put the stovepipe hat on and make a campaign speech for the presidency.

Materials:
- Construction paper (red, white, and blue)
- Tape
- Scissors
- Pencil
- Glue

Variations: Vote for the best campaign speech and elect a new president.

Put democracy to the test with a mock election. Your family can vote for anything and everything, such as where to go on your next vacation, what to have for Sunday dinner, who has which chores, and so on.

Practical Tips: Make the hat out of stiff paper so it will hold up longer and be easier to work with.

Make hats whatever colors you like—they don't have to be black like the original.

Cherry Cake

The name Washington reminds people of the word "cherries." Legend has it that Washington chopped down a cherry tree and when his father asked him who did it, he replied, "I cannot tell I lie. It was me, Father." Here's a tasty recipe you can whip up for your Presidents' Day celebration.

Time: 45 minutes (including baking time)

Complexity: Easy—Adult assistance recommended

Ingredients:
- Chocolate cake mix
- 1 can cherry pie filling
- Frosting
- Cherries
- Tube of icing

What to Do:

1. Mix up the package of chocolate cake mix and pour into the rectangular pan. Pour the can of cherry pie filling on top and swirl it into the batter with the spoon.

2. Bake cake according to package directions and let cool.

3. Frost cake and top with icing and cherries arranged in the shape of a tree. Your guests will love the surprise filling that keeps the cake moist and flavorful!

Materials:
- 9" x 12" cake pan
- Spoon
- Oven

Variation: Use other cake-top decorations.

Practical Tips: Don't swirl the cherry pie filling too much or you'll lose the pretty design.

Be sure the cake is fully baked by using a toothpick to test. The cake is done if the inserted toothpick comes out clean.

March

ST. PATRICK'S DAY
March 17

It's time to watch out for wee folk—Irish leprechauns, that is! It's also time for "the wearing o' the green" as we honor the patron saint of Ireland, Bishop Patrick, and everything Irish. St. Patrick introduced Christianity into Ireland during the fifth century. According to legend, he used the shamrock, or three-leaf clover, to teach his converts about the Holy Trinity. Legend also tells that St. Patrick performed many miracles, including chasing snakes out of Ireland.

In Ireland they honor St. Patrick with a national holiday and a week of religious festivities. Celebrations in the U.S. include parades and parties with green food and drink. People who are Irish (and most other folk) wear green clothes to get into the holiday spirit. Almost everyone claims to have a little Irish in them on this special day.

Shamrock Shake

This thick, mint-flavored shake is cool and refreshing. It's a St. Patrick's Day tradition worth repeating.

Serves: 1

Time: 5 minutes

Complexity: Easy

Ingredients:
- 2 cups milk
- 1 banana
- 1/2 cup mint ice cream

Materials:
- Blender
- Large glass
- Spoon or straw

What to Do:

1. Put all ingredients into the blender and cover.
2. Blend until smooth and creamy, about 30 to 45 seconds.
3. Pour into the large glass and serve immediately.

Variation: Tint light-colored ice cream or frozen yogurt green. Or substitute pistachio ice cream for mint.

Practical Tip: For a thicker shake, use 1 cup of ice cream and 1 cup of milk.

Magic Green Crystal Garden

Abracadabra! Here's an activity that magicians young and old find amazing. And it's the perfect way to turn your world green on St. Paddy's Day.

Time: 30 minutes (plus hours to grow crystals)

Complexity: Challenging—Adult assistance recommended

What to Do:

1. Dampen the pieces of brick, clay-pot chips, and sponge. Place them in the large glass jar, fishbowl, or terrarium.

2. Pour a few drops of the green food coloring over the broken bricks, clay pieces, and sponge.

3. In the small bowl, combine the ammonia, liquid bluing, and water. Slowly pour over bricks, clay pieces, and sponge.

4. Sprinkle salt over the top of the liquid. The garden will begin to grow in the next few hours, so check back every now and then to see how it's coming along.

5. While you wait, make some leprechauns to hide in the magic garden. Cut pictures of leprechauns out of coloring books or draw your own. Color them, and set them carefully in the garden so they can hide among the strange-looking crystals.

Materials:
- Large glass jar, fishbowl, or terrarium
- Pieces of brick
- Clay-pot chips
- Sponge
- Green food coloring
- Small bowl
- 4 tablespoons ammonia
- 4 tablespoons liquid bluing (available in laundry section of grocery stores)
- 4 tablespoons water
- Salt
- Paper or coloring books with leprechauns
- Crayons

Variation: Use different colors of food coloring.

Warning: Do not sniff the ammonia!

Leprechaun Glasses

Put these glasses on and suddenly the whole world looks green.

Materials:
- Green tagboard
- Scissors
- Green cellophane
- Glue
- Pipe cleaners
- **Optional:** stapler

Time: 20 minutes

Complexity: Easy

What to Do:

1. Cut round or shamrock-shaped frames out of the green tagboard.
2. Cut out the center of the frames for eyeholes.
3. Cut the cellophane into pieces that will cover the eyeholes.
4. Glue the cellophane over the back of the holes.
5. Poke a small hole on each side of the glasses, insert pipe cleaner, and twist to secure. Or staple a pipe cleaner to each side of the glasses.

Variations: Use different colors of cellophane instead of green.

Color clear plastic pie liners with a permanent green felt-tip pen and use instead of the cellophane.

Practical Tip: Decorate the frames with markers or stickers.

SHAMROCK PARTY

Here are some fun ideas for making your St. Patrick's Day party extra special.

Shamrock Cake

- Bake three heart-shaped cakes and join them together at their tips to form a shamrock. Or bake four cakes to make a lucky four-leaf clover.
- Frost with green-tinted icing and top with gold coins or use a decorator tube and create tiny shamrocks all over the cake.

Shamrock Decorations

- Cut out oodles of giant shamrocks from green construction paper.
- Tape the shamrocks to the walls, use them as place mats, or hang little ones from the ceiling.
- Make a shamrock mobile instead of the heart mobile described for Valentine's Day (page 20).

Rainbow Wall

- Cut out rainbow colors from construction paper or use a large sheet of white paper and color a rainbow with felt-tip pens or crayons.
- Tape your creation to the wall to form a giant rainbow wall.

Pot o' Gold

- Set a small table at the end of the rainbow with a large pot full of gold-coin candies or other treats.
- Pick some clovers and sprinkle them onto the tablecloth, with handfuls of gold coins here and there on the table.

Extra Touches

- Play Irish music in the background, something from the Irish Rover Boys or another group.
- Dress up as a leprechaun and have your guests do the same.
- Request that everyone wear as many green articles of clothing as possible. Award a (green) prize to the one who wears the most green.

Materials:
• Tin foil
• Fork
• Oven, preheated to 400°
• Bowls

Stuffed Potatoes

St. Patrick's Day is the perfect time to serve traditional Irish favorites, such as corned beef and cabbage, and lots of potatoes. These potatoes will add a little pizzazz to your St. Patrick's Day dinner.

Time: About 1-1/2 hours

Complexity: Moderate—Adult assistance recommended

Ingredients:
• Potatoes (1 for each person)
• Cheddar, jack, and/or jalapeño cheese
• Bacon bits, ground beef, and/or cubed ham
• Green onions, cooked peas, and/or broccoli florets
• Chili or beef stroganoff
• Salt, pepper, Mexican seasoning, and/or Cajun seasoning

What to Do:

1. Wash and prick the potatoes with the fork, then wrap them in tin foil and pop them into the oven for about an hour (check to see if done by inserting fork).

2. While the potatoes bake, prepare your stuffings. Shred, cut, and cook each ingredient as desired. Put each ingredient in a separate bowl.

3. Serve each guest one potato on a plate or in a bowl, then let them help themselves to their choice of stuffings!

Variations: Use just the potato skins instead of the whole potatoes. Fill with taco stuffings, pizza toppings, or hamburger fixings.

Practical Tip: Offer the potato stuffings "cafeteria" style or put everything on the table and have a "pass-around."

Leprechaun Detector

Worried about sneaky little leprechauns creeping up and surprising you? Afraid they'll steal away all your gold candy? Here's a way to keep the wee folk away!

Time: 20 minutes

Complexity: Easy

What to Do:

1. Buy some little bells at a hobby store or collect several small metal objects, like keys.
2. Tie the objects together with yarn.

Materials:
- Bells or several small objects, like keys
- Yarn
- Tack or ceiling hook

3. Attach the yarn to the ceiling so the door will brush against the objects when it opens. When a leprechaun (or anyone) enters, the objects will rattle and warn you that someone is there.

Variation: Tie the bells around door knobs instead of hanging them from the ceiling.

Practical Tip: Don't let the bells hang down too far or they'll catch in the door as it closes.

Hot Potato

Ouch! This fast-moving game is a great party activity. And you don't really have to use a hot potato, any potato will do—as long as it's not a mashed potato!

Time: 20–30 minutes

Complexity: Easy

What to Do:

1. Have the players stand in a circle about an arm's length from each other.
2. Give the "hot" potato to one player with instructions to toss it to any other player as quickly as possible because it's "hot."
3. Continue playing. Players are out of the game if they drop the potato or hold it more than 3 seconds.

Materials:
- Potato

4. The last player left is the winner.

Variations: Wrap the potato in tin foil so it looks like it just came out of the oven.

Have the players take a step back each time the potato hits the ground.

Have the players try to catch the potato one-handed to make the game more challenging.

Practical Tip: Use a softball or Nerf ball instead of a potato.

FIRST DAY OF SPRING
March 21

Spring has sprung! The first day of spring arrives on the vernal equinox, when the sun, heading north, crosses the plane of the earth's equator. Day and night are approximately equal in length on this day.

Spring officially arrives before the weather actually changes in many areas of the country. March winds can blow your hair, snap your flags, and fly your kites! People welcome spring by preparing their gardens, cleaning their windows, and starting new projects.

Homemade Bubbles

Welcome spring by filling the air with soap bubbles. All you need is a nice day and a few household items to blow these bubbles.

Time: 30 minutes or more

Complexity: Easy—Adult assistance recommended

What to Do:

1. In the small bowl or container mix the water, glycerin, dish detergent, and sugar or Karo syrup (makes the bubbles last longer).

2. Make a blower by one of the following methods: bend a wire into a circle, allowing part of it to be the stem; use a plastic straw or several straws taped together; punch a hole in the bottom of a paper cup and blow into the cup; or save a plastic six-pack holder and staple a dowel or stick to the holder.

Materials:
- Bowl or other small container
- 2 cups warm water
- 6 tablespoons glycerin (available at drugstores)
- 6 tablespoons liquid dish soap
- Dash of sugar or Karo syrup
- Blower (wire; plastic straw and tape; paper cup; plastic six-pack holder, stapler, and dowel or stick)

3. Dip the blower in the bubble liquid and blow, blow, blow!

Variation: Add food coloring to the mixture to make colorful bubbles.

Practical Tip: Blow or move blower slowly to make the best bubbles.

Popcorn Flowers

These fun-to-create popcorn flowers make beautiful spring bouquets! Have a little extra popcorn for your gardeners to munch on after the project is complete.

Time: 30 minutes

Complexity: Easy

What to Do:

1. Pop the popcorn, reserving some to eat after the flowers are completed.
2. Put handfuls of the popcorn in plastic baggies and add powdered tempura paint to each one.
3. Shake well to distribute paint all over the popcorn for a colorful blossom effect.
4. Cut stems and leaves out of the green construction paper and glue them to the tagboard.
5. Glue on the colored popcorn to make spring flowers.

Variations: Instead of coloring the popcorn with tempura paint, buy already colored popcorn, usually available at candy stores, gourmet food stores, and variety stores.

Materials:
- Popcorn
- Popcorn popper
- Plastic baggies
- Powdered tempura paint
- Tagboard, 8-1/2" x 11"
- Green construction paper
- Glue
- Scissors

Use cotton balls instead of popcorn. Color them the same way as described here for the popcorn.

Practical Tips: Be sure not to eat the paint-colored popcorn, even though it is nontoxic and very tempting.

Keep paper towels handy in case the powdered paint comes off on hands.

MAKING KITES

Go, fly a kite! After a long winter it's fun to get outside and run around. Kids can make their own kites out of many different papers and fabrics. Just keep in mind that kites should be strong yet lightweight.

Suggested Kite Coverings: Old sheets, fabric remnants, newspaper, brown package wrap, Christmas paper or gift wrap, plastic garbage bags, "Rip-stop fabric" (available at fabric stores), cellophane, tissue or crepe paper, department store bags, Mylar or other plastic sold by the yard, lining material, or construction paper

Practical Tip: Make sure that you have a large-enough piece before you begin cutting your kite. You can seam pieces together, if necessary.

Materials for Decorating: Felt-tip pens, watercolors, crayons, poster paints, construction paper cut-outs, posters, tie-dyed fabric, glitter, sequins, stickers, or rickrack

Practical Tip: Draw, paint, or glue on decorations, but don't overload it with excess weight or it won't fly well.

What to Draw: Superheroes, geometric designs, flowers, hearts, rainbows, clouds, birds, planes, monsters, dragons, names, messages, people, faces, or animals

Practical Tip: Be sure to make big, bold, bright designs, filling in with lots of color, so you can see the artwork from a distance.

Frame: Kite frames can either be made from wood or plastic. Wooden dowels or bamboo will work, as will plastic rods that may be found at plastics or hardware stores. The dowels should be about 1/4 inch in diameter, and if they are wooden, should be soaked for a few hours to allow for more flexibility. You'll need two dowels, 30-inches and 24-inches long, for the common diamond kite.

Tails: Most kites will spin if they don't have a tail. A tail keeps the kite balanced and upright. It's important to remember that wind resistance is the purpose of the tail, not weight. The friction of the wind blowing over the tail helps keep the kite upright.

Suggestions for Tails: Ribbons, rosettes, paper cups, fabric swatches, tissue paper, paper fans, or construction paper designs

Attach the tails with staples, safety pins, paper clips, tape, or small rings; or sew them on if you like. Make sure the tail is long—at least six times the width of the kite. Most mistakes are made by trying to use tails that are not long enough for the kite. It's better to have one too long than too short.

Diamond Kite

Get ready for kite-flying season. Construct this easy-to-make kite ahead of time so it'll be ready to fly on the first windy spring day.

Time: 1 hour

Complexity: Challenging—Adult assistance recommended

What to Do:

1. Notch the two wooden dowels at each end with the scissors or knife. Or buy pre-notched dowels.

2. Measure down the 30-inch dowel and mark off 8 inches. Measure down the 24-inch dowel and mark off 12 inches.

3. Cross the pieces at right angles to form a "+" shape at the two marks. Tie or tape the dowels together. Add some glue for strength and let it dry completely.

4. Run a string around the outside of the dowels, through their notched ends, to form a frame. Tape around the ends to keep the string secure.

5. Measure and cut the fabric, allowing a seam for folding and gluing, sewing, taping, or stapling.

Materials:
- 1 30-inch wooden dowel
- 1 24-inch wooden dowel
- Scissors or knife
- Ruler or tape measure
- String or yarn
- Tape (masking or duct)
- Glue
- Fabric
- Kite string
- Kite tail

6. Poke two holes in the center of the kite and tie a string loosely through the holes, coming back out the back of the kite.

7. Attach another string to this loop, add the tail, and you're ready to fly.

Variation: Cut all materials in half and make a mini-kite.

Practical Tip: Use lightweight materials for better aerodynamics.

Spring Butterflies

Butterflies are a sure sign of spring. Make these butterflies out of craft materials to keep inside.

Time: 30 minutes

Complexity: Easy–Moderate

What to Do:

1. Color small bowls of water with the food coloring.

2. Using the eye dropper, scatter drops of colored water onto the round coffee filters and watch the colors bleed and blend.

3. While the filters dry, draw eyes and body details on the wooden clothes pins.

4. Gather each coffee filter up in the center and clip with a clothespin.

5. Make antennae for each butterfly by inserting a pipe cleaner into the end of the clothes pin and twisting it secure.

Materials:
- Food coloring
- Small bowls
- Water
- Coffee filters
- Eye dropper
- Wooden clothes pins (the pinching kind with the hinge)
- Pipe cleaners
- Felt-tip pens (all colors)

6. Bend the ends of the pipe cleaner.

Variations: Use tissue paper instead of coffee filters and use several sheets in different colors for a multilayered, translucent effect.

Decorate the butterfly body with sequins, glitter, and other decorations.

Make caterpillars from green pompoms glued to a large real or paper leaf (with a "bite" taken out) for a before-and-after exhibit.

Practical Tip: Be sure the coffee filter is dry before you gather it up or it may tear.

April

APRIL FOOLS' DAY
April 1

April Fools' Day may have originated in festivals celebrating the return of spring, when people feel silly and full of fun. Ancient celebrations seem to have lasted from the vernal equinox (about March 21) until April 1. However the practice of playing pranks on April 1 began, they're a fun way to celebrate the return of spring.

Celebrate April Fools' Day by playing lots of tricks and jokes on friends and family. It's the one day we can make fools of ourselves by becoming tricksters, jokers, and magicians. Just remember, though, that what goes around comes around, so don't do anything mean or hurtful. It's all just for fun!

Pig Snout

Soo-ee, pig, pig, pig! April Fools' Day is the perfect day to act a little "foolish." It's a hoot to wear a fake nose while pretending that nothing's different.

Time: 15 minutes

Complexity: Easy

What to Do:

1. Cut the cardboard egg carton apart into individual egg holders.
2. Use the felt-tip pens to color an egg holder (pig snout) pink or another color or design.
3. Poke or draw two nostril holes in the end of the snout.
4. Staple a rubber band or piece of elastic to the sides of the snout to hold the snout in place around your head.

Materials:
- Cardboard egg carton (with flat bottom)
- Scissors
- Felt-tip pens
- Large rubber band or piece of elastic
- Stapler

Variations: Use dixie cups instead of an egg carton.

Make other animals' noses, such as an elephant's trunk out of a toilet-paper or paper-towel tube.

Practical Tip: Make sure the rubber band or elastic is not too tight.

BACKWARDS PARTY

Everyone feels a little backwards once in a while—some people even put their clothes on backwards from time to time by mistake. April Fools' Day gives people a chance to act backwards and goofy on purpose! Celebrate this day with a "Sdrawkcab Ytrap" (that's "Backwards Party" spelled backwards!).

Invitations

Invite your friends to your Backwards Party by writing the invitations backwards. For example: "Emoc ot ym Sdrawkcab Ytrap!" Or write the information the opposite of what you really mean: "I'm not having a party. You're not invited! It's not at my house. And it's not a Backwards Party!" Tell them to dress backwards or to wear the opposite of what they normally wear.

Decorations

Decorate your party room upside down and backwards. Turn the chairs facing the wrong way or set them upside down. Place the tablecloth wrong side up and the plates, cups, and silverware upside down. Hang streamers from the ceiling and tape the balloons at the bottom of the streamers. Hang posters upside down, welcome guests with "Good-bye" instead of "Hello," and walk backwards when showing your guests to the party room.

Games

Play all your favorite games, but play them backwards or the opposite way. For example, instead of playing "Musical Chairs," play "Quiet Chairs." Tell the players to find a chair when the music begins, not when it stops. Instead of playing "Pin the Tail on the Donkey," play "Pin the Donkey on the Tail." Give the winner a booby prize and the loser the real prize.

Activities

Make T-shirts with puffy paints, backwards, so they can only be read in the mirror. Or write to each other in code with the alphabet letters written backwards as the code.

Food

Serve an upside-down cake. Offer ice-cream cones with the cone on top (served in a bowl). Serve drinks in bowls, cake in cups, and ice cream on plates.

Party Favors

Send the guests home with prizes wrapped inside-out. Make sure there are lots of funny booby prizes, like a bag of dog treats, a giant pair of underwear, a record by an old musical group, or a hideous statue of Elvis.

Goofy Grab Bag

Oooh, what's that? Here's a goofy guessing game to play at your April Fools' party.

Time: 45 minutes

Complexity: Easy–Moderate

What to Do:

1. Place the goofy items in the large paper bag.
2. Have one player reach in and feel an object without looking at it. Blindfold the player, if desired.
3. Have the player describe the object and guess what it is. If right, the player gets to keep the item. If wrong, the player selects another player who must keep the item.
4. Have the next player take a turn. Continue playing until all the players have guessed an item.

Variations: Place different kinds of candy bars in the bag. Have the players reach in, grab a candy, and try to guess what it is.

Materials:
- Large paper bag
- 6 or more small goofy items such as: giant underwear, gummy worm candy, already chewed gum in a pouch, dog biscuit, hair net, toy false teeth, rubber snake, slice of frozen pizza sealed in a bag, diaper, prune, broken toy, Jell-O in a sealed bag, ice cube in a sealed bag, and so on
- **Optional:** blindfold

Play musical grab bag where the bag is passed around a circle until the music stops. Whoever has the bag must reach in, grab something, and identify it without looking at it.

Put in a bunch of items just for one player who "grabs and guesses" until making a mistake. Each player keeps all the stuff correctly named. Reload the bag between players.

Practical Tips: Make sure nothing in the bag is wet or has sharp edges.

Make sure players don't pull items out of the bag accidentally, which ruins the fun.

Silly Simon Says

You don't always have to do what Simon says. Kids of all ages will enjoy this variation of the Simon Says game that gives them a chance to add their own creativity to the fun.

Time: 30 minutes

Complexity: Easy–Moderate

What to Do:

1. Have the players stand in a circle.

2. Choose one player to be "Simon" or "It." Simon is to call out true or false statements and act them out in an attempt to get the other players to copy the actions.

3. Here's how to play: Simon says "Jump like a kangaroo," and since this is true, all players should jump around like a kangaroo, just like Simon does. After a few seconds, Simon might say, "Tweet like a bird," "Slither like a snake," or "Fly like a jet." Simon acts out appropriately as the other players follow. Suddenly Simon says something that doesn't make sense, such as "Fly

Materials:

• Enough space for the players to form a circle

like a rabbit." Simon can either pretend to fly or hop like a rabbit in an effort to get the other players to do the same. Players who do follow Simon are out. Players who don't follow Simon stay in the game.

4. Continue playing until only one player is left. That player is the winner.

Variations: Have cards made up ahead of time so players don't have to think up anything. Simon can simply read a card and do what it says.

Have players take turns being Simon instead of just having one player be Simon. This will add extra chaos to the fun.

Practical Tips: Keep the game moving fast so it stays challenging.

Help the players with ideas if they can't think of any. If the game goes on too long with one player being Simon, have another player be Simon for a while.

PASSOVER
Date Varies

Pesach or Passover begins an eight-day celebration commemorating the delivery of the Jews from slavery in Egypt. It's celebrated on the fourteenth of the lunar month of Nisan (March or April). A central part of the Passover celebration, Seder is the ceremony in which families retell the story of the Exodus from Egypt and explain the symbols of the Passover meal.

To prepare for Passover, people clean their houses, wash dishes, and empty refrigerators of foods, especially leavened (regular) bread. On the first night of Passover, families gather to celebrate with the Seder meal; they eat matzo (unleavened bread), drink wine or grape juice, and eat a sumptuous feast. As part of the ceremony, children ask their elders about the customs of Passover—children are included in all areas of Passover as much as possible, to help pass on the drama of the celebration to the next generation.

Haroseth

Haroseth is a traditional spread made during Passover. The ingredients resemble the mortar used to build the pyramids when the Jews were slaves. Sometimes the mixture can taste bitter depending on the herbs used, but this one is sweet and tasty. It tastes great on matzo.

Time: 20 minutes

Complexity: Easy

Ingredients:
- 1 cup chopped apple
- 1/2 cup chopped walnuts or almonds
- 2 teaspoons cinnamon
- 1 teaspoon honey
- 1 tablespoon grape juice or sweet wine
- Matzo

Materials:
- Spoon
- Serving bowl

What to Do:
1. Mix the apples, nuts, and cinnamon with the honey and juice.
2. Serve on matzo during traditional ceremony.

Practical Tip: Have younger children use a nut chopper to chop up the fruit and nuts.

Matzo

Unleavened bread, like matzo, reminds Jews that their ancestors couldn't wait for dough to rise before they escaped from Egypt—they carried matzo with them while fleeing and ate it flat. This year you can make your own matzo.

Time: 30 minutes

Complexity: Moderate—Adult assistance recommended

Ingredients:
- 3-1/2 cups flour
- 1 cup water

What to Do:

1. Mix and knead the flour and water.
2. Roll out the dough on a floured surface, and then transfer it to the greased cookie sheet.
3. Prick the dough several times with a fork and cut into squares with a knife.
4. Bake for 10 to 15 minutes or until lightly brown.

Materials:
- Rolling pin
- Cookie sheet, greased
- Knife
- Fork
- Oven, preheated to 475°
- Large bowl
- Decorated napkins

5. Serve three on top of each other, covered with a decorated napkin.

Variation: Make place cards for each guest by writing names on the small matzo crackers using a toothpick dipped in food coloring.

Practical Tip: During the meal, kids are encouraged to "steal" parts of the matzo and hide them until the dinner is nearly finished, only to be discovered and the last bits eaten so the meal can formally end.

Paper Flowers

Passover is also a celebration of spring. Make these bright paper flowers to welcome spring and to decorate the Seder table.

Time: 30 minutes

Complexity: Easy

What to Do:

1. Cut ten sheets of your favorite colors of tissue paper into 8-inch or 10-inch squares and lay them on top of each other.

2. Accordion pleat the tissues together and tie them off with the strong string in the center.

3. Wrap one end of the florist's wire around the center, and keep the rest of the wire straight to use for holding the flower.

Materials:
- 10 sheets of tissue paper (all colors)
- Scissors
- Strong string
- Florist's wire

4. Gently pull out the first tissue from the pleat, then the second, and so on until you've finished five on one side. Turn the flower over and repeat. Turn the flower upside down and repeat for both sides, until you have a colorful fluffy flower.

5. Arrange your flowers in a vase and set them on the table.

Variation: Spray the flowers lightly with your favorite perfume.

Practical Tips: Use thin paper—thick paper will not fold or pull apart easily.

When pulling the tissue out, pull gently and slowly to avoid tearing.

Passover Sponge Cake

Enjoy this traditional Jewish dish usually made in a special pan during Passover. It's tasty anytime of the year.

Serves: 10–12

Time: 30 minutes

Complexity: Challenging—Adult assistance recommended

Ingredients:
- 10 eggs
- 1-1/2 cups sugar
- 1 lemon
- 1/2 cup potato starch
- 1/2 cup pancake meal
- Powdered sugar

Materials:
- Large bowl
- Electric mixer
- Large spoon
- Medium bowl
- Grater
- Rubber spatula
- Ungreased 10" tube pan
- Oven, preheated to 350°
- Knife
- Passover plate

What to Do:

1. Separate the egg yolks from the egg whites.
2. Beat the egg whites in the large bowl until frothy.
3. Slowly add 1/2 cup of the sugar and continue beating until the egg whites become stiff and shiny.
4. Add the remaining cup of sugar to the egg *yolk* in a medium bowl and beat with the electric mixer until smooth and creamy.
5. Grate the rind off of the lemon and add to egg-yolk mixture.
6. Squeeze the juice from the lemon and add to egg mixture (watch for seeds).
7. Using the rubber spatula, fold the potato starch and pancake meal into egg whites, gently but thoroughly.
8. Pour into the tube pan and bake for 1 hour.
9. Remove from the oven and invert pan over the counter. It is important to tradition to cool the cake upside down. When cool, loosen the edges with the knife and turn onto the Passover plate.
10. Dust with powdered sugar.

Practical Tip: Traditional Passover food is served in special Passover dishes. Check to see if those you're serving follow this observance.

EASTER
(Date Varies)

Easter falls on the Sunday following the first full moon after the vernal equinox, between March 22 and April 25. The principal Christian festival, Easter celebrates the resurrection of Jesus Christ from the dead.

Easter is a joyous celebration that usually includes church services, family dinners, and Easter egg hunts. Sneaking into houses, hiding Easter eggs and leaving baskets of goodies, the Easter bunny is also a favorite part of this holiday to children.

By the way, eggs—so prominent at Easter time—are a universal symbol of new life. Be sure to hard boil plenty of eggs for your Easter decorations.

Group Egg Decorating

Here's a way to include the whole family in your egg decorating.

Time: 15 minutes

Complexity: Easy

What to Do:

1. Pass out eggs to everyone at the table.

2. Have everyone draw hair on an egg, then pass it to the right. Have the next person add eyebrows.

3. Continue passing the eggs and have each person draw a part of the face—eyes, cheeks, nose, mouth, ears, moles, eyelashes, chin, and freckles. See what your original egg looks like when all the features have been added.

Materials:
- Hard-boiled eggs (one for each person)
- Permanent felt-tip pens or small markers

Variation: Let everyone draw all the features on an egg—with their eyes closed.

Practical Tip: Have sample cartoon eyes, noses, and mouths on display for ideas.

Candle Eggs

These beautiful candle eggs will add the right touch to your Easter dinner table. Just make sure that no one tries to crack them for breakfast!

Time: 1 hour

Complexity: Challenging—Adult assistance recommended

What to Do:

1. Hollow out several eggs by gently poking a small hole in one end of each egg with the sharp pin or turkey skewer. Scramble the egg inside with the skewer, then let the egg drip out into the small bowl. Rinse clean. Set the eggshells in the egg carton.

2. Melt some old candles or paraffin wax and wax coloring in the double boiler over low heat.

3. Place the funnel over the opening of the egg. Carefully pour the wax into the hollow eggshell in the carton.

4. When the eggshell is full, insert the wired wick into the egg, centering it with a piece of tape for support.

5. Allow the wax to cool and harden, then break off the shell and buff the candle with a soft rag.

6. Heat the bottom end of the candle to soften, then press on flat surface to make it stand up. Or use a candle holder.

Materials:
- Several eggs
- Pin or turkey skewer
- Small bowl
- Egg carton
- Old candles or paraffin wax (available in the baking section of grocery store)
- Wax coloring
- Double boiler
- Small funnel
- Wired wicks
- Tape
- Soft rag

7. Light your candle egg and watch it glow.

Variations: Use several different colors of wax. Layer the colors, letting them cool between additions.

Add glitter and metallic confetti to make your egg sparkle.

Color the wax with old color crayons instead of buying wax coloring.

Practical Tip: Be sure egg shell is dry inside before you fill it.

Batik Eggs

Here's a nice change of pace from ordinary purple and pink Easter eggs. Batik is an Indonesian method of hand-printing textiles by brushing wax on the parts not to be dyed. This activity calls for masking tape instead of wax, but the effect is just as interesting.

Time: 30 minutes

Complexity: Easy–Moderate

What to Do:

1. Cut out designs from masking tape.
2. Stick the tape on the eggs and dip the eggs in the dye.

Materials:
- Hard-boiled or hollow eggs
- Masking tape
- Scissors
- Egg dyes
- Cups or bowls

3. Remove the tape when dry.
4. Repeat the sticker process, overlapping some colors before dipping eggs in another color. Work from light to dark colors. Tape over previous color if you wish to retain a particular shade or let them bleed together.

Variation: Instead of tape, use white crayon to resist the dye.

Practical Tip: Use bacon tongs to hold the egg to avoid coloring fingers.

Rainbow Eggs

These colorful eggs will brighten up any Easter basket.

Time: 30 minutes

Complexity: Easy–Moderate

What to Do:

1. Dissolve the egg dye in 2 tablespoons of water in a cup. Add 2 or 3 drops of vinegar.
2. Dampen a piece of cloth with water and wrap it around the egg.
3. Using the eye dropper, drop spots of different colors of dye on the cloth.
4. Twist the cloth tightly around the egg so the colors blend together.

Materials:
- Hard-boiled or hollow eggs
- Egg dyes or food coloring
- Cups of water
- Vinegar
- Eye dropper
- Pieces of cloth

5. Unwrap the egg and let it dry.

Variation: Add glitter to the egg coloring for sparkle.

Practical Tip: Wear rubber gloves to avoid coloring fingers.

Eggshell Mosaic

For once it's okay to smash eggs! But make sure you pick up all the pieces—you'll need them for this activity.

Time: 30 minutes

Complexity: Easy

What to Do:

1. Break the colored eggshells into small pieces.
2. Outline a design on paper or tagboard with the felt-tip pen or marker.
3. Spread glue in one area of the design and fill in with eggshell bits, leaving a slight gap between each piece. Do not cover up your outline. Continue until your design is filled.
4. Allow your mosaic to dry, and then hang it up on a wall.

Materials:
- 6–8 colored eggshells
- 8-1/2" x 11" paper or tagboard
- Felt-tip pen or marker
- Glue
- Varnish

Variation: Decorate Easter eggs as mosaics. Just dye a batch of eggs the traditional way, then remove the shells and glue them onto a blown egg. Cover the eggs with varnish to preserve them.

Practical Tips: Make the eggshell pieces small enough so they're flat but not so small that they become difficult to handle. Spread the pieces onto a plate and press your fingertips in the shells, then transfer to paper.

Use black paper or another dark color for contrast.

Egg Bunny

It's impossible to hatch your hard-boiled Easter eggs into chicks, but you can transform them into darling bunnies. Wanna-be surgeons and designers will love creating these cute critters.

Time: 45 minutes

Complexity: Easy–Moderate

What to Do:

1. Lay a hard-boiled egg on its side and glue on pompoms for feet and a tail. Glue them on slightly under the egg to keep the egg from rolling.
2. Glue on wiggly plastic eyes at the pointy front end.

Materials:
- Hard-boiled eggs
- 5 small pink or white pompoms per egg
- Glue
- 2 wiggly plastic eyes per egg
- Felt-tip markers (red and black)
- Felt (pink and white)
- Scissors

3. Draw on a nose with the red marker and whiskers with the black marker.
4. Cut out ears from the pink felt and small rectangular teeth from the white felt. Then glue the ears on top and the teeth under the nose and whiskers.

Natural Easter Egg Dyes

Do your Easter Eggs look the same year after year? Try some natural dyes for a change. Remember that these colors won't be as bright as the dyes you're used to.

Golden Tan—cook eggs in a small amount of water with brown onion skins.

Pink—soak eggs in a bowl with pickled beets or cranberry juice.

Yellow—dip eggs in a mixture of 1 teaspoon turmeric with 2/3 cup hot water and 1/4 teaspoon vinegar.

Brown—place eggs in 1 tablespoon of instant coffee dissolved in 2/3 cup hot water and 1/2 teaspoon vinegar.

Red—peel off the outside skins of several red onions, put into 2 cups of water, and boil with eggs for 1/2 to 1 hour.

Violet Blue—collect some violet blossoms and set eggs in hot water with the blossoms overnight.

Lavender—add 2 teaspoons of lemon juice to the violet water to get lavender, or soak eggs in grape juice.

Green—add 1/4 teaspoon of baking soda to the violet bowl and the eggs will turn green; or purchase some liquid chlorophyll and soak the shells in that for awhile.

Pink and Blue Pastels—rub cranberries and blueberries over the eggs for a soft, blended coloring.

Panorama Egg

What a view! A fun Easter scene is hidden inside this beautiful panorama egg. It does, however, take time and careful work to create this masterpiece.

Time: 3 hours

Complexity: Challenging—Adult assistance recommended

What to Do:

1. Pour the sugar into the large bowl.

2. In the small bowl, stir together several drops of food coloring and one egg white.

3. Add the colored egg white to the sugar and knead until color is blended thoroughly.

4. Spray the egg mold with vegetable-oil spray, and then press sugar into it. Pack it in tightly and allow to harden for exactly 2 hours.

5. Leaving a shell at least 1/2-inch thick, gently scrape sugar out of the egg mold. Carve out small openings at both ends of the egg so you'll have a peephole when the two halves are put together. Dry overnight.

6. Prepare royal icing by combining 3 egg whites, powdered sugar, and cream of tartar. Beat for 7 minutes. Blend in food coloring.

Materials:
- 4 cups sugar
- Large bowl
- Food coloring
- 4 egg whites
- Small mixing bowl
- 4"– 6" plastic or metal egg mold (available at craft stores)
- Vegetable-oil spray (such as Pam)
- 1/2 pound powdered sugar
- 1/2 teaspoon cream of tartar
- Electric mixer
- Decorator icing tube and tip
- Miniature items (candies, flowers, bunnies, chicks, cut-up Easter card figures)
- Easter grass

7. Squirt a small amount of icing in the center of the shell and add the miniature items.

8. Squirt icing around the edge and seal the two halves together. Let dry. Add icing around the sealed edges and on top with a fancy decorator tip, and top with tiny flowers.

9. Peek inside and see the display of miniature items.

Baker's Clay Easter Basket

A tisket, a tasket, a homemade Easter basket! Here's a fun basket to make and bake for Easter.

Time: 30 minutes (plus baking time)

Complexity: Moderate—Adult assistance recommended

What to Do:

1. Mix up a batch of baker's clay by combining the flour, salt, and water.

2. Roll dough flat, to 3/8 inch, and cut into 1-inch-wide strips.

3. Cover the cookie sheet with tin foil, and then place the small oven-proof bowl upside down on it.

4. Lay three strips of dough across the bottom of the bowl, with 1/2-inch space in between each strip. Lay three more strips on top, at right angles, carefully weaving them in and out of the first three strips. Add more strips, weaving them in along the sides, until the bowl is covered.

5. Roll excess dough into two long snakes and twist them together like a peppermint stick. Place the twisted coil around the bottom of the bowl. Make a handle the same way, and lay it

Materials:
- 4 cups flour
- 1 cup salt
- 1-3/4 cups water
- Rolling pin
- Knife
- Small, oven-proof bowl
- Cookie sheet
- Tin foil
- Oven, preheated to 250°
- Varnish (such as Verathane)
- Acrylic paint
- Pipe cleaner, ribbon, or string

flat on the cookie sheet. The curve of the handle should be the same length as the diameter of the bowl and the two ends should curve up so they can be inserted into the bowl when both have been baked. Poke a hole in each end of the handle and in the top sides of the basket.

6. Bake until firm, 2 to 3 hours. Remove from oven and allow to cool.

7. Remove the dough from the bowl and varnish it for added protection and color.

8. Attach handles with pipe cleaners, ribbons, or string. Use for an Easter basket.

Practical Tip: Include sugarless treats in your Easter basket: furry bunnies, chicks, and ducks; Easter storybooks; seeds to plant in the spring; nuts and trail mix; stickers; plastic eggs filled with party favors; crackers; playdough; or tickets to an Easter movie.

Washcloth Bunny

Making most homemade stuffed animals is hard, but not this adorable little bunny. And it's a great substitute for some of those Easter basket sweets.

Time: 30 minutes

Complexity: Moderate—Adult assistance recommended

What to Do:

1. Place the washcloth flat on the table.

2. Tightly roll one corner to the center of the cloth. Keep the rolled section in place as you turn the cloth around and roll the opposite corner toward the center.

3. Turn over.

4. With the rolled side down, fold the washcloth in half. Then fold back about 2 inches from one end.

5. Place a rubber band around this section to form the bunny's head.

Materials:
- Washcloth (pink, blue, or white)
- Rubber band
- Ribbon
- Wiggly plastic eyes
- Glue
- String
- Yarn
- Cotton ball

6. Tie a ribbon over the rubber band.

7. Glue on wiggly plastic eyes, a yarn nose, and string whiskers to the head.

8. Glue on the cotton ball for a tail.

Variation: Tie-dye the washcloth to make a multicolored bunny. Or use a little creative twisting and tying and see if you can come up with a chick, duck, or kitten.

Practical Tip: Help younger children with the construction of the bunny since it seems to require more than two hands when your hands are small and not as experienced. For safety, draw on eyes with a permanent marker and sew on nose and whiskers if you're going to give the bunny to a baby.

Giant Easter Egg

This giant Easter egg looks like it was laid by a dinosaur! Put it in an Easter basket or hang it up to welcome the Easter Bunny.

Time: 45 minutes

Complexity: Easy—Adult assistance recommended

What to Do:

1. Blow up the balloon and tie a 2-foot piece of thread to the bottom of it.
2. Cover the entire balloon with starch or watered-down glue, using the large paint brush.
3. Wrap the crochet thread around the balloon in one direction, leaving small gaps about 1/2-inch wide so the balloon isn't completely covered. Wrapping doesn't have to be perfect, but it should be somewhat even.

4. Apply another light layer of starch or glue on top of the thread and wrap with another layer of crochet thread in another direction.
5. Repeat one more time until the balloon is covered with crochet thread. (There will be gaps, much like crocheted lace, but the balloon should be fairly well covered with thread.)

Materials:
- Crochet thread (pink, blue, or yellow)
- Balloon
- Starch or white glue
- Large paint brush
- Scissors

6. Hang the balloon from the bottom thread to dry for about 24 hours.
7. When fully dry, pop the balloon and gently pull it out of the thread.
8. Hang the giant egg from the ceiling or place it in a giant Easter basket.

Variations: Use multicolored thread. Although crochet thread works well, you might want to try different yarns and threads for variety.

When the egg is dry, cut a hole in the center and fill it with a stuffed animal or special treat.

You can also flatten the end of the egg by pressing on it gently so it will stand on end.

Practical Tips: Work quickly before the glue or starch dries, or add more when necessary.

Handle the egg with care after it dries as it may cave in if you squish it.

Marshmallow Eggs

Kids of all ages love the ooey, gooey, stuck-to-your-finger mess of marsh-mallows. These marshmallow eggs are sure to be a hit with such a crowd.

Time: 30 minutes (plus time for setting)

Complexity: Easy—Adult assistance recommended

Ingredients:
- Bag of marshmallows
- Margarine or vegetable-oil spray (such as Pam)
- Cornstarch
- 12-ounce bag of chocolate chips
- 1/4 cup margarine
- Decorator frosting tube

What to Do:

1. Grease the plastic egg molds with margarine or vegetable-oil spray, to make removing the marshmallow eggs easier.

2. Melt a bag of marshmallows in the lightly greased, large saucepan over low heat.

3. Pour the melted marshmallows into the plastic egg molds. Allow to set, about 2 hours.

4. When the marshmallow eggs are set, ease them out of the molds and onto the cookie sheet sprinkled with corn-starch. Dust the marshmallows with more cornstarch and let dry, uncovered, for several hours.

Materials:
- Plastic egg molds (available at craft stores)
- Large saucepan, lightly greased
- Stove
- Cookie sheet
- Double boiler or microwave
- Waxed paper

5. Melt the chocolate chips with the 1/4-cup margarine in the double boiler or microwave. Shake excess cornstarch from eggs and set on waxed paper. Spread with chocolate glaze. Chill until firm (about 1 hour). Decorate with frosting tube.

Variations: Color marshmallows with food coloring.

Sprinkle on decorative sprinkles or chocolate for added interest.

Practical Tip: For best results, don't rush the setting and drying times.

EARTH DAY
April 22

America the Beautiful—and let's keep it that way. Earth Day was organized by environmentalists in 1970 and has become more and more popular each year.

Kids have taken action to help the environment in the past few years, forming environmental clubs and organizations.

Earth Day is a day to become more aware of environmental problems. And, it's a day to take action and show you care.

Trash Contest

Take pride in your community! Hold a contest and see who can collect the most trash in half an hour or half a day.

Time: Optional

Complexity: Easy

What to Do:

1. Gather your family and friends together, give everyone a decorated bag in which to collect stuff, set your watches, and take off.

2. Treat the winners (they're all winners) to cookies and milk after the race. Give a special prize to whomever collected the most trash. Stash the trash in a trash can—and don't forget to recycle!

Materials:
- Decorated bags
- Gloves

Practical Tips: Pair younger kids up with older kids or adults.

Be careful picking up broken glass.

Earth's Layers

Anyone who's ever tried to dig a tunnel to China knows that the Earth has many layers. This geological work of art represents the layers of the Earth's formation. It's fun, easy to do, and makes a beautiful gift or decoration.

Time: 45 minutes

Complexity: Easy–Moderate

What to Do:

1. Collect the layering items in the small bags or bowls.

2. Use a folded piece of sturdy paper or large spoon to add a layer to the jar. For example, fill the folded paper with sand and pour it as evenly as possible in the bottom of the jar.

3. Add a second layer of pebbles or whatever you like. It doesn't have to be perfect—the Earth's layers are not perfect. You might have some layers at a slant to make it more realistic.

4. Fill the jar to the top with layers and glue down the lid.

Materials:
- Medium open-mouth jar with lid
- 8–10 items for layering, such as sand, pebbles, shells, seeds, rice, dry beans, popcorn seeds, birdseed, and pasta
- Small bags or bowls
- Sturdy paper or spoon

Variation: Instead of collecting a wide variety of items for the layers, just use white sand or salt and color it with chalk. Pour a small amount of sand or salt on newspaper and gently rub a large piece of colored chalk over it. Set that layer aside and continue the process until the rest of the sand or salt is colored. Layer into the jar. When finished, insert a toothpick into the jar and gently pull it out along the inside of the jar to create an interesting effect. You can also make small birds, trees, and other outlines using this method.

Practical Tip: Don't tilt the jar too far or the layers may mix. Fill it to the very top and seal the lid to prevent it from mixing up if it accidentally tips over.

DESIGNS OF NATURE

The Earth is a work of art in itself. Discover the beauty of the Earth on this special holiday with these designs.

Time: 1 hour or more

Complexity: Easy–Moderate

Tree Rubbings
What to Do:

1. Tape paper to the bark of a tree and gently rub a peeled crayon over it until the bark pattern comes through.
2. Label the rubbing with tree type.
3. Make a variety of tree rubbings and compare the different textures.

Nature Rubbings
What to Do:

1. Collect nature items and place one item under a piece of paper.
2. Rub a peeled crayon over it until the image appears.
3. Overlap different items and use other colors to make unique designs.

Track Casting
What to Do:

1. Find animal tracks at the beach, zoo, barnyard, forest, park, or backyard.
2. Follow directions on Plaster of Paris package and mix with water.
3. Stir in a handful of sand.
4. Pour into the track and let harden (it doesn't take very long).

Materials:
- Lightweight paper
- Tape
- Crayons
- Small nature items, such as leaves, twigs, flowers, bushes, herbs, and even small dead insects
- Plaster of Paris
- Sand
- Water
- Pail with pouring lip
- Paint
- Brush
- Sheets of paper
- Rolling pin

5. Carefully pick up the cast and brush off the dirt.
6. Make a cast of your own hand or footprint too.

Leaf Print
What to Do:

1. Collect a variety of dry leaves.
2. Cover one side of each leaf with paint, then place leaves on a sheet of paper until you have a nice design.
3. Place another sheet of paper on top of the leaves and roll with the rolling pin.
4. Peel up the paper and leaves to see the design.

Practical Tip: Collect and set out all the items you're going to use ahead of time.

May

MAY DAY
May 1

Since ancient times people have celebrated May Day with dances, maypoles, and parades. Romans feasted and worshipped the goddess of flowers, Flora. Swedes held ceremonial battles on horseback between Summer and Winter. The English honored the legendary outlaw Robin Hood.

Many May Day celebrations feature a tall decorated tree called a maypole. In history, bringing the maypole in from the woods was a ritual in itself. People also went into the woods before dawn to pick flowers and branches to decorate the tree with. Children wrapped streamers around the maypole.

In the United States this holiday is primarily for children. They make paper May baskets filled with flowers and candy to hang on their friends' doors. They still dance around maypoles, which are more often basketball poles than trees. However you celebrate May Day, it's the perfect time to get outside and enjoy the weather.

Pine-Cone Bird Treat

By May Day birds have returned to most of North America. Your neighborhood birds will love dining on this tasty peanut-butter-and-seeds treat.

Time: 30 minutes

Complexity: Easy

What to Do:

1. Tie the yarn to the top of the pine cone.
2. Spread peanut butter into the crevices of the pine cone.
3. Roll the pine cone in the birdseed or wheat germ.
4. Tie the yarn to a tree branch and watch birds flock to dinner.

Materials:
- Large pine cone
- Colorful piece of yarn (2–3 feet long)
- Peanut butter
- Birdseed or wheat germ
- Spatula or spoon

Variation: Mix oatmeal and water together to create a paste. Spread it on the pine cone and roll in birdseed.

Ice-Cream Cone May Baskets

It's a May Day tradition to make May baskets and hang them on friends' doors. Here's a quick and easy basket that's also edible!

Time: 20 minutes

Complexity: Easy

What to Do:

1. Fill an ice-cream cone with candies, flowers, or small toys.

2. Cut a large circle out of the plastic wrap or cellophane and lay it over the top of the cone.

3. Cut the ribbon into two 2-foot lengths.

4. Wrap the two ribbons around the rim of the cone and tie at opposite sides.

5. Bring the four ends up and tie together in a bow to form a handle.

6. Repeat steps 1 to 5 for each basket you want to make.

Materials:

- Ice-cream cones, one per basket
- Basket fillings (candies, flowers, or small toys)
- Scissors
- Plastic wrap or cellophane
- Narrow ribbon, 4 feet per cone

Variation: Use a paper cup instead of an ice-cream cone for each basket.

Practical Tip: Handle cones carefully so they won't break. Have extras handy.

Topiary Garden—
Plants in Animal Shapes

Get a little goofy in the garden! It's fun to create and tame these garden pets—you can make a dog, a cat, or even a brontosaurus!

Time: 1 hour

Complexity: Challenging—Adult assistance recommended

What to Do:

1. Bend the hangers and wire into an animal-shaped frame. (Remember, it doesn't have to be perfect!)

2. Soak the sheet moss and sphagnum peat moss in the tub of water until they are good and wet (about 5 minutes).

3. Squeeze out most of the water from the sheet moss and push it into the frame as a lining. This forms the animal's shape.

4. Push the sphagnum moss inside the frame as stuffing. This is the animal's innards.

5. Fill in the outline with pieces of moss and make sure the innards are fully packed.

Materials:
- Wire coat hangers
- Flexible wire for shaping (available at hardware stores)
- Sheet moss
- Sphagnum peat moss
- Tub of water
- Plants that are about 4 inches long (creeping fig, ficus vine, or small leaf, needlepoint, jubilee, glacier, or itsy-bitsy ivy)
- Screwdriver
- Hairpins

6. Wash the soil off the roots of the other plants.

7. With the screwdriver, make holes about an inch apart in the moss. Insert the plants' roots into the holes.

8. Lay the remaining plants along the outside of the frame, pinning them into place with the hairpins. Use many plants if you want it completely covered and you can't wait until it grows in.

9. Water every 2 to 3 days, or when it seems to be drying out.

Practical Tip: Keep your animal in shape by trimming it occasionally and pinning down its new growth. And remember to talk to your new pet often.

Growing Porcupine—Potato Plant Holder

Everyone will love watching this plant take shape. It looks like a porcupine as it grows.

Time: 30 minutes

Complexity: Easy—Adult assistance recommended

What to Do:

1. Cut off the top of the potato.
2. Use the potato peeler or melon baller to hollow out the potato, leaving about a 1/2-inch shell.
3. Put a moist cotton ball inside the potato. Sprinkle some seeds on top of the cotton ball.
4. Glue the buttons on the outside of the potato for eyes, and stick the Popsicle sticks or toothpicks in the bottom of the potato for feet.
5. Set the potato creature near the light and water every day until it grows "prickly" like a porcupine. Then water twice a week as the porcupine takes shape.

Materials:
- Potato
- Knife
- Potato peeler or melon baller
- Cotton ball
- Mustard seed, birdseed, or grass seed
- 2 buttons
- Glue
- 4 Popsicle sticks or toothpicks

Variation: Instead of a porcupine, make a Mr. or Mrs. Potato Head. Use felt-tip pens to draw a face. The seeds grow into hair.

Coloring Flowers

Calling all future scientists! Here's one experiment that's guaranteed to produce colorful results.

Time: 15 minutes

Complexity: Easy—Adult assistance recommended

What to Do:

1. Cut about 2 inches off the bottom of the flower stems.
2. Fill the vase with water.
3. Put several drops of food coloring into the water.
4. Stand the flowers in the water for several hours. Eventually the petals will begin to turn the color of the water in the vase as the flowers "suck up" the colored water through their stems.

Materials:
- Freshly cut inexpensive flowers (carnations, daisies, or daffodils)
- Scissors or knife
- Vase
- Water
- Food coloring

Variation: Try making a flower more than one color by splitting the stem in half and standing each half in a different color of water.

Practical Tip: Add a stalk of celery to see better what is happening.

Sprouting Seeds

Get ready for the gardening season by germinating these seeds indoors. It's a great way to learn about nature and to produce some tasty beans.

Time: 20 minutes

Complexity: Easy

What to Do:

1. Soak the beans in the dish of water overnight.

2. Rinse the beans.

3. Tape the beans to the inside of the sandwich baggy, as shown.

4. Cover the beans with the moist paper towel.

5. Cut a "house" shape out of the green construction paper to fit around the bag and make it look like a "green house."

6. Tape the house to the baggy, and then tape the baggy to a window that receives a lot of light.

Materials:
- 3 beans (pinto beans work well)
- Dish of water
- Sandwich baggy
- Tape
- Moist paper towel
- Green construction paper
- Scissors
- Round orange-juice containers or small pots
- Potting soil

7. In a few days the beans will begin to germinate. When they outgrow the baggy, transplant them to the round orange-juice containers or small pots filled with potting soil.

8. After a few weeks transplant the seeds into the ground, and soon you'll have your own home-grown beans.

Variation: Experiment with a variety of seeds.

Practical Tip: This works best in a sunny, warm window.

Dirt Dessert

This dessert looks like a flowerpot filled with dirt and flowers, but it's really a yummy treat. There are two ways to make Dirt Dessert—the original way or the quick way.

Original Recipe—Pudding and Cookie Pie

Serves: 6–8

Time: 20 minutes

Complexity: Moderate—Adult assistance recommended

Ingredients:
- 1 cup powdered sugar
- 1 8-ounce package cream cheese
- 1/2 cup margarine, softened
- 2 3-1/2-ounce packages instant vanilla pudding
- Milk (for instant pudding)
- 1 12-ounce container Cool Whip
- 1-1/2 packages (20 ounces) Oreo cookies
- Gummy worms

Materials:
- Clean, unused 8" pot (plastic or clay)
- Tin foil
- Plastic flowers
- Blender

What to Do:
1. Combine the powdered sugar, cream cheese, and margarine in the blender.
2. Mix the instant vanilla pudding according to package directions and fold in the Cool Whip. Combine the pudding and cream-cheese mixtures.
3. Line the pot with the tin foil.
4. Crush the Oreo cookies.
5. Put half of the cookie crumbs into the pot. Add the cream mixture and then the other half of the cookie crumbs.
6. Decorate the top of the dessert with plastic flowers and gummy worms. Refrigerate until serving time.

Easy Recipe—Ice Cream and Cookie Pie

Serves: 6–8

Time: 20 minutes

Complexity: Easy

Ingredients:
- Ice cream
- 1 16-ounce box chocolate wafer cookies
- Gummy worms

What to Do:
1. Line the pot with the tin foil.

Materials:
- Clean, unused 8" pot (plastic or clay)
- Tin foil
- Plastic flowers

2. Fill the pot with the ice cream.
3. Crush the cookies.
4. Cover the ice cream with the cookie crumbs.
5. Decorate the top of the dessert with the plastic flowers and gummy worms.
6. Keep in freezer until serving time. Allow to thaw for a few minutes before digging in!

CINCO DE MAYO
May 5

Here's a holiday for everyone who roots for the underdog! Cinco de Mayo is the Mexican national holiday recognizing the anniversary of the Battle of Puebla on May 5, 1862. That day, Mexican troops, outnumbered three to one, pulled together to defeat the French forces of Napoleon.

Mexicans everywhere celebrate this anniversary with parades, dances, and speeches. Children break open piñatas and feast on the treats that pour out. The celebration continues into the night with spectacular food and fireworks. This Mexican holiday is especially popular in the southwestern part of the United States.

Musical Instruments

Everybody loves a Cinco de Mayo parade! Make your parade extra special with homemade musical instruments. Then dress up in bright clothes and hats and make music!

Jingly Bracelet

Sew bells onto elastic, fit the elastic around your hand, and sew to fit. Then slip over your wrist and shake.

Tambourine

Fill tin-foil pie pans with seeds or beans and staple or glue-gun the pans together. Shake. Use heavy-duty paper plates instead of pie pans for a softer sound.

Rhythm Sticks

Tap wooden dowels or hollow bamboo sticks together to make a rhythm sound.

Rhythm Blocks

Staple sandpaper to two small wooden blocks and rub them together to make a swishy sound.

Variation: Offer a concert for your relatives in the backyard during a picnic celebration.

Maracas

Kids love to experiment with many different kinds of musical instruments, especially rhythm instruments. Maracas—often heard in Mexican music—are fun to make and add a happy beat to any music.

Time: 45 minutes

Complexity: Moderate—Adult assistance recommended

What to Do:

1. Combine the flour and water in the large bowl until you get a thick paste.

2. Place a handful of popcorn kernels into the balloon, and then carefully blow it up and tie it.

3. Tape the toilet-paper tube or half a paper-towel tube to the balloon so it forms a handle.

4. Cut the newspaper into 1-inch strips and tear the tissue paper into medium-sized pieces.

5. Dip the strips of newspaper into the flour-and-water paste, and then wrap them around the balloon and tube, being sure to cover them completely several times. Stuff some paper up into the tube before covering it.

6. Cover the balloon and tube with two layers of the torn tissue paper.

Materials:
- 1/4 cup flour
- 2–3 tablespoons water
- Large bowl
- Spoon
- Toilet-paper or paper-towel tube
- Tape
- Balloon
- Popcorn kernels
- Newspaper
- Scissors
- Colorful tissue paper
- Pin
- Felt-tip pens or stickers
- **Optional:** oven, preheated to 450°

7. Let dry for 24 hours or bake in oven for 5 to 10 minutes.

8. When the shell is hard, pop the balloon with a pin inserted directly through the shell.

9. Decorate with the felt-tip pens or stickers. Shake.

Variation: Fill the maracas with different seeds, beans, or sand.

Practical Tip: This can be messy, so cover your work area with newspaper.

Piñata Party

Why not host a Piñata Party on Cinco de Mayo? Decorate the room in bright colors, serve some tasty Mexican treats, and end the fun with this piñata filled with surprises.

Time: 30 minutes

Complexity: Easy

What to Do:

1. Fill the large paper bag with the toys, candies, stickers, or other treats.

2. Gather the bag at the top and tie it closed with the cord or rope.

3. Decorate the bag with the wrapping paper, crepe paper, or paint.

4. Tape the crepe paper streamers to the bottom of the bag so they will hang down.

5. Hang the piñata from the ceiling with the remaining rope or cord.

6. Have the guests gather around the piñata, not too close though.

7. Blindfold one player with instructions to take three swings at the piñata with the broom handle. If it breaks open, the other players grab what falls out.

Materials:
- Large paper bag
- Small toys, candies, stickers, or other treats
- Long cord or rope
- Bright wrapping paper, crepe paper, or paint and paint brushes
- Crepe paper streamers
- Tape
- Blindfold
- Broom handle

8. If the first player doesn't break the bag open, have another player try. Continue until the bag breaks open.

Variations: Use a lightweight box instead of a bag.

Have the guests make individual piñatas.

Practical Tips: Make sure all the guests are well away from the swinging broom handle so nobody gets hurt.

When the bag breaks open, immediately tell the blindfolded player to stop swinging.

Have some extra goodies on hand in case some of the players don't get any from the piñata.

Burrito Buddies

Serve a whole meal in one hand with this burrito. Both kids and adults will enjoy this popular Mexican food.

Serves: 4

Time: 20 minutes

Complexity: Easy—Adult assistance recommended

Ingredients:
- 4 flour tortillas
- 1 9-ounce can refried beans
- 1/2 cup Cheddar and/or Monterey Jack cheese, grated
- Margarine
- 1 cup sour cream
- 2 avocados
- Mild taco sauce

What to Do:
1. Fill the tortillas evenly with refried beans.
2. Spread the grated cheese evenly among the tortillas.
3. Fold the tortillas in half or roll them up.
4. Melt a little margarine in the frying pan on medium-low heat.
5. Place a filled tortilla in the pan, turn the heat up to medium, and cook for 3 to 4 minutes, until the underside of the tortilla begins to turn brown.

Materials:
- Spoon
- Grater
- Frying pan
- Stove
- Spatula
- 4 plates

6. Turn with the spatula and cook for a few more minutes.
7. Serve on plates with sour cream, avocado, and taco sauce.

Variation: Add other Mexican foods to your burrito. Fill with leftover dinner meats, cooked ground beef, other cheeses, onions, chili peppers, or whatever you like. Offer bowls of condiments and let the family choose what they want to add to their basic burrito.

Practical Tips: It's easier to fill the tortilla with beans and cheese before you place it in the pan, but many cooks prefer to set the tortilla in the pan and then fill it.

Be sure to watch the burrito brown—it cooks quickly.

Tortilla Crispies

Replace greasy potato chips with this healthy, Mexican-style treat. Serve them at your Piñata Party.

Serves: 4–6

Time: 20 minutes

Complexity: Easy—Adult assistance recommended

Ingredients:
- 12 6-inch corn tortillas
- Vegetable-oil spray (such as Pam)
- 1/2 teaspoon salt
- **Optional:** salsa

What to Do:

1. Place the tortillas on a cutting board.

2. Spray the tortillas with the vegetable-oil spray until lightly covered.

3. Sprinkle half of the salt over the tortillas. Turn tortillas over and repeat.

4. Place tortillas on top of each other and cut into quarters.

5. Spread the tortilla pieces out on the cookie sheet.

Materials:
- Cutting board
- Knife
- Cookie sheet
- Oven, preheated to 400°

6. Bake for 8 to 10 minutes, until crisp and lightly browned.

7. Allow to cool. Serve with salsa or plain.

Variations: Omit the salt if you prefer.

Sprinkle on Mexican seasoning, seasoned salt, or Parmesan cheese.

Practical Tips: Make sure the chips are cool before eating them.

Let the leftovers cool completely, and then store them in an airtight container.

Cinco de Salsa Dip

Here's a great dip to go with your Tortilla Crispies. It tastes even better when it's made with fresh ingredients.

Serves: 4–6

Time: 20 minutes

Complexity: Easy—Adult assistance recommended

Ingredients:
- Vegetable-oil spray (such as Pam)
- 1 9-ounce can refried beans
- 1/2 cup Cheddar cheese, grated
- 1/2 cup Monterey Jack cheese, grated
- 1/2 cup sour cream
- 1 package taco seasoning mix
- 1 tomato, chopped
- 1 3-ounce can chopped olives

What to Do:

1. Spray the cookie sheet or oven-proof platter with the vegetable-oil spray.

2. Spread the refried beans on the cookie sheet or platter.

3. Sprinkle on both cheeses.

4. Bake for 8 to 10 minutes, until hot and bubbly. Remove from oven.

Materials:
- Cookie sheet or oven-proof platter
- Spoon
- Oven, preheated to 400°
- Small bowl

5. Combine the sour cream and taco mix in the small bowl. Spread over the beans and cheese.

6. Sprinkle on the chopped tomato and chopped olives.

7. Serve with Tortilla Crispies or other chips or vegetables.

Variations: Use canned bean dip instead of refried beans.

Use mozzarella or American cheese instead of Cheddar and Monterey Jack.

Spread guacamole over the sour-cream layer. Add chopped green onions, chopped mild chili peppers, or other Mexican seasonings.

Use a microwave plate and heat in the microwave instead of the oven.

Practical Tip: Allow the bean-and-cheese layer to cool a few minutes before adding the sour cream so it won't melt.

MOTHER'S DAY
Second Sunday in May

Mother's Day was first observed in 1907 at the request of Anna M. Jarvis of Grafton, West Virginia, who asked her church to honor all mothers on the second anniversary of her mother's death. In 1914 Congress passed a resolution establishing a national Mother's Day. It's a day to express publicly our love and respect for mothers.

Some say that a Mother's Day of sorts, called "Mothering Sunday," existed in the Middle Ages. During this time children often left home at a fairly young age to become apprentices. They were allowed to visit their home on one Sunday each year, Mothering Sunday. Bringing small gifts or cakes home for their mothers, they visited and worked around the house for the day.

Today, many children buy carnations or corsages for their mother to wear on this holiday. Many also make mom breakfast in bed, take her out to brunch or dinner, or send her a card to say thanks.

Potpourri Ball

Mmm—something smells good! This potpourri ball adds a pleasant scent to drawers or closets.

Time: 15 minutes

Complexity: Easy

What to Do:

1. Cover the tennis ball with glue and roll it in the potpourri until it's completely covered.

2. Let dry for 1 hour.

Materials:
- Tennis ball
- Glue
- Potpourri (available at craft stores)
- Ribbon

3. Tie the ribbon around the ball.

4. Hang in a closet or place in a drawer.

Variation: Roll the ball in seeds instead of potpourri to make an attractive decoration.

Practical Tip: Put a thick coat of glue on the ball.

PRESERVING FLOWERS

Kids will be proud to present mom with these decorative flowers on Mother's Day.

Dried Flower Bouquet—Hanging Method

Time: 1–2 weeks

Complexity: Easy

What to Do:

1. Tie the flower stems together loosely.
2. Hang the flowers upside down in a dark room or closet, leaving the door open to provide some circulation.
3. Check them in a week or two, when they should be dry.
4. Wrap them in the tissue paper and give to mom.

Materials:
- Fresh flowers
- String
- Tissue paper

Variation: Press the flowers instead of drying them. Then make a collage to hang on the wall.

Practical Tip: Start this *early* since it takes awhile to dry the flowers.

Dried Flower Bouquet—"Buried Alive" Method

Time: 2 weeks

Complexity: Easy

What to Do:

1. Cover the bottom of the box with cornstarch.
2. Arrange the flowers in the box so they are not touching each other.
3. Slowly add more cornstarch until the flowers are completely covered.
4. Uncover the flowers in about two weeks and wrap them in the cellophane.

Materials
- Fresh flowers
- Large box
- Cornstarch
- Cellophane

Variation: Use borax instead of cornstarch.

Practical Tip: Be patient!

Picture Frame

Here's a simple, inexpensive way to frame favorite photos for mom to display.

Time: 15 minutes

Complexity: Easy

What to Do:

1. Cut a triangle in the back of the margarine top, as shown, and fold back to make a stand.

2. Punch a hole in the top of the lid.

3. Glue a circle of felt or a doily on the lid.

4. Glue the photo onto the felt or doily.

5. String the yarn through the hole and hang the frame up, or tie a decorative ribbon through the hole and stand it up.

Materials:
- Plastic top from a margarine container
- Scissors
- Paper punch
- Glue
- Felt or paper doily
- Photo
- Yarn or ribbon

Variation: Attach magnet tape to the back of the frame to make a refrigerator magnet.

Practical Tip: Have an adult help younger kids cut the lid.

Homemade Bubble Bath

Every mom needs to get away from it all every once in a while. Here's a gift to make for Mother's Day that will give mom an opportunity to take some time out for herself.

Time: 15 minutes

Complexity: Easy

What to Do:

1 Place the Epsom salts in the glass jar.

2. In the small bowl combine the glycerin with two drops of the food coloring and a few drops of the perfume.

3. Add the mixture to the Epsom salts and stir thoroughly.

4. Use a piece of paper to make a label for the jar. Write "Mom's Bubbles" or whatever you like on the label, and then tape it to the jar.

5. Tie the ribbon around the jar.

Materials:
- 3 cups Epsom salts (available at drug stores)
- Glass jar with lid
- Small bowl
- Spoon
- 1 tablespoon glycerin
- Food coloring
- Perfume
- Paper
- Felt-tip pens or crayons
- Scissors
- Tape
- Ribbon

Variation: Carve a perfumed soap into a heart shape or the first letter of mom's name. Tie it with a ribbon or a pretty washcloth.

Practical Tip: Give mom a few hours off so she can enjoy her gift.

Gumdrop Corsage

After mom is done wearing this colorful corsage, maybe she'll want to eat it! (But don't let her.)

Time: 30–45 minutes

Complexity: Moderate

What to Do:

1. Out of the posterboard cut a circle the same size as the doily. Glue the doily to the circle.

2. Poke a pipe cleaner into the flat side of each gumdrop to form flower centers on stems.

3. Cut small scalloped circles out of the tissue paper.

4. Push three or four of the tissue circles onto the end of each pipe cleaner. Then push the circles up to the gumdrops to form the petals around the flower centers.

Materials:
- Small sheet of posterboard, 8-1/2" x 11"
- 5" round paper doily
- Scissors
- Glue
- 6–8 green pipe cleaners
- 6–8 gumdrops (all colors)
- Tissue paper (all colors)
- Skewer
- Ribbon, 1-foot long

5. With the skewer, poke holes in the doily-covered posterboard (one hole for each flower).

6. Insert the pipe cleaners into the doily and back out again so the ends of the pipe cleaners are in the front of the doily.

7. Twist the pipe cleaner stems together and tie with the ribbon. Make a bow with the remaining ribbon.

Variation: Make paper flowers out of construction paper and glue them to strips of green construction paper for stems. Write promises to mom on the stems, such as "I will clean my room" or "I will wash the dog." Then do them!

Baked French Toast

Surprise mom on her special day with this easy-to-make breakfast-in-bed presentation.

Serves: 3–6

Time: 45 minutes

Complexity: Easy—Adult assistance recommended

Ingredients:
- 1/4 cup margarine
- 1/2 cup brown sugar, firmly packed
- 1/2 teaspoon cinnamon
- 2 eggs
- 1/4 cup milk
- 6 slices French bread
- 1–2 tablespoons powdered sugar
- 12 ripe strawberries, sliced
- **Optional:** syrup

What to Do:

1. Melt the margarine in the small saucepan on the stove. Or melt it in the microwave-safe bowl in the microwave. Pour into the oven-proof pan.

2. In one small bowl, combine the brown sugar and cinnamon. Sprinkle over the melted margarine.

3. In the other small bowl, combine the eggs and milk. Stir until well blended.

4. Dip a slice of the bread in the egg-and-milk mixture, coating both sides. Place in the oven-proof pan. Repeat for the other slices of bread.

Materials:
- Small saucepan or microwave-safe bowl
- Stove or microwave
- Oven-proof pan
- 2 small bowls
- Spoon
- Tin foil
- Oven, preheated to 375°

5. Pour the remaining egg-and-milk mixture over the bread, cover with tin foil, and bake for 25 minutes. Take the foil off and bake for 10 more minutes.

6. Sprinkle the powdered sugar on top of the French toast and top with the sliced strawberries. Serve with syrup, if desired.

Variations: Use regular bread instead of French bread.

Substitute other fruit for the strawberries.

Practical Tips: Present the Mother's Day breakfast to mom in bed on a tray covered with a fancy napkin. Add the newspaper, a card, a flower, and juice or coffee.

Make sure an adult can help out with the cooking. Or substitute foods that don't have to be cooked, such as cereal, a croissant, or a fruit cup.

MEMORIAL DAY
May 30 or Last Monday in May

Memorial Day began around 1868 as a day to honor those who died in the Civil War. Celebrations in most cities and towns included colorful parades led by Civil War veterans and programs with speeches and patriotic songs. People decorated veterans' graves with flowers, ribbons, and flags. Memorial Day became a federal holiday in 1971.

Today, soldiers from all wars are honored on Memorial Day. Flags are flown at half-mast in honor of the dead, and graves are decorated with flowers, wreaths, and miniature flags. Some communities still hold parades and programs, but others observe a quiet holiday. For many, this holiday has become a day to remember all family members and friends who have died.

Crepe-Paper Poppies

Red flowers called poppies are traditionally worn on Memorial Day in memory of the soldiers who died on European battlefields where poppies grew. On Memorial Day, veterans organizations sell real and artificial poppies and donate the proceeds to help disabled veterans. Buy some poppies and try making your own, too.

Time: 20 minutes

Complexity: Easy

What to Do:

1. Cut two 4-inch circles out of crepe paper for each poppy.
2. Place one circle on top of the other.

Materials:
- Red crepe paper
- Scissors
- Green pipe cleaners
- Safety pins

3. Poke two small holes in the center of both pieces of crepe paper.

4. Put the end of one pipe cleaner up through one hole, bend it, and bring it back down through the other hole.

5. Twist that end of the pipe cleaner around the longer end of the pipe cleaner to form a stem.

6. Attach to clothing with a safety pin.

Memorial Day Wreath

Family gatherings have become popular on Memorial Day since it became a three-day weekend. Hang this wreath on your door to remind everyone what the holiday is really about.

Time: 30–45 minutes

Complexity: Moderate

What to Do:

1. Cut stars out of the posterboard in a variety of sizes, using the cookie cutters or stencils as a guide.

2. Spray glue on the stars and sprinkle glitter on them.

3. Tape a piece of the curling ribbon to the back of each star. Curl the ribbon with the scissors.

4. Glue the stars, ribbon-side down, to the wreath. Allow to dry.

Materials:
- Star-shaped cookie cutters or stencils
- Posterboard (red, white, and blue)
- Spray adhesive glue
- Glitter
- Curling ribbon (red, white, and blue)
- Tape
- Glue
- Scissors
- Styrofoam wreath (available at hobby stores)

5. Hang on the front door to greet visitors.

Variations: Use a wreath cut out of posterboard or cardboard.

Instead of stars, decorate the wreath with red, white, and blue wrapped candies.

Practical Tip: Use pins to reinforce the stars if they fall off. Just stick a pin through them into the Styrofoam to secure them.

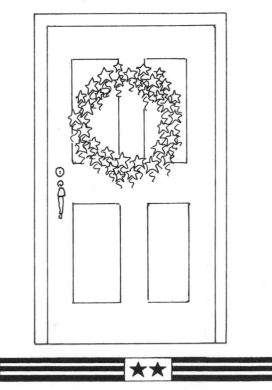

Patriotic Windsock

Instead of flying a flag on Memorial Day, make this red, white, and blue windsock. It's also great to hang up on the 4th of July.

Time: 45–60 minutes

Complexity: Challenging—Adult assistance recommended

What to Do:

1. Sew or glue the red and blue pieces of fabric together along the 18-inch sides, allowing a 1-inch overlap.

2. Cut the red fabric into 1-inch strips, starting at the unglued end and cutting to where the blue and red fabric meet.

3. Glue the top of the blue fabric to the outer rim of the embroidery hoop. The fabric should be long enough to go all the way around the hoop with an inch overlapping itself to make a seam.

4. Glue the overlapping blue fabric together. Do not glue the red fabric together.

5. Cut eight to ten 2-inch stars out of the felt and glue them to the blue portion of the windsock.

Materials:
- 12" x 18" red piece of nylon parachute fabric (available at fabric stores)
- 12" x 18" blue piece of nylon parachute fabric
- 3 squares of white felt
- 5" embroidery hoop (available at fabric and craft stores)
- Glue gun
- Scissors
- 3 feet of twine or string
- **Optional:** sewing machine or needle and thread

6. Cut the twine or string into three even pieces. Cut three small, evenly spaced holes in the blue portion of the windsock near the rim.

Poke one piece of string through each hole and tie them onto the hoop. Tie the three pieces of the string together about halfway up and again at the end of the strings. Hang up.

Variation: Make a windsock from paper instead of fabric. Decorate the paper first with felt-tip pens or paint. Wrap the paper around an oatmeal box, attach crepe-paper streamers to the bottom, and tie the top with three pieces of twine.

Practical Tip: Use caution around the glue gun—it's very hot. Have two people work on the project together.

June

FATHER'S DAY
Third Sunday in June

The earliest known observance of Father's Day was back in 1908, a year after the first Mother's Day. In 1936 the National Father's Day Committee formed to promote this day honoring dads. The committee also has the difficult task of selecting a Father of the Year. Father's Day became a permanent U.S. holiday in 1972.

On this day children, young and old, take time to tell their fathers how much they mean to them. Some give cards and gifts to their fathers, while others show their appreciation with gifts of action, such as doing household chores, washing the car, or mowing the lawn.

Writing a Poem for Dad

Let dad know how much he's loved on this day by writing a special poem about him. Include the poem on a card or have it framed for a gift.

Time: 15 minutes

Complexity: Easy

What to Do:

1. Think about dad—what he likes to do, what makes him special, funny things he says—and write it all down. Remember, poems don't have to rhyme; they just have to express feelings.

2. Read the poem during dinner, slip it into his coat pocket before he goes to work, or recite it on his answering machine at work.

Materials:
- Paper
- Pen or pencil

Variations: Give dad a poetry book instead of writing a poem.

Read the poem on a tape recorder and give dad the tape for a lasting memory.

Practical Tip: Look through family albums for inspiration.

Father's Day Stencil Card

Parents love to display their children's artwork on their refrigerators. Dad will proudly "show off" this easy-to-make stencil card on his special day.

Time: 15 minutes

Complexity: Easy–Moderate

What to Do:

1. With the pencil draw an outline of dad in the middle of one of the sheets of construction paper.

2. Cut out the outline of dad, creating a hole in middle of the paper that's shaped like dad.

3. Glue the sheet with the hole in it on top of the other sheet of construction paper so dad's shape is the color of the second sheet of paper.

4. Fold the ends of the paper to the middle so the front of the card looks like double doors to the inside of the card.

5. Write something on the outside of the card like "My Two Favorite Words Are . . ." Then write something on the inside like "Dad's Home!"

Materials:
- 2 sheets of construction paper (different colors)
- Pencil
- Scissors
- Spray adhesive or glue
- Felt-tip pens or markers
- **Optional:** envelope

6. Use the felt-tip pens to add details like hair, a face, and clothing to the picture of dad.

Variation: Ask dad to sit near a wall, shine a bright light on the side of his face, and create a silhouette on the wall to trace on a sheet of paper. Glue the silhouette to a large 8-1/2" x 11" card.

Practical Tip: To draw the shape of dad more easily, find a full body photograph and trace the outline.

"Dad" Book

Make dad feel like a celebrity by creating a book about him. It's sure to be #1 on his reading list.

Materials:
- Construction paper (white or colored)
- Stapler or paper punch and yarn
- Felt-tip pen
- Glue
- Scissors
- Family photos
- **Optional:** old magazines

Time: 30–60 minutes

Complexity: Easy

What to Do:

1. Staple several sheets of the construction paper together, or punch two holes along the sides of the sheets and tie them together with yarn.

2. Draw or glue a photo of dad's head on the front cover, and then draw a body wearing a costume like Superman's, SuperDad's, or another design you like.

3. Make up a title for the book such as "SuperDad!" or "The World's Greatest Dad" and write it on the front cover. Write "Written by (your name)" on the front cover, too.

4. Inside the book draw pictures of things dad likes to do, eat, play, and so on.

5. On one or more pages write a short story or poem about why your dad is special.

Variations: Cut out pictures of things dad likes instead of drawing them.

On the front of the book write "I love dad because . . ." On the inside pages write and draw pictures explaining why you love dad.

Or, write down a list of dad's favorite sayings or expressions.

Practical Tip: Young children can make short books and older children longer ones.

Miniature Backyard Golf

Putt, putt! Here's an activity the whole family will enjoy on Father's Day. Play individually or in teams.

Time: 30 minutes

Complexity: Easy

What to Do:

1. Make holes for the course by setting cans on their sides.
2. Make obstacles by turning chairs upside down, cutting holes in boxes to send balls through, and thinking up your own creative ideas with items around your house and yard.
3. Get the family together and play. Give everyone three tries to hit a ball through or around each obstacle. If they miss, they lose their turn. If they make it, they get to keep going.
4. Change the course after each game.

Variation: Keep score. Whoever completes the course in the fewest number of strokes, wins.

Materials:
- Metal cans, various sizes
- Chairs
- Boxes
- Scissors
- Baseball bats, broomsticks, or golf clubs
- Golf or ping-pong balls

Personalized Baseball Hat

Dads love hats. Maybe they wear them because they're in fashion. Maybe it's to keep their heads warm or protect them from the sun. Or maybe it's because they're losing some of that hair. No matter why dad wears a hat, he's sure to love this one.

Time: 30 minutes

Complexity: Moderate—Adult assistance recommended

What to Do:

1. With the felt-tip pens draw a design on the front of the white baseball hat. You might draw golf clubs, a fish dad would love to catch, a favorite team logo, or dad's nickname.
2. Sew the pieces of fabric onto the back of the hat to provide extra protection from the sun.

Materials:
- White baseball-style hat
- Permanent felt-tip pens
- 2 pieces of fabric, 4" x 6" long
- Needle
- Thread

Variation: Pin or glue items onto the hat that are associated with dad's interests, such as golf tees, baseball pins, ski badges, fishing lures, or old concert tickets.

Practical Tip: Omit the flaps if you want the hat to come together quickly and easily without sewing.

Necktie Cake

Dads often get neckties for Father's Day gifts. This year make dad a tie he can eat—a cake shaped and decorated like a tie.

Time: 30 minutes

Complexity: Easy—Adult assistance recommended

Ingredients:
- Cake mix (any flavor)
- 1 can frosting mix
- M & M candies

What to Do:

1. Mix up the cake mix according to package directions. Fill the paper cupcake holder with batter, and then pour the rest of it into the rectangular cake pan.

2. Bake according to package directions. Allow to cool.

3. Cut the cake in half lengthwise. Lay the pieces of the cake end to end on the cardboard covered with tin foil.

4. Place the cupcake at one end of the cake.

Materials:
- 1 paper cupcake holder
- Cupcake tin
- Rectangular cake pan
- Oven
- Knife
- Cardboard covered with tin foil
- Frosting knife

5. Cut the other end of the cake into a V-shape.

6. Frost the cake and decorate it with M & Ms to create a polka-dot tie.

Variations: Decorate the cake with other candies or use frosting in a tube with different tips to create a design.

Copy the design of one of dad's real ties.

Practical Tips: It's easier to frost a cut cake if you freeze it for a while first.

Blueberry Muffins

Greet dad on Father's Day morning with these homemade blueberry muffins. He'll love the special treatment.

Yields: 12 muffins

Time: 30–40 minutes

Complexity: Moderate—Adult assistance recommended

Materials:
- Oven, preheated to 375°
- Muffin tin
- Paper muffin cups
- Large bowl
- 2 large spoons
- Medium bowl
- Spatula

Ingredients:
- 1-1/2 cups flour (white, wheat, or a combination of both)
- 2 teaspoons baking powder
- 1 teaspoon baking soda
- 1/2 teaspoon salt
- 1/2 teaspoon nutmeg
- 1 egg
- 1/4 cup vegetable oil
- 1/2 cup sugar
- 3/4 cup milk
- 2 cups blueberries (fresh or frozen)

What to Do:

1. Place the paper muffin cups in the muffin tin.

2. In the large bowl, combine the flour, baking powder, baking soda, salt, and nutmeg until well blended.

3. In the medium bowl, combine the egg, vegetable oil, sugar, and milk until well blended.

4. Pour the egg mixture into the flour mixture and stir until combined. Do not overmix.

5. Fold the blueberries into the mixture. Batter will be lumpy.

6. Fill each paper muffin cup 1/2 to 3/4 full.

7. Bake for 20 minutes, or until muffins are lightly browned.

8. Remove muffins from muffin tin and allow to cool.

Practical Tip: Serve to dad warm with milk or coffee.

JUNETEENTH
June 19

HAPPY "JUNETEENTH"

Celebrated by African Americans throughout the country, but especially in Texas and the South, this special holiday recalls the day in 1865 when Union General Granger proclaimed the slaves of Texas free. Although President Lincoln issued his Emancipation Proclamation on January 1, 1863, slavery did not really end until the Union victory in April, 1865. According to legend, the slaves in Texas were not freed until June because the news was either withheld so that one last crop could be harvested or delayed because of slow mule travel or the murder of the messenger.

Juneteenth was originally celebrated in Texas and Louisiana. The celebration soon spread to Arkansas, Oklahoma, California, Alabama, and Florida as African Americans moved to these states. Today, it's celebrated throughout the country with picnics, games, and lots of food. Join in one of the many activities and celebrations in your community or host your own Juneteenth celebration.

West African Ginger Ale

Ginger ale, a favorite drink in West Africa, has a spicy taste that tickles the tongue. It will liven up any Juneteenth meal.

Serves: 8–10

Time: 30 minutes

Complexity: Easy—Adult assistance recommended

Ingredients:
- 2 quarts water
- 1/2 pound fresh ginger, peeled and thinly sliced
- 1/2 cup fresh lemon juice
- 1 cup honey
- Ice cubes

Materials:
- Medium saucepan
- Stove
- Large spoon
- Strainer
- Large pitcher

What to Do:
1. In the medium saucepan, combine 2 cups of water and the ginger. Simmer over medium heat for 20 minutes.
2. Stir in the lemon juice and honey. Let cool completely.
3. Strain the ginger mixture into the large pitcher.
4. Add the rest of the water and ice cubes. Let stand until chilled, and then serve.

Iron-On Crayon T-shirts

Here's an opportunity to wear your own art. Create African designs, pictures of famous black historical figures, or black-history art for this special celebration.

Time: 30–45 minutes

Complexity: Moderate—Adult assistance recommended

Materials:
- White T-shirt, mostly polyester with some cotton in it
- Textile dye crayons (available at craft stores)
- 4 sheets of blank white paper
- Towel or newspaper
- Ironing board
- Iron
- Scissors
- Colorful beads

What to Do:

1. Pressing firmly, draw a design on a sheet of the paper with the textile crayons. The design will turn out backwards on the shirt, so draw the pictures or letters accordingly.

2. Place a towel or layers of newspaper on the ironing pad. Then place a sheet of the unprinted white paper on the very top. This will prevent color from bleeding onto the ironing pad.

3. Place the T-shirt on the ironing pad with a sheet of blank paper between the front and the back of the shirt to prevent the colors from transferring to the opposite side of the shirt. Lay the designed paper face-down on the fabric with a piece of the blank paper on top of it to prevent the colors from smearing onto the iron.

4. Set the iron to the cotton setting with no steam. Iron until the image becomes slightly visible through the paper.

5. Carefully remove the designed paper. The design will come out in brilliant colors and will remain on the fabric permanently.

6. Cut a fringe design along the bottom of the sleeves and the bottom of the T-shirt. Attach large, colorful beads to each of the fringe strands and tie them on securely.

Variation: Fringe a pair of knit pants, such as bicycle pants, and add beads to those strands too.

HAPPY "JUNETEENTH"

Blackberry Surprise

Food is an important part of Juneteenth celebrations. This blackberry dessert is like a cobbler but is cooked on the stove instead of in the oven. It's delicious served with ice cream on the side.

Serves: 6

Time: 30 minutes

Complexity: Moderate—Adult assistance recommended

Ingredients:
• 5 cups blackberries
• 2/3 cup sugar
• 2/3 cup water
• 1 teaspoon vanilla extract
• 1-3/4 cups flour
• 2 tablespoons sugar
• 2-1/2 teaspoons baking powder
• 3/4 teaspoon salt
• 1/3 cup margarine, cut into pieces
• 1/2 cup + 3 tablespoons milk
• Ice cream

What to Do:

1. In the frying pan, combine the blackberries, 2/3 cup sugar, and water. Bring to a boil over medium heat, stirring occasionally.

2. Reduce to low heat and simmer for approximately 5 minutes, until thickened.

Materials:
• 10" frying pan with lid
• Stove
• Spoon
• Medium bowl
• Tablespoon
• Serving bowls

3. Stir in the vanilla.

4. While the blackberries are simmering, combine the flour, 2 tablespoons of sugar, baking powder, and salt in the medium bowl.

5. Cut the margarine into the flour mixture until it's crumbly.

6. Stir in the milk to make a soft dough.

7. Drop 12 heaping tablespoons of dough into the simmering blackberries.

8. Cook uncovered for 10 minutes. Then cover and cook for another 10 minutes.

9. Divide into serving bowls. Serve with ice cream.

Variation: Instead of blackberries, use another favorite berry, peaches, or plums.

Practical Tip: Keep margarine chilled until ready to use to make it easy to cut into crumbs.

Sweet Potato– Peanut Butter Tarts

Sweet potatoes and peanut butter sounds like an unusual combination. But this dessert blends them together to make a sweet and tasty treat.

Yields: 18 tarts

Time: 1 hour

Complexity: Challenging—Adult assistance recommended

Crust Ingredients:
- 2-1/2 cups flour
- 1 teaspoon baking powder
- 1/4 teaspoon salt
- 8 tablespoons (1 stick) margarine, cut into pieces
- 1/2 cup smooth peanut butter
- 1/3 cup ice water

Filling Ingredients:
- 2 medium sweet potatoes (1 pound)
- 8 tablespoons (1 stick) margarine, softened
- 1-1/2 cups sugar
- 1 teaspoon vanilla
- 1 teaspoon cinnamon
- 1/4 teaspoon salt
- 1 cup evaporated milk
- 2 large eggs, beaten
- Vegetable-oil spray (such as Pam)
- 1/4 cup heavy cream, chilled
- 2 tablespoons powdered sugar

Materials:
- Large bowl
- Large spoon
- Waxed paper
- Medium saucepan
- Stove
- Potato peeler
- Mixer
- Rolling pin
- Cookie cutter or cup
- Muffin tin
- Fork
- Oven, preheated to 350°
- Knife

What to Do:

1. First make the crust. In the large bowl, combine the flour, baking powder, and salt. Cut in the margarine and peanut butter until crumbly.
2. Sprinkle in water until the dough is moist enough to hold together.
3. Roll the dough into a ball, wrap it in waxed paper, and chill for 1 hour.
4. Next make the filling. In the medium saucepan, cook the sweet potatoes in boiling water until tender (about 25 minutes). Drain and cool slightly, then peel and mash.
5. Combine the potatoes and softened margarine. Stir until the margarine melts.
6. Stir in the sugar, vanilla, cinnamon, and salt. Then beat in the milk and eggs. Chill until ready to use.
7. Roll half of the dough out until it's about 1/8-inch thick. Use a cookie cutter or cup to cut the dough into circles. Repeat until all the dough is used.
8. Spray the muffin tin with vegetable-oil spray. Place the dough circles into the muffin cups, press into sides, and prick the bottom and sides of the dough with a fork.
9. Fill each muffin cup with 1/4 cup of the filling.
10. Bake for 10 minutes, then run a knife around the inside of each cup, lift out, and cool.
11. Whip the cream and powdered sugar until soft peaks form. Top each tart with whipped cream and serve immediately.

FIRST DAY OF SUMMER
About June 21

The first day of summer arrives at the summer solstice, when the sun's distance from the celestial equator is greatest. This is also the longest day of the year in the northern hemisphere—the Arctic Circle experiences daylight for twenty-four hours.

The arrival of summer also officially welcomes summer vacation. School is out, there's no more homework, and hot weather is finally here! Start planning the special outings, daily activities, chores, and goals for summer now before those endless summer days magically slip away.

Pinwheel

The warm summer winds have arrived. Carry this homemade pinwheel outside and watch it spin and spin.

Time: 20 minutes

Complexity: Moderate

What to Do:

1. Cut a sheet of the construction paper into a 9-inch square.
2. Decorate both sides with the felt-tip pens and glitter.
3. With the ruler, draw diagonal lines from the corners so they cross in the middle.
4. Cut along the lines *almost* to the middle.

Materials:
- Construction paper
- Scissors
- Felt-tip pens
- Glitter
- Glue
- Ruler
- Thumbtack
- Pencil or wooden dowel
- Tape

5. Bend every other corner to the middle and poke the thumbtack through the tips and the center of the pinwheel.

6. Push the thumbtack into the pencil or dowel, near one end, leaving space between it and the pinwheel. Blow the pinwheel or swing it through the air.

Summer Activity Calendar

Summer brings vacations to far-away and not-so-far-away lands, lazy days at the beach, and countless ball games and activities. Whatever this summer brings to your family, a calendar of your plans will keep the whole family on track.

Time: 15–30 minutes

Complexity: Easy

What to Do:

1. With the ruler and pen or marker make a grid with five spaces down and seven spaces across on each sheet of paper or tagboard. Write June, July, and August on the top of the grids. Fill in the appropriate dates on these months.

2. Fill in the days you already have plans for (birthdays, vacations, when to start packing for vacation, the day summer school starts, Father's day, Juneteenth, the 4th of July).

3. Brainstorm with your family about what they want to do on the rest of the summer days. Fill in the calendar with your plans.

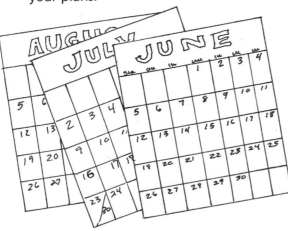

Materials:

- 3 sheets of construction paper or tagboard
- Ruler
- Felt-tip pen or marker
- Thumbtack

Suggestions: Make a pizza. Go to the zoo. Start a collection. Make paper dolls. Learn a code. Read a murder mystery. Camp in the backyard. Have a sleepover party. Go skating. Make a crossword puzzle. Learn to braid hair. Collect bugs and classify them. Visit your grandparents. Go to a movie. Walk to town. Read comics all day. Go fishing. Collect cans for money. Have a lemonade stand. Try some temporary tattoos. Have a carnival. Start a dog-washing service. Climb a tree. Practice skateboarding. Learn the latest dances. Try out for a drama production. Write a short story. Create a cartoon character. Go to the beach. Learn the harmonica. Have a jacks marathon. Design clothes. Make a race car. Change your hairstyle. Create a computer game. Make it to the 9th level in Super Mario 3.

4. Hang the calendar up in the kitchen or somewhere everyone will see it every day.

Variation: Use a pre-existing calendar to write your summer plans on.

Practical Tip: Use another calendar for reference when you're filling in the correct days and dates of your summer calendar.

Sand Picture

Ahhh, the smooth feel of sand slipping between your toes. You don't have to be at the beach to make these beautiful sand pictures. Wherever you make them, they'll remind you of sunny days at the beach.

Time: 30 minutes (plus drying time)

Complexity: Moderate

What to Do:

1. Put sand in the plastic containers and add a few drops of food coloring—a different color for each container.

2. Cover and shake the containers or stir until the sand is completely colored.

3. Spread the colored sand out on newspaper for a few minutes and let it dry while you color more.

4. Using the pencil, draw a design on the tagboard or cardboard.

5. Spread glue on the outline of the design.

6. Cover the outline with one color of sand. Shake the excess sand back into its container.

7. Spread glue onto another area of the design, and then fill it in with another color of sand. Repeat until your entire design is complete.

8. Allow to dry (about an hour). Hang up on a wall.

Materials:
- Sand
- Several plastic containers with lids
- Food coloring
- Newspaper
- Heavy tagboard or cardboard
- Pencil
- Glue

Variation: If you're at the beach, clear a smooth area of sand. Then draw a simple design in the sand with a stick. Fill in the areas with a fine layer of colored sand, creating a tropical scene, multicolored parrot, or colorful flower.

Practical Tip: Do this activity outside or in a garage or basement where you won't mind the sand that gets left behind.

Homemade Hurricane

Hold onto your hat, it's hurricane season! Here's a fun way to learn more about this awesome windstorm.

Time: 20 minutes

Complexity: Easy

What to Do:

1. Attach the Tornado Tube to a bottle according to package directions.

2. Fill one bottle with water, food coloring, and glitter.

3. Close the bottles using the tube, then turn the bottles over so the water is on top.

4. Swirl the top bottle to create a whirlpool, and watch the hurricane appear as the water moves to the bottom bottle.

5. Add a little boat to the bottle if you want some more excitement.

Materials:
- 2 plastic soda or water bottles (2-liter size)
- Tornado Tube (available at toy or school supply stores)
- Water
- Food coloring
- Glitter
- **Optional:** miniature toy boat

Variation: Make oceans in a bottle by filling the bottle with 2/3 water and 1/3 oil, adding glitter, sequins, or sparkles, and sealing with the cap.

Practical Tip: Try to figure out what's happening and why.

Frisbee Golf Tournament

In Beaver, Oklahoma, they hold a cow-chip-throwing contest this month. If you don't have any cow chips lying around, well, you're lucky. You can have just as much fun with Frisbees as with the authentic chips.

Time: 20 minutes

Complexity: Easy

What to Do:

1. With the acrylic paints, paint designs or your names on the Frisbees. Let them dry.

2. Set up your Frisbee golf course in the yard. Use objects such as sticks, boxes, or

Materials:
- Frisbees (one for each player)
- Acrylic paints
- Paint brushes
- Large yard
- Felt-tip pens or small cards with numbers on them

tables that the Frisbees must land in or hit. Number each goal with felt-tip pens or small cards.

3. Have the players toss their Frisbees to each goal, one at a time. Keep score by counting how many "strokes" it takes to land on or around each goal.

Variations: Give each player a different-colored Frisbee instead of painting them.

Use plastic lids from ice-cream pails instead of real Frisbees.

Practical Tip: Let the players practice awhile before you start the game.

Homemade Badminton

Here's a great game for the beach or the backyard that you create yourself.

Time: 15 minutes

Complexity: Moderate

What to Do:

1. Bend the wire hanger into an oval shape, so it looks like a racquet.

2. Twist the ends of the hangar together to make a handle.

Materials:
- Wire hanger
- Nylon stocking
- Yarn or string
- Nerf ball, sponge, or ping-pong ball
- Volleyball net or long string

3. Pull the nylon stocking over the top and wrap it tightly around the handle.

4. Wrap yarn or string around the handle to make it secure and easy to hold.

5. Hit the Nerf ball, sponge, or ping-pong ball back and forth across the volleyball net or long string stretched between two trees.

Cooling Fan

Sometimes the hot summer weather can be too much. Make this fancy fan to keep your cool.

Time: 20 minutes

Complexity: Easy

What to Do:

1. Glue ribbon, lace, or string across the top side of the construction paper. Cut to fit.

2. With the felt-tip pens, crayons, or colored pencils make a colorful design on the rest of the paper.

3. Add the glitter, sequins, or puffy paints to the design.

4. Fold the paper into 1/2-inch creases back and forth accordion-style.

5. Tape the bottom end closed. Fan yourself when you get hot.

Materials:

- Construction paper or cardstock, 11" x 14"
- Ribbon, lace, or string
- Glue
- Scissors
- Felt-tip pens, crayons, or colored pencils
- Glitter, sequins, or puffy paints
- Tape

Variations: Use two pieces of colored paper, each a different color, to make a two-tone fan.

Make a giant fan with an extra-large piece of paper.

Fold the fan first, and then decorate every other strip one way and the alternate strips another way. Then you'll have two designs depending on how you hold the fan.

Practical Tip: The cardstock paper makes a more powerful and sturdier fan, so use it if you're really hot.

Homemade Strawberry Ice Cream

You'll need the whole family to make this frosty treat. But the results are simply delicious!

Yields: 2-1/2 cups

Time: 30–45 minutes

Complexity: Moderate

Ingredients:
- 1 cup heavy cream
- 1 cup milk
- 1 egg, beaten
- 1/2 cup sugar
- 1 teaspoon vanilla
- 1/3 cup strawberries, diced
- 20 cups crushed ice
- 1-1/2 cups rock salt

What to Do:

1. With the electric mixer, mix the cream, milk, egg, sugar, vanilla, and strawberries together in the small can.

2. Cover the small can and set it inside the larger can.

3. Layer about 10 cups of the crushed ice alternately with about 3/4 cups of the rock salt in the space between the cans.

Materials:
- Electric mixer
- 1-pound-size empty coffee-style can with lid
- 3-pound-size empty coffee-style can with lid
- Table knife
- Large spoon
- Bowls
- Spoons

4. Cover the large can and roll it back and forth between two family members for about 10 minutes.

5. Open the outer can and empty the remaining ice and water.

6. Lift out the small can, wipe the lid dry, and remove the lid.

7. Using the knife, scrape the ice cream from the sides of the can and stir well.

8. Cover the can and place it inside the large can again.

9. Repack the large can with another 10 cups of crushed ice and 3/4 cup salt.

10. Cover and roll for 5 more minutes.

11. Serve in bowls.

Variation: Substitute other fruits for the strawberries.

Practical Tip: Mix the ingredients in a bowl first if desired, and then pour into the small can.

July

CANADA DAY
July 1

While people in the United States celebrate Independence Day on the 4th of July, Canadians celebrate on July 1 in remembrance of the 1867 confederation of their country. Although loyal to Great Britain, regions of Canada wanted to unite to form their own government. On July 1, 1867, the British government approved their plan and the Dominion of Canada became an independent country.

Canada Day is celebrated much like the 4th of July in the U.S., with parades, picnics, and fireworks. Since the Independence Days of Canada and the U.S. are so close together, a week-long International Freedom Festival is held each year in bordering Windsor, Ontario, and Detroit, Michigan. The Detroit River separates the two cities and the river is central to the festivities, which include fireworks, water parades, sky diving, concerts, and art exhibits.

Crayon Melt

Here's a creative way to use all those worn-down crayons in the bottom of the crayon bucket. Melt the crayons into a Maple Leaf design in honor of Canada Day.

Time: 2-1/2 hours (including melting time)

Complexity: Easy

What to Do:

1. Lay the newspaper over the work area and place a sheet of construction paper in the center.
2. Sharpen the crayons, collecting the shavings in bowls by color.
3. Arrange the shavings on the construction paper in a Canadian leaf design, flag, or other shape.

Materials:
- Newspaper
- Construction paper
- Pencil or crayon sharpener
- Crayons
- Bowls

4. Carefully carry the picture outdoors on a hot, still day and leave it to melt for a few hours in the sun.

Variation: Melt under a low-heat iron using paper towels on top to absorb the wax and protect the iron.

Practical Tip: Don't make the design too detailed because the colors may run into each other as they melt.

Paper Firecrackers

Fireworks displays are central to both Canada Day and 4th of July celebrations. Real firecrackers are dangerous to play with—these paper firecrackers are a fun alternative. They can really make a bang!

Time: 5 minutes

Complexity: Easy

What to Do:

1. Cut a piece of paper into a square of about 7 or 8 inches.

2. Fold the square in half so the bottom edge of the sheet comes within 1/2 inch of the top edge.

Materials:
- Paper
- Scissors

3. Fold the square in half again from side to side so the flap is on the inside. Crease the fold well.

4. Hold the paper firecracker tightly between your thumb and index finger at the open corner where the paper is only two thicknesses thick.

5. Quickly flick your arm and wrist downward. The inside flap of the paper will pop out and make a loud snap.

Fishing Hole

Canada is famous for its great fishing. If you can't trek to the north woods, try fishing at home with this activity.

Time: 30 minutes

Complexity: Easy

What to Do:

1. Make a fishing pond by rounding the corners of one sheet of the posterboard.

2. Cut out fish, alligators, turtles, and frogs from the construction paper. Use the felt-tip pens to add details. Attach a paper clip to the mouth area of each animal. This will be your "hook."

Materials:
- Several sheets of posterboard (blue or green)
- Construction paper
- Scissors
- Felt-tip pens
- Paper clips
- Dowels or rulers
- Yarn or string
- Magnet tape

3. Tie a piece of yarn or string about 2 feet long to the dowel or ruler. Attach a small piece of magnet tape to the end of the string and start fishing.

Ice-Cream Pie with Leaf Design

I scream, you scream, we all scream for ice cream. Keep cool on Canada Day with this yummy ice-cream pie. Make it with Maple Nut and Rocky Road ice cream or your two favorite flavors.

Serves: 8–10

Time: 30 minutes

Complexity: Easy

Ingredients:
- 2 flavors of ice cream (1 quart of each)
- Chocolate cookie pie crust
- Chocolate sauce
- Whipped cream

Materials:
- Ice-cream scoop
- Knife
- Bowls or plates
- Spoons
- **Optional:** tiny Canadian flag, microwave

What to Do:

1. Soften one carton of ice cream on the counter or in a microwave.
2. Spread a thin layer of the chocolate sauce on the crust.
3. Spread the softened ice cream on the crust, filling the pan a little over half full. Smooth the ice cream with the knife and place the pie in the freezer for about an hour.
4. Soften the other carton of ice cream.
5. Spread a layer of the chocolate sauce over the first layer of ice cream.
6. Add a second layer of ice cream to the pie, creating a mound. Freeze for another hour.
7. Drizzle more chocolate sauce over the pie. Return to the freezer until ready to serve.

8. When ready to serve, create a leaf design with the whipped cream on the top of the pie.

9. If desired, stick in a small Canadian flag.
10. Cut the pie into slices and serve in bowls or on plates.

Variation: Make your own pie crust: mix crushed chocolate wafers or cookies with a little melted butter and press into a pie pan.

Practical Tip: Be sure to refreeze between ice-cream fillings for easier handling.

Maple Nut Bars

These yummy maple nut bars are a tasty way to celebrate the independence of the Maple Leaf nation.

Yields: 12–16 bars

Time: 1-1/2 hours

Complexity: Moderate—Adult assistance recommended

Bar Ingredients:
- 2 cups flour
- 1/2 teaspoon baking soda
- 1/2 cup brown sugar, packed
- 1/2 cup margarine, softened
- 1 cup pure maple syrup
- 1 egg
- 2 teaspoons vanilla
- 1 cup walnuts
- Vegetable-oil spray (such as Pam)

Frosting Ingredients:
- 1/2 cup margarine, softened
- 2 ounces cream cheese, softened
- 1 tablespoon brown sugar, packed
- 3 tablespoons pure maple syrup
- 1/4 cup + 2 tablespoons powdered sugar

Materials:
- 2 medium bowls
- Large spoon
- Large bowl
- Electric mixer
- Oven, preheated to 325°
- Baking pan, 8" x 8"
- Toothpick
- Cooling rack
- Frosting knife

What to Do:

1. First make the bars. In a medium bowl, combine the flour and baking soda. Mix well and set aside.

2. In the large bowl, use the electric mixer to combine the brown sugar and the margarine. Add the maple syrup, egg, and vanilla. Beat until smooth.

3. Combine the flour mixture and the walnuts with the sugar mixture. Do not overmix.

4. Spray the baking pan with vegetable-oil spray, and then pour in batter.

5. Bake for 40 to 45 minutes or until a toothpick inserted in the center comes out clean. Allow to cool for 15 minutes, and then turn it upside down on the cooling rack and allow to cool completely.

6. Make the maple frosting. In a medium bowl, combine the margarine and cream cheese, using the electric mixer. Add the brown sugar and maple syrup and beat until smooth.

7. Slowly add the powdered sugar and mix until smooth. Add more powdered sugar if the frosting seems thin.

8. Spread frosting on the bars.

Variation: Sprinkle nuts on top on the frosted bars, too.

FOURTH OF JULY
July 4

Oooh, aah! The 4th of July means brilliant fireworks and jubilant parades in America today. But we also try to remember what we're celebrating—the anniversary of the signing of the Declaration of Independence in 1776, when the Continental Congress declared the United States of America independent from Great Britain.

In the preamble to the Declaration of Independence, Thomas Jefferson wrote that "all men are created equal" and that they have a right to "life, liberty, and the pursuit of happiness." The declaration also contains a section listing twenty-eight grievances against King George III of Great Britain, and a section that terminated the allegiance of the colonies to the British Crown.

Berry Sparkler Sundaes

This blueberry-and-strawberry sundae is always delicious, especially on hot July days. It's also very fitting for the 4th of July because it's red, white, and blue.

Time: 15 minutes

Complexity: Easy—Adult assistance recommended

Ingredients:
- Vanilla frozen yogurt or ice cream
- Blueberries
- Strawberries
- Lemon extract
- Colored sugar cubes

What to Do:

1. Scoop the frozen yogurt or ice cream into bowls and top with the blueberries and strawberries.

Materials:
- Ice-cream scoop
- Bowls
- Spoons
- Match or lighter

2. Soak the colored sugar cubes in the lemon extract. Place a cube on top of each sundae, and light it.

3. Serve immediately.

Variation: Top your sundaes with sparkly pipe cleaners for artificial flames.

Practical Tip: Watch young children around flames.

Homemade Map

The 4th of July presents the perfect time to learn more about our country. You can explore different areas of the country without leaving home by making a homemade map of the whole country, a state, or individual communities.

Time: 1 hour or more

Complexity: Moderate

What to Do:

1. If you're using the plywood option, paint the wood with green paint.

2. Design a map on paper using an existing map as a reference. Using your design as a model, transfer the map to the plywood or tagboard.

3. Include geographical features such as rivers, lakes, and mountains; favorite points of interest such as amusement or national parks; and homes of friends and relatives.

4. Paint a street that goes across the map and past favorite points of interest along the way. Fill in the details with paint or make structures out of construction paper and glue them on.

5. Paint the board with shellac to protect it.

Materials:
- Large piece of plywood or green tagboard
- Paint
- Paint brushes
- Map
- Paper
- Pencil
- Construction paper
- Scissors
- Glue
- Shellac

Variation: Make a map from fabric. Make the "country" out of green fabric, appliqué on the points of interest, and add details with permanent felt-tip pens.

Practical Tip: If you want to make a really large map, buy plywood in small sections for easy storage, and then assemble them at home.

PATRIOTIC COSTUMES

Planning on attending a local 4th of July parade? Join in the fun instead of watching from the sidelines. Here are two costumes to wear as you march down the street and celebrate the Red, White, and Blue.

Giant Firecracker

Materials:
- 2 sheets of heavy red tagboard
- Stapler
- Scissors
- Sparkly pipe cleaner
- Headband
- Red shorts

What to Do:

1. Staple the ends of the red tagboard together to form a tube.
2. Cut out two eyeholes.
3. Bend the sparkly pipe cleaner around the top of the headband to look like a fuse. Put the headband on.
4. Put on red shorts.
5. Slip on the tube. Keep your hands down at your sides and hold the tube up with your fingers. March down the street.

Paul Revere

Materials:
- Piece of cloth
- Marker
- Red, white, and blue clothing
- Paul Revere style hat (from costume or thrift store)
- Hobby horse or homemade one out of brown construction paper

What to Do:

1. With the marker make a sign on the cloth that reads "The British Are Coming," or make it funny and write "The British Aren't Coming Anymore!" or "The Parade Is Coming!"
2. Dress in red, white, and blue clothes.
3. Hop on the hobby horse and ride through town warning the villagers.

Variation: Come as another famous character from history, such as George Washington with an ax and a handful of cherries or Thomas Jefferson writing the Declaration of Independence.

Homemade Water Slide

The 4th of July usually means hot weather. Cool off on a homemade water slide.

Time: 15 minutes (to set up)

Complexity: Easy

What to Do:

1. Lay the plastic piece out on a clear area of the lawn. Don't put it too close to trees, shrubs, birdbaths, or anything else that you might run into accidentally.

2. Secure the corners of the plastic in the ground with tent hooks or heavy (but not sharp) objects.

3. Turn the hose nozzle on the "spray" setting and set it at the edge of the plastic, with the water running down lengthwise.

4. Run, slip, and slide, making up contests as to who can go the fastest or farthest, who can do the most spins, and so on.

Materials:
- Plastic sheet, tablecloth, shower curtain, or large garbage bag
- Tent hooks or heavy (but not sharp) objects
- Hose with spray nozzle

Variations: Gather all the neighborhood kids together and stage a water war. Use squirt guns, water balloons, or lunch baggies filled with water and tied off (add a few drops of food coloring for a special effect). Or fill a bucket with sponges and water and toss them at each other. Or hurl plastic buckets full of water at each other and use umbrellas or cookie sheets as shields.

Practical Tip: Move the water slide to a new place after half an hour to avoid damaging the lawn.

Balloon Pop

Here's a harmless way to add a little "fireworks" to your 4th of July party. It's full of laughs, cackles, and pops!

Time: 15 minutes

Complexity: Easy

What to Do:

1. Cut the paper into small slips.
2. Write riddles, jokes, or funny sayings on the slips of paper. Or write stunts, such as "Kiss a friend," "Sing 'America the Beautiful,'" or "March around in a circle, backwards, with eyes closed."
3. Roll up the paper and insert one slip into each balloon.
4. Blow up and tie the balloons.
5. Put all the balloons on the floor.

Materials:
- Paper
- Scissors
- Pen or pencil
- Balloons (red, white, and blue)

6. Have the guests sit on the balloons and try to pop as many as they can, collecting the slips of paper as they go. The person with the most slips of paper wins but has to do all the stunts won or read all the jokes and riddles collected.

Variation: Put candy inside the balloons instead of messages.

Practical Tip: Play this game in a large, clear room. Be sure to pick up all balloon pieces after the game so little ones don't put them in their mouths.

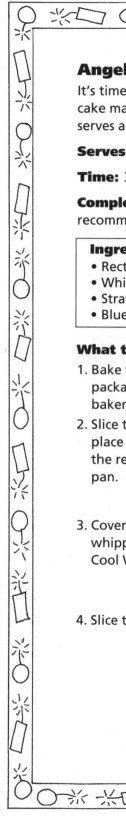

Angel-Food Flag Cake

It's time to show the flag! This angel-food cake makes an impressive centerpiece and serves a lot of hungry people!

Serves: 8–12

Time: 30 minutes

Complexity: Easy—Adult assistance recommended

Ingredients:
- Rectangular angel-food cake
- Whipped cream or Cool Whip
- Strawberries
- Blueberries

What to Do:

1. Bake the angel-food cake according to package directions or buy a cake from a bakery.

2. Slice the cake and place the pieces into the rectangular glass pan.

3. Cover the cake with whipped cream or Cool Whip.

4. Slice the strawberries.

Materials:
- Knife
- Rectangular glass pan
- Spoon
- Small plates
- Forks

5. Decorate the cake with the strawberries and blueberries in a flag design.

6. Refrigerate until serving time.

Variation: Use a regular cake instead of angel food. Add other fruits to the top of the cake.

Practical Tip: Don't refrigerate the cake longer than an hour or the whipped cream will get hard.

BASTILLE DAY
July 14

On this day in 1789, citizens of Paris captured and nearly destroyed the Bastille, a state prison. Although it actually held few prisoners, the Bastille was a symbol of the cruel French monarchy. Under the king, the rich paid no taxes on their land and lived luxuriously while the poor endured heavy taxes and starvation. Anyone who spoke out against the injustice was thrown into prison. The fall of the Bastille prison thus marked the beginning of the French Revolution that overthrew the monarchy and sought a democratic government.

People worldwide celebrate Bastille Day to remember democratic ideals. Grand parades, block parties, dances, and music are part of this joyous celebration. As in the U.S., fireworks are enjoyed at dusk.

French Crepes

Celebrate Bastille Day with French crepes. These thin pancakes are filled with fruit and topped with whipped cream or syrup.

Serves: 4

Time: 1 hour

Complexity: Moderate—Adult assistance recommended

Ingredients:
- 1-1/2 cups flour
- 1 tablespoon sugar
- 2 cups milk
- 2 eggs
- 1 teaspoon vanilla
- 2 tablespoons margarine, melted
- Vegetable-oil spray
- 1 cup fresh strawberries, sliced
- Whipped cream or berry syrup

Materials:
- Large bowl
- Electric mixer
- Large spoon
- Frying pan
- Stove
- Spatula

What to Do:

1. In the large bowl, combine the flour, sugar, milk, eggs, vanilla, and margarine. Beat until smooth.
2. Refrigerate for 30 minutes.
3. Spray the frying pan with vegetable-oil spray and heat over medium.
4. Pour in enough batter to cover the bottom of the pan. Batter should be thin. Cook until lightly browned, turn, and cook until other side is lightly browned.
5. Remove to a plate. Fill with sliced strawberries and fold over both sides. Serve with whipped cream or berry syrup.

Homemade Candles

The French use a lot of candles in their festivities. These candles symbolize the burning of the Bastille.

Time: 30–45 minutes

Complexity: Moderate—Adult assistance recommended

What to Do:

1. In the double boiler, slowly and carefully melt the candles or paraffin with dye or coloring.
2. Fill the milk carton 1/2 full with small ice cubes.
3. Set a long wick in the center.
4. Pour the wax over the ice.
5. Add more ice cubes to fill the carton, and then add the rest of the wax.
6. When the wax has cooled (about 15 minutes), pour off the water.
7. When the wax is completely firm, tear off the carton and you'll find what's left of the Bastille! It's a candle!

Materials:
- Candles or paraffin
- Candle dye or food coloring
- Double boiler
- Stove
- Milk carton
- Small ice cubes
- Long wicks

Variation: Use old broken crayons to add color.

Practical Tip: Use extreme caution around hot wax.

French Revolution Game

Here's a game for the whole family. It's a lot like the game Battleship, but you're looking for French flags.

Time: 30 minutes

Complexity: Moderate

What to Do:

1. Using a permanent felt-tip pen, make a grid eleven spaces across and eleven down on the top of the four box pieces. Use the ruler to make the lines straight.

2. Number from one to ten across the top, allowing an empty space in the upper left-hand corner.

3. Skipping the first square again, write the letters R-E-V-O-L-U-T-I-O-N down the left-hand column.

4. Cover the grids with clear Contact paper, then set the box top and bottom at right angles so your opponent can't see inside.

5. Decide who wants to be the revolutionist and who wants to be the monarch. Then, mark five French flags on your upper grid with a water-based felt-tip pen (not permanent) without your opponent seeing.

Materials:
- 2 dress-size boxes, about 11 inches or more in length and width
- Permanent felt-tip pens
- Ruler
- Clear Contact paper
- Water-based felt-tip pens
- Damp cloth

6. Take turns trying to guess where the other player's flags are hidden by calling off points on the gird such as R–8, I–5, and so forth. If your guess is correct, your opponent must tell you. If you're wrong, your turn is over. Whoever first guesses where all five of their opponent's flags are wins the game.

7. When the game is over, wipe the grid clean with a damp cloth and start again.

Variation: Hide only one flag to make the game extra challenging.

Practical Tip: Be sure to mark down what numbers you have called at the bottom grid so you won't repeat yourself.

August

SUMMER VACATION DAYS

Technically August doesn't have any holidays in it, but when you think about it, the whole month is like one long holiday! August is vacation month, that special time of year when parents cram their kids into the back seat of their compacts and head for Vacation City, using the narrowest, windiest scenic routes they can find. After an hour's chorus of "Are We There Yet?" to the tune of "99 Bottles of Beer on the Wall," everyone's a little batty.

August is also a month of togetherness for many families, when everyone breaks away from hectic schedules to play with each other. It's a great time to explore new lands or just to hang out together in your own community.

Learning Sign Language

Learn a new language while you're traveling—sign language. Practice the American Sign Language alphabet until you know it by heart. Then spell your name, your friends' names, street signs, and short sentences. If you learn it with somebody else, you'll be able to talk to each other without making a sound—and nobody can eavesdrop.

Travel Box

Don't forget to pack a travel box as you load up the car for vacation. Fill it with things to keep busy with during those long car, plane, or train trips.

Time: 30 minutes

Complexity: Easy

What to Do:

1. Glue old postcards or travel pictures to the tin container or box.

2. Cover the box with clear Contact paper.

3. Tape the cereal box inside the decorated box to hold books, pads of paper, and postcards.

4. Tape the orange-juice can upright in one corner of the decorated box to hold pens, pencils, and crayons.

5. Tape the envelope inside the decorated box to hold stickers, paper dolls, and other small items.

6. Fill the box with travel items mentioned under materials.

Variations: Instead of a box, fill a backpack or carry-bag with lots of travel items.

Prepare a travel box as a gift for a friend or relative going on a trip. Wrap each item up in gift wrap and include a note to open one new item every day or hour of the trip.

Practical Tip: Don't forget to include old favorites, such as a blanket, teddy bear, or pillow.

Materials:

- Tin container, cigar box, old lunch box, cardboard box, or other carrying case
- Postcards and/or pictures from travel magazines
- Glue
- Scissors
- Clear Contact paper
- Cereal box
- Orange-juice can
- Legal-size envelope
- Wide packing tape
- Stuff to put inside, such as sticker books, coloring books, dot-to-dot books, activity books, comic books, paperback books, song books, crayons, markers, white glue, small scissors, pads of paper, hand-held video games, small radio or cassette player with headset, blank and recorded tapes of songs or stories, small toys or dolls, action figures, puppets, small travel games, slinky, playdough, silly putty, Etch-a-Sketch, magic slates, View Master, the beginning of a postcard collection, address books, stationery, grooming items, nonperishable snacks, juice boxes, flashlight, or Band-Aids

Traveling Checkerboard

"Are we almost there?" This checkerboard with magnetic pieces is a great way to keep riders occupied on car and plane trips.

Time: 30 minutes

Complexity: Easy

What to Do:

1. Using the black marker and the ruler, draw a grid on the cookie sheet with sixty-four squares, eight across and eight down.

2. Color the squares alternately with the red and black markers so your cookie sheet looks like a checkerboard.

3. Cut the magnet tape into small pieces and stick them to the bottom of the checker pieces.

4. Have a checker tournament on your new board in the car—the pieces won't slip off when you go over a bump.

Materials:
- Cookie sheet
- Permanent markers (red and black)
- Ruler
- Magnet tape
- Scissors
- 24 checker pieces

Variations: Make your own checker pieces out of baker's clay. (See recipe on page 21.)

Play chess instead of checkers on your new travel board by sticking magnet tape to the bottom of chess pieces.

Practical Tip: Keep the pieces in a large baggy when you're not playing so you won't lose any.

Alphabet Highway

A, B, C, D . . . Finding letters in alphabetical order on signs and license plates is a favorite car game that can be played on any road with signs.

Number of Players: 2 or more

Time: Open

Complexity: Easy

What to Do:

1. Watch for signs or license plates along the road and pick out words that contain letters you need. Start with "A" and continue picking out words with the other letters in order. Two players cannot pick the same letter from the same sign.

> **Materials:**
> • A road with plenty of signs

2. Play until someone gets through the entire alphabet or you reach your destination.

Variations: Call out words that begin with the letter of the alphabet you are on. Or instead of words, locate objects that begin with the letters of the alphabet, in order. For example, if you see a car, call out "A—automobile, C—Car, or F—Ford."

Limit players on the left side of the car to signs on the left side of the road; players on the right side of the car to signs on the right side of the road.

Practical Tip: Give younger players a few seconds head start or assistance from adults.

Name That Tune

Who's up on the Top 40? Find out by playing this guessing game with a radio.

Number of Players: 3 or more

Time: Open

Complexity: Moderate

What to Do:

1. Turn the radio dial slowly across your portable radio and stop each time you get to a tune.
2. Whoever correctly names the tune first gets a point. Another point is awarded if the player can also name the artist.

> **Materials:**
> • Portable radio
> • Pen or pencil
> • Paper

3. Keep score on paper. Play until someone gets ten points or you reach your destination.

Variation: Sing or hum a song and have the others guess the title.

Practical Tip: If a song goes on too long and no one can name it, move on.

Materials:
- Pen or pencil
- Paper

The DJ Game

Try guessing song titles based on one-word clues. You'll be surprised at how many song titles you remember.

Number of Players: 2 or more

Time: Open

Complexity: Easy

What to Do:

1. Have one player think of a popular song and say only one word from the song, such as "Happy" from "Happy Birthday to You."

2. The next player tries to guess the song. If the player guesses a song that contains the right word, but is not the song the first player was thinking of, the player who guessed gets one point. The player who guessed then takes a turn at choosing a song.

3. The player gets two points for a correct guess. Then the player who chose the first song has to choose another one (this gives the guesser more chances to get more points).

4. If the player who is guessing cannot name a song using the key word, the player who thought of the song gets two points and must announce what the song was. The turn goes to the guesser.

5. Keep score on paper. Play until someone gets ten points or you reach your destination.

Variation: Describe a song instead of giving a word clue, such as "a song about water." Play the same as above.

Practical Tip: Designate someone to keep score.

Happy Birthday
Jingle Bell Rock
99 Bottles of Beer
Good Old Summer Time
Take me out to the Ball Game
Let the Sun Shine In.

Name Chain

Good spellers are needed for this fast-moving game. See how long you can keep the chain going.

Number of Players: 2 or more

Time: Open

Complexity: Moderate

What to Do:

1. One player says a first name.
2. The next player says another first name, but it must begin with the last letter of the previous name. For example, the first player says JohN, the

Materials:
• A quick mind

second player says NicK, the third player says KathY, the fourth player says YvonnE, and so forth.

3. If you stump your opponent, your opponent gets an "N." The first one to spell "Names" is out of the game.

Variation: Use cities, foods, animals, and lots of other categories.

Practical Tip: Don't say names that end in the letters x, q, or z.

Nick, Kate, Ellen, Neil,

What's His Name?

Here's a variation on the old "20 Questions" game.

Number of Players: 3 or more

Time: Open

Complexity: Easy

What to Do:

1. One player thinks of a person, real or fictional, but famous or at least known to the group. (Include cartoon characters.)
2. The other players take turns asking "yes" or "no" questions.
3. Limit the guesses to twenty or keep going until someone guesses or all give up. If someone guesses correctly, move on to the next player.

Materials:
• **Optional:** pens or pencils
• **Optional:** paper

Practical Tips: Here are some good questions to begin with: "Is it a male/female? Is it a child/adult? Is it real/fictional? Is it famous/friend? Is it animal/human? Is it cartoon/story character? Is it in show business/politics?"

Some good characters to try are Bugs Bunny, Santa Claus, Grumpy, Cookie Monster, Yourself.

Write down the answers to the questions so you won't repeat questions and to help figure out who it is.

Materials:
- Flashlights (2 per team)
- Paper
- Pens or pencils
- Cards or paper with Morse code on it (one per player)

Flashlight Messages

Everyone gets a thrill out of sending and receiving secret messages. When night falls, use flashlights and the Morse code to play this secret-message game.

Time: 30 minutes

Complexity: Challenging

What to Do:

1. Split the players up into partners or teams of four or six players each.

2. Split the partners or teams across the yard, making as large a space between them as possible. Half of each team will be sending the message while the other half receives it.

3. Give half of each team a simple message to send to their partners. Use messages like "Time for dessert," "Go into the house," "Sing a song."

4. Teams send the message by using long and short flashes of light for the dashes and dots of the Morse code. Use a waving light to signal "Ready for message" and "Please start over." Also, be sure to have senders pause between each letter and pause longer between words.

5. Give a prize to the first team to send and receive the message correctly.

6. Play again but have different players send and receive another message.

Variation: Instead of giving light signals, give sound signals by using a whistle or harmonica. You'll need a different sound maker for each team.

Practical Tips: Keep the messages simple.

Teams need to pay attention to their own partner and decode the message quietly so they don't help other teams figure it out.

Teams can invent their own way to signal word breaks.

International Morse Code

A	•—	N	—•
B	—•••	O	———
C	—•—•	P	•——•
D	—••	Q	——•—
E	•	R	•—•
F	••—•	S	•••
G	——•	T	—
H	••••	U	••—
I	••	V	•••—
J	•———	W	•——
K	—•—	X	—••—
L	•—••	Y	—•——
M	——	Z	——••

Gorp

This high-energy food is a must for any camper. Give everyone a baggy full and head out for a long hike.

Time: 5 minutes

Complexity: Easy

Ingredients:
- Nuts, such as peanuts, cashews, almonds, walnuts, hazelnuts, sunflower seeds, and dried coconut
- Dried fruit, such as raisins, apricots, dates, apples, candied pineapple, and banana chips
- M & Ms and/or Reeses Pieces
- Yogurt-covered raisins and/or peanuts

Materials:
- Large bowl or bag
- Large spoon
- Zip-lock baggies

What to Do:
1. In a large bowl or bag mix equal amounts of the nuts, fruit, and candy.
2. Fill a baggy full of the mixture for each camper.

Variation: Make an all-fruit or all-nut mix.

Practical Tip: Gorp makes you thirsty, so bring a thermos of water along on your hike.

S'mores

Gather around the campfire and make S'mores. Sandwiches never tasted so good as these made with graham crackers, chocolate, and gooey marshmallows.

Serves: 6

Time: 15 minutes

Complexity: Easy—Adult assistance recommended

Ingredients:
- 12 marshmallows
- 3 chocolate bars
- 6 large graham crackers

What to Do:
1. Break the graham crackers and chocolate bars in half.
2. Place the chocolate halves on six graham cracker halves.

Materials:
- Long barbecue fork or roasting stick
- Napkins

3. Roast the marshmallows over the fire, and then stick two marshmallows on each chocolate-covered graham cracker. Use the plain graham cracker halves to top the sandwiches.
4. Press closed, let the heat of the marshmallow melt the chocolate bar, and eat.

Variation: Use mint-flavored or dark-chocolate bars.

Practical Tip: Don't burn the marshmallows. Golden-brown marshmallows make the best-tasting S'mores.

OVERNIGHT CAMPOUT

August is the perfect time to have a campout—the weather's warm, the stars are out, and all you need are some campers and a few pieces of camping equipment to make it happen. Kids will love this outing even if it's only in your backyard.

Invitations

Write the party details with a permanent felt-tip pen on tiny flashlights or packages of dried camp food. Or cut out tiny construction-paper tents that open up and write the party details inside the tents. Send or hand deliver the campy invitations to guests.

Decorations

Use tents, sleeping bags, or whatever you plan to use in your campout as decorations. Place the camping gear on a nearby picnic table. Set out flashlights, comics, snacks, and so on. If your campout is at home, make the area look like a mountain camp by drawing a mural of a mountain to tack on the fence.

Activity

Have a nighttime scavenger hunt in the backyard. Split the guests up into two teams and give each team a list of items to find. Set a time limit to collect everything. Tell them not to take anything that is not on their list, because it might be on the other team's list. Include such things as "a bug, a leaf, some litter, a toy, a piece of garden hose, a gardening tool, and some camping equipment." Whoever collects the most things on their list wins.

After the traditional ghost stories, tell funny stories and jokes before going to sleep.

Food

Serve traditional campout food, such as hot dogs, baked beans, and S'mores for dessert.

Favors

Send your guests home with small flashlights, comic books, freeze-dried camp food, compasses, or other camping equipment.

Variation: Have a family campout in your backyard. Look at the stars and share camping memories.

Practical Tip: If it rains, move the party indoors and hang up a paper moon and stars.

September

LABOR DAY
First Monday in September

Labor Day isn't a day to labor—on the contrary, it's a day to relax. It all began in 1882 when a New York workers' union declared the first Monday in September a day to honor all workers. The new holiday was first observed on September 5, 1882, with a parade in Union Square and speeches about better working conditions, shorter work days, and higher wages. A few years later, in 1894, Labor Day became a national holiday. (Many other countries honor workers on May 1, the traditional May Day.)

Today this holiday marks the end of summer vacations, the reopening of schools, and the beginning of fall activities. State fairs, picnics, and visits to friends are common outings for many families on this day of relaxation.

Family Excursions

Labor Day weekend is your last chance to check off the remaining items on your summer activity list. So pack up the family and take an overnight vacation or a one-day trip to a local fun spot. Here's a list of suggestions.

- Visit the zoo and imitate the animals.
- Go to the park and have a scavenger hunt.
- Pack your lunch in backpacks and take a bike trip.
- Go to an ice-skating rink and cool off.
- Take in a matinee movie and bring your own favorite candy.
- Visit a farm and learn what it's like to be a farmer.
- Go to a planetarium and watch the stars in broad daylight.
- Have a bring-something-to-share picnic with other families and sample new foods.

- Visit a rest home and bring along a fun activity or game to play with the residents.
- Go out to lunch at a foreign restaurant and taste new foods.
- Go to a sports event, wear the team colors, eat vendor's food, and root for the home team.
- Go to a local park and get a game of Frisbee going.
- Get up early, watch the sunrise, and have a breakfast picnic.
- Go to a lake and float boats, fish, or swim.
- Learn a new sport such as horseback riding, golf, or badminton.
- Take a short train ride to a nearby town—and back again.

Lemonade Stand

Fresh, squeezed lemonade is a real thirst-quencher. Setting up and running a lemonade stand is a great way to make a little spending money during hot weather.

Time: 20 minutes

Complexity: Easy–Moderate

Ingredients:
- 6 lemons
- 6 cups cold water
- 6–12 teaspoons sugar
- Ice cubes

What to Do:

1. Cut the lemons in half.
2. Squeeze the lemons over the juicer or by hand into the pitcher.
3. Add water and sugar according to taste and stir until well blended.
4. Add ice to keep it cold.
5. Set up a table, make colorful signs, and serve lemonade over ice cubes in cups to thirsty customers. Charge ten cents a glass and five cents for refills.

Variations: Make pink lemonade by adding three to four strawberries to the lemon juice and whirling it in a blender until smooth.

Materials:
- Knife
- Large pitcher
- Large spoon
- Plastic or paper cups
- Table
- Large sheet of paper or tagboard
- Markers
- **Optional:** juicer

Set up other weekend businesses, such as selling arts & crafts made during the summer; tutoring a younger child in needed back-to-school subjects; performing chores for neighbors, such as mowing lawns, weeding gardens, or washing windows; collecting recyclable items that can be turned in for cash; or washing cars or bikes.

Practical Tips: If it's a really hot day, freeze the lemonade before opening for business and serve icy slushes to overheated customers.

Make the lemonade with clean hands and utensils and keep it cool in a cooler with plenty of ice.

Lemonade 10¢

SPORTS MARATHON PARTY

Here's a winning party idea for sports enthusiasts. They'll love the exercise and variety of activities.

Decorations

- Decorate the party room or backyard with sports equipment, such as baseball bats, footballs, and mitts.
- Put up posters of favorite athletes, set out sports cards, and hang pennants.
- Make the tablecloth look like a giant scorecard, game board, or large sports pennant.
- Use the sports pages for place mats, and set up a table centerpiece of Ace bandages, Ben-Gay, baseballs, sports cards, and anything related to sports.

Games

- Set up lots of different games for people to play, such as croquet, badminton, softball, lawn bowling or lawn darts (safety ones), basketball, and miniature golf.
- Have tournaments or marathon games, make up new rules for old games, or have rotations where everyone plays a game until time is called. Then have everyone rotate to the next game.

- Teach everyone a new version of "Capture the Flag." Divide the group into two teams. Give each member of one team a small rag of one color; the other team's members rags of a different color. Players put the ends of the rags into the backs of their pants. When play begins, set everyone free to run and grab as many of the opposite rags as they can. The team that first gets all the other team's rags, wins.

Food

- Ask everyone to bring lunch in a decorated bag. Encourage interesting, intriguing, and attractive artwork on the bags. Set all the bags on the table. At lunch time, have the youngest party guest choose one of the decorated lunch bags. Work up to the oldest. This way everyone gets a new lunch, perhaps something unfamiliar. Share the surprise of finding what's inside.
- Have plenty of sports drinks, such as Gatorade, available.

Burger Dogs

Hamburgers don't have to be round. These hotdog-shaped burgers will please everyone at your holiday picnic.

Serves: 4

Time: 15 minutes

Complexity: Moderate—Adult assistance recommended

Ingredients:
- 1 pound lean ground beef
- 4 slices of American cheese
- 4 hotdog buns
- Condiments (mustard, catsup, relish, onion, tomato)

Materials:
- Grill
- Spatula
- Plates
- Napkins

What to Do:
1. Shape the ground beef into four logs about 6 to 7 inches long.
2. Grill until browned and cooked, about ten minutes, turning once.
3. Top with cheese slices.
4. Serve in hotdog buns with condiments.

Space Invader Salad

This salad may look a little "alien" at first, but closer examination reveals that it's made with common ingredients that are nutritious and tasty. It's a good way to include some other food groups at your picnic or barbecue.

Serves: 4

Time: 10 minutes

Complexity: Easy

Ingredients:
- 1 cup cottage cheese
- 1/4 cup shredded carrots
- 2 tablespoons raisins
- 4 slices of pineapple
- A variety of additives, such as cherry halves, dried fruit, chow-mein noodles, chopped nuts, coconut, carrot circles, celery sticks, and so on

Materials:
- Large spoon
- Medium bowl
- 4 plates

What to Do:
1. In the medium bowl, mix the cottage cheese with the shredded carrots and raisins, reserving a few raisins to use for eyes or other decorations.
2. Scoop the mixture onto four plates.
3. Top each scoop with a pineapple slice to begin the space invader's face.
4. Decorate the face with the additives to make creatures from Mars.

BACK-TO-SCHOOL

As summer draws to a close, it's time to get ready for school again! It's a time to assemble school supplies and gym clothes, organize study areas in the home, and adjust to new schedules. It's an exciting and sometimes scary time for kids. They'll have new teachers, classes, friends, and responsibilities. The beginning of the new school year can also be emotional for parents—whether children are entering kindergarten or ninth grade, they've reached another milestone in their lives.

Preparing for the school year may be an elaborate or simple task for your family. Each family is different. However you prepare for the school year, just make sure you're ready when that first bell rings.

Educational Place Mats

Learn fun new facts while eating breakfast with educational place mats. They're easy to make, so change them as each "subject" is mastered.

Time: 30–45 minutes

Complexity: Easy—Adult assistance recommended

What to Do:

1. Decorate a sheet of white construction paper using felt-tip pens, crayons, and glitter, or glue on magazine pictures of a favorite hobby or interest. For example, draw or glue down pictures of dinosaurs from a coloring book.

2. Outline the drawings or pictures in black felt-tip pen and label them. (Name the dinosaurs, for example.)

3. Cover both sides of the paper with the clear Contact paper, allowing the Contact paper to extend 1/8 inch beyond the construction paper as a border.

Materials:
- White construction paper
- Felt-tip pens, crayons, and/or glitter
- Glue
- Scissors
- Clear Contact paper
- **Optional:** old magazines or coloring books

Variations: Try a star chart of the constellations, different types of insects, baseball stars, different kinds of fish, varieties of flowers, colors, maps, foreign words and phrases, pictures of famous buildings and sites worldwide, pictures of famous people, or breeds of dogs, cats, or horses.

Practical Tip: The Contact paper is tricky to use so adults should assist with this.

Pasta Pencil Holder

Everyone loves to eat pasta in spaghetti, soups, and salads, so why not use pasta to create interesting crafts—like this pencil holder made out of alphabet pasta?

Time: 45 minutes

Complexity: Easy—Adult assistance recommended

What to Do:

1. Spread the alphabet pasta out on the newspaper.
2. Use the paint brush to brush a thick coat of the glue on the jar, and then roll the jar in the pasta, picking up the pieces as you go. Fill in any bare areas with leftover letters.
3. Allow the glue to dry.
4. Go outside and spray the letters on the jar with a favorite color of enamel paint and allow to dry.
5. Fill with pencils or other school supplies.

Materials:
• Alphabet pasta
• Newspaper
• Empty jar or can
• White glue
• Paint brush
• Enamel spray paint

Variations: Color the alphabet noodles before gluing them to the jar by soaking them in a mixture of food coloring and vinegar or alcohol for a few minutes. Allow them to dry on a paper towel. Roll the glue-covered jar in the noodles, and then spray with clear Verathane or another varnish.

Color the noodles with a felt-tip pen.

Use a variety of pasta noodles, beans, seeds, or other items to cover the jar.

Practical Tips: For safety, use a plastic jar instead of a glass one.

Decorate the lid if you plan to close the jar.

Homemade Rubber Stamps

Kids can't wait to make their own special marks on paper, letters, and reports with these homemade rubber stamps.

Time: 45–60 minutes

Complexity: Moderate

What to Do:

1. Draw a design such as your name, hearts, stars, or "I Love You" messages on the wood with the pen or pencil.

2. Cut rubber bands into pieces that will fit the design.

3. Brush the rubber cement on the design and carefully place the pieces of the rubber bands on top of the design. Let dry for 5 to 10 minutes.

4. Press the rubber stamp on the ink pad and then on paper.

Variation: Cut designs out of thick posterboard and glue them onto wood blocks for a different kind of stamp.

Materials:
- Small block of wood (approximately 3" x 5" or smaller)
- Pen or pencil
- Scissors
- Rubber bands
- Rubber cement
- Ink pad
- Paper

Practical Tip: Keep the designs simple so it will be easier to make an exact fit with the rubber bands.

Creating Study Space

It's hard to do homework at the kitchen table. Here are some ideas to help you create a fun but functional study space for the upcoming school year.

- Set up a special table or desk for study. Make sure it's the right size.
- Set up a bookshelf. Stock it with a good dictionary and other reference books.
- Hang up a calendar to keep track of project deadlines and upcoming events.
- Get a good supply of pencils, pens, erasers, rulers, paper, and art supplies.

- Invest in a computer for the whole family to use.
- Cover an entire wall with clear Contact paper, and then write on the walls with water-based magic markers. Put learning posters underneath the Contact paper for studying the parts of the body, world geography, or multiplication tables. Add some game boards.
- Buy a section of corkboard at a lumber store and nail it to all or part of one wall. Frame it with wood to make it more attractive. You can leave the cork showing or cover it with a favorite fabric and change the fabric as you like. Use thumbtacks to display artwork, notes, and pictures.

- Make a map mural. Find a map of your local area, the U.S., the world, or other geographical areas, and pin it to corkboard. Stick pins in favorite or familiar places and attach colored yarn to show distances. Circle places you've been to.

- Buy a plastic paper-towel holder and screw the holder into the bedroom wall at arm's level. Fill it with a roll of butcher paper (available at art stores). Make sure that the paper unrolls against the wall. Create pictures right against the wall, or cut off a piece and work at an easel or desk.
- Nail or glue strips of Velcro horizontally or vertically on the wall. Also sew small bits of Velcro onto stuffed animals, light jackets, and any kind of cloth toy or item. Stick them on the Velcro strips. This is a handy way to show off a stuffed animal collection or keep track of jackets.
- Create some new storage areas to help keep rooms neat and clean. Collect ice-cream tubs and cover them with fabric, wallpaper, or paint. Stack them on their sides or set them on shelves. Old lunch boxes make good storage containers for small things—plastic figurines, jewelry, or crayons.

Personalized School Bag

This personalized school bag is a great help to students carrying all those books, papers, and pencils to school. Each bag will be unique.

Time: 30–60 minutes

Complexity: Moderate—Adult assistance recommended

What to Do:

1. With the pencil draw a picture or design, such as a favorite cartoon character, superhero, or your name, on the canvas bag.

2. Draw over the pencil lines with the fabric crayons, pressing hard.

3. Lay the canvas between a few layers of damp paper towels.

4. With the iron on a low setting, press the paper towels until they're dry.

Materials:
- Plain canvas carry bag (white or off-white)
- Pencil
- Fabric crayons
- Paper towels
- Iron and ironing board
- **Optional:** newspaper, vegetable peeler, scissors

5. Peel off the paper towels and repeat until the crayon wax is gone from the bag and only the color is left.

Variations: To add extra color, peel the paper off of the fabric crayons. Grate the crayons into separate color piles on the newspaper. Sprinkle colors inside the design outlines and press with the iron as described above.

After the bag has been colored with the crayons and pressed, dye the bag in a favorite color. The crayon color will resist the dye color, leaving the design on a colorful background.

Practical Tips: For safety make sure adults do the ironing part of this activity.

Paper towels don't need to be damp if you don't have any water handy.

Don't pile the shaved crayon peelings too thickly inside the design or it will be difficult to iron off the wax.

Fruit Leather

Like the fruit rolls sold in grocery stores, this fruit leather is a hit with kids and parents because it's sweet and nutritious.

Time: 15 minutes (plus cooking time)

Complexity: Moderate—Adult assistance recommended

Ingredients:
- 2-1/2 cups fruit puree, such as plums, apricots, peaches, or nectarines
- Vegetable-oil spray (such as Pam)

What to Do:
1. Spray the nonstick pan or cookie sheet with the vegetable-oil spray and set aside.
2. In the medium saucepan, bring the fruit puree to a boil and stir until it thickens.

Materials:
- Nonstick pan or cookie sheet
- Stove
- Medium saucepan
- Large spoon
- Oven, preheated to 250°
- Plastic wrap

3. Pour the mixture onto the pan or cookie sheet and spread to 1/4-inch thickness.
4. Bake for 2 to 3 hours, until dry and no longer tacky.
5. Carefully tear the fruit up into smaller pieces and roll the pieces up in the plastic wrap. Store in refrigerator.

Variation: Cover a cookie sheet with heavy-duty plastic wrap, pour thickened fruit mixture on, and place in the sunlight for 2 to 3 days.

Apple Boats

What more could a person ask for in a snack? This refreshing, high-protein after-school snack covers three food groups. But the best part is that kids will love eating it.

Time: 10 minutes

Complexity: Easy—Adult assistance recommended

Ingredients:
- 2 green apples
- 1/4 cup peanut butter, chunky style preferred
- 3 tablespoons peanuts, chopped
- 1/4 cup Rice Krispies
- 3 tablespoons raisins
- 2 slices Cheddar cheese

Materials:
- Knife
- Small bowl
- Spoon

What to Do:
1. Cut the apples in half and remove their cores, leaving hollows for the peanut-butter mixture.
2. In the small bowl, combine the peanut butter, peanuts, Rice Krispies, and raisins.
3. Spoon the mixture into the prepared apple halves.
4. Make sails with triangular pieces of cheese set on top and stuck in the peanut-butter mixture.

GRANDPARENT'S DAY
First Sunday following Labor Day

Grandparent's Day, celebrated on the first Sunday in September following Labor Day, began in 1978 to honor those special people we call Grandma and Grandpa.

It's a day for grandchildren to send their grandparents cards and gifts but also just to spend time with them to show their love! It's also a day for family stories. Kids will be amazed at what their grandparents remember about their parent's childhood as well as other tales from their family's history.

"I Love You" T-shirt

Grandparents delight in showing off arts and crafts made by their grandchildren. This personalized T-shirt is sure to become a favorite item in their wardrobe.

Time: 30–45 minutes

Complexity: Easy–Moderate

What to Do:

1. Use the puffy paints to write "I Love You" or another message on the front of the T-shirt. Also, outline your hand with the puffy paints and carefully write "Grandma" or "Grandpa" inside the hand.

2. Color the inside of each letter with a permanent felt-tip pen in a light shade.

3. Wrap up and give to your grandparent.

Materials:
- Large white T-shirt
- Puffy paints
- Permanent felt-tip pens

Variations: Have your picture made into a decal, cut it out in the shape of the "I Love You" sign, and have it pressed onto the shirt. Outline in puffy paints and give to a grandparent.

Make your own design or special message on the shirt.

Practical Tips: Allow to dry thoroughly before wrapping.

Wash the T-shirt in cold water.

Puzzle Picture

Grandparents never tire of looking at pictures of their grandchildren. Here's a picture they'll have to put together—it's a puzzle made out of a favorite photo.

Time: 45 minutes

Complexity: Moderate

What to Do:

1. Enlarge a funny or cute photo of the grandchildren at a photo or copy store.

2. Using the spray adhesive or photo mount spray, glue the photo onto the piece of tagboard. Be sure to glue the entire photo to the tagboard.

3. When the glue is dry, draw puzzle-piece shapes on the back of the tagboard with the felt-tip pen.

4. Cut along the lines to form the puzzle pieces. Don't make them too small or too large.

5. Put all the pieces in the box or large envelope (which you can also decorate) and your surprise picture is ready.

Materials:
- Photo of grandchildren
- Tagboard
- Spray adhesive or photo-mount spray
- Felt-tip pen
- Scissors
- Box or large envelope

Variation: If you have any pictures of grandchildren and grandparents together, even better.

Practical Tip: When put back together, the puzzle photo can be mounted on tagboard and framed. Hobby stores also have special glue for bonding together completed jigsaw puzzles.

Grandparent Interview

This activity gives kids a chance to pretend they're reporters. It's also a fun way for them to discover new things about their grandparents and their family history.

Time: 1 hour

Complexity: Easy

What to Do:

1. Make a list of questions to ask during the interview. Some good ones are: What was life like for you when you were my age? What were your parents and siblings like? What was school like? What did you want to do when you got older? What was my parent like as a child?

2. Pretend to be a reporter and interview the grandparent. Record the interview on an audio- or videotape for a lasting memory.

Materials:
- Pen or pencil
- Paper
- Quiet and comfortable place
- **Optional:** tape or video recorder

Variations: Take turns asking questions to each other.

Take notes during the interview and write a story about the grandparent afterwards. Give a copy of the story to the grandparent.

Practical Tip: Be a good listener.

Family Tree

Grandparent's Day is the perfect time to gather information together and create a family tree. Kids will enjoy chatting with their grandparents and discovering where they came from and who they are related to.

Time: 45–60 minutes

Complexity: Easy

What to Do:

1. Ask your grandparents from both sides of the family to tell you the names of all your relatives, as far back as they can remember. Write the names down on a piece of paper, grouped in families.

2. Draw a tree trunk on the brown construction paper, cut it out, and glue it onto the posterboard.

3. With the black felt-tip pen, write your name in the center of the trunk.

4. Cut two branches out of the brown construction paper, one for your mother's family and one for your father's family. Label each branch with the appropriate family's last name.

5. Add more branches for extending family groups and glue them onto the posterboard.

6. Cut leaves out of the green construction paper and write the names of your relatives on the leaves.

7. Assemble the leaves together in family groups and glue them onto the branches. Repeat for all family members until you have a full family tree with lots of branches.

Materials:
- Sheet of paper
- Pen or pencil
- Large sheet of white posterboard
- Fine-tipped black felt-tip pen
- Construction paper (brown and green)
- Scissors
- Glue

Variations: Use photos or draw pictures of your family members instead of or in addition to writing their names on the tree.

Add details to the tree, such as birthdates, places of birth, and so on.

Give the tree some fruit by having the kids be apples and the adults be oranges. Or have the girls be apples and the boys be oranges.

Instead of a tree, make a circus, pyramid, fan, rainbow, staircase, or other grid for building your genealogy chart.

Practical Tips: Make a rough draft of the chart and then transfer it to the posterboard.

Talk to other relatives and go through old photo albums if grandparents are not available to talk to.

ROSH HASHANAH
(Date Varies)

Rosh Hashanah means "head" or beginning of the New Year. It occurs on the first day of the Jewish month of Tishri and marks the beginning of an observance covering ten days, culminating with Yom Kippur, the solemn Day of Atonement.

Originally a harvest festival, Rosh Hashanah is celebrated at the new moon. The shofar, a ram's-horn trumpet, is sounded at sundown and the festivities begin with a special holiday meal. In the days that follow, Jews reflect on the year past and their hopes for the year ahead. Many attend services at temples or synagogues.

The Jewish High Holy Days end with Yom Kippur, the Day of Atonement, which is considered the holiest Jewish holiday. It's a day for fasting, repentance, and seeking forgiveness.

Apple and Honey Treat

Serve a traditional sweet treat on Rosh Hashanah to assure the family that the coming year will be "a sweet year."

Time: 20 minutes

Complexity: Easy—Adult assistance recommended

Ingredients:
- Apples
- Jar of honey
- Hallah (white bread usually twisted into a braid but served smooth and round during this holiday)

What to Do:
1. Cut the apples into slices and remove the cores.
2. Place the apple slices on the serving plate with pieces of hallah.

Materials:
- Knife
- Serving plate

3. Dip into honey and eat.

Variations: Core an apple and fill it with honey. Dip apple wedges into the apple well.

Slice the apples crosswise to make circles, remove the cores, and place on plate. Fill the holes with honey. Serve with dates and almonds.

Warning: Honey should not be served to children under two.

Pop-Up Greeting Card

A pop-up greeting card is a fun way to carry Rosh Hashanah wishes to family and friends. It's also a great way to begin a new year.

Time: 30 minutes

Complexity: Moderate

What to Do:

1. Cut a rectangle out of the blue construction paper and a smaller one out of the white paper.

2. Fold the white rectangle in half.

3. Make two small cuts at the fold on an angle.

4. Put glue around the edges of the white paper.

5. Glue the white rectangle inside of the blue one. Let the glue dry.

6. Fold the card in half.

7. Open the card, fold the center piece outward while the outer edges remain folded inward.

8. Press the card shut to crease it again.

9. On the outside write something about a special friend, like a memory of something fun you've done together. You might write "I have a special friend

Materials:
- Blue construction paper
- White paper
- Glue
- Scissors
- Felt-tip pens

who loves to play baseball." Then open the card and write around the pop-up part something like, "Happy New Year to my friend." On the pop-up part write the friend's name so it jumps out in 3-D: "Benjamin Samrick!"

Variation: Make up your own design for the card.

Practical Tip: Adults might need to help younger kids with the folding part of this card.

Holiday Fruit Pizza

Honey cakes and pieces of apples dipped in honey symbolize a sweet year to come and are popular at Rosh Hashanah. It's also customary to eat "funny fruit" or fruit you haven't eaten before or for a long time during Rosh Hashanah.

Serves: 8–10

Time: 20 minutes

Complexity: Moderate—Adult assistance recommended

Ingredients:
- Refrigerator sugar-cookie dough
- 2 8-ounce packages of cream cheese
- 1-1/4 cups sugar
- 1/2 teaspoon vanilla
- Sliced fruits (kiwi, guava, papaya, or other favorites)
- 2-1/2 tablespoons cornstarch
- 1/2 cup cold water
- 1 cup orange juice
- 1/4 cup lemon juice

What to Do:

1. Slice the cookie dough into thin circles, then press the circles together and smooth them into a round pizza pan so there are no holes between the slices.

Materials:
- Knife
- Round pizza pan
- Oven
- Electric mixer
- Small saucepan

2. Bake according to package directions, until lightly browned.

3. Mix the cream cheese with 1/4 cup of the sugar and the vanilla. Spread on top of the cooled dough. Top with sliced fruits in a circular pattern.

4. Dissolve the cornstarch in cold water. Add orange juice, lemon juice, 1/2 cup cold water, and 1 cup sugar.

5. Pour the mixture into the small saucepan and heat over low heat until thick. Cool, then spoon over fruit.

6. Refrigerate for 1 hour, and then cut into wedges and serve.

Variation: Choose a variety of different fruits to decorate the dough and make a design with the fruit.

Practical Tip: Cut the fruit in thin slices and allow space between the fruit to fill with glaze.

October

COLUMBUS DAY
Second Monday in October

Celebrated on the second Monday in October, Columbus Day honors Christopher Columbus's arrival in the Bahamas on October 12, 1492. Columbus Day has become a controversial holiday in recent years, especially for Native Americans, as it marks the beginning of European domination over their lands. Many historians do not believe that Columbus was the first to discover America or that he was a hero. Nonetheless, the holiday serves as a tribute to the New World rather than one particular man.

The first Columbus Day celebrations in the U.S. took place on October 12, 1792, in both New York and Maryland. President Franklin D. Roosevelt proclaimed Columbus Day a federal holiday on October 12, 1937. In 1968, President Lyndon B. Johnson moved the holiday to the second Monday in October to create a three-day weekend. Today we celebrate this holiday with parades and parties.

Sailor's Delight

Ships ahoy! This healthy snack looks like sailing ships. Pretend they're the Niña, Pinta, and Santa Maria and have them for a treat on Columbus Day.

Time: 10 minutes

Complexity: Easy

Ingredients:
- Cantaloupe
- Cherries
- Grapes
- Raisins
- Cheese slices

What to Do:
1. Cut the cantaloupe into sizable slices, keeping on the rind.

Materials:
- Wooden skewers
- Knife
- Plates

2. Push a cherry, grape, and raisin to the end of each skewer.
3. Poke two holes on opposite ends of each cheese single and poke a skewer through the holes to form sails.
4. Add more fruit on top of the cheese and stick the skewer into the cantaloupe.

Variations: Use paper sails instead of cheese; write the names of the ships or pirate logos on the paper sails.

Use toothpicks instead of skewers.

Columbus Diorama

Re-create Columbus's world in miniature. All you'll need are a few basic craft supplies and your imagination.

Time: 30–60 minutes

Complexity: Moderate

What to Do:

1. Place the shoe box on its side and begin re-creating the scene of Columbus landing in America inside it.

2. Use paint, crayons, or markers to color the inside of the box. Color a sky at the back and top. Add clouds, land, and ocean. Extend the ocean onto the bottom side of the box.

3. Glue sand to the edge of the land to create a shoreline.

4. Make trees out of construction paper and glue them to the land.

5. Glue glitter and fish cut out of construction paper to the ocean.

6. Make ships out of walnuts. Crack the walnuts in half, remove the nuts, and fill them with playdough. Make sails out of paper taped or glued to toothpicks to stick into the playdough. Or make ships out of construction paper. Place the ships on the ocean.

7. Use your imagination to add other details to the scene.

Materials:
- Shoe box
- Paint, crayons, or markers
- Paint brushes
- Construction paper
- Scissors
- Tape
- Glue
- Walnut and nut cracker
- Playdough
- Toothpicks
- Glitter
- Sand

Variations: Cut a hole in the lid of the box and put the lid back on the box. Cut holes in the top of the box so light can come in. Peer through the hole to see your scene.

Use a larger box

Practical Tip: Plan out your scene before you get started.

Around the World Game

Christopher Columbus explored the world by sailing to new lands. You can explore the world by playing this game. Keep a map handy to identify the places you're "traveling" to.

Time: 30 minutes

Complexity: Easy–Moderate

What to Do:

1. Before the game, fill the suitcase with items from around the world.

2. Have the players sit in a circle with the map or globe in the middle.

3. Give the suitcase to a player. Tell the player to open the suitcase and pull something out without looking. After closing the suitcase, the player is to look at the item and tell the other players what the item is and where it came from.

4. Tell the player to find the location on the map or globe. If the player cannot find the location, the player seated on the right gets to try. Continue until someone identifies the item and locates it correctly.

Materials:
• Suitcase
• Items from different parts of the world, such as a fan from China, maracas from Mexico, jewelry from Africa, a book from Russia, tea from England, mittens from Alaska, a lei from Hawaii, a clock from Switzerland, and so on
• World map or globe

5. Award a point to the player who gets the correct answer.

6. Continue passing the suitcase around the circle until everyone has had a turn.

Variation: Use food from around the world. Go to an international food or import store and buy candy, cookies, crackers, or other foods from various countries. Put the food items in a picnic basket. Let the players keep the treats they pull from the basket.

Practical Tip: Have clues ready in case the players have trouble identifying where the items came from. Or let the players put their fingers on the map and call out "hot" or "cold" as they trace a path to the right location.

Columbus Spaghetti

This spaghetti recipe uses tuna instead of red meat—just the way sailors might have made it while at sea.

Serves: 4

Time: 45 minutes

Complexity: Easy—Adult assistance recommended

Ingredients:
- 1 small garlic clove, chopped
- 2 tablespoons olive oil
- 3 tablespoons parsley, chopped
- 1-1/2 cups canned Italian tomatoes in juice, chopped
- 1 can (10 ounce) tuna in water, drained
- 1 pound spaghetti noodles, cooked
- **Optional:** 3 tablespoons margarine, Parmesan cheese

What to Do:

1. Sauté the garlic in the olive oil until lightly browned.
2. Add the parsley. Stir and cook for 30 seconds.
3. Add the tomatoes and their juice. Simmer uncovered over low heat for 20 to 25 minutes, stirring occasionally.
4. Break the tuna into small chunks and add to the sauce, mixing well.
5. Remove from the heat and stir in the margarine, if desired.
6. Serve over the cooked spaghetti noodles. Add Parmesan cheese, if desired.

Materials:
- Stove
- Medium saucepan
- Large spoon
- Large serving bowl

Variations: Serve the sauce over other types of pasta instead of spaghetti, such as twisted macaroni or wheel-shaped pasta.

Buy enriched spaghetti made from spinach or other vegetables. Or serve over rice for a Spanish taste.

Practical Tip: Use your favorite can or jar of spaghetti sauce if you want to save time. Just add the tuna as you heat the sauce, and dinner will be ready in a jiffy.

UNITED NATIONS DAY
October 24

This holiday commemorates the founding of the United Nations in 1945. The United Nations is an organization of nations who work together to secure peace throughout the world. Fifty nations signed the initial charter; today over 150 are members.

Perhaps the best known UN agencies are UNICEF (United Nations Children's Fund), which works to improve the health and welfare of children and mothers, and WHO (World Health Organization), which successfully eradicated small pox from the earth. The office of the High Commissioner for Refugees is also, unfortunately, very active.

On this holiday people take time to learn about the traditions, food, and people of other nations.

International Flags

Here's a creative way to appreciate the flag of our country as well as the flags from other countries.

Time: 30 minutes

Complexity: Easy

What to Do:

1. Create new designs for the U.S. flag using red, white, and blue construction paper. Try to have your new design represent something special about this country.
2. Make flags for other countries. Choose colors and designs that represent something about the countries.

Materials:
- Construction paper (all colors)
- Scissors
- Glue
- Pictures of flags of the world

3. Talk about your flags and the designs you chose. Then look at the pictures of the real flags to see how your flag compares.

Variation: When the flags are complete, guess which country they represent before the flag-maker tells you.

AROUND THE WORLD PARTY

Kids are intrigued with the foods, customs, and life-styles of other countries. Have a party on United Nations Day to celebrate the diversity in our world.

Time: 2 hours

Complexity: Moderate

What to Do:

1. Send out invitations on postcards from different parts of the world. Or make your own postcards from cut-up maps. Write the party details in with the black felt-tip pen. Ask the guests to dress in clothes that represent another country and to bring a food dish from that country to share at the party.

2. Decorate the party room with posters, travel brochures, and postcards from different parts of the world. Hang flags from different countries from the ceiling or the walls.

3. Cut out shapes of other countries from construction paper and glue or tape them to full sheets of construction paper and use as place mats.

4. Play a variety of music from other countries during the party.

5. Ask trivia questions from different parts of the world. Or play a game of "Where in the World Is Carmen Sandiego?"

6. Send the guests home with small flags or other souvenirs from different countries.

Materials:
- Maps
- Black felt-tip pen
- Globe
- Food from different countries (brought by your guests)
- Flags, souvenirs, posters, travel brochures, postcards, and music from different countries
- Construction paper (all colors)
- Scissors
- Glue or tape

Variation: Ask each guest to bring a set of stamps from a different country. Provide stamp books, and exchange stamps so everyone goes home with a beginning international stamp collection. For more information on UN stamps, write: United Nations Postal Administration, P.O. Box 5900, Grand Central Station, New York, NY 10017.

Practical Tip: Assign a different country to each guest so a wide variety of countries are represented at the party.

HALLOWEEN
October 31

Halloween is an ancient celebration combining Druid rites and Christian customs. Thousands of years ago European Druids began the new year on what is now November 1. They believed it was the beginning of winter, that winter and summer were at war, and that on the night before the new year, the army of winter, including ghosts, goblins, and witches, would approach. People tried to frighten these evil beings away by building huge bonfires and wearing masks and animal skins. When Christianity arrived, November 1 became All Saints' Day or All Hallows' Day. And the night before this day was known as All Hallows' Eve, or Halloween.

What originated as a frightening holiday has become a fun holiday for kids, who continue the tradition of dressing up in costumes. The best part for many kids is going out into the night "Trick or Treating." Like the ghosts and goblins they imitate, if they aren't given candy treats, they just might pull some trick on you.

Skeleton Person

What's more scary than a skeleton showing through a person? This spooky drawing will thrill trick-or-treaters on Halloween.

Time: 30 minutes

Complexity: Easy

What to Do:

1. In heavy black felt-tip pen or crayon draw a skeleton on one of the large sheets of white paper

2 Place another sheet of paper over the skeleton. Tape them together so they won't slip apart.

3. Draw a second picture on the outer sheet of paper, covering the skeleton with a face, hands, clothes, and shoes.

Materials:
- 2 large sheets of white paper
- Heavy black felt-tip pen or black crayon
- Crayons (all colors)
- Tape

4. Tape the resulting picture to the window with a light behind it or hold it up to a lamp, so that the skeleton shows through the person.

Variation: Personalize your skeleton by adding a photograph of a family member to the outer drawing.

Practical Tip: Make the picture at night and tape it on the window, then watch the surprise when the sun shines through it in the morning.

HORRIFIC HAUNTED HOUSE

Eeeeeeeeekkk! Everyone likes to get a little spooked on Halloween. These tips will help you turn your garage into a spooky maze of surprises.

- Hang spiderwebs made from yarn, or buy stringy stuff at the store and squirt it all over as your guests walk in.
- Make a headless horseman. Stuff old clothes with newspapers and set a pumpkin in its lap for its head. Paint a face on the pumpkin with glow-in-the-dark paint.
- Paint "eyes" all around the room with glow paint or use glow-in-the-dark stickers.
- Play a ghost record or a tape of creaky sounds and eerie screams. Or make your own scary sounds. Blow across the tops of different sized bottles to make weird moaning sounds; breath heavily into a large empty bucket or bin to make an echo sound; and scream into a paper tube.

- Create tunnels from large cardboard boxes or card tables and blankets for the victims to crawl through.
- Set up silly gravestones with your guests' names on them.
- Have the guests put their hands in bowls of Jell-O and Slime and tell you what they feel as you introduce yourself as Dr. Frankenstein. Cold baked beans, spaghetti, and oatmeal also work well.
- Ask friends to be "dead" bodies that suddenly come to life. Wrap them up in sheets.
- Wear costumes to suit your theme, such as the Mad Scientist, Frankenstein's Laboratory, the Witch's Cottage, and so on.

COSTUMES

The most memorable Halloween costumes are often homemade. Here are some fun and spooky costumes that are easy to make.

Pumpkin

Here's the perfect costume to wear while you're waiting for "the great pumpkin" to arrive.

Time: 30–45 minutes

Complexity: Challenging—Adult assistance recommended

What to Do:

1. Cut two large circles out of the orange fabric.

2. Sew the circles together, leaving openings for legs, arms, and head.

3. Turn the top over 1/2 inch and run a drawstring through it.

Materials:
- Orange fabric
- Scissors
- Needle
- Orange thread
- String
- Green felt
- Old newspapers, tissues, fabric, or pillows
- Green tights and shirt or pajamas

4. Cut out a green hat from felt in the shape of a pumpkin stem.

5. Sew two pieces of string onto the hat to tie under your chin.

6. Put on the green clothes, slip on the pumpkin suit, and stuff it with newspapers, tissues, fabric, or pillows.

7. Pull the drawstring closed.

Variation: With a black marker draw a face on your pumpkin after it's sewn together.

Practical Tip:

Make sure the costume is comfortable, especially if it's going to be worn for an extended period of time.

Quick Favorites:

Mummies are spooky favorites. Tie-dye an old white sheet so that it has splotches of red all over it. Allow it to dry. Cut or tear the sheet into strips and wrap it around your body. Add some make-up to your face for the "long dead" look. Or use a plain sheet or a flowered one for a tropical mummy. Be sure to leave mouth, nose, and eyeholes.

Glow-in-the-Dark Skeletons will chill your bones. Put on black clothes, such as tights, a shirt or leotard, gloves, and socks. Attach glow-in-the-dark masking tape where bones are, cutting rounded edges for the ends.

Pinocchio and Gepetto make a great pair traveling together. Pinocchio wears a white shirt, red or black shorts, suspenders made from braid trim, a Peter Pan hat, and a long putty nose. Gepetto wears knickers, a big billowing shirt, a hat, and glasses. Attach yarn to the shoulders, hands, and knees of Pinocchio, draw on "joints" with eyebrow pencil, and attach the yarn ends to a wooden "X." Then have Gepetto "work" the Pinocchio puppet.

Peter Pan or Robin Hood, two old favorites, wear green tights and leotards or green pajamas (you can use the pajamas later for sleeping). Cut jagged edges on a green shirt for both, and add a hat, feathers, and a belt with a homemade cardboard knife attached.

Raggedy Ann wears an old dress, a white apron with a small red heart on it, and white tights with red tape wrapped around the legs. Add a red yarn wig for hair, draw on some freckles with eyeliner, and brush on lots of blush.

Superman, Spiderman, and the Incredible Hulk are quick and easy superhero costumes. The bodies are made from tights and leotards, or pajamas—red and blue for Superman, red for Spiderman, and green for Hulk. Superman wears colored jockey underwear over the tights, a cape, and a big letter "S" on the front of his shirt; Spiderman wears a fishnet cap and a spider on the front of his shirt; and Hulk pads his body with fabric or towels and wears cut-off jeans.

Mickey Mouse is a perennial favorite. Wear black tights, a blue shirt, red shorts with big white felt buttons on the front. Then add a black piece of rope for the tail. Glue black tagboard ears to a headband. Put on black socks over the shoes if you don't have black shoes. Add make-up for whiskers, and color the nose red.

Guess What It Is Game

What's in the bag? Great Green Gobs of Greasy Grimy Gopher Guts? This traditional Halloween game always provides plenty of thrills and chills as the guests feel the foreign objects.

Time: 30 minutes

Complexity: Easy

What to Do:

1. Put the fruits and vegetables, or "innards," in the plastic bags. Cover them with the brown paper bags so the players can't see what's inside.
2. Tell a scary story as you pass around the "innards" and have the guests feel what's inside. Or sing "Great Green Gobs of Greasy Grimy Gopher Guts."

Materials:
- Fruits and vegetables that resemble body parts, such as an old, softening carrot for a finger, Jell-O for a liver, large cooked macaroni noodles for intestines (guts!), cooked spaghetti for brains, 2 large peeled grapes for eyeballs, popcorn kernels for teeth, a canned apricot half for a tongue, and a soft, ripened tomato for a heart
- Plastic bags
- Brown paper bags

3. Have the players guess what they are really feeling. Award a prize to the player who gets the most answers right.

Variation: Use your imagination to come up with other body parts.

Practical Tip: Show the players what the items really are after the game is over.

Apple on a String

Here's an apple-eating game that's just as tricky as bobbing for apples, but you won't get wet playing this game.

Time: 15 minutes

Complexity: Easy

What to Do:

1. Hang the apples from the ceiling on long pieces of string.
2. Say "Go" and have the players eat the apples without using their hands.
3. The first player to finish an apple is the winner.

Materials:
- Apples
- String
- Scissors

Variation: Make the game easier by using marshmallows or doughnuts instead of apples.

Practical Tip: Encourage the players to use a shoulder to help them "capture" the apple and eat it.

Crystal Ball Piñata

Look into the magic crystal ball and see your future. Goodies are in store for you if you have this crystal ball at your party—it's a piñata!

Time: 30 minutes

Complexity: Moderate

What to Do:

1. Blow up a large balloon and cover it with papier-mâché (follow package directions on how to apply), or cover the balloon with liquid starch and crepe paper. Allow it to dry.

2. Paint the ball black and sprinkle on glitter. Allow it to dry again.

3. Cover with glow-in-the-dark star stickers.

4. Cut open a small hole at the top and fill with candies.

Materials:
- Large balloon
- Papier-mâché or crepe paper and liquid starch
- Black paint
- Paint brush
- Glitter
- Glow-in-the-dark star stickers
- Scissors or knife
- Small candies
- String
- Plastic bat

5. Tie with string and hang from the ceiling.

6. Turn off the lights, let the ball glow in the dark, and then take turns swinging the bat.

Variations: Instead of painting the ball black, use black crepe paper.

Paint on stars with glow-in-the-dark paint instead of using stickers.

Fill the piñata with small magic tricks or made-up fortunes instead of candy.

Practical Tip: Use caution when swinging at the piñata. Don't turn all the lights off.

Gauze Ghost

What's Halloween without a ghost? Use this spooky ghost as a table centerpiece—or hang it from the ceiling to greet the witches and monsters who stop by for a Halloween treat.

Time: 10 minutes

Complexity: Moderate—Adult assistance recommended

What to Do:

1. Use the scissors to round the corners of the 6-inch piece of gauze or cheesecloth.
2. Pour the liquid starch into a bowl and dip the gauze or cheesecloth in it completely.
3. Set the bottle on the newspaper.
4. Drape the wet gauze or cheesecloth over the bottle and allow it to dry for 24 hours.

5. After completely dry, use the black felt-tip pen to draw a face on the ghost.
6. Place the ghost on your table for a centerpiece or thread string through the top of the ghost and hang it from the ceiling.

Materials:
- 6" square of surgical gauze or cheesecloth
- Scissors
- Liquid starch
- Bowl
- Newspapers
- Empty soap or drink bottle
- Black felt-tip pen
- **Optional:** string

Variations: Color the liquid starch with food coloring to make a colorful ghost.

Glue on wiggly plastic eyes instead of drawing them on or glue on eyes and a mouth cut out of felt.

Practical Tips: This is messy, so use plenty of newspapers.

Although the ghost will retain its shape once the starch dries, it is still delicate and should be handled with care.

Jack-O'-Lantern Candy Holder

Everybody likes to make jack-o'-lanterns for Halloween. Most are carved out of pumpkins, which are too messy to hold candy. Here's a jack-o'-lantern that doubles as a container for trick-or-treat goodies.

Time: 30–45 minutes (plus drying time)

Complexity: Easy–Moderate

What to Do:

1. Cut the newspaper into 1-to-2-inch strips.

2. Blow up the balloon and tie it.

3. Cover the balloon with newspaper strips dipped in the flour-and-water paste or liquid starch.

4. Cover the whole balloon two or three times, and let it dry completely (2 to 3 hours or overnight).

5. Pop the balloon and paint the ball orange. Add some black eyes, a nose, and a mouth.

6. Cut a zigzag-patterned top off of the pumpkin holder, poke holes in the sides, and attach a piece of the yarn for a handle.

Materials:
- Newspaper
- Scissors
- Balloon
- Flour-and-water paste or liquid starch
- Orange paint
- Black paint
- Paint brush
- Yarn
- Shellac

7. Shellac the holder and allow it to dry.

Variation: Make a witch's head or a big bat instead of a pumpkin.

Practical Tip: This is messy, so work over newspapers and wear a smock.

Materials:
- Saucepan
- Stove
- Candy thermometer
- Large bowl
- Medium bowl
- 2 large spoons
- Plastic wrap

Popcorn Pumpkins

Pop up a batch of popcorn and make these Halloween treats. They look and taste great

Time: 45–60 minutes

Complexity: Moderate—Adult assistance recommended

Ingredients:
- 2 cups white corn syrup
- 1 tablespoon vinegar
- 1 teaspoon salt
- 2 teaspoons vanilla
- Orange food coloring
- Green food coloring
- 1 medium bowl popped popcorn
- 1 small bowl popped popcorn
- Butter
- Raisins

What to Do:

1. Heat the corn syrup, vinegar, and salt in the saucepan until it reaches 250° on the candy thermometer.

2. Add the vanilla, and then pour 2/3 of the mixture into the large bowl and color it with the orange food coloring.

3. Pour the remaining mixture into the medium bowl and color it with the green food coloring.

4. Pour the hot orange mixture onto the medium bowl of popcorn. Mix well with a spoon. Pour the hot green mixture onto the small bowl of popcorn. Mix well with a spoon.

5. When the popcorn is warm (not hot), use buttered hands to form the orange into balls and the green into stems. Press the pumpkins and stems together while they're still warm.

6. Press in raisins to make faces. Wrap the popcorn pumpkins in plastic wrap.

Variation: Omit raisins, but cut out facial features from black construction paper and glue onto the plastic wrap.

Practical Tip: Work quickly but keep hands buttered to prevent burnt fingers.

Jack-O'-Lantern Oranges

Kids get a lot of candy on Halloween. Here's a treat that's sweet and delicious naturally. And best of all, it looks like a jack-o'-lantern.

Time: 20 minutes

Complexity: Easy—Adult assistance recommended

Ingredients:
• Oranges
• Can of frozen orange juice

What to Do:

1. Cut the tops off of the oranges in a zigzag pattern.
2. Lift off the tops and scoop out the insides.
3. Draw jack-o'-lantern faces on the outsides of the shells with the black permanent felt-tip pen.
4. Mix up the can of frozen orange juice according to package directions. Squeeze the juice from the orange pulps and mix with the orange juice. Pour the juice into the orange shells and set in the freezer for several hours.

Materials:
• Knife
• Spoon
• Pitcher
• Black permanent felt-tip pen

5. To eat, set on counter for a few minutes to partially thaw, or peel back the orange shells.

Variation: Fill the orange shells with orange sherbet or vanilla pudding tinted orange. Decorate the orange shells with chocolate frosting.

Practical Tip: Make these at night and freeze overnight so they're ready to go in the morning.

Halloween Punch

Here's a fruity, spicy punch that warms you up. It's a must for a Halloween party.

Time: 30 minutes

Complexity: Easy—Adult assistance recommended

Ingredients:
• 1 pumpkin
• 1 quart apple juice
• 1/2 cup lemon juice
• 5 cloves
• 1 teaspoon nutmeg
• 2 cinnamon sticks

What to Do:

1. Clean out the pumpkin, removing all seeds and strings.

Materials:
• Knife
• Large spoon
• Paper towel
• Felt-tip pens
• Large pan
• Stove

2. Blot the inside with a paper towel.

3. Draw a jack-o'-lantern face on the outside of the pumpkin with the felt-tip pens and refrigerate.

4. Prepare punch by mixing the apple juice, lemon juice, cloves, nutmeg, and cinnamon sticks in a large pan and bringing the mixture to a boil.

5. Simmer for 10 minutes. Serve in the pumpkin shell.

Variation: Fill the pumpkin with favorite soup or stew and serve for lunch or dinner.

Dracula's Blood Yogurt and Ice-Cream Mixture

This creepy drink is sure to bring kids running up for refills. It's made with fruit, yogurt, and ice cream.

Serves: 6

Time: 5 minutes

Complexity: Easy

Ingredients:
- 16 ounces plain yogurt
- 1/2 teaspoon vanilla
- 1 10-ounce package frozen strawberries
- Ice cubes
- Strawberry ice cream

Materials:
- Blender
- 6 tall glasses

What to Do:
1. Mix the plain yogurt, vanilla, and frozen strawberries in the blender until smooth.
2. Pour the mixture into tall glasses with ice cubes or chill.
3. Top with a spoonful of strawberry ice cream.

Variation: Try another flavor of ice cream instead of strawberry.

Floating Hand

Yipes! There's a hand floating in the Halloween punch! Don't worry—it's scary, but safe.

Time: 10 minutes (plus freezing time)

Complexity: Easy

Ingredients:
- Red drink mix
- Water

What to Do:
1. In the pitcher mix up the red drink mix according to package directions.
2. Fill the new rubber glove with the red drink. Tie the end with string.
3. Put the filled glove in the freezer and allow it to freeze.

Materials:
- Pitcher
- Large spoon
- String
- New rubber glove
- Fine scissors

4. When frozen, cut the glove off carefully and float the remaining "frozen hand" in a bowl of punch.

Variation: Serve a red hand made of frozen Jell-O.

Practical Tip: Wash and clean the rubber glove thoroughly to remove any residues before using it.

Baked Pumpkin Seeds

Don't let all those pumpkin seeds you pulled out of your pumpkin go to waste. Bake them up and pop them in your mouth—delicious!

Time: 45 minutes

Complexity: Easy—Adult assistance recommended

Ingredients:
- Pumpkin seeds
- 3–4 tablespoons margarine
- **Optional:** salt or seasoning

What to Do:

1. Spoon pumpkin seeds out of a pumpkin.

2. Clean the pumpkin seeds.

Materials:
- Large saucepan
- Stove
- Cookie sheet
- Large spoon
- Oven, preheated to 350°

3. Melt margarine in a large saucepan and mix in the seeds.

4. Spread the seeds out on the cookie sheet, sprinkle with a little salt or seasoning, if desired, and bake, stirring about every 10 minutes, until they are crispy (about 45 minutes). You can eat the shell and all!

Variation: Omit the margarine if you prefer.

November

VETERANS DAY
November 11

We celebrate Veterans Day on November 11, the day when World War I ended on the eleventh hour of the eleventh day of the eleventh month of 1918. The holiday, originally called Armistice Day, became Veterans Day in 1954 to honor veterans from all wars.

On this day the president or one of his representatives lays a wreath of flowers at the Tomb of the Unknown Soldier in Arlington National Cemetery in Virginia. The memorial actually comprises three tombs that represent all the unidentified soldiers who lost their lives in WWI, WWII, and the Korean Conflict.

Today the holiday is sometimes celebrated on the Monday closest to November 11. Whenever they observe it, many communities hold parades or programs in honor of this day of remembrance.

Flag T-shirt

Show the red, white, and blue. It's easy to turn a plain, white T-shirt into a patriotic flag to wear on this special day.

Time: 30–45 minutes

Complexity: Moderate—Adult assistance recommended

What to Do:

1. Cut stripes out of the red iron-on fabric.
2. Cut stars out of the blue iron-on fabric.
3. Arrange the stripes and stars on the white T-shirt in any shape or design you like. You can form the American flag (traditional except for the blue stars), or you can create a new look for the stars and stripes.

Materials:
- Red iron-on fabric
- Blue iron-on fabric
- White T-shirt
- Iron
- Scissors

4. Iron on the fabric and wear your shirt proudly for the day.

Variation: Outline the stars and stripes with red and blue puffy paints for a 3–D effect.

Practical Tip: Use a star-shaped cookie cutter or other predrawn star to help you make your stars exact.

Thank-a-Veteran Card

Today would be a nice day to send a veteran a special card, to thank him or her for supporting our country. Send the card to a veteran you know or call your local Veterans Administration office for names.

Time: 30 minutes

Complexity: Moderate

What to Do:

1. Glue the red and blue sheets of construction paper together.

2. Fold the paper in half.

3. Cut several small stars or one big star out of the front of the card so you can see the inside of the card, which will be the other color.

4. Open the card up and set it on the newspaper. With the eye dropper, drop diluted white poster paint on the bottom right-hand side of the inside of the card.

5. With the straw, blow the paint upwards causing a wispy branchlike design. Repeat if necessary to cover the inside card with more "bursts" of white paint, creating a "star-spangled" sky lit up with "fireworks."

Materials:
- 1 sheet of red construction paper
- 1 sheet of blue construction paper
- Glue
- Scissors
- Newspaper
- Eye dropper
- Straw
- White poster paint, slightly diluted with water
- Paint brush

6. With the white paint, write "Oh, say, can you see . . ." on the outside of the card. Then write "Thanks for protecting our country!" on the inside of the card.

Variations: Use white paper and red and blue paint to make "bursts" of "fireworks."

Add glitter before the paint dries.

Practical Tip: Young children may have a hard time understanding how to blow on straws because they're used to sucking on them. Give them a quick lesson by having them blow a scrap of paper off the table. You might also cut a small slit at the top of the straw, which will keep them from inhaling and won't interfere with blowing.

THANKSGIVING
Fourth Thursday in November

Turkey Day! The first Thanksgiving was held by the Pilgrims in Plymouth, Massachusetts, after their first harvest sometime around 1621. They invited Native Americans to join in the celebration, and all enjoyed a feast of deer, goose, duck, oysters, eel, bread, fruit, and cornmeal pudding.

President George Washington proclaimed November 26, 1789, a national Thanksgiving Day, so people could offer thanksgiving and prayer for prosperity, freedom, and hope. The day was not accepted nationally, however, until 1863, when President Lincoln declared Thanksgiving to be the last Thursday in November. President Franklin D. Roosevelt moved the holiday to the fourth Thursday in November in 1941.

Today Thanksgiving is usually celebrated as a family day rather than a public holiday. Families gather together and eat too much turkey, stuffing, cranberry sauce, sweet potatoes, and pumpkin pie. Then they all take a nap!

Turkey Napkin Rings

Thanksgiving dinner can be very messy—be sure to have plenty of napkins and napkin rings on the table. These turkey napkin rings complement your holiday table.

Time: 30 minutes

Complexity: Easy

What to Do:

1. Cut the cardboard tubes into 1-1/2-inch rings.
2. Glue ribbon around each cardboard ring.

Materials:
- Cardboard tubes, such as paper-towel tubes
- Scissors
- Colorful ribbon
- Glue
- Brown paper or cloth napkins
- Construction paper

3. Cut out a turkey face from construction paper, leaving a flap at the neck to glue onto the ring. Cut the flap in half, fold it in different directions, and glue it upright to the tube, as shown.

4. Stuff a napkin through each ring to make a turkey body and back feathers.

Turkey Place Mats

Kids can contribute to the holiday meal by making these turkey place mats.

Time: 30 minutes

Complexity: Easy—Adult assistance recommended.

What to Do:

1. Cut out scallop shapes from three sides of the brown construction paper, leaving one long side straight. Use as much of the paper as you can to make it large.

2. Cut another scallop shape from the orange paper, but smaller than the brown.

3. Cut another scallop shape from the yellow paper, again smaller.

4. Glue the yellow scallop onto the orange. Glue the orange scallop onto the brown.

5. Cut a small turkey head from the red construction paper and glue it onto the yellow paper.

Materials:
- Construction paper (brown, orange, yellow, and red)
- Scissors
- Glue
- Clear Contact paper

6. Cover the turkey mat with clear Contact paper, cut off excess paper, and set the mat at the table.

7. Make a place mat for each person who will be at your holiday meal.

Variation: Instead of turkey, make fall leaf designs using the same technique.

Practical Tip: Adults should help with Contact paper as it's tricky to manage.

Thanksgiving T-Shirt

Kids enjoy eating turkey, but they'll also enjoy wearing turkey T-shirts made with colorful iron-on transfers.

Time: 30–45 minutes

Complexity: Easy—Adult assistance recommended

What to Do:

1. Cut a turkey shape out of the paper or fabric.
2. Paint the underside of the turkey. Mix the colors as you paint to create the different colors on the turkey.
3. Place the turkey on the T-shirt.
4. Cover the turkey with plain white paper and iron according to transfer directions. The heat will transfer the paint to the T-shirt and create a beautiful print.
5. Carefully remove the paper and turkey to see your design.

Materials:
- Paper or fabric
- Scissors
- Water-based iron-on transfer paint (available at hobby stores)
- Paint brush
- T-shirt that's at least 60 percent synthetic
- White paper
- Iron

Variation: Cut out leaf shapes from paper or fabric or use real leaves. Use the same technique to make prints.

Practical Tip: Make sure you use a synthetic T-shirt or the transfer will not take well.

Hand Turkey Puppet

Gobble, gobble! These turkeys make great leading characters in a Thanksgiving play.

Time: 30 minutes

Complexity: Easy

What to Do:

1. With a pencil trace your hand on a paper plate.
2. Cut out the paper handprint.
3. Cut "feathers" out of the construction paper and glue them onto the fingers of the paper hand.
4. Draw a face on the turkey with the crayons or markers and tape or glue a Popsicle stick to the back of the paper hand.

Materials:
- Paper plate
- Pencil
- Scissors
- Glue
- Construction paper
- Color crayons or markers
- Popsicle stick
- **Optional:** tape

Variations: Use real feathers (available at hobby stores) instead of paper.

Draw on the turkey's face with puffy paints for a 3-D effect.

Instead of gluing the puppet to a Popsicle stick, cut out two paper plates in the shape of your hand and glue all edges of the hand together except the wrist side. Decorate one or both sides of the hand. Slide the puppet onto your hand like a glove and use during your puppet show. Or decorate an old glove as a turkey.

Practical Tip: Be sure to let the puppet dry before using it or it may fall apart.

Pine-Cone Turkey

Create these holiday turkeys to decorate the holiday table or to keep as pets.

Time: 20 minutes

Complexity: Easy

What to Do:

1. Cut small, medium, and large scallops out of the construction paper.

2. Glue the scallops to the pine cone for the turkey's feathers.

3. Cut a head out of the construction paper and glue onto the pine cone.

4. Glue the wiggly plastic eyes onto the head.

5. Cut feet out of the brown construction paper and glue onto the bottom of the pine cone.

Materials:
- Pine cone
- Construction paper (brown, red, orange, and yellow)
- Glue
- Wiggly plastic eyes

Variation: Instead of construction paper, use colored or natural feathers from a hobby store.

Practical Tip: Glue is tricky to use on a pine cone, so work slowly and carefully. Don't use too much glue.

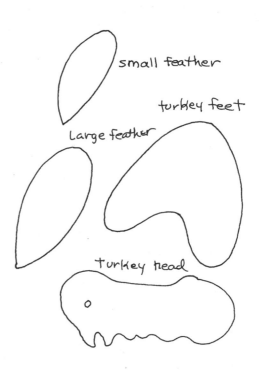

small feather

turkey feet

Large feather

turkey head

Dream Catcher

The legend of the dream catcher comes from the Ojibwa, who believe that the night air is filled with dreams, both good and bad. The dream catcher captures the dreams that float by. The good dreams slip through the center hole and slide down to the person sleeping below, while the bad dreams get tangled in the web. Make your own dream catcher in honor of the Native Americans at the first Thanksgiving.

Time: 1 hour

Complexity: Challenging—Adult assistant recommended

What to Do:

1. Glue or twist a hoop together.
2. Tie one end of the web material you are using to the hoop.
3. Begin stitching a web by looping the web material completely around the hoop. Be sure to catch each loop about itself before going to the next one, as shown. Space the stitches evenly apart, pulling loops tight to the hoop.
4. Start a second row by following the same steps for the first row, but go around the middle of the loops from the first row instead of the hoop. Periodically add beads, trinkets, or charms to the web.

Materials:
- Hoop material, such as willow twig, basket reed, pipe cleaner, embroidery hoop, or grapevine
- Glue
- Web material, such as thread, yarn, string, dental floss, or fishing line
- Fastener, such as a leather strip, leather shoe lace, yarn, or narrow ribbon
- Feathers
- Beads, small trinkets, or charms

5. Continue adding rows until you have a hole in the center the size you desire. Tie a small knot at the end of the web material to hold it in place.

6. Attach feathers to the web by gluing them to the hoop or inserting them into small openings in the hoop.
7. Tie a fastener to the hoop to hang the dream catcher up by.

Variation: For another web style, start as above, but in the second row loop around the same point as the first row.

Practical Tip: Work slowly and carefully for best results.

Totem Pole

A totem pole identifies a family or clan with carved or painted symbols of family ancestry and mythical or historical incidents. Surprise your family or Thanksgiving guests with your own family totem pole.

Time: 45–60 minutes

Complexity: Easy

What to Do:

1. Clean the cans and remove paper labels.
2. Glue the rim or edge of each can to another can, making a stacked totem pole.
3. Cut out strips of construction paper to fit the size of the can labels.
4. Using the felt-tip pens, fabric scraps, or yarn pieces, decorate the strips with faces or symbols representing your family.
5. Glue the decorated strips onto the totem pole.
6. Set your totem pole near the front door to greet visitors.

Materials:
- 5–7 cans the same size
- White glue
- Construction paper (all colors)
- Fabric, paper, and yarn scraps
- Felt-tip pens
- Scissors

Variation: Make face caricatures of your visitors so they can see themselves as they arrive. Use costume jewelry, yarn for hair and mustaches, and other items to personalize each face.

Practical Tips: Be sure the cans you use have been emptied since you won't be able to use them once they're glued together.

Let the glue dry thoroughly before using the totem pole.

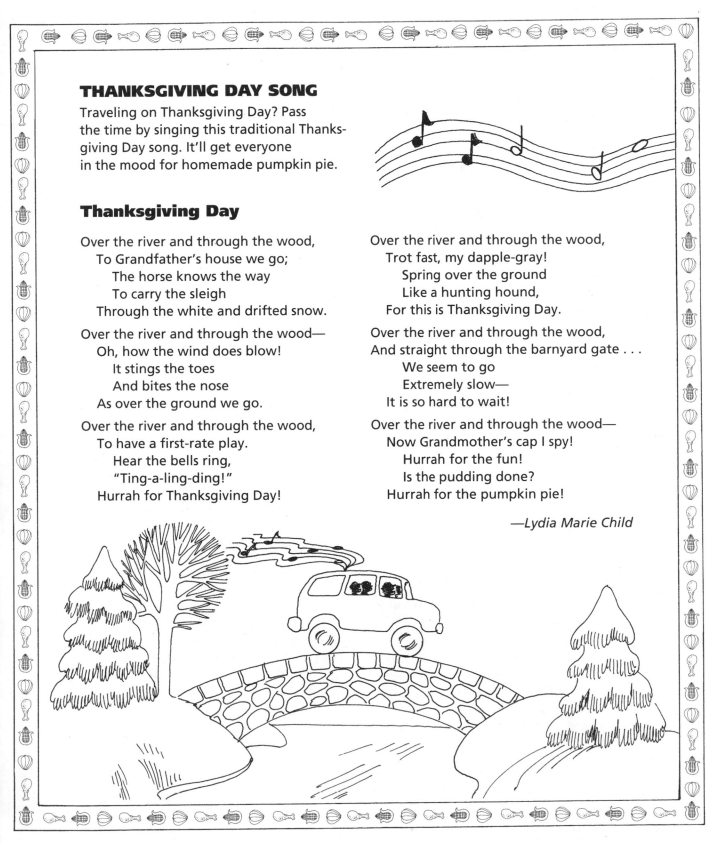

THANKSGIVING DAY SONG

Traveling on Thanksgiving Day? Pass
the time by singing this traditional Thanksgiving Day song. It'll get everyone
in the mood for homemade pumpkin pie.

Thanksgiving Day

Over the river and through the wood,
  To Grandfather's house we go;
    The horse knows the way
    To carry the sleigh
Through the white and drifted snow.

Over the river and through the wood—
  Oh, how the wind does blow!
    It stings the toes
    And bites the nose
As over the ground we go.

Over the river and through the wood,
  To have a first-rate play.
    Hear the bells ring,
    "Ting-a-ling-ding!"
Hurrah for Thanksgiving Day!

Over the river and through the wood,
  Trot fast, my dapple-gray!
    Spring over the ground
    Like a hunting hound,
For this is Thanksgiving Day.

Over the river and through the wood,
And straight through the barnyard gate . . .
    We seem to go
    Extremely slow—
It is so hard to wait!

Over the river and through the wood—
  Now Grandmother's cap I spy!
    Hurrah for the fun!
    Is the pudding done?
Hurrah for the pumpkin pie!

—*Lydia Marie Child*

THANKSGIVING DAY CELEBRATION

Here are some ideas to make your Thanksgiving Day celebration extra special.

Decorations

- Hang up autumn mobiles to give the party room an outdoor look and to add some fall colors. Collect a bunch of leaves and pine cones from the yard. Tie colored yarn around each leaf or pine cone. String a long piece of yarn kitty-corner from one corner of the party room to the other, then repeat from other corners. Hang leaves from yarn. Or cut out tree branches from brown construction paper and tape them to a wall or on top of a tablecloth. Then glue the leaves and pine cones to the tree branches.

- Decorate the table with a display of Indian corn, colorful gourds, and leaves in a big wicker or cornucopia basket. To make your own cornucopias, curve brown construction paper into a cone shape and place corn and gourds inside. Lay it on its side and add more corn, gourds, and leaves tumbling out.

- Hollow out a pumpkin and fill it with flowers or fall leaves. Or cut a pineapple in half, hollow it out, attach a construction paper or felt turkey head for one end and use the pineapple leaves for the tail end. Fill it with fruit salad.

Activities

- After everyone is served and ready to eat, go around the table during mealtime and have each person tell what they are thankful for. This is a good time to share stories about what each one appreciates about life, friends, family, and so on. If you get a chance, write these down and save them to read at next year's Thanksgiving gathering.

- Ask a friend from another country or culture to make something traditional from their heritage. Then exchange dishes and enjoy the new foods during the meal.

Game

- Have the guests sit in a circle and begin a rhythm by having them first slap their legs, then clap their hands, then snap their fingers. Each time they snap their fingers one guest must name something to be thankful for, taking turns around the circle. If players miss the beat and can't come up with something, they are out of the game and the rest continue.

Food

- Make individual pumpkin pies for your guests that reflect their personalities. Buy or make graham-cracker shells for each guest in individual aluminum pans. Make pumpkin pie filling according to directions on the can and pour into the shells. Bake for 20 to 25 minutes or until done. Allow to cool. Create eyes, nose, and mouth with candy corn. Create hair with whipped cream.

Turkey-Shaped Cheese Appetizer

Serve an appetizer that looks like a turkey! Your guests will gobble it up.

Serves: 6–8

Time: 30 minutes

Complexity: Easy—Adult assistance recommended

Ingredients:
- 2 cups whole almonds
- 2 8-ounce packages cream cheese
- 2 5-ounce jars favorite cheese spread (Cheddar, pimento, bacon)
- 1/4 cup chopped green onions
- 1 teaspoon Worcestershire sauce
- Breadsticks

Materials:
- Jelly-roll pan
- Oven, preheated to 375°
- Electric mixer
- Medium bowl
- Large spoon
- Platter
- Scissors
- Construction paper
- Tape

What to Do:
1. Bake the whole almonds in a single layer in the jelly-roll pan for 10 minutes. Allow to cool.
2. With the electric mixer, mix the cream cheese and cheese spread together until smooth.
3. Stir in the green onions and Worcestershire sauce.
4. Shape the cheese into a turkey body (a round mound) and tail. Place on the platter.
5. Stick half a breadstick in one end of the cheese to form a turkey neck and several at the other end to form a tail.
6. Cut out a paper head from the construction paper and tape it onto the single breadstick.
7. Cover the turkey body and tail with almonds to form feathers.
8. Cut out feet from brown construction paper (or use bread sticks). Place them at two points around the body.
9. Serve with crackers.

Variation: Use a variety of nuts and/or crackers instead of just almonds.

Practical Tip: Keep refrigerated until serving time.

Cran-Apple Cider

Welcome your Thanksgiving Day guests with this hot drink. It's berry delicious!

Serves: 6–8

Time: 10 minutes

Complexity: Easy—Adult assistance recommended

Ingredients:
- 1 pint cranberry-juice cocktail
- 1 quart apple juice
- 1 cup water
- 6 whole cloves
- 2 cinnamon sticks
- 1 lemon, sliced thin

Materials:
- Large saucepan
- Strainer
- Stove
- Mugs

What to Do:
1. Mix the cranberry-juice cocktail, apple juice, water, cloves, cinnamon, and lemon together in a large saucepan.
2. Heat and strain.
3. Serve warm in mugs to cold guests.

Variations: Substitute other fruit drinks for apple juice.

Serve this drink cold.

Practical Tip: Keep the cider warm all day in a coffee warmer or Crockpot.

Ice-Cream Turkeys

They didn't have ice cream at the first Thanksgiving Day feast, but there's no reason you can't indulge in these ice-cream turkeys today!

Time: 15 minutes

Complexity: Easy—Adult assistance recommended

Ingredients:
- 1 cup flaked coconut
- Ice cream (chocolate, toffee, or toasted almond)
- Candy corn
- Raisins

Materials:
- Oven, preheated to 375°
- Cookie sheet
- Ice-cream scoop
- Small bowls
- Spoons

What to Do:
1. Spread out the coconut on the cookie sheet and toast in the oven until lightly brown. Allow to cool.
2. Scoop out one round ball of ice cream per person for the turkey bodies. Roll the ice-cream balls in the toasted coconut and place in small bowls.
3. Place two candy corns in the front of each ice-cream ball for beaks, two raisins for eyes, and form tails with candy corn. Serve immediately.

Pumpkin Ice-Cream Pie

Why not make a pumpkin ice-cream pie instead of the traditional pumpkin pie this year? It's easy, different, and refreshing.

Serves: 8

Time: 30 minutes

Complexity: Moderate—Adult assistance recommended

Ingredients:
- 1 cup plain canned pumpkin (not filling)
- 1/4 cup sugar
- 1/4 teaspoon cinnamon
- 1/4 teaspoon ginger
- 1 quart vanilla ice cream
- 1 graham-cracker pie crust
- **Optional:** whipped cream

Materials:
- Medium bowl
- Large spoon
- Large bowl
- Knife
- Plate or bowls
- **Optional:** electric mixer

What to Do:

1. In the medium bowl, mix the pumpkin, sugar, and spices together.

2. Soften the ice cream in the large bowl.

3. Add the pumpkin mixture to the ice cream and stir until well blended. Use an electric mixer, if desired.

4. Spoon the mixture into the pie crust and smooth the top. Place in a freezer for several hours, until firm.

5. Allow to thaw for a few minutes before serving. Add whipped cream to top, if desired. Serve on plates or in bowls.

Variation: Use eight mini pie crusts instead of one large one.

Pumpkin Cookies

These pumpkin cookies are sure to be a hit with pumpkin-pie lovers.

Yields: 3 dozen

Time: 20 minutes

Complexity: Moderate—Adult assistance recommended

Ingredients:
- 1/2 cup margarine, softened
- 3/4 cup brown sugar, packed
- 1 egg
- 1 teaspoon vanilla
- 1 cup canned pumpkin
- 2 cups flour
- 1 teaspoon baking soda
- 1 teaspoon cinnamon
- 1 teaspoon nutmeg
- 1/2 teaspoon ginger
- 1 cup raisins
- Vegetable-oil spray (such as Pam)

What to Do:

1. In the large bowl, mix the softened margarine and brown sugar. Beat at low speed until smooth.
2. Add the egg, vanilla, and pumpkin and beat until smooth.
3. Add the flour, baking soda, cinnamon, nutmeg, and ginger and mix well.
4. Stir in raisins.

Materials:
- Large bowl
- Electric mixer
- Tablespoon
- Cookie sheet
- Oven, preheated to 350°
- Spatula

5. Spray the cookie sheet with vegetable-oil spray.
6. Drop batter by tablespoons onto cookie sheet, about 1 inch apart.
7. Bake until edges begin to brown, about 15 minutes. Cool and serve.

Variations: Make cookies without raisins.

Decorate cookies with chocolate or yellow-tinted frosting.

Practical Tip: Make sure adults help with the mixer and oven for safety.

December

HANUKKAH
(Date Varies)

This eight-day celebration, often called the Festival of Lights, commemorates the victory of a small group of Jews led by Judah Maccabee over the Syrians and Greeks. It's also a celebration of the rededication of the Temple at Jerusalem, which was recovered by the Maccabees in 165 B.C. The holiday begins on the 25th day of Kislev, third month of the lunar year, which usually falls in December near the time of the winter solstice.

Hanukkah is a joyous celebration in both the home and in the synagogue. Each night one candle on the menorah—a lamp with eight candles, one for each day of the holiday, and one extra candle with which to light the others—is lit until all eight are burning brightly. This recalls the "miracle of the lamp" when the victorious Jews returned to worship in the damaged temple to find only enough oil for the "eternal light" to burn for one day. But instead it lasted for eight days. During the eight days of Hanukkah, families often play games, sing songs, and exchange gifts.

Hanukkah Greeting Card

Friends and family love receiving homemade cards, especially if they're made by kids. This one is simple to make.

Materials:
- Blue construction paper
- White glue
- White yarn
- Pen or marker

Time: 30 minutes

Complexity: Easy

What to Do:

1. Fold a piece of the blue construction paper in half to form a card.
2. Drizzle white glue on the cover to form the six-pointed star of David.
3. Place white yarn over the glue. Allow the glue to dry.
4. Write a Hanukkah message inside.

Variation: Make potato-print cards featuring the Star of David by cutting a potato in half. Pin on a paper pattern of a six-pointed star, then trace around the pattern with the point of a knife, not too deeply. Remove pattern and cut away the area until the star stands out 1/4 inch. Dip the potato star in white paint and print on blue paper or vice versa.

Dreidel Game

A dreidel is a top with four sides, each with a Hebrew letter on it, that is used to play a Hanukkah game. Play this game of chance with the whole family.

Time: 1 hour

Complexity: Easy

What to Do:

1. Shape a piece of clay into a cube with a pointed end. Trim with a table knife to make the sides flat and the point sharp.

2. Gently push a sharpened dowel or pencil into the middle of the clay.

3. On each of the four sides draw one of these Hebrew letters: Shin, Hay, Gimel, and Nun.

4. To play, give every player about ten pennies, nuts, or candies. Each player must put one penny, nut, or candy into the middle of the table (the pot).

5. Then the players take turns spinning the dreidel. The letter that comes up determines whether the players win or lose.

   Shin = the player adds two to the pot.
   Hay = the player takes half the pot.
   Gimel = the player takes the whole pot.
   Nun = the player does nothing.

6. When the pot is gone, each player adds one more penny, nut, or candy, and play continues until one player has collected everything.

Shin	Hay	Gimel	Nun
שׁ	ה	ג	נ

Materials:
- Clay
- Table knife
- Sharpened dowel or pencil
- Marker
- Pennies, nuts, or candies

Variations: Make up your own rules to go with each side of the dreidel.

Make a dreidel out of wood or cardboard.

Practical Tip: Have a reference chart handy to help you remember the rules until you've learned them.

Menorah Candle Necklace

You will love wearing this Menorah Candle Necklace during Hanukkah. Add one charm to the necklace each day, just as you light a candle each night.

Time: 30 minutes (plus baking time)

Complexity: Moderate—Adult assistance recommended

What to Do:

1. Make baker's clay by combining the flour, salt, and water and kneading it until well mixed.

2. Make eight candle charms with the baker's clay. Stick a paper clip into the top of each charm so it can later be attached to the necklace.

3. Place the baker's-clay charms onto a tin-foil-lined cookie sheet and bake for 1 to 2 hours (until firm). Allow to cool.

4. Paint or color the charms.

Materials:
- Ribbon or chain
- 4 cups flour
- 1 cup salt
- 1-3/4 cups water
- Paper clips
- Tin foil
- Cookie sheet
- Oven, preheated at 250°
- Acrylic paints and paint brushes or permanent markers

5. Slip one charm onto the ribbon or chain necklace each day of the holiday until you have all eight charms on at the last day.

Variations: Instead of candles, make the Star of David, dreidels, or other charms to attach to the necklace.

Make a bracelet or a pin to wear each day.

Star of David

Symbolizing Judaism, this Star of David is a creative decoration for Hanukkah. Set it on a table or hang it from the ceiling.

Time: 45 minutes

Complexity: Moderate

What to Do:

1. Out of the posterboard cut two equal-sided (equilateral) triangles with 8-inch sides.

2. Place one triangle upside down on top of the other so they make a star shape.

3. Glue the triangles together.

4. Outline the star with glue and stick on toothpicks for a border.

5. Fill one section of the triangle with glue, and then with the macaroni noodles. Repeat with the other sections until the star is filled with noodles. Allow to dry.

6. Paint with blue paint.

Materials:

- Posterboard (white or blue)
- Ruler
- Pencil
- Scissors
- Glue
- Toothpicks
- Macaroni noodles
- Paint (blue)
- Paint brush

Variation: Use a variety of materials to fill the star, such as tissue paper, glitter, beads, seeds, or pictures of family members in a collage.

Practical Tip: Allow to dry completely before painting.

Potato Latkes

No Hanukkah meal is complete without Potato Latkes. They're delicious and fun to make, too.

Serves: 4

Time: 30 minutes

Complexity: Moderate—Adult assistance recommended

Ingredients:
- 4 potatoes, grated
- 1 egg
- 1 small onion, chopped
- Dash of salt
- 1 tablespoon flour
- Margarine
- Sour cream or applesauce

What to Do:

1. Mix the grated potatoes, egg, onion, salt, and flour in the medium bowl.

2. Drop large rounded spoonfuls onto the hot frying pan, greased with margarine.

Materials:
- Medium bowl
- Spoon
- Frying pan
- Stove
- Spatula

3. Fry on both sides until brown.

4. Serve hot with sour cream or applesauce.

Variation: Add shredded cheese.

Practical Tip: Serve immediately for best taste.

Sufganiyyot (Orange Donuts)

Israelis celebrate Hanukkah by making and eating orange-flavored donuts. They're fun and easy to make, but require adult supervision while cooking.

Yields: 1-1/2 dozen (depending on size of donuts)

Time: 30 minutes (plus 1 hour rising time)

Complexity: Easy—Adult assistance recommended

Ingredients:
- 3/4 cup orange juice
- 1/4 pound margarine, melted
- 1/4 cup granulated sugar
- 2 packages dry yeast
- 3 cups flour
- 2 eggs, beaten
- Dash of salt
- Vegetable oil for cooking
- Powdered sugar for dusting

What to Do:

1. Mix the orange juice, melted margarine, and granulated sugar together in the medium saucepan and heat until luke-warm. Sprinkle in the yeast and stir until it's dissolved.
2. Add the flour, eggs, and salt, and mix to a smooth dough.
3. On a lightly floured cutting board or counter, knead the dough until it is springy.

Materials:
- Medium saucepan
- Large spoon
- Large cutting board or large surface to knead on
- Medium bowl, greased
- Large frying pan
- Stove
- Spatula or tongs
- Paper towels
- Paper bag

4. Place the dough in the medium greased bowl, cover with a paper towel, and let rise for half an hour.
5. Knead again, shape into donut rings, and let rise for half an hour more.
6. In the large frying pan, fry the donuts in 2 inches of hot oil until golden brown, turning once with a spatula or tongs.
7. Drain on paper towels.
8. Put some powdered sugar in a paper bag, add donuts, and shake to cover with the sugar.

Variations: Although not traditional, substitute lemonade for the orange juice to make lemon donuts.

Frost the donuts with orange frosting or eat plain.

Practical Tips: If the dough gets sticky, add a little more flour.

Use caution around hot oil. Turn pan handles inward and use a back burner.

CHRISTMAS
December 25

Kids of all ages love this Christian holiday that commemorates the birth of Jesus Christ. Many Christmas customs come from the story of Christ's birth. People give each other gifts because the Three Wise Men, or Three Kings, brought gifts to the baby Jesus. Other customs come from older holidays. Burning the Yule log, for example, comes from a northern European holiday called Yule. And the tradition of the Christmas tree began in Germany from Druid tree worship.

Did you know that Santa Claus was a real person? He began as a kind bishop named St. Nicholas who lived in the fourth century. He passed out gifts to children and poor people in secret. Only with the poem "A Visit from St. Nicholas," by Clement Clarke Moore, did Santa Claus acquire reindeer, a red suit, and a sleigh full of toys.

No matter which Christmas traditions your family follows, Christmas is the perfect season for the whole family to gather together. It's also a great opportunity to create your own family traditions.

Snow-Storm Jar

Capture winter in a jar. This easy-to-make snow-storm jar is a gift anyone will appreciate.

Time: 15 minutes

Complexity: Easy

What to Do:

1. Fill the jar with baby oil or corn syrup, and a little water.
2. Add glitter, star sparkles, metallic confetti, or other decorations to act as snow.
3. Glue the tiny Christmas figurine to the inside of the lid with glue, and then put glue around the lid and seal it shut.

Materials:
- Small glass jar with lid, such as a baby-food jar
- Baby oil or corn syrup
- Water
- Glitter, star sparkles, or metallic confetti
- Glue
- Tiny Christmas figurine

4. When dry, turn the jar upside down and give it a shake. Then watch the "snow" fall on the tiny figurine.

GIFT WRAP

Wrap up your gifts with love using materials you already have at home.

Tin Foil

Materials:
- Tin foil
- Tape
- Permanent felt-tip pens (various colors)
- Scissors

What to Do:

1. Crinkle and then smooth out the tin foil.
2. Wrap the gift, then color in the smooth areas with colored permanent felt-tip pens. Leave some of the fold lines uncolored for a stained-glass look.

Practical Tips: Allow the ink to dry thoroughly before handling.

Wrap the top and bottom of gift boxes separately so each box can be opened without ripping the paper.

Construction Paper

Materials:
- Construction paper
- Tape
- Glue
- Scissors

What to Do:

1. Wrap the gift with construction paper.
2. Cut out "clues" to the gift and glue them onto the construction paper. For example, if the present is some fish hooks for Dad, cut out some colorful fish. If the present is perfume for Mom, cut out a picture of a skunk or a flower.

Variation: Draw the clues on the construction paper with felt-tip pens or crayons.

Brown Paper Bags

Materials:
- Brown paper bags
- Scissors
- Construction paper
- Tape

What to Do:

1. Place the gift inside a brown paper bag, fold over the top, and cut along the edge to give it a curved look.
2. Top the bag with construction paper eyes and place a bow under the cut edge to make a "Christmas Frog." Try other animals using this technique.

Other Ideas:

- Decorate gift boxes with pompoms, glitter, sequins, magazine pictures, wiggly plastic eyes, funny faces, stickers, or bows.
- Make "curls" for the top of boxes by cutting wrapping paper into 8-inch strips and pulling scissors along the unprinted side, gently but firmly, to make the ribbon "curl," much as you would curling ribbon. Tape a bunch of curls onto the packages.
- Find attractive pictures from Christmas cards or wrapping-paper designs and re-create the designs with construction paper or felt. Top the boxes with your creations. (If you make it from felt it can be used as an ornament later.)

Santa Countdown

Here comes Santa Claus! Count down the days until Santa arrives with this Santa chain. Each link in the chain represents one day—cut one off each day until Christmas.

Time: 30–45 minutes

Complexity: Easy

What to Do:

1. Roll a sheet of white construction paper into a cone. Glue or tape it together. Trim the bottom of the cone so it will stand up straight and even.

2. With a red marker or felt-tip pen color the top third of the cone for Santa's hat.

3. With markers or felt-tip pens draw eyes, a nose, and a mouth on one side of the cone under the hat.

4. Glue on cotton balls for eyebrows, sideburns, a beard, and hair.

5. Glue a cotton ball to the top of the cone.

6. Out of red, green, and white construction paper cut twenty-four strips, each about 1-1/2 inches wide by 6- or 7-inches long. Number the strips from one to twenty-four.

7. Make a paper chain by gluing one strip into a circle and then linking another strip through it and gluing it together. Continue until all twenty-four strips are linked together.

Materials:
- Construction paper (white, red, and green)
- Glue
- Tape
- Scissors
- Markers or felt-tip pens (red, green, and black)
- Cotton balls

8. Glue or tape one end of the paper chain to the top or bottom of Santa's hat.

9. Cut off one link each day until Christmas.

Variation: Make a Christmas tree out of a piece of green construction paper rolled into a cone. Cut out circles from construction paper to make ornaments for the tree. Number the ornaments from one to twenty-four, and then tape them to the tree. Attach a cut-out star to the top. Pull off an ornament each day until Christmas.

Practical Tips: Make this at the beginning of December so you will have twenty-four days to cut the chain links apart. Or only attach as many links to your chain as you have days left until Christmas.

Cut the links off at the same time each day.

Advent Calendar

Waiting for Christmas is hard. This Advent Calendar provides something to look forward to during the countdown.

Time: 30 minutes

Complexity: Easy

What to Do:

1. Cut twenty-five "doors" in one piece of tagboard and glue it on top of the other piece.

2. Inside the doors attach small candies or notes, each telling where a small treat is hidden. Or write down a special activity you plan to do with a friend or family member, such as "Visit Santa," "Read *The Night Before Christmas,*" "Sing Christmas Carols," "Go Gift Shopping," and so on.

3. Close the doors and seal them shut with stickers.

4. Number the doors on the outside from one to twenty-five.

Materials:
- 1 sheet red tagboard
- 1 sheet green tagboard
- Scissors
- Glue
- 25 candies or notes
- 25 stickers
- Felt-tip pen

5. Open a door in numerical order each day to find a treat, message, or something to do.

Variation: Have a series of Advent books and read a new story each day.

Practical Tip: Make sure the candies are wrapped so insects won't get into them.

Candy-Cane Sleigh

Santa is not the only one who rides in a sleigh. This decoration features a cute mouse. It will last for years—unless someone eats the runners off the sleigh.

Time: 30 minutes

Complexity: Easy

What to Do:

1. Wrap the lidless box with Christmas wrapping paper, or decorate it with felt-tip pens and ribbons.

2. Set the box open-side up on the table. Glue the candy canes to opposite sides of the box for the runners of the sleigh.

3. Make a mouse by gluing the wiggly plastic eyes to the gray pompom.

4. Glue the small black pompom on the gray pompom for a nose.

5. Cut ears out of the pink felt and glue them onto the top of the gray pompom.

6. Glue yarn to the bottom of the gray pompom for a tail.

Materials:
- Small box (without lid)
- Christmas wrapping paper or felt-tip pens and ribbons
- Tape
- 2 candy canes
- Glue
- Large gray pompom, approximately 1-1/2"–2" in diameter
- 1 tiny black pompom
- 2 wiggly plastic eyes
- Pink felt
- Yarn (pink, black, or gray)
- Scissors

7. Set the mouse in the sleigh, with its tail hanging over the edge of the box.

8. Use as a table or tree decoration.

Variation: Make lots of different kinds of animals to set in the sleigh. Or fill the sleigh with tiny Christmas candies.

Practical Tip: When gluing the candy canes onto the box, hold each one in place for a few seconds to make sure the glue has taken hold. Allow to dry thoroughly before handling.

Yule-Log Centerpiece

This traditional Christmas decoration makes a great centerpiece for all of your holiday meals.

Time: 30 minutes

Complexity: Easy—Adult assistance recommended

What to Do:

1. Brush or spray a thin coat of glue on the log and sprinkle with glitter.
2. Melt wax in the center of the log and set the large round candle on the melted wax so it will stick to the log.
3. Glue small fir cones or other small decorations around the candle.

Materials:
- Log, about 20" long and 4" high
- Glue
- Glitter
- Wax
- Large round candle
- Small fir cones or other small decorations
- Ribbons
- Tree ornaments

4. Add ribbons and tree ornaments to the log. Place in center of the table.

Practical Tip: Be careful not to burn yourself with the hot wax.

Christmas Candles

People used candles to adorn Christmas trees before the days of electricity. Use these paper candles to give your Christmas tree an "old-fashioned" look.

Time: 30–45 minutes

Complexity: Easy

What to Do:

1. If you're using paper-towel tubes, cut them in half.
2. Glue or tape red construction paper around each tube.
3. Wrinkle the gold foil into flame shapes, one for each tube, and glue them to the inside of the tubes, but make sure the top of each flame sticks out.
4. Set the "candles" on the tree by placing them over upturned branches.

Materials:
- Paper-towel or toilet-paper tubes
- Red construction paper
- Glue
- Tape
- Scissors
- Gold foil gift wrap

Variation: Make the candles as decorations instead of tree trimmers. Set them on colorful plastic lids. Add glitter, lace, ribbon, or holly.

Practical Tip: If your tree does not have many upturned branches or the candles seem insecure on the tree, use florist wire to secure.

Santa Pencil

Have fun using this Santa pencil when you're writing your Christmas wish list. Make a few extra pencils to give to teachers or friends.

Time: 30 minutes

Complexity: Easy

What to Do:

1. Stick the pointed end of the pencil halfway into the Styrofoam ball.

2. Remove the ball, add a little glue to the eraser end of the pencil, and insert the eraser end of the pencil into the ball.

3. Cut the red felt into a square, and then fold or roll it into a cone shape for a hat.

4. Glue the hat together, and then glue it onto the Styrofoam ball.

5. Using the felt-tip pens, draw a face on the ball.

6. Glue cotton balls onto the Styrofoam ball for a beard, hat trim, and hat topper.

7. Allow to dry.

Materials:
- Pencil (red or green)
- Styrofoam ball, approximately 1"–1-1/2" in diameter
- Red felt
- Cotton balls
- Felt-tips pens (red and black)
- Glue
- Scissors

Variations: Personalize the pencils by portraying family members and friends instead of Santa. Decorate to suit their features, then place the pencils on the tree or give them as Christmas gifts.

Add wiggly plastic eyes and cheeks colored with a pink felt-tip pen. Write the name of friends or family members along the side of the pencil.

Practical Tip: Separate the cotton balls into smaller pieces to make eyebrows and other smaller details.

Twelve Days of Christmas Gifts

"On the first day of Christmas . . ." Act out this popular Christmas song by giving your true love (or best friend) a gift on each day of Christmas, beginning on Christmas Day and ending on January 5, the day before Epiphany.

What to Do:

1. Using "The Twelve Days of Christmas" as a guide, write down your own version of the song on index cards. Change each stanza to fit a small gift you plan to give someone special. For example, you might write, "On the first day of Christmas my true love gave to me—a sweet-smelling candle made of fresh bayberry."

2. Choose two things to give your true love for the second day, three for the third, and so on, until you have twelve. You might include such things as two matching socks, three shiny apples, four scented soaps, five candy bars, a six-pack of soda, seven stickers, eight chocolate gold coins, nine bath beads, ten sticks of gum, eleven colorful pencils, and a dozen blueberry muffins.

3. Decorate each index card with Christmas stickers or markers, and set one card with a gift on the doorstep of your special friend each night of the twelve days of Christmas, then ring the bell and run away.

4. Sign the card on the last day.

Materials:
- 12 index cards
- Christmas stickers or markers
- Pen or pencil
- 12 small gifts

Picture-Frame Ornament

Here's a way to decorate the tree with a familiar smiling face year after year!

What to Do:

1. Make baker's clay by combining the flour, salt, and water and kneading it until well mixed.

2. Make several shapes, such as Christmas trees, stars, or stockings.

3. Cut out the centers of the shapes, leaving a 1/2-inch frame. Stick a paper clip or other metal hanger in the top of each frame and bake for 1 to 2 hours (until firm). Allow to cool.

4. Paint and then glue a piece of felt to the back to hold photos, leaving a gap at the top to slip them in. Slip in family photos and hang the ornaments on the tree.

Materials:
- 4 cups flour
- 1 cup salt
- 1-3/4 cups water
- Knife
- Paper clips or metal picture hangers
- Cookie sheet
- Oven, preheated to 250°
- Acrylic paints
- Paint brush
- Glue
- Felt
- Photos

No-Bake Clay Ornaments

These ornaments look like Christmas cookies—but don't eat them, they're for your Christmas tree.

Time: 30–45 minutes (plus drying time)

Complexity: Easy—Adult assistance recommended

What to Do:

1. In the medium saucepan, bring water to a boil, then remove from heat.

2. Stir in the salt and cornstarch.

3. Return to low heat and cook until dough becomes difficult to stir.

4. Pour dough onto waxed paper. Allow to cool.

5. Knead until smooth, then roll dough to 1/8-inch thickness and cut with Christmas cookie cutters.

6. Poke a hole in the top of each ornament with a toothpick. Allow to dry for 2 to 3 days. Store the leftover dough in an airtight container.

7. Paint with acrylic paint.

8. Attach string through the hole in the top of the ornaments and hang on the tree.

Materials:
- 1-1/2 cups water
- Medium saucepan
- Stove
- 2 cups salt
- 1 cup cornstarch
- Large spoon
- Waxed paper
- Roller
- Christmas cookie cutters
- Toothpick
- Acrylic paint
- Paint brush
- String

CHRISTMAS CAROLING

Get into the holiday spirit. Gather your family and friends together and go caroling through the neighborhood, local hospital, or retirement community.

Jolly Old Saint Nicholas

Jolly Old Saint Nicholas,
Lean your ear this way!
Don't you tell a single soul
What I'm going to say;
Christmas Eve is coming soon;
Now you dear old man,
Whisper what you'll bring to me;
Tell me, if you can.

Johnny wants a pair of skates;
Susy wants a sled;
Nellie wants a picture book,
Yellow, blue, and red;
Now I think I'll leave to you
What to give the rest;
Choose for me, dear Santa Claus;
You will know the best.

Up on the House-Top

Up on the house-top reindeer pause,
Out jumps good old Santa Claus;
Down through the chimney
with lots of toys,
All for the little ones' Christmas joys.

First comes the stocking of little Nell;
Oh, dear Santa, fill it well;
Give her a dolly that laughs and cries,
One that will open and shut her eyes.

Refrain:
Ho, ho, ho! Who wouldn't go!
Ho, ho, ho! Who wouldn't go!
Up on the house-top click, click, click,
Down through the chimney with good
Saint Nick.

We Wish You a Merry Christmas

We wish you a Merry Christmas,
We wish you a Merry Christmas,
We wish you a Merry Christmas,
And a happy New Year.

Good tidings we bring to you and your kin,
Good tidings for Christmas and a happy
New Year.

We all know that Santa's coming,
We all know that Santa's coming,
We all know that Santa's coming,
And soon will be here.

Good tidings we bring to you and your kin.
Good tidings for Christmas and a happy
New Year.

We wish you a Merry Christmas,
We wish you a Merry Christmas,
We wish you a Merry Christmas,
And a happy New Year.

Practical Tips:

- Bring along hot apple cider to keep the group warm between songs.
- Carry candles to light while you are singing.
- Wear red, white, and green clothes.

Cookie House

Work together to build this cookie house. Remember to set aside a few extra cookies for your hardworking construction workers to nibble on.

Time: 1 hour

Complexity: Moderate

What to Do:

1. From the cardboard cut out a roof to fit the box.
2. Glue, tape, or staple it onto the box.
3. Frost the cardboard box with royal icing (see recipe below), and then cover the box with cookies.
4. With the cookies make doors, windows, shingles, and designs for the outside of the house.

Variations: Make a candy house, using the same technique, or make it a combination of both.

Use graham crackers instead of cardboard for house walls and roof. "Glue" together with royal icing.

Practical Tip: Use up leftover Halloween candy as house decorations. Also make candy fences, flowers, paths, and trees. Put it all on a large Christmas tray.

Materials:
- Cardboard box about the size you want your "house" to be
- Cardboard scrap
- Scissors
- Glue, tape, or stapler
- Cookies
- Mixer
- Large bowl
- Damp towel

Royal Icing Recipe

Ingredients:
- 1 egg white
- 1/2 teaspoon cream of tartar
- 1 16-ounce package powdered sugar

What to do:

1. Beat the egg white with the cream of tartar until foamy.
2. Add powdered sugar, then beat until stiff peaks form, about 7 minutes.
3. Keep the bowl covered with the damp towel when not using—it dries fast and hard.

Taffy Candy Canes

Be a little daffy, pull some taffy! Everyone will enjoy working on this project, especially when it's time to taste the results.

Yields: 2 dozen

Time: 45 minutes

Complexity: Moderate—Adult assistance recommended

Ingredients:
- 1-1/4 cups sugar
- 1/4 cup water
- 2 tablespoons white distilled vinegar
- 1-1/2 teaspoons butter
- 1/2 teaspoon peppermint extract
- Red food coloring

What to Do:

1. Combine the sugar, water, vinegar, and butter in the medium saucepan.
2. Cook over medium heat until sugar is dissolved, stirring constantly.
3. Lower the heat and continue to cook without stirring, to 260° on the candy thermometer (or until a small amount of syrup forms a firm ball when dropped in very cold water).
4. Remove from heat and stir in the peppermint extract.
5. Pour half the mixture into the buttered pan.
6. Color the remaining half with red food coloring. Allow to cool a few minutes.
7. With clean, lightly buttered hands, pull the taffy until it becomes a satiny opaque look and begins to feel a little stiff (about 6 to 8 minutes).

Materials:
- Medium saucepan
- Stove
- Candy thermometer
- Large spoon
- Buttered pan, such as a cookie sheet with a lip
- Waxed paper

8. Take one strand of white and one of red and twist together, then form into candy-cane shapes. Allow to cool on waxed paper.

Variation: Use a variety of food coloring to make the taffy, then make all sorts of shapes and designs for the holiday.

Practical Tip: Be sure the taffy has cooled enough before you pull it so you won't burn your hands.

Rice Krispy Christmas Trees

Make Rice Krispy Christmas Trees to decorate your home or gobble up during those special Christmas TV programs.

Serves: 6–8

Time: 20 minutes

Complexity: Moderate—Adult assistance recommended

Ingredients:
- 1/4 cup butter
- 40 marshmallows
- Green food coloring
- 5–6 cups Rice Krispies
- Red-hot candies
- Powdered sugar

Materials:
- Large saucepan
- Stove
- Large spoon
- Large plate or cookie sheet

What to Do:

1. Melt the butter and marshmallows in the large saucepan over low heat.
2. Add a few drops of green food coloring.
3. Stir in the Rice Krispies.
4. Quickly shape into trees, then add the red hots for ornaments. Place on a plate or cookie sheet.
5. Sift a small amount of powdered sugar over the top for "snow."

Variation: Make other shapes or designs with cookie cutters.

Red-Nosed Reindeer Drink

Here's a warm drink for cold winter nights. Named after our favorite reindeer, this drink is popular around the Pole and might turn your nose red.

Serves: 6–8

Time: 10 minutes

Complexity: Easy—Adult assistance recommended

Ingredients:
- 1 16-ounce bottle apple juice
- 1 16-ounce bottle cranberry juice
- 1 16-ounce bottle lemon-line soda
- 3 cinnamon sticks
- Tiny candy-cane stirrers

Materials:
- Large saucepan
- Stove
- Mugs

What to Do:

1. In the large saucepan mix the apple juice, cranberry juice, and lemon-lime soda with the cinnamon sticks.
2. Heat, and then serve in mugs with tiny candy-cane stirrers.

Variation: Mix together a variety of drink flavors to create your own recipe.

EXTRA IDEAS

A Time of Giving

The true meaning of Christmas is about giving of yourself. Spend some of the holiday time giving to others as a family.

- Make gifts and donate them to charitable organizations. Check first to see what they need and can accept.
- Prepare extra goodies to give to the local senior citizens' center or nursing home.
- Invite a single person to Christmas dinner—an elderly neighbor, a college student away from home, or a soldier.
- Ask that one gift be made in your name to a charitable organization.
- Join in a walkathon that benefits a needy group.
- Adopt a hungry child in another part of the world. Remember that this is a year-round commitment.
- Collect toys and clothes from the neighborhood and donate them to a local homeless shelter. (Check first to see if they can accept second-hand goods.)

KWANZAA
December 26–January 1

Kwanzaa is an African-American holiday based on the traditional African winter harvest festival. The holiday was created by Dr. Maulana Karenga in 1966. Kwanzaa, which means "first fruit" in Swahili, focuses on seven principles that contribute to the unity of the black family. It also focuses on developing community with a sense of African-American cultural heritage.

Each night families talk about one of the seven principles and how it can be applied to their daily lives. The seven principles are "umoja" (unity), "kujichagulia" (self-determination), "ujima" (collective work and responsibility), "ujamaa" (cooperative economics), "nia" (purpose), "kuumba" (creativity), and "imani" (faith). Children play a central role in this celebration. They light the Kinara (a seven-place candle holder), recite and explain the principles, help prepare special foods, and make music and dance presentations. Gifts are traditionally exchanged on the last day of Kwanzaa.

Karamu Feast Tabbouleh

A high point of Kwanzaa is the Karamu or feast. Karamu foods, like this recipe, incorporate the Kwanzaa colors of black, red, and green.

Serves: 4

Time: 1-1/2 hours

Complexity: Easy—Adult assistance recommended

Ingredients:
- 2 cups boiling water
- 1 cup bulgur wheat
- 1 cup fresh parsley, finely chopped
- 1/2 cup mint, finely chopped
- 1/2 pound tofu, finely chopped
- 2 tomatoes, finely chopped
- 1/2 cup black olives
- 1/4 cup lemon juice
- 1/4 cup green onions, chopped
- 2 tablespoons olive oil
- 1/2 teaspoon salt
- 1/2 teaspoon black pepper
- Leaf lettuce

Materials:
- Medium saucepan
- Stove
- Strainer
- Medium bowl

What to Do:

1. Pour boiling water over the bulgur wheat and soak for 1 hour.

2. Pour off water and drain well.

3. In the medium bowl combine the bulgar wheat with the remaining ingredients. Serve with leaf lettuce.

African Animal Necklace

Jewelry is an important part of African dress. Wear this necklace during Kwanzaa or anytime.

Time: 30 minutes (plus baking time)

Complexity: Easy—Adult assistance recommended

What to Do:

1. Make baker's clay by combining the flour, salt, and water and kneading it until well mixed.

2. Shape the dough into African animals, such as an elephant, a lion, a zebra, and a giraffe, or use animal cookie cutters.

3. Poke a hole at the top of each animal, then bake for 1 to 2 hours, until firm.

4. Paint your animals appropriate colors, allow to dry, then string one animal onto a black satin cord and tie a knot so it will stay in one place.

Materials:
- 4 cups flour
- 1 cup salt
- 1-3/4 cups water
- Medium bowl
- Animal cookie cutters
- Cookie sheet
- Oven, preheated to 250°
- Spatula
- Paint
- Paint brush
- Black satin cord

5. Add a second animal and repeat, until your necklace is complete.

Variation: Make a beaded necklace from red, black, and green baker's clay, by making tiny little balls of the three colors, poking a hole through the center, baking, and stringing through strong thread to make a necklace.

Practical Tip: Don't make the animals too big.

Kwanzaa Candles

On each night of Kwanzaa, one of seven candles in a holder (a Kinara) is lit. Three red candles on the right represent struggle, three green candles on the left represent the future, and a black one in the middle is for African people everywhere. Kinaras are usually homemade—make this one for your home.

Time: 30–45 minutes

Complexity: Easy

What to Do:

1. Wash and dry the cans or jars.
2. Spread newspaper out on your work area and paint the cans or jars red, green, and black. Paint them solid colors or with designs.
3. Place a candle in each can or jar.
4. Place the candles on a table or mantel. Light one candle each night of the holiday.

Materials:
- 7 small cans or jars, empty, without sharp edges
- 7 small votive candles (3 red, 3 green, and 1 black)
- Enamel paint (red, green, and black)
- Paint brushes
- Newspaper

5. After lighting the candle, talk about the principle honored on that day and how it applies to you.

Variations: Decorate the jars or cans with colorful cloth or paper, torn tissue paper, or wide ribbons.

Glue the jars onto a candelabra made of wood or posterboard.

Practical Tip: Be careful around the lit candles. Place a juice-can lid or dish under the candle to protect furniture from leaking wax.

Sweet-Potato Cookies

These yummy, African-style cookies have an unusual cookie ingredient—sweet potatoes. The cookies turn out bright orange and cakelike, with good nutrition along with good taste.

Yields: 2-1/2 dozen

Time: 30 minutes

Complexity: Easy—Adult assistance recommended

Cookie Dough Ingredients:
- 5 tablespoons margarine
- 1/8 cup sugar
- 1/2 teaspoon lemon juice
- 1/2 teaspoon nutmeg
- 1/8 cup honey
- 1 egg
- 1/2 cup raw sweet potato, finely grated
- 1-1/4 cups flour
- 3/4 teaspoon baking powder
- 1/4 teaspoon baking soda
- 1/4 teaspoon salt

Lemon Glaze Ingredients:
- 1/2 teaspoon margarine
- 1 tablespoon lemon juice
- 3/4 cup powdered sugar
- 1/2 tablespoon water

Materials:
- Large bowl
- Electric mixer
- Large spoon
- Teaspoon
- Cookie sheet
- Oven, preheated to 350°
- Medium bowl
- Spatula

What to Do:

1. With the electric mixer, combine the margarine and sugar in the large bowl until creamy.
2. Blend in the lemon juice, nutmeg, honey, and egg.
3. Fold in the sweet potato.
4. Add the flour, baking powder, baking soda, and salt. Stir until well blended.
5. Place rounded teaspoons onto the ungreased cookie sheet.
6. Bake for 6 to 8 minutes.
7. Make the glaze by combining ingredients in the medium bowl and stirring until smooth. Add water by the drop until the glaze is easy to spread on cooled cookies.
8. Spread glaze on cooled cookies.

Variation: Decorate the cookies with frosting and sprinkles in Kwanzaa colors. Use chocolate for black.

INDEX

INDEX

Order Form

Qty.	Title	Author	Order No.	Unit Cost	Total
	A Bad Case of the Giggles	Lansky, B.	2411	$14.00	
	Free Stuff for Kids	Free Stuff Editors	2190	$5.00	
	Girls to the Rescue	Lansky, B.	2215	$3.95	
	Kids' Holiday Fun	Warner, P.	6000	$12.00	
	Kids' Party Games and Activities	Warner, P.	6095	$12.00	
	Kids' Pick the Funniest Poems	Lansky, B.	2410	$14.00	
	The New Adventures of Mother Goose	Lansky, B.	2420	$15.00	
	Subtotal				
	Shipping and Handling (see below)				
	MN residents add 6.5% sales tax				
	Total				

YES! Please send me the books indicated above. Add $2.00 shipping and handling for the first book and 50¢ for each additional book. Add $2.50 to total for books shipped to Canada. Overseas postage will be billed. Allow up to four weeks for delivery. Send check or money order payable to Meadowbrook Press. No cash or C.O.D.'s, please. Prices subject to change without notice. Quantity discounts available upon request.

Send book(s) to:

Name _____

Address _____

City _____ State ____ Zip ____ Telephone ( ) _____ P.O. # (if nec.) _____

Payment via: ☐ Check or money order payable to Meadowbrook Press (No cash or C.O.D.'s, please)

Amount enclosed $ _____   ☐ Visa (for orders over $10.00 only)

☐ MasterCard (for orders over $10.00 only)

Account # _____ Signature _____ Exp. Date _____

A FREE Meadowbrook Press catalog is available upon request.
You can also phone us for orders of $10.00 or more at 1-800-338-2232.

Mail to: Meadowbrook, Inc., 18318 Minnetonka Boulevard, Deephaven, MN 55391

(612) 473-5400   Toll-Free 1-800-338-2232   Fax (612) 475-0736